GASLIGHT

Also by Femi Kayode

Lightseekers

GASLIGHT

FEMI KAYODE

MULHOLLAND BOOKS

LITTLE, BROWN AND COMPANY

NEW YORK BOSTON LONDON

To Nneka.
For the space
and everything within.
For the love
and all it made possible.
For always.

———————————

Copyright © 2023 by Femi Kayode

Mulholland Books / Little, Brown and Company
Hachette Book Group
1290 Avenue of the Americas, New York, NY 10104
mulhollandbooks.com

First North American Edition: November 2023
Previously published in Great Britain by Raven Books, June 2023

Mulholland Books is an imprint of Little, Brown and Company, a division of Hachette Book Group, Inc. The Mulholland Books name and logo are trademarks of Hachette Book Group, Inc.

The publisher is not responsible for websites (or their content) that are not owned by the publisher.

The Hachette Speakers Bureau provides a wide range of authors for speaking events. To find out more, go to hachettespeakersbureau.com or email hachettespeakers@hbgusa.com.

Little, Brown and Company books may be purchased in bulk for business, educational, or promotional use. For information, please contact your local bookseller or the Hachette Book Group Special Markets Department at special.markets@hbgusa.com.

ISBN 9780316536646
LCCN 2023932913

Printing 1, 2023

LSC-C

Printed in the United States of America

GENESIS

Let them come for him during Sunday service.

They should wait for him to walk to the altar. Let him check that the cameras are placed as he directed during rehearsals. Give him time to mumble some gibberish as prayers. Some in the congregation will swoon and the ushers will rush to break their falls. This is not the right moment.

A lot is at stake. Arresting Bishop Jeremiah Dawodu during his televised sermon is no joke. Timing and sequence are critical, so please follow the steps as we agreed.

Start with my disappearance. He would have told everyone I travelled to be by myself. Let the police know this is a lie to cover why calls to my mobile phone are going to voicemail. If they wave this away as insignificant, point them to the driver who never picked me up and my car still parked in the garage. They might claim I've not been missing long enough to suspect foul play. It's okay. Just make sure they get to the house. Leave the rest to me.

At the Sunday service, let him urge the congregation to sit. Wait for him to welcome the viewers at home and ask everyone to turn their Bibles to the passage he's chosen to misread. The more confident he is that he's the centre of attention – The Anointed One – the better.

He will hide his outrage when they come. His bodyguards will come forward, ready to defend their man of God. The elders will protest. One or two will pull the police aside and

1

offer them something. Let this be. The point would have been made. The unholy hand of suspicion is upon their bishop.

If they take him away, I hope it's in handcuffs. This should humble him. He won't be able to wave with false calm, urging his church to pray for him. No raised fists, proclaiming the devil a liar. If you can't make this happen, no pressure. From this point, a lot will be out of your hands.

The coming weeks will be hard to get through but don't worry. I'll be with you every step of the way. Trust me. Everything is in place. It is time.

Let's get to work.

BOOK I

Total pressure exerted is equal to the sum of the partial pressures in a mixture.

Dalton's Law

The Light shines in the darkness, and the darkness did not comprehend it.

John 1:5 (NASB, 1995)

BROTHERS AND SISTERS

I can't look away from the other side of the road. That'll be us later, stuck and trapped. I dread it already.

'You can at least fake some interest?' Kenny says, petulance mixed with irritation.

I turn from the static scene of cars heading towards Lagos. 'Do I look bored?'

Kenny side-eyes me, then hisses. 'We've been in this car for almost an hour and—'

'Eighty-two minutes to be exact. But I can't complain since you've used Folake to—'

'I didn't use anyone!'

I'm still miffed she went through my wife to ask my help. 'So, why didn't you come to me directly?'

'Because I don't like how you make me feel every time church comes up.'

I raise a sardonic brow. 'Like a whimsical escapist?'

'See?' She glowers. 'That's why I went to Folake first.'

'No, Kenny Girl.' She hates Dad's pet name for her, even more than I detest his 'Kenny Boy' for me. 'You went to Folake because you know murder makes it perfectly legit for me to say "I told you so."'

'He didn't murder his wife,' Kenny whispers, nodding in the direction of her driver's clean-shaved head.

I snort but lower my voice. 'Everyone knows.'

'Not from me.'

I suck in air – one Mississippi, two Mississippi, three – and exhale. 'He's practically the most famous murder suspect on earth right now.'

'*Suspect* is the keyword here,' Kenny snaps.

'How you don't find suspecting a pastor of murder disturbing, worries me deeply.'

'It's the devil at work. Why would Bishop kill his wife? There's nothing to remotely suggest she's dead. It's a conspiracy.' She kisses her teeth loudly. 'So many haters out there.'

I blink. It's hard to reconcile this accomplished career woman in her late forties with language at my teenage daughter's level. My younger sister's religious fervour confounds me. How did we get here?

'You don't know the world, Philip,' Kenny continues with pity reserved for the naïve. 'It's firmly under the devil's control.'

'And this world somehow has your pastor's wife hidden away somewhere?'

'Bee-shop,' she corrects. My sarcasm ranks lower than my mislabelling.

'Whatever. His wife's missing, and even if he's God's personal assistant, the spouse is always the number-one suspect.'

'That's why we need your—' Kenny's phone rings. 'We're still in traffic, sir,' she says with reverence into the handset. 'It's not that bad, but still slow.'

It is bad. The road I've nicknamed 'Highway of Evangelical Churches of Nigeria' is chaos. The snail-paced traffic starts just before the 'Goodbye to Lagos' signage and graduates to near standstill as another billboard welcomes you to Ogun state.

'We're moving now,' Kenny continues. 'The road is clearing a bit. We should be there in about half an hour—'

I scoff, taking in my surroundings with resignation. Unless we are airlifted, her optimism is doomed. The megachurches lining both sides of the road are the only sign of order. A town planner would have an apoplexy at the jumbled mass of petrol stations, retail shops, informal markets and bus stops connecting one church estate to another. There's no method to the madness that spills onto the road, narrowing a width created for three cars to two at the best of times.

'Ah, he feels very honoured, o. It's no bother at all.'

My double take is pointed. Kenny ignores me. I return my attention to the road. After megachurch estates, schools are next on the road's claim to fame. From kindergartens through high schools with boarding options to university campuses; they're all here. Tuition fees are printed in large, colourful starbursts with facilities listed as endless bullet points on massive billboards. The schools' intimidating entrance gates seem designed to reassure prospective students of protection from the bedlam on the road. I'm not sure they succeed.

Kenny ends the call. 'The elders are waiting.'

'They can spend the time praying for a miracle.'

'Don't.'

I keep my face on the road to hide my smirk.

*

Two hours and twenty-three minutes later, in a plush boardroom more befitting of a Fortune 500 company than a church, nine men and four women stare at us like we just interrupted a heated discussion on plummeting stock prices. There's more tension here than in the Pentagon's situation room during the ambush of Osama bin Laden.

'Good afternoon, sir,' Kenny says as she walks around the wide and long conference table, curtsying. I try to guess the elders' rankings by how low she dips before each one. The greeting goes on until Kenny gets to the man closest to an empty leather chair at the head of the table. Early- to mid-fifties. He'd be good looking without the scowl. Dark-skinned, clean-shaven. The sprinkling of grey on his hair and the way he clasps his hands together gives him a stern headmaster aura. Kenny's knees touch the ground. The resident Deputy Jesus, I bet.

'Is this him?' His voice booms. A man used to addressing large crowds. 'The psychologist?'

'Yes, sir.' Kenny looks at me, and my heart warms at the affection beaming from her. 'This is my brother, Dr Philip Kehinde Taiwo. He's an investigative psychologist,' she announces.

I wave, as uncomfortable with the pride in her voice as the full rendition of my name and profession. Kenny moves to the woman next to Deputy Jesus. She makes to kneel, but the older woman stops her, pulling Kenny into an embrace.

'I was just telling them they shouldn't have bothered you,' the woman says, her eyes on me.

'Ah, auntie, not bother me, ke? How can I not be bothered when the devil is not resting?' Kenny looks at me as she puts her arms around the woman's shoulders. 'Phil, this is Bishop's mother-in-law, Mrs Kikelomo Bucknor.'

I try to hide my surprise. Having the mother of the possible victim here throws me. I'll have to proceed with more sensitivity than the unbridled candour I'd planned.

Mrs Bucknor gives me the once-over. I can't read her beyond her weary demeanour. Her face is bare of discernible make-up, and apart from the tiredness around her eyes, her light skin glows with health. She wears an ìró and bùbá that would have looked ostentatious if not for the simple knot of the matching gèlè on her head. No jewellery. No wedding band. Affluence oozes from her like it's the only adornment she needs.

'So, you're also a twin,' a female elder says, as though doubting Kenny's assertion.

'Yes, ma,' I respond stiffly. Hard to be gracious with thirteen pairs of eyes trained on you.

Mrs Bucknor turns to Kenny. 'Two sets of twins in one family. What a blessing!'

While I doubt my mum would agree, I find the way Mrs Bucknor spoke curious. Her tone was flat, without the wonder I've come to expect whenever my family tree comes up. Then again, the woman's son-in-law is being accused of murdering her daughter. Not quite a hurrah moment.

'Please have a seat,' Deputy Jesus orders me.

I comply and find myself opposite him.

'My name is Pastor Abayomi George. I'm the assistant general overseer of Grace Church.'

I was right. Second-in-command.

'Let me introduce the elders,' – He gestures at Mrs Bucknor – 'as Sister Kenny said, this is our First Lady's mother, Mrs Bucknor ...'

Decades of sibling coding goes into the look I give Kenny across the room: *You go to a church where the pastor's wife is called 'First Lady'?* She narrows her eyes in a reprimand that eerily reminds me of our mum. I turn back to Pastor George.

'Next to her is Pastor Richard Nwoko. He heads our finance ...'

To preserve my sanity, I decide to save remembering the names and titles for when – *if* – I take the case. I scan the room as the introductions drone on. None below middle age. The female elders don African print attires, reflecting good taste and skilled tailors. The men look dapper in three-piece suits and ties. How they are not uncomfortable is beyond me. Despite the cooling effect of the air-conditioning, the strain in the room makes me feel like unbuttoning my cotton shirt.

'Our leadership is made up of a lot more people, with several heads of departments across the globe. But due to the delicate nature of this assignment, we thought it prudent to keep things, er, discreet for now.' Pastor George looks around as if to confirm he has delivered his speech as agreed.

All, except Mrs Bucknor, nod. The rest look like kids in detention; defensive and ready to flee rather than go through what's to come.

To ease the tension, I put on my most genial smile and lie. 'I'm honoured to be here. How can I be of service?'

FIRST LADY

'Dr Taiwo, I'm sure you're aware of our current situation,' Pastor George begins. 'Our general overseer was arrested yesterday on suspicion of involvement in his wife's disappearance.' He pauses, looks around as if to confirm his summation is accurate. The elders nod with varying depths of sighs.

'This is a matter of great concern to us as the church leadership. As much as we're concerned for our First Lady's safety—'

Mrs Bucknor raises a hand. 'I still think this is unnecessary.' She turns to Kenny on her left. 'She'll be back any day now, and the police will be sorry.'

Before Kenny can speak, Pastor George touches Mrs Bucknor's right shoulder gently. 'We discussed this and you agreed.'

Mrs Bucknor doesn't look at Pastor George but her eyes flit from Kenny to me. Is that a plea in her eyes? Or a challenge?

'It just seems like a waste of time when we all know the truth.' Mrs Bucknor leans closer to Kenny, as if to apologise for all the trouble of bringing me. Why do I sense she doesn't want me here?

11

'And the truth being...?' I ask in Pastor George's direction.

'We all understand how the pressure of being the general overseer's wife can take its toll,' he says. 'Our First Lady takes time off to be by herself several times a year. We've never worried. We just give her space.'

'You mean it's possible she's away somewhere with no TV, no phone or internet, and no access to any media channel broadcasting her husband's arrest?'

I tried not to sound sarcastic, but the way Pastor George's scowl becomes even more intimidating proves I failed.

'We know how this must sound to an outsider but First Lady is known for taking these retreats. Ask anyone.' Pastor George looks around again. Bobbing heads urge him on. 'We all assume she discusses her whereabouts with Bishop before leaving, but no one has ever questioned her decision to take these leaves of absence when it suits her.' The knots on his brow smoothen as he speaks; his face becomes as neutral as his tone. I don't think he likes their first lady.

'You assumed she told her husband but she hadn't? So, he doesn't know where she went?' I look around the room.

'He doesn't,' Pastor Nwoko says, louder than necessary. The elders murmur their agreement. 'The police swooped on our church, committed this blasphemous act, and we have no way of proving First Lady is somewhere recuperating, and will soon be home.'

'So, the pastor admits he doesn't know where his wife is?' I ask again, my gaze settling on Pastor George.

'Bishop,' he corrects and continues smoothly, 'and no, he doesn't. He said she left home after he came here to the church office but that they did discuss her going away.'

'The bishop was away from home for how many days?'

'We had a special programme. Seven days of fasting and praying,' Pastor Nwoko says, defensive, as if my enquiry came with judgement. 'Bishop has been known to be in the cathedral for days on end, waiting on the Lord for a prophetic word—'

'And you can all vouch that in the days leading to his arrest,' I pause to look around the room, 'the bishop never went home?'

'Absolutely,' Pastor Nwoko says loudly, above everyone's affirmation.

'Without doubt,' Mrs Bucknor adds less robustly.

'It's true,' Kenny says. 'When work permitted, I also attended the programme. Bishop never left Graceland.'

'Your first lady was absent during such an important programme?' I ask the room. 'And no one thought that was strange?'

The elders look at each other like actors figuring out who has the next cue.

Pastor Nwoko eventually shakes his head like the reluctant bearer of unpalatable news. 'Our First Lady is young and quite impulsive.'

Mrs Bucknor throws him a look that could freeze boiling water.

'I'm sorry,' he says insincerely. 'But, if we want Dr Taiwo to help us, we must say things as they are, not how we wish them to be.' He turns to me. 'Our First Lady is a lovely woman, but she's recently become prone to youthful exuberance and unpredictable moodiness. We forgive this on account of her age.'

I steal a glance at Mrs Bucknor, but she's arranged her face into a blank slate.

'How old is the first lady?' I ask.

'She'll be thirty in two months,' one of the three female elders answers, eager to ease the awkwardness in the air. 'I'm the one organising the women's conference in honour of her birthday.'

Thirty is not young but I concede it might be for the 'first lady' of a megachurch. It's hard to picture these elders kowtowing to a woman at least two decades younger than the average age in the room.

'And the bishop?' I can't seem to drop the article before the man's title, just as the elders can't stop using his title as his first name. Their reverence is obvious, even in the way they now stare at me. Like they've never considered their leader had something as human as a birth date.

'Fifty-two,' Kenny says from across the room, her hand back on Mrs Bucknor's shoulders, squeezing in support.

'Is this his first marriage?'

'Of course,' Pastor Nwoko answers, his irritation evident. 'He was focused on his ministry while waiting on the Lord for the right helpmeet.'

The man's zeal is tedious. I write quickly to mask my impatience. 'Children?'

No response. I look up from my notepad.

'Bishop and his wife are still waiting on the Lord for the fruit of the womb,' Pastor George answers sombrely.

'And they've been married for what?'

'Five years and a couple of months,' Kenny answers gently since everyone's focused on Mrs Bucknor's impassive face.

I read from my notes. 'So, the bishop's wife goes missing—'

'Her name is Sade. *Fo-la-sa-de*,' Mrs Bucknor says sharply.

'And she's not missing—' Pastor Nwoko throws in.

'For lack of a better word,' I say to the man, while giving Mrs Bucknor an apologetic look. I'd also hate it if my child's existence was reduced to her marital status. To deflect from my shame, I focus on Pastor Nwoko. 'We don't know her whereabouts, which technically means she's missing.' I go back to reading off my notepad. 'The first lady goes missing for three days, and her husband, who's not been home for those days, can't say where she is. You all say this is normal, yet yesterday – making a total of five days since she was last seen – the police arrested the bishop on suspicion of murder?'

There's silence, until Pastor Nwoko says with uncharacteristic solemnity, 'That would be a credible summary of the current situation.'

'What about kidnap?' I broach tentatively. 'Perhaps she's—'

Pastor George shakes his head. 'We explored the possibility. But no demand for ransom has been made as of now.'

'So, why can't you all, A, wait for your first lady to appear and all this will be cleared up, or B, send out a search party while trying to convince the police no foul play has occurred? Option B is especially easy with a good lawyer.'

Mrs Bucknor lets her guard down enough to give me a grateful look. 'Is that not what I've been saying?'

I guessed right. She doesn't want me here.

'It's not that simple, Dr Taiwo,' Pastor Nwoko says. 'Given the public nature of Bishop's arrest, we need to show the congregation that due diligence is being done. We need answers. We need to know who reported First Lady as missing, or worse, killed. The police claim it was an anonymous tip-off.' He hisses with a downward curve of his lips, leaving no doubt as to his unchristianly impression of law enforcement and whoever tipped them off.

I frown. 'You don't think it's an anonymous tip?'

'No, we don't,' Kenny says with a reassuring smile at Mrs Bucknor. It's strange she can't sense the woman's ambivalence about my presence. But then, my sister is like that. Loyal without reservation. Supportive without questioning.

'Enemies are at work,' Pastor Nwoko adds, but he's looking around as if the culprit is in the room. 'Those who will do anything to bring the man of God down. We want to know who they are and what they must have told the police. Our God will punish them.'

Murmurs of 'amen' and 'in Jesus' name' ripple across the room. The irony of hiring someone to look for culprits to deliver to a forgiving God for punishment appears lost on them. I write in my notepad, more for dramatic impact while waiting for their loud piety to fizzle out.

When the room quietens, I glance at Mrs Bucknor. 'I'm sorry, ma, but I've got to ask. What if the police are right?'

'Phil!' Kenny exclaims into the gasps around the table.

My eyes stay on Mrs Bucknor, and I keep my voice gentle. 'For me to look into the matter, I've got to consider what the police know, and why they made the arrest. And if they believe the first lady is, er, well—'

'Nothing has happened to my daughter.' Mrs Bucknor's gaze is unwavering, her tone clipped.

The elders agree with more amens and sprinklings of 'the devil is a liar'. Their expressions dare me to contradict them.

I can't back off. 'The police must have something that points to foul play. If that's the case—'

'But who would want First Lady dead?' Pastor Nwoko cuts in loudly. Mrs Bucknor flinches, and Kenny pulls her closer. There's rebuke in the way the other elders stare at Pastor Nwoko, who now looks to Pastor George for support.

'If we consider that possibility,' Pastor George says, 'then I'm afraid we have to ask who would want Bishop framed for such a crime.'

If he's being framed. I don't say this out loud, but the way Deputy Jesus is looking at me, I suspect he's thinking the same thing.

THE WAR AT HOME

It is almost 9 p.m. when we drive through the gates of Graceland Church Estate, into the mayhem and on our way back to Lagos. It's no worse than I anticipated but now, my mind is occupied. I quiz Kenny about the elders and time passes swiftly as she explains the hierarchy and dynamics of leadership in Grace Church. Her feedback confirms my suspicion: unravelling how and why Bishop Dawodu would be implicated in his wife's disappearance won't be a breeze.

'Sister Kikelomo sees herself as the mother of the church,' Kenny says when I ask about the older woman.

'She's not an elder like the others?'

Kenny shakes her head. 'No, but she might as well be. I met her when I started going to Grace Church. We were both in the professional women's support group.'

Kikelomo Bucknor didn't come across as a career woman but then people are rarely what they look, sound or dress like. Or what they call themselves. I had learnt this the hard way. 'She's a professional at what?'

'Civil engineer at the Ministry of Works. She's retired now though.'

Ah. I wasn't so far off, after all. 'When?'

Kenny frowns. 'I think it was after Sade married Bishop.'

'So, her status in the church rose after her daughter's marriage?'

Kenny gives me a sharp look. 'Don't say it like that. Yes, her church responsibilities increased when Sade became First Lady but she was due for retirement anyway.'

'No husband?'

Kenny shakes her head. 'He's late. Quite a while back from what I hear.'

A widow who never remarried and wears no wedding band. Curiouser. 'What's her relationship with the bishop?'

'Quite close,' Kenny answers without hesitation. 'Bishop calls her his mother, and encourages everyone to see her like that. That's why she can't believe any of the nonsense the police are saying.'

Perhaps that would explain her reticence about my presence. Her belief in her son-in-law's innocence is intertwined with her loyalty to him as her pastor. But should both supersede the concern around her daughter's whereabouts?

'Pastor George,' I say, recalling the flat way the man spoke of Sade Dawodu. 'How does he get along with the bishop's wife?'

Kenny's shrug gives off an 'it is what it is' vibe. 'Rocky, but not in a disruptive way. There's the age difference. Sade's young and dynamic. She has exciting ideas for youth programmes, wants sex education workshops for single women and all that. Pastor George is more traditional but is forced to be respectful because she is First Lady. So, there's some friction when they're in the same space. We don't think much of it because we understand that it's mostly a conflict of ideologies.'

'And you?' We've just crossed into Lagos. The traffic has eased somewhat. It's chaotic, but moving.

'What about me?' Kenny raises a suspicious eyebrow.

The ease with which she refers to the first lady by her first name has not escaped me. 'What's your relationship with her?'

Kenny takes a deep breath and looks away. I give her time to compose her thoughts. When she's not spitting Holy Ghost fire, my sister can be profoundly percep-tive. Being an auditor – an exceptionally successful one in a male-dominated field – gives her a skill for analysis that few can match. A skill she appears to suspend on all church-related matters.

'She's not happy,' Kenny says after a long pause.

'She told you?'

Kenny turns to face me, and even in the semi-darkness of the car, I see her reluctance to share. Too bad.

'How do you know she's unhappy?' I press on.

'Because I just know,' Kenny retorts sharply. She sighs when my silence tells her I'm not budging. 'Look, she's kind of my friend even if she's Bishop's wife. She took me as an aunt of sorts—'

'She doesn't have friends her own age?'

Kenny gives me a warning side-eye and continues, 'I'm sure she did before she married Bishop. But after, I don't think it was easy for people to relate with her the same way any more. Especially in the past year, she just seemed to keep more to herself. We used to hang out a lot, especially after prayer meetings when everyone was gone. All that stopped months ago, and when I asked her, she would say everything is fine, she's just busy that's all.

Even when I sensed she was lying, I tried to give her space.
But I could sense she was lonely.'

'And she goes on personal retreats?'

Kenny searches my face for traces of irony. Finding none,
her brow creases and she bites her lower lip the way she
does when she's about to pick her words carefully. 'The
church can be a pressure cooker, Phil. You saw those elders.
Constantly bickering, so much politics. Bishop can take
it. He's older, experienced and more mature. Besides, he's
walking in his ministry. You know, obeying God's calling is
his life. Sade didn't ask for all of that. She just wants to live
her life. That can't be easy for someone so young.'

'You like her,' I say with a smile. My sister sees good
in everyone. A strange trait for someone trained to see the
fault lines in trends and numbers.

'So, you'll take the case?' Kenny asks eagerly.

I won't be railroaded. 'I'll consider it.'

'Consider fast,' she snaps, cutting short the sibling affection in the air. 'Bishop is languishing in jail.'

'Oh, please! It's only been a day.'

'One night in a Lagos prison might as well be ten years.
Especially if you're innocent!'

'He'll get bail,' I say confidently.

Kenny shakes her head. 'He says no bail. Bishop wants
the law to take its course.'

Who, but the reckless or naïve, would take such a stance?
'But he's entitled to a bail hearing, at least.'

'His ways are not our ways,' Kenny announces so cryp-
tically, I can't say whether she's referring to God or the
bishop. 'I'm sure he'll tell you his reasons when you speak
with him.'

'*If* I speak with him.'

'Come on, Philip. You know how much this means to me.'

In spite of my misgivings, my professional curiosity is on high alert. I'm getting bored with teaching at the Police College while waiting for Folake's sabbatical to be over. Plus, it's almost a year since the near-death experience of my last case. It's time to enrich my résumé in readiness for our return to the States. I know former colleagues in law enforcement who'd give a body part to investigate a case like this.

'I'll let Pastor George know my decision tomorrow.' I try to sound non-committal as the driver steers the car towards the staff residential area of the University of Lagos campus.

'It's too late to come in,' Kenny says when we are parked in front of my house.

I slot my notepad and pen into my laptop bag's side pocket. 'I'll greet them for you. Greet Dele and the kids.'

'The kèfèrí will hear.'

I chuckle at Kenny's description of her husband. Dele Bhadmus is an atheist of note. The success of their union should rank as the eighth wonder of the world. It has produced four freakishly balanced teenagers and provided baffled entertainment at every family gathering.

'It's like Hillary and Reagan as a couple,' Folake once said of my sister's marriage. 'As unthinkable as it would be fascinating.'

I thank the driver with a 1,000 Naira note. He protests but takes the money when I insist it's for his kids, a little something for keeping their father out so late. Kenny adds her gratitude on her driver's behalf with a torrent of prayers in Yoruba which I wave off as I hurry towards my front porch.

'If you think this is one of your Disney family shows, you're sorely mistaken, young lady!' Folake's anger is loud and unmistakable. My hand freezes on the doorknob. 'We don't bang doors in this house simply because things aren't going our way!'

Lara. Again. What wouldn't I give to go back to the time before she turned fifteen. After my day, I'm not looking forward to dealing with the sullen alien who has replaced my sunny daughter. I take a deep breath, count to ten and turn the knob.

'Except if I ever spoke to my own mother that way, you've no right to even look at me like that.'

When Folake reverts to Nigerian-mother mode, jettisoning the accent and sentence structure acquired after over two decades of living in the States, there's trouble.

'Talk to your daughter because I'm done!' Folake says as soon as she sees me.

'What happened?' I ask Lara, standing defiant in the centre of the living room.

'She started it, Dad, all I—'

'Who started what? Am I your mate?' Folake thunders.

Lara knows better than to answer.

I give Folake our 'I'll handle this' look. She storms past me and heads upstairs.

'You were saying?' I ask as soon as I hear our bedroom door close.

'Nothing.' Lara is her mum's mini-me, clothed in teenage angst as she crosses her arms over her chest.

'You were ready to tell me just now.'

'And I was gagged, wasn't I? So, nothing happened.'

Where's my little girl who'd have hugged me as soon as I come home? Where's our Miss Fix-it, who'd put together any electronic gadget in less time than it took her to pull it apart? Our bookworm who'd quote Tolkien while thrashing her brothers at a Minecraft? Despite saying I'll handle the situation, I'm at a loss what to say to this stranger.

'Omolara,' I say gently. 'Talk to me. Why are you so angry?'

The way Lara wipes the sudden tears breaks my heart. I move closer, ready to embrace and console. She steps backwards, out of my reach. This cuts deep.

'You promised we were coming home!' Lara accuses me, her eyes throwing angry darts.

'Home? What do you—'

'When we were leaving the States, you both said we were coming home.'

'But it's true,' I say, somewhat relieved. My daughter misses her life in America. I can relate.

'It's not. This is not home. The people aren't that nice. It's hot and noisy. Everyone speaks at once. There's dust everywhere. The roads are a nightmare. The internet is even slower than the traffic which means you can't get anywhere. Literally! The food is overrated. Who needs all that spice, day in, day out?'

'But you didn't feel like this when we first arrived?' I ask when it seems she's run out of steam.

'Well, things change. I miss my friends. My school. Our neighbourhood. I wanna go back home.'

'Nigeria is your home,' I say, feeling like a fraud.

'No. You guys are, like, forcing it to be home, but it's not!'

I've mulled this notion more times than I should, so I take the defensive. 'First of all, no matter how upset you might be, don't raise your voice to me. Second, no one's forcing anything. Mum's sabbatical will be over soon and we—'

'I want to go now,' she pleads, tearful.

'Why?' No answer. 'Why now, Lara?'

We're like this for less than a minute, but it feels much longer. Lara says nothing but her eyes dare me to keep pushing. I am tired.

'Maybe you should go to your room now. We can talk more when you're ready?'

Lara gives a 'whatever' shrug and I don't have the strength to caution her. I'm more concerned she'll do something to raise her mother's ire further. If that happens, no one – not her brothers now hiding in their rooms or me – can save her from Folake's wrath.

'Omolara,' I call when she's halfway up the stairs.

She stops and glares at me like I'm the Grinch who stole Christmas.

'Whatever you do, do not slam your door.'

TRUTH OR DARE

The smell of incense wafts from the bathroom. Folake is taking a long soak, her go-to calming ritual. Perhaps it's for the best. I'm not sure she's ready to hear Lara's turnaround about being back in Nigeria. Besides, experience has taught me to wait for her legal mind to process things. Failure to do this almost certainly results in an argument she'll win. No one spars with Professor Afolake Taiwo without having their ducks aligned. Backed into a corner, my wife is brutal. Give her time to think things through, she might go easy on you and let you lose gracefully.

I sit on the bed and bury my head in my palms. Lara's outburst hit me more than I care to admit. More so, her words echo my feelings about what I privately call 'our Nigerian Experiment'.

Are we home? If we are, is this where we want to call home especially when we've got a choice?

I look around the bedroom. We've done our best to upgrade it from the university's standard furniture, but it's a still a far cry from our living space in San Francisco. Adjacent to the built-in wardrobe, there's a crack in the wall, so deep it has inspired more nightmares of the house splitting in two than I care to remember. No matter how many coats of paint we use on the ceiling, nothing can hide the dipping of the boards, swollen with age and rot. Our application to the university's maintenance department has been in since we moved in seventeen months ago.

This is not home. I know this. But with five months to the end of her sabbatical, I'm getting the feeling Folake won't agree with me. Her silence on the future worries me, so naturally, I don't bring it up. Choosing to let time decide our next steps seems the wise course of action, especially since our reason for leaving the States remains between us. An insurmountable wedge that compromises any leverage I might have, while strengthening her resolve.

Sleep won't come, so I change into my old USC Alumnus tee with matching joggers and head towards the storeroom we converted to what could pass for a study.

I google 'Sade Dawodu'. It's unnerving to find nearly all references to the missing woman occur in relation to her mega-popular husband. I scroll through social media sites, check numerous articles on Grace Church; mentions of the first lady come across as an aside. In the pictures, she's almost always next to the bishop; he smiles with a gregarious charm at the cameras, while she looks demure, like she's too shy to take the spotlight from him.

And she could if she wanted to, because Folasade Dawodu is stunning. She's slender and stands almost shoulder to shoulder with the bishop who is not of average height. Her light skin glows with health, and even perfectly made-up, the similarity to her mother is so uncanny they could pass for sisters.

I'd have skipped the documentary if it wasn't for the tag; #PrayforFirstLady which started trending from the day the bishop was arrested, along with #IstandwithBishop. It's an old twelve-minute video profiling the work of a non-governmental organisation called 'Girls in Control'. A fresh-faced Sade Dawodu appears. The graphics type out her name and identify her as one of the trustees of the NGO.

'Girls in Control is dedicated to supporting young girls to acquire and actively use their agency,' Sade Dawodu says to the camera. She is glowing, sporting a white T-shirt emblazoned with '#CONTROL' and blue jeans. A far cry from the ultra-glamorous wife of Bishop Dawodu. Her voice is sonorous, with a lilt and enunciation suggesting private schooling. 'We live in a world where traditions, culture and parents play such a crucial role in how young people see the world and the choices they make. The pressure on girls is much more, and they struggle to meet expectations which are often in conflict with their needs, or ambitions.'

I fast forward when another trustee comes on and presents the different activities Girls in Control does to empower girls between eight and eighteen years old. I'm impressed. The programmes are practical: employing counsellors, peer review models and even family therapy to support teenagers who have challenges communicating with their parents. I should share this with Folake. The way the situation with Lara is going, I'm not averse to outside help.

'I love being a trustee because early on in my life, I wanted to be a doctor because it was what my parents wanted for me. I never considered what I wanted and that cost me many years of unhappiness.' Sade Dawodu's voice comes up over visuals of young girls in different activities. 'This is why I love the work we do at Girls in Control. Because if there had been something like this when I was growing up,

I'm sure I would have been able to think for myself, stand up for myself and, perhaps, challenge what I thought society expected of me.'

I check the date. Uploaded two years ago but I can't confirm when it was produced. More trustees and volunteers speak, and the documentary ends with Sade Dawodu, the staff and several young girls waving at the camera and shouting, 'I am in control!'

The Sade Dawodu in this video contradicts my image of the 'first lady' of a megachurch. Not once did she quote a Bible verse or come across as patronising. I can see why Kenny likes her. I like her, at least this version of her. I hope the police are wrong, and the elders are right regarding Sade Dawodu's well-being.

I type 'Bishop J. Dawodu' in the search box. The topmost results are of the arrest. Several videos seem to have been uploaded by attendees of the now infamous service. Some started recording from the moment the police were prevented from approaching the pulpit. Others focused on the bishop as he stopped the sermon and urged the police to come forward. Many video segments tagged with #IstandwithBishop show him regally holding out his hands to be cuffed.

'God is good!' The bishop hollers as the cameras either switch back to the shocked faces of the elders I recognise from earlier or to the wailing congregation.

I click on some of the bishop's sermons. Messages of a good God promising prosperity only to the faithful and tithe-payers abound. Motivational talks about pursuing and attaining success and wealth. Nothing new. Yet, the man's charisma pulls me in. He speaks plainly, but with the command that reminds me of Barack Obama, accent and all. His approach to breaking down the scriptures is accessible and his advice practical. In spite of my misgivings about new-age Pentecostal pastors, I find myself listening to Bishop Dawodu longer than I intended. It doesn't take deep self-analysis to figure out why.

Reverend August Freeman.

It's been years since the pastor of First Baptist Assembly in downtown Los Angeles crossed my mind. But watching Bishop Dawodu preach brings back memories of the man my twin brother credits for our ambivalent relationship with organised religion. The same sing-song cadence in their sermons. A conviction in their tone, reminiscent of Martin Luther King's speeches. A charm that invites everyone, without judgement. Wit combined with a pragmatic approach to the gospel that's both contemporary and relatable. It was hard not to like Reverend Freeman, just as it is to resist the magnetism of Bishop Dawodu.

Nope. Don't go there. Thinking of Reverend Freeman is a sure-fire way to say no to Kenny and the elders. Pack it in. It's in the past. Decades ago. I am older now. Wiser, I hope. Less impressionable.

Are you? a little voice whispers, like a dare.

I pretend I don't hear it. Besides, it's getting late, and I'm on school drop-off tomorrow. I'm about to logout when the bishop calls on the choir to join him in a worship song. The singing starts before the camera swings to the mammoth-sized choir, all dressed in robes made from ankara. The lead singer looks familiar, handsome and clad in a form-fitting grey suit. The sound production is top-notch and I'm as riveted by the music as by the mood it has evoked in the congregation. One moment, Bishop Dawodu was this dynamic, commanding presence and the next, he's on his knees in worship.

The sudden change of tone from the bishop's one-man show to an all-out ensemble performance is mirrored by the editing style of the footage. Quick and sharp, barely resting for more than a second on a shot. I click pause, move the cursor back slightly, reduce playback speed and play again.

There it is.

Sade Dawodu is standing, but her hands are not raised nor her eyes closed in worship. Her expression reminds me of the one her mother threw Pastor Nwoko when he misspoke. Disdain mixed with something I can't put my finger on. I play it back again. Pause, play. Pause, play. The woman's eyes are on her kneeling husband.

Interesting. I check the upload date: a week short of eleven months ago. I take a screenshot of the scene and zoom in on the first lady. Stripped of the distractions around her, the scorn in her eyes is unmistakable. Now, it seems directed at me. I stare at the image as if willing it to animate, for the eyes to blink and the lips to move.

'*Where are you?*'

I close the laptop sharply when I realise I spoke out loud.

It's only when I settle in bed and pull Folake close that I'm able to shake off my unease. But even as sleep claims my tired body, Sade Dawodu's eyes taunt me: frozen in time and unwilling to reveal what went before.

Or lies ahead.

KICKSTART

The previous night's tension lingers in the air, even after Folake leaves for her early class. Tai and Kay's relief that I'm on school-run duty would be hilarious if I wasn't so preoccupied with what my decision to take Sade Dawodu's case would mean for my day.

Lara stomps downstairs, prompting instant silence from her brothers. She walks to Kay and places my old Nikon 300 on the dining table.

'Stop using any old rag to clean the lens. I've reset it. You shouldn't get the error message now.'

'Thanks!' Kay says with a mouthful of what should be his lunch.

'Six hundred Naira. I want cash. Have it ready by evening.'

All mouths hang open. In all the time Lara has been the resident Miss Fix-it, she's never asked to be remunerated.

'But—' Kay starts to protest.

'No buts. I've emptied the data on it. Locked in my Cloud. You pay, I release.'

Before I can intervene, Lara gives me a barely audible, 'Good morning, Dad. Gonna wait in the car,' and walks out.

'Why she trippin'?' Kay wonders aloud and wipes bread-crumbs off his mouth while slugging his backpack on his shoulder. He's more careful with the camera. Before touching it, he wipes his hands carefully and checks all the different components before storing it away in its special-purpose bag.

'Gotta admit she's cheaper than a pro,' Tai says, as he puts away his books, wraps his sandwich in foil and places it in his bag's side pouch.

My twin boys are now seventeen, identical in looks but different in attitude. Tai will eat at precise times. Kay, anytime – his lunch box just became his breakfast and I bet his backpack is filled with leftovers he raided from the fridge. Tai is more like me. He'll avoid conflict at all costs. Even witnessing an altercation distresses him. Taking after his mother, Kay lives for battle.

'Dad, please?' Kay pleads. 'Six hundred? Seriously? Where am I gonna get—?'

'You've got savings, use it,' I say, sharper than necessary. While a part of me is impressed at seeing my tech-savvy daughter seek compensation for a service we've all taken for granted, the other part worries at the abruptness of the demand. Not to mention the blackmail to ensure her brother pays up.

The drive through the university campus to the staff school is silent. Lara is the last to leave the car. She stares straight ahead, not looking at the school gates. My heart leaps. Maybe she wants to talk. Just as I'm about to prompt her, she squares her shoulders, mumbles goodbye and is out.

It takes a lot to stop myself from running after her. I swear if she turned back for even a second, I'd cancel all my plans for the day and whisk her somewhere for a proper father–daughter chat. Like old times.

I hold my breath and wait. But Lara doesn't look back.

*

'This is good,' Abubakar Tukur says as he blows smoke into the air, away from my face. We are standing outside his office, next to an overflowing ashtray. 'Brilliant in *pact*.'

More than a year of working with him, I'm only just getting used to the Police College commandant's penchant for replacing the *f*s in words with *p*s, and then vice versa. I've noticed he does this more when he's excited or agitated, forcing me to listen more carefully.

'A*p*ter the great work you did with the Okriki Three case, we managed to get some funding that allowed us to give you a contract—'

'A temporary contract,' I correct him, still amused by how the man's fondness for me makes him elevate my status above a part-time lecturer's pay grade. Since the feeling is mutual, I generally let the issue of my unpaid promotion slide. I admit a healthy savings account in US dollars helps.

Abubakar bends to stub out the cigarette. When he rises, his broad, dark face is bright with excitement. His police uniform gives him a stately air, making him appear taller and broader than my 6' 2" frame.

'Semantics. The *p*act is you're here. If you crack this case, we might well be on our way to start a *p*ull-*p*ledged criminology department here.'

'First of all, I don't *crack* cases.'

A dismissive snort this time. 'You know what I mean. Despite the *publicity* you shunned after the Okriki case, we still got a lot of goodwill from those who knew what you did. But with this one, you can't escape the media.'

'Whoa! Wait there.' I raise my palms to ward off the image of paparazzi hanging outside my home and office. 'Besides, this woman might appear tomorrow.'

'That's tomorrow. *Today*, you've been hired by one of the largest churches in the country to find her.'

'I'm not finding her. I told you—'

Abubakar waves an impatient hand. 'I know, I know. Husband framed, you find who and why. All well and good but how will you do all that if you don't find her first?'

My expression must have given it away that I'm still figuring this out because Abubakar rubs his palms together in glee and breaks out in a torrent of Hausa.

'Babu wata jayayya daga gareni! I am in.'

'In where?'

'In with whatever you want *prom* me. That's why you came to see me, right? And why you're tolerating my smoking even when you hate it.'

I chuckle aloud. The commandant has always been quick on the uptake.

'The investigative team. I need to know who tipped them off.'

'You want the case file?'

I nod. 'That and access to the investigating officers.'

'Where's the case? HQ or local?'

I shake my head. 'No idea. I only know where the bishop's being held.'

'That's a start. Where?'

I check the notes I transferred onto my phone. 'Ikoyi Model Prison.'

Abubakar frowns. 'He doesn't stay on his church estate?'

I shrug, not bothering to challenge the idea of a church belonging to any one person. 'He's got a guest house there. The church and estate are listed as his business address, but his residential one is in Ikoyi.'

Abubakar nods again, his frown deepening. I know he's mentally exploring his formidable network for the fastest and most reliable source of the information I need. As he brings out another cigarette, I speak in a rush before he lights up again.

'Any chance you know anyone at the prison?'

*

Within minutes of leaving his office, Abubakar has forwarded me the contact details of the chief warden of the Ikoyi Model Prison, along with a text message that he has booked an appointment for me with Bishop Dawodu for tomorrow.

This makes me less than present during my class on interrogation techniques. Fortunately, it employed role play rather than theoretical frameworks, so I listen, give guidance and facilitate discussions while hoping for it all to end so I can get back to the missing First Lady.

In my office, an email from Pastor George is waiting for me. A very measured correspondence on the Grace Church letterhead that expressed 'delight' regarding my decision to take the case, asked me to sign the attached non-disclosure agreement and return it as soon as I am able. How progressive; a church requesting an NDA. I'm surprised it's less than three pages rather than the grand treatise I'd have had to wade through if I was taking a similar case in the States. I append my electronic signature and click 'send'.

With classes done and Folake on pick-up duty, I've got a few hours to kill before braving the traffic home. I bring out my pile of multi-coloured Post-it notes, and start writing.

Blue. *Facts*. What is known, verifiable in the public domain and by third parties.

Red. *Red Flags*. Answers leading to more questions, creating new leads that must be followed.

Green. *Lines of Enquiry*. I start compiling some questions and make a rudimentary list of who to ask. Every elder of course. Then, there must be other people. Select church staff? What about the bishop's home? Who works there? Sade Dawodu's friends? Family members? Definitely must talk to Mrs Bucknor. But first, I call Kenny.

'You didn't tell me you accepted the job,' she says as soon as I tell her my request.

Lawdermercy! 'You wanted me to send you a special memo?'

'Ehen, is that how you talk to your sister who brought you a lucrative contract?'

'You want a finder's fee?' I snap and don't wait for what I know will be a sharper rejoinder. 'Can you make me a list or not?'

'Of First Lady's close friends? I'm not sure she has that many. I told you last night.'

'Yes, but she must have had close relationships before she became First Lady.'

'Let me think. I know there's the head of one charity she volunteers with, and then there's Margie, a doctor in Canada. They went to university together and one time when I was travelling to Toronto, and she gave me some things to—

'A *written* list, Kenny. Please. I can't keep all this info in my head right now.'

'Have you heard of Facebook?' she asks caustically.

'I've got news for you. Your First Lady has zero social media presence.' The silence is so long I check if the call has dropped. 'Kenny?'

'That's strange. She was so active on social media. I'm not on those platforms apart from LinkedIn, but I know quite a number of people follow her on Twitter and Facebook.'

'So, what happened? Because there's no sign of Sade Dawodu in Zuckerbergville or Twittersphere.'

'Let me think.' Kenny sounds like she's not even listening to me any more. 'So strange.'

I don't have time for this. 'Do that. Gotta go.'

I hang up. I'll have to look into why Sade Dawodu's presence on the internet has been reduced to only mentions in relation to her husband. And check the timing of her non-activity on social media.

I tear out a purple-coloured Post-it. *Research*.

Orange. *Timelines*. The trajectory of events leading to now. Finding connections. Checking for linkages.

Abubakar was right. The path of least effort would be to find Sade Dawodu first. That is, assuming the elders' version of events is true and the police have made a grave mistake in their haste to arrest the bishop. The first forty-eight hours of tracking a missing person are critical, with the clock starting when the person went missing, not when someone noticed they'd disappeared. After seventy-two hours, the police tend to assume the worst. I don't know enough to guess the window for a positive outcome in Nigeria. Without a viable database or a working national identity card system, I'm guessing finding a missing person must rely on a combination of luck and prayers.

Theoretically, a missing person is anyone whose whereabouts cannot be confirmed and where the circumstances of disappearance are distinctively out of character. If the elders are to be believed, this definition does not apply to Sade Dawodu. Given their insistence that the first lady is merely *absent*, the most prudent thing for the police to do would be to wait for her to reappear. Since they haven't, one must ask what else they know.

Get the case file asap. In an ideal world, this would be my starting point. I'd have access to the file and to everyone on the case. They would be clear that I am working in the best interests of the case, to ensure the best possible outcome. If a crime has been committed, my job would be to ensure that the prosecution has an airtight case. If there was no foul play, I'd have saved millions in taxpayers' money. Not here though, and certainly not this case. The police will not welcome my interference. Especially when they know who's paying my bill. I need Abubakar to get that file but I can't afford to wait for him.

I tear out a purple Post-it and write. *Bishop Dawodu.*

Who's this man accused of a crime that might not have been committed?

VERY IMPORTANT PRISONER

Bishop Jeremiah Dawodu walks in and the room shrinks further. His impressive frame is accentuated by the navy-blue blazer that's so tightly fitted you'd think every inch of his body was measured before a single stitch was sewn. Well-trimmed, greying moustache and close-cropped hair give the impression that he just walked in from a barbershop.

'Dr Taiwo?'

His handshake is firm, patting the back of my hand like a politician greeting an ardent fan. I shake off memories of Reverend Freeman. That infectious smile. The easy camaraderie that makes you feel you've found an ally for life.

Focus, Philip, the little voice orders.

'Wonderful,' Bishop Dawodu says as he pulls out a plastic chair and points to the other one I just stood up from. 'Bless you. Please, please let's have a seat.'

We're meeting in the tiny interrogation room arranged for us by the chief warden. The walls are a drab grey with dark stains of dubious origin that I'd rather not think about. The one small window looks onto the backyard where rusted body parts of vehicles lie and brown khaki uniforms hang out to dry on crudely made clothing lines. But all these seem to retreat as soon as the bishop sits and gives me another warm smile. His energy is positive, his aura so relaxed you'd think he's the manager of a five-star restaurant and not a guest of the Nigerian prison system.

I'm taken aback by his congeniality, his crisp cotton shirt, ironed trousers with a brown leather belt matching the tone of his pointed shoes. His cologne fills the room, a woody scent with undertones of something. Bergamot?

'So, you're Sister Kenny's brother?' he asks.

Pleasantries give me time to study him. He asks where I lived in the States, about my children and how they are acclimatising. My responses are brief. When he asks where I worship, I take out my mobile phone.

'Do you mind if we record this conversation?'

He flicks his wrist. A Patek Philippe watch peeks out of the cuffs. I press record.

'What's your take on what you're being accused of?' I keep my tone light, my body language unthreatening.

Perfectly manicured nails wave dismissively through the air. 'Ridiculous. My wife is perfectly fine and should be home soon.'

I expected this but not the near beatific expression. 'So, the police have it all wrong?'

'Of course, they do. But who can blame them? Some mischievous person has chosen to use the unique dynamics of my marriage to discredit me. The police are just doing their job. I bear no ill will.'

'Any idea who this mischievous person or persons might be?'

He shrugs. 'I'm a servant of the Most High and that makes me a target of the devil. It could be anyone.'

'You can't hazard a guess? Something I can work with?'

'To be honest, I really don't care. If I had my way, you wouldn't be here. I told the elders there's no need for all this but they were insistent. And don't get me wrong, I understand why they feel they have to act since they can't trust the police to do the right thing. I walk in faith. My wife will be home soon and all this will be over. To your question though, no, I don't know who could have spread the malicious lies that led to my arrest. But it has to be someone who knows Sade goes away for her personal and spiritual retreat.'

I've interviewed enough suspects to know this is not the typical reaction to a murder accusation, let alone an arrest. The bishop's eyes are clear, not dilated; his gestures expressive, not manic. The demeanour of someone at peace with himself and his situation. Weird.

I switch tack. 'How are things between you and your wife?'

'Blessed. Of course, we've had our challenges, but God has always helped us through.' He pauses, but the smile doesn't falter as he chooses his words. 'I'm sure you know our union has not been blessed with a child. This causes a lot of tension within the church.' His smile wobbles, and sadness fills his eyes. 'I understand their concern. It's not a good look for a general overseer to be in my situation. But who can question the will of God?'

'The tension is only within the church?' I ask gently. In spite of myself, there's something about the way the bishop conducts himself that draws me to him. He speaks calmly, without judgement and grounded in reality. I'd expected platitudes, Bible quotes, the devil at work and all that nonsense. Rather, this man seems to appreciate how his relationship with his wife may be misconstrued and used against him. There's no aggression or defensiveness about him. Just resignation.

He lets out a deep breath. His smile disappears completely and he looks away from me as if embarrassed. 'We're spirit beings, but still flesh, Dr Taiwo. My wife and I. There are times when it worries us, when it seems our prayers are falling on deaf ears. Or that God is testing us beyond what our faith would allow. I must admit, it hits her more than me. I have the church to keep me busy, and well, she has a bit more time on her hands to question the will of God. So, yes, the tension spills over into our home, and when that happens, I know she needs a break, so I give my blessing for her to take it.'

I nod. 'Is it her or you? I mean, the problem?' It's a delicate balance between probing and being invasive, so my tone is tentative, allowing him to choose not to answer.

He chuckles, amused at my unease. 'Dr Taiwo, I assure you our situation has led to more uncomfortable questions before. I can write a book on the tests and questionnaires we've gone through over the past years. You can relax. That said, we've seen many doctors, and the verdict is the same. We are both healthy and there's no medical reason why my wife cannot carry a baby to term.'

I frown. 'To term? You mean...?'

'I mean my wife has conceived before but we lost the baby in the first trimester,' he says calmly, his gaze steady.

'When was this?' I keep my voice neutral. This is information that the elders are either not aware of or chose not to share. Its bearing on the matter at hand is yet to be determined.

'About three and half years into our union. We were overjoyed, but chose to keep it between us till we were sure. With hindsight, maybe we shouldn't have. Maybe we should have proclaimed our testimony and not doubted God's promise. Perhaps then, people wouldn't look at my wife like she's barren and somehow less than worthy of her role as First Lady of Grace Church. I regret that.'

'The choice to keep the pregnancy secret was yours?'

He nods, still avoiding my gaze. 'You have to understand, Dr Taiwo, we had waited so long. Prayed so hard. And when it happened, I'm ashamed to say, I was surprised. I couldn't take it in my stride like it was an expected miracle. I wanted us to hold on to that precious news for just a little while, get used to it even, before letting everyone in.'

Are those tears in the man's eyes? I look down at my recorder, cursing my decision not to carry my notebook so I can pretend to be taking notes. I'm not prepared for this level of vulnerability from a man who leads a congregation of millions. It's humbling to witness.

The awkward pause gives the bishop time to compose himself. When I look up, he's all smiles again.

'But we moved on. The Lord has done it before and Sade and I know He'll do it again. We just have to be patient and prayerful.'

The bishop speaks of his wife like he's unaware of the charges against him. His inflections suggest warmth every time he mentions her name with an almost paternal indulgence. My mind races to the upload date on the YouTube video I viewed two days earlier. If Sade was recovering from a miscarriage months earlier, perhaps that would explain the resentment I observed in that image? Perhaps she was angry at a situation where her husband placed her needs below his commitment to the church.

'Tell me about the last time you saw her,' I ask.

Perhaps because it's a question he knew I'd ask or has been asked by the police, there's no lightness in his tone. Or hesitation. 'I had a board meeting at Graceland. She was supposed to be there, but that morning, she was low in spirit and I felt she wouldn't be able to handle the pressures of the church leadership, so I asked her to stay at home to rest. By the time I returned in the evening, she had given the staff the day off and cooked me a very nice dinner. It's what she does when she wants to go away. But this time, I don't know why it didn't sit well with me. I'm not proud of it but we had a fight.'

A well-prepared response. He'll expect me to ask what transpired during the fight, so I don't.

The bishop looks like someone about to confess something grievous. 'I take full responsibility. I didn't expect her to leave the next day. I expected a romantic evening with my wife, but instead she told me she needed space.'

A sharp intake of breath follows more regretful head shaking. There's a brokenness about him that makes me want to pat his broad back in comfort. I resist the urge.

'She said terrible things. That I don't care about what she's going through, and I care more about the church than our marriage. That she feels like a failure and I'm not doing anything to help her.'

'Maybe she wanted you to come with her this time?' I suggest, proffering understanding for his plight and a different perspective. Empathy without judgement makes interviewees less guarded.

It works. Bishop Dawodu looks at me as though my question hadn't occurred to him. He frowns, then nods slowly, like an insight is just dawning. The silence stretches as he stands and walks to the small window. I watch him as he appears to focus on the broken-down vehicles that dot the landscape.

Just as I start considering if I should change my line of questioning, he turns to me with a rueful smile. 'If that's what she wanted, she had a strange way of showing it. In fact, there was a time—' He looks away as if considering the wisdom of saying more, then adds, 'I was worried her illness was coming back.'

'Her illness?'

'It's not something I've ever shared with anyone, but since you're here to help, I guess it's okay.' He holds my gaze. 'Sade has a history of mental illness.'

'You knew this before or after marriage?' I try to sound neutral. Mental health is highly correlated with the unintended disappearance of missing persons. But this is not information I want to divulge to a murder suspect.

'Only after. By the time we married, she was out of therapy and off medication, so I never knew until after the miscarriage when the illness made a resurgence.'

'Did she get help after the miscarriage? Therapy? Medication?'

'We should have but we didn't. She insisted she was fine, and I felt whatever she was going through was normal. Who waits more than three years to be pregnant, then loses the baby and is in perfect health? Mental or otherwise. So, I agreed that she didn't need anything but prayers and support. I thought I was right until that night.'

'She showed symptoms similar to her behaviour after the miscarriage?'

46

He nods. 'Worse. Much worse. The things she said. And the violence.' He frowns again, as if figuring out a puzzling clue. 'Quite unlike her. I couldn't explain it.'

'Violence? From her?' He doesn't strike me like someone who'd claim the 'victim' role in a domestic altercation.

He pulls his shirt collar down. Long scabs and welts across his neck disappear into his collar bones. 'It took everything within me to maintain my peace. She even threatened me with a knife. It was the security guard who helped me restrain her and made her drop it.'

I try not to ponder on how two men 'made' a woman do anything, so instead I ask, 'What did you do then?'

'I left the house. I drove back to Graceland and spent the night at our house there. The next day, we started our seven-day special programme. I assumed she left for her retreat and didn't call because she was still angry and if I'm honest, I was also angry.'

'So, you never followed up with her after?'

He looks remorseful. Again, his eyes glisten with tears. 'I should have. I know that now. But I was angry. Hurt.'

'You told no one about this?'

He shakes his head, avoiding my gaze, and in an act of unexpected inelegance, he wipes his eyes with the sleeves of his crisp shirt. 'I couldn't. I was too ashamed.'

'Then, the police came.' I say this to prompt any information different from what he and the elders have shared about the events leading to his arrest.

He waves a hand around the room. 'And here we are.'

So, nothing new. I don't know the bishop enough to determine whether he's capable of murder, but I've interviewed enough murderers to know that if Sade Dawodu has come to any harm, the chances that her husband did it are getting lower than statistics indicate. His genuineness about what happened the night before Sade left home, his admission of bad judgement and remorse are testimony that any smart person would know doesn't help their case. Except if it's true.

I change tack. 'I'm told you refused to ask for bail?'

He comes back to sit across from me again. The smile is back. He crosses his legs and opens his palms into the air. 'Where would my faith be if I can't trust the truth to vindicate me?'

'But being here?' I gesture around the room. 'This can't be easy.'

He smiles wider and wags a teasing finger at me. 'Apostle Paul wrote some of his most inspired letters to the church from prison.'

I give him a pointed look. 'These are hardly the same conditions.'

His smile becomes rueful. 'Touché, Dr Taiwo. What can I say? Some of the staff here are church members. Plus, for 125,000 Naira a night, I'm remanded in the VIP quarters. I have my own room and I can order meals from any restaurant. But make no mistake, it is still prison.'

'Beats being in the general population,' I quip.

'But doesn't beat being free of the suspicion that I murdered my wife,' he says, smile gone. 'That's a burden no preferential treatment can lift.'

We are both quiet. His wife's absence hangs in the air, heavy with the possibility that he might be wrong.

He sits back on the plastic chair, and cocks an eyebrow at me. 'Perhaps you think I'm playing martyr. After all, why else would I refuse bail until my wife comes back?'

Under the circumstances, frankness seems the best policy. 'Bishop, I don't know you well enough to know if you're playing at being a martyr. If you are, it's a high price to pay given what you're being accused of.' The bishop's bearing slumps slightly and uncertainty creeps into his eyes. I quickly add, 'But, I'm also inclined to think that can only mean one thing.'

'What's that?' There's hope in his tone.

Compassion makes me answer more honestly than I should. 'You're convinced your wife is alive and will be home soon.'

BE PREPARED

Stay focused. Always. The people around him will do everything to maintain the appearance of his power and anointing. Let them do their jobs. Let the lawyers deliberate, the police ask questions, and the media speculate. Let the whole congregation murmur, grumble and whisper. Remember, we want to force scrutiny. To unpeel his mask of righteousness. We need all eyes on him, probing.

Expect the worst. I couldn't think of every possible way he and his people will try to counter all I have put in place. Leave nothing to chance. Destroy the dossier I gave you. Nothing must be traceable to you. Do not be tempted to keep anything. There are copies with people ready to move at the right moment. On your word.

It took a lot to get the medical records, but I needed you to have some context, especially about those days in university. You can see how the doctor showed me I was not 'crazy' or 'unstable'. How he helped me through my grief after Daddy died and I flunked out of medical school. That file is for your eyes only. Keep it that way. We don't need him using it to justify what I have done. Burn it when you're done reading.

Don't let your guard down. Don't allow anger make you rush things. Trust that I planned that he would put up a fight. Even when it seems like he's winning, don't despair. Remember: the greater his illusion of victory, the sweeter the fall.

Above all, be strong.

A TALE IN BLOOD

'You believe him?' Chika asks as soon as we settle down with our food. We've chosen the least noisy corner, away from the music videos playing on TV screens and customers shouting their orders.

'It's a gut feeling,' I say, digging into my food. 'I'm not quite sure how to read the guy. Something's not adding up.'

'And yet, your gut says he didn't kill his wife? I'm confused,' Chika says ruefully.

'It's his personality that confuses me. Look, this guy's the leader of a church with millions of members across the globe. Forbes ranked him as one of the top twenty richest pastors in the world. I expected a bit more arrogance, some entitlement even. But he's actually quite cool, level-headed, approachable, even humble enough to admit his poor handling of the quarrel with his wife.'

'Ah, I get it now. Because the suspect didn't fit into your preconceived notion of what a megachurch pastor should be, your gut says he's innocent?'

If anyone has earned the right to tease me, it's Chika Makuochi. I wave a cautionary finger at him. 'He has a solid alibi. He was at the church that night.'

Chika holds up a piece of meat, frowning. He has an abhorrence of the innards of a cow. 'He could've killed her before going to the church to establish his alibi.'

I can't argue against this logic without the case file to establish a timeline. For the umpteenth time, I pray Abubakar comes through.

'Fair point,' I grudgingly concede, as I put the fork aside and use my fingers to deal with the fried fish. Delicious. 'By the way,' I continue, 'I hope you don't expect me to pay for this meal because Ghana High is not some new joint you discovered. I practically grew up here.'

Chika rolls his eyes. 'I could tell from the way they greeted you.'

He's won our ongoing contest of discovering the best bukas around Lagos three consecutive times. But not this time. Months ago, when I came here with my dad – his medical practice is around the corner – it was like a home-coming. The place has graduated from being a makeshift shack to a full-fledged restaurant, but the food hasn't changed. Still the best jollof rice on this side of Lagos.

Chika downs his bottled water. 'Anyway, it's my treat. A celebration of sorts.'

'Of what?' I ask, mouth full.

'Today marks a year when we met in Port Harcourt.'

How fortuitous to be taking my second case exactly a year after the first. 'A lot has happened, eh?'

'Adaora's going to be one next month.'

Despite knowing that I wouldn't have met Chika other-wise, I try not to connect the turbulence of my last case to my godchild's birth. The dangers Chika and I encountered while investigating the vigilante killing of three undergraduates in Port Harcourt were nothing compared to our various worries for our families in Lagos. Chika was dealing with a heavily pregnant wife while I was agonising over a bad patch in my marriage brought on by my paranoia.

'Time flies, eh? And nothing's changed. I'm still using you as a sounding board.'

Chika cocks an eyebrow while waving at a nearby waitress. 'Is that what I am now? A sounding board?'

'Well, you could be more if you use your contacts to track any activity on the first lady's phone. Can you?'

'Maybe.' Chika holds up his empty bottle and points at the refrigerator behind the waitress. 'What makes you think the police don't have it already?'

'I'm assuming I won't get the case file in time to make critical deductions. Besides, no harm in getting evidence that corroborates whatever they've got.'

'And you call me a control freak,' Chika scoffs.

'I'm not controlling,' I sputter in protest. 'I just want access to information that hasn't been curated.'

'How's that not controlling?' Chika says as the waitress comes over with two bottles of water.

I wait for her to retreat then lean forward. 'I know how hard it is to get phone records, but if anyone can do it, it's you. Please?'

'It's borderline illegal.'

'Which is why I'm asking you.'

'Thank you,' Chika retorts, unimpressed by my dubious compliment. 'Anyway, I might know someone but it's going to cost. You have her number?'

I take out my phone to text the request to Kenny just as Abubakar's message appears.

I.O. will take you thru the C.S. B there at 1500 hrs.

A walk through the crime scene by the investigating officer? I check the clock on the phone screen. 2:17 p.m.

I lick my fingers, grateful I'm almost done. 'How would you like to be more than a sounding board and telephone hacker?'

*

An hour later, Chika steers his Pajero into a secluded part of Ikoyi.

Chika whistles. 'God business is good business.'

I can't argue. Bishop Dawodu lives on a street where old money effortlessly meets the new. Massive mansions hide behind tall walls and high gates. The distance between one entrance gate and the next is easily a quarter of a mile.

'You have arrived,' the GPS says.

'I think it's that one,' I say, pointing to a battered Peugeot with the Nigerian Police insignia.

Chika brings the car to a stop behind it.

'This is fun,' he says as we alight.

'Stop it. Someone might be dead.'

He grins. 'My idea of fun is not everyone's.'

I give him a stern glance, which he ignores by smiling even wider. Chika's brand of humour takes getting used to, especially when one forgets his past life as a mercenary.

We walk through the open gates and an impressively muscled security guard strides in our direction. Just as we are about to introduce ourselves—

'They are here for me!' a loud voice calls out.

The security guard retreats to his station and the owner of the voice grounds a cigarette butt on the concrete inter-locks. He's almost painfully skinny with tobacco-stained teeth and a head full of hair sprinkled with pockets of grey. He's not in uniform but I can make out a Police Force logo on the white T-shirt he wears under his previously white polo shirt.

'Ibrahim Dobra,' he says when he gets to us. 'Inspector,' he adds quickly, his head bopping with delight. 'Dr Taiwo? I've heard so much about you.'

'I hope good things.' I offer a handshake. 'Sorry we're late. The traffic, you know.' I gesture towards Chika, 'This is—'

Inspector Dobra's eyes widen. 'Chika Makuochi?'

'You know me too?' Chika asks, uncharacteristically unable to hide his surprise.

Dobra turns to me, speaking in a rush, 'I read the case study of your work on the Okriki Three. Brilliant work. That's why I am so glad you are interested in this case.'

Chika and I exchange quick looks. A fan wouldn't hurt. Not like we have a choice since Dobra is already usher-ing us past a signboard with the fading lettering: 'POLICE CRIME SCENE. DO NOT ENTER.'

'You're not the lead investigator?'

'No, no,' Inspector Dobra says, gingerly skipping up the steps to the front door. 'That would be Detective Bello. We are both with the Special Crimes and Investigations Unit. I'm sure you know of us.' He turns to Chika with a smile. 'In the regular force, he would be a deputy commissioner and I'd be a superintendent. So, he's the boss, although I don't report to him directly.'

'I thought he was the one coming to meet with us,' I cut in.

If Inspector Dobra hears the disappointment in my tone, it doesn't dampen his enthusiasm. 'He couldn't be here, so he sent me.'

Damnit. I was really hoping to meet the lead I.O. I'm bursting with questions for this Detective Bello. For now at least, best to meet Dobra's excitement with some interest. It will be foolhardy to fritter away the opportunity to study the crime scene simply because I did not get the tour guide of my choice. I plaster a game-on smile on my face and follow Inspector Dobra through the front doors of the Dawodu mansion. Behind me, Chika chuckles. He's not fooled.

Opulence meets us. High ceilings held up by pillars. Bulkheads of pristine plaster of Paris, with intricate patterns which must have taken months to achieve. Marble tiles, furniture upholstered in rich damask and side tables of polished teak. Life-size framed pictures of the bishop and his wife occupy every available wall space not covered by velvet curtains. It looks like the lobby of a grand hotel.

A musky smell fills the air. The house hasn't been aired since it got its crime scene status. It takes a lot not to ask that the huge windows be opened. Despite the abundant space around me, I feel closed in.

Dobra hands us gloves and plastic bags.

'I'm sorry we're not as sophisticated as what you must be used to in America,' he says, 'but I did a three-month course in Aberdeen on CSI, and I try to replicate what I've learnt as much as possible.'

I pull on the gloves and put a plastic bag over each shoe. Chika and Inspector Dobra do the same. They look ridiculous. I'm sure I do too.

'We came as soon as we got the search warrant four days ago, sealed the premises and left everything as is.' He lowers his voice, looks around quickly. 'Apart from the I.O.s who were here, no one knows what we saw here. It's all in the file, though. Come, please.'

Dobra leads us past a living room at least four times the size of mine.

'There was nothing much there. We gathered strands of synthetic hair, most likely from the victim's wig, and lots of fingerprints belonging to the suspect and his wife. Their servants, too. We also have traces of his hair on the furniture here.' He pauses at the transition between the living room and the dining area. 'Here's where things got really interesting.' He gestures for us to come closer. 'See here. Can you see the blood smear?'

I peer at the wall labelled '1' by a square of hand-cut cardboard paper.

'This was our first sign of foul play, just as the tip-off informed us.'

'You tested the blood?' I ask.

Dobra nods. 'We get the results fast because the labs are privately owned. We were able to make the match with Mrs Dawodu's blood type within twenty-four hours.' He points to the blood on the wall. 'And there was more here …'

Twenty-four hours? Even I know that's unusually fast. 'Wait. How come you got a match so quickly? Did you have the victim's blood type on file?'

Dobra's squints, then cocks his head to one side like he's trying to recollect a detail he never considered as significant. 'I think it's the detective. He said something about contacting the victim's doctor. Or was it clinic? I'm not sure.'

Chika shakes his head at me. Don't push it, his eyes say. This is not the time or place to question the ethics of a physician divulging personal information to the police without so much as a subpoena. I pack it in the red-flag corner of my brain and nod at Dobra as if everything he just said made perfect sense.

'Over here,' – Dobra says, pointing to the dining area – 'you'll see more bloodstains although not as much as in other places.'

Small dots of dried blood on the cream-coloured marble top of the dining table. I recall the scars and welts on the bishop's neck.

'No blood match was done on the suspect?'

Dobra frowns as if my question is beside the point. 'I'm sure it was, but he's alive, ko? It's the ones that match with the victim we were more interested in.'

How a crime is committed is as important as the crime itself. For one, it can determine premeditation or argue for a case of self-defence. The way Dobra waved off my enquiry is worrisome.

'See here?' Dobra is walking and pointing to the floor. The pristine tiles have a long trail of blood. 'I wasn't expecting this level of inceptive evidence on a first walk around.'

Dobra is showing off, and I can tell Chika is getting frustrated by the need to maintain our status as the young investigator's heroes. I give him a look that says it's okay to ask questions. Besides, I need to concentrate and the inspector's non-stop commentary is not helping.

'What evidence?' Chika asks.

Dobra seems startled by the question, then a broad smile spreads across his face. 'Ah, Mr Makuochi. I forget you're not an investigator like Dr Taiwo.'

Chika tries to look apologetic for his demotion in the inspector's estimation. Dobra doesn't notice.

'Basically, there are three types of ...'

There's something about the dried blood on the wall. The pattern of spread.

'... so, you get it now?' Dobra continues. 'Inceptive evidence indicates whether a crime has been committed.'

In the absence of my Nikon 300, my phone will have to do. I turn on the flash.

'And all evidence that a crime was committed can be found on the one scene?' Chika asks. From the eagerness in his tone, I know he's lost interest in Dobra's patter and is now just distracting him to allow me work.

I take pictures of the blood smears from different angles. On some shots, I switch off the flash. Will be good for comparisons later.

'Not at all. Corroborative evidence comes from anywhere ...'

I preview the pictures, then compare with the marks on the wall. I switch mode to photos and use the panorama function. A wider view of the wall proves to be quite informative.

'Like if the murder weapon is discovered far from the scene?' Chika asks with the earnestness of a teacher's pet.

'Yes, yes, you get it.' Dobra is delighted his tutoring is paying off. 'But you'd need the suspect's fingerprints on the victim or at the crime scene to corroborate the evidence as the same on the gun. See? Corroborative evidence!'

I zoom in on the photos. A pattern is emerging. Focusing on the larger sized smear could sidetrack an observer from the dots about three inches away from it. Dots of blood that seem sprayed rather than spurts, which would have led to drips from the splatter. Also on the wall is a rather large island of dried blood. No spread. Just caked in a spot, as if poured like icing on a cake.

'So, you get it? There is also indicative evi—' Dobra is saying, as he walks past the cardboard sign labelled '2' towards a door further down the corridor.

'Where does this lead?' I cut in, pointing at the trail of dried blood on the tiled floor.

'Ehen, this is where it gets even more damning for the suspect.' Dobra steps over cardboard square '3'. I switch my iPhone's camera to video mode, press record and follow behind Chika.

'He must have dragged her as she was bleeding down this corridor into their bedroom, which is right there.' Dobra walks on and points towards a door.

Something's not adding up. 'Inspector, do you reckon the victim was still alive when she was dragged on the floor?'

'Definitely,' Dobra answers, confident. 'There were several bloodstains in the bedroom indicating some struggle there. Come, I'll show you.'

'Wait, please.' I beckon to Dobra and Chika. 'If the victim was alive and perhaps struggling as she was being dragged, perhaps by her hair or a limb, why is the trail of blood so consistent in size and density?'

I click on gallery to share the pictures I took, but just then, Kenny's text message comes in.

Why? You made progress?

I swallow an irritated swear, excuse myself to Dobra and type quickly.

Just send the number if you have it!

I turn back to Dobra and Chika, drawing their attention to my phone screen. I press play on my recording and hand the phone to Chika to hold up. 'See, if I were dragging a struggling person, and they were bleeding, surely they'd move this way and that.' I move my shoulders jerkily, hands in the air. 'Then, the blood wouldn't have a consistent pattern of distribution. Even if the person was shot or stabbed in the butt and being dragged on it, the consistency of the blood spread on the floor would change as the person shifts their weight while struggling.'

'Ah, I see what you mean, Dr Taiwo, but the evidence is irrefutable. Come, come and see.'

I can see Chika gets my point but Dobra is not easily convinced. We follow the officer into the bedroom. There are so many square cardboards here, I'd hate to break it to the officer that it only corroborates my evolving hypothesis.

'The blood is everywhere.' Dobra points. 'See ... here ... and there.'

'The weapon? Where did you find it?' I ask.

'Under the bed. There.' He points again.

'Let me guess, when you ran the prints, there were only two: the bishop's and his wife's.'

'No,' Dobra answers with a hint of triumph. 'The security guard's, too.'

'The same one outside?' Chika asks.

'As luck would have it, yes.'

'Can I speak with him?' I'm already heading out.

The security guard looks bewildered as we approach him. Our meeting at the gate had been too brief to make any impression. Now, standing at attention as we get to the security post, I study him. Early thirties. Well groomed, with a box-cut reminiscent of the sprinter Carl Lewis. His bearing shows an athletic body under the uniform. A pistol is holstered on his right side. His walkie-talkie is so shiny, it could have been bought yesterday.

I greet him and ask his name.

'Samson Adamu,' he says in a stiff manner. I know when my American accent won't help. I turn to Chika. He takes the cue, breaks out in rapid pidgin, and Samson visibly relaxes.

'Oga shout my name,' Samson says when Chika asks about the night in question. 'I come tink say arm robber don pass me enter the house. I come run inside. Wetin I see, ehn?'

'Wetin you see?' Dobra asks, more forcefully than I know Chika would have.

'Na madam o! She come hol Bishop for neck like this.' Samson pulls his own collar to indicate the tightness of the first lady's grip and rolls the blacks of his eyes. 'She come hol knife over im head. Na like say devil enter madam bodi.'

I make a face at Chika when he wants to translate. I get it: First Lady had Bishop by neck and threatened to kill him. A lot more dramatic than the bishop's account but materially similar.

'I come dey beg madam make im give me knife ...'

The pidgin gets more frenetic. I concede defeat.

Chika comes to my rescue. 'He joined the bishop to plead with the wife. She then dropped the knife.' He turns to Samson. 'Wetin come happen?'

'Bishop tank me well, well. E come commot house. Me, I just siddon here dey pray make devil no come dis house again.'

'The madam didn't go out?' I ask.

Samson shakes his head.

'And Bishop no come back?' Dobra asks. I sense dread in his tone.

'No be for dat night, sha,' Samson answers confidently.

'Why didn't you tell us this when I questioned you?' Dobra shouts. His armpits are pools of sweat.

Samson opens his palms to air, perplexed. 'You no aks me, o. You aks weda na me dey duty. I say yes.'

'I asked if you saw anything unusual!' Dobra screams, agitated.

'Haba. Wetin dey unusual for husband and wife quarrel? You no get wife? Jus dis morning, my own woman chop small craze and ...'

If there were a chair nearby, Dobra would have sunk into it. Gone is the effusive officer we met earlier, in his place is a deflated man contemplating the magnitude of his error. Overconfidence is a typical rookie mistake in forensic science. Placing too much trust in what is observed without due consideration to the human stories around the very evidence under investigation. I detest shoddy police work but I like Dobra enough to feel sorry for him as he shrinks before our eyes.

To be fair, the whole police force must take responsibility, not just Inspector Dobra. Making such a public arrest, even for the purpose of 'questioning', solely based on inceptive evidence is unusual. Poor calculation. Hasty conclusions. Under the scrutiny of a competent legal defence, no matter the numbered cards, none of the evidence could be used to convict Bishop Dawodu for murdering his wife. It might take some time, perhaps even require the importation of forensic expatriates to give their expensive expert opinion. The conclusion will be what Dobra now suspects. Every bloodstain, smear and spot at the crime scene is a well-positioned stage prop.

BACKSTAGE

'You think she set it all up?' Chika asks, as we head to his car.

Although I'm staring at the burgeoning traffic, my mind is still at Bishop Dawodu's house, reliving our tour of the carefully laid-out crime scene. Whoever did that wanted the blood trail to tell a damning story.

'Everything was done to give the impression of a violent struggle,' I muse aloud.

'But there *was* a struggle,' Chika says. 'That security guy, Samson, witnessed it.'

I turn to him. 'He attests to the fact that there was an argument where Sade was threatening her husband with a knife. His version aligns with what the bishop told me.'

I give Chika a brief rundown of the bishop's account of the fight with his wife, leaving out the more personal details.

'He could've planned the whole story with the security guard.'

'Except witnesses can confirm he was at Graceland till the time of his arrest.'

'They could have communicated via phone, or Samson could have visited his boss at Graceland. They had enough time to make their stories add up.'

'Fair enough. So, for argument's purpose, we must assume the bishop didn't leave at the time Samson said he did. He killed his wife, somehow neglected to rid the house of any sign of struggle. We have to assume that something as basic as cleaning up after himself is beneath him. He then carried his wife's body, possibly with the same security guy's help, and dumped it somewhere?' I recall the crispness of the bishop's dressing, the attention to detail, even while in prison, and shake my head. 'Doesn't add up. Too messy. Too easy.'

'What if the body is somewhere in the house or buried there?' Chika speculates aloud but I know he's just challenging my hypothesis. 'I mean the yard is big enough.'

It's on the tip of my tongue to ask Chika to turn the car back towards the bishop's residence. Common sense prevails. While Inspector Dobra might not have the experience needed to read a crime scene accurately, he struck me as fastidious enough to have searched that house from top to bottom. A seven-day-old cadaver in humid Lagos would smell, except if stashed in a very large freezer which could not be hidden. Our walk around the large compound before leaving the flustered Inspector Dobra didn't show signs of freshly dug soil in any part of the well-manicured gardens and lawns.

'Those blood splatters aren't random,' I reiterate, more confident than before.

'What makes you so sure?' Chika asks, curious rather than provoking.

I explain the science of blood splatter and the wealth of information it can provide about a crime scene. Experienced killers are good at covering up foul play. Chika knows this as a former mercenary, but few killers are ever at the scene when the police or investigators are trying to determine *how* a crime was committed. In a premeditating state, a killer has control over everything before and after the act of killing – the type of weapon, the angle of attack, even the positioning of the body and so many other factors, except one: how blood flows.

'Every contact leaves a trace,' Chika says after I am done. 'They taught us that in sniper training.'

'Exactly. And every trace tells a story.'

'So, the blood at the house—?'

'Did not splatter unpredictably, which tells a different kind of story from the one it was supposed to tell. Of course, there was an attempt to make it all look random, but because it's hard to predict the trajectory of fluid, the specificity of the spread is a dead giveaway. The blood pattern at the scene is a fake trace, meaning contact is doubtful.'

'But why would Sade frame her husband for her supposed death?'

I throw Chika a sharp stare. He knows better than to think I'd jump to such a conclusion. 'I didn't say the wife set him up. I'm saying she would be my number-one suspect.'

'Isn't it the same thing?'

'Except if she's not planning to come back, what would she gain?'

'Maybe she wants to punish him for something? Scare him even, and with his popularity, maybe embarrass him? Or blackmail him? Maybe she wants to leave him and he's not agreeing?'

Based on the bishop's psychological profile of his wife, all these questions are valid.

'And with all that already achieved, shouldn't she be home by now?' I muse aloud.

'Good point,' Chika says, as he parks his car across from mine. 'Either way, it's looking like your bishop is innocent. Your job's done.'

*

'That's quite a leap, Sweet,' Folake says from the bed as I undress, while giving her a rundown of my day, skipping the parts my NDA prevents me from sharing.

'Not really,' I say. 'It didn't take massive levels of deduction. The facts were there.'

I plop next to her, still keyed up about the day's events but too tired to shower just yet. Folake tends to ask questions only a lawyer would, which came in handy at the times I had to write reports to support a case proceeding to trial or convince the district attorney to drop one.

Folake sets aside the *Harvard Law Review* and removes her reading glasses. 'I just think you should be careful not to jump to conclusions. It's up to the prosecution to determine whether the weight of evidence against the bishop warrants a trial. They won't proceed unless they are relatively sure of a guilty verdict. From what you're saying, an acquittal is very possible which won't be a good look for the police or the state.'

'But going by the crime scene, someone's trying to frame him.'

'You've only confirmed what the elders suspected. You were hired to find out *why* the bishop might have been framed, and you've not done that.'

Trust Folake to cut right to the chase.

'How will I do that if the wife is still missing?' I ask aloud.

'How were you planning to do it when you thought she was dead?' Folake asks.

Her question stays with me well after she drops off to sleep and I am just about to get up to wash the day's grime off me. She does have a point. Even if I hate to admit it, deep inside, I know my eagerness to have this over and done with has a lot to do with my disdain for the assignment itself.

Organised religion and I have a turbulent relationship. As a child, I was mandated along with my siblings to go to Saint Stephen's Anglican Church with my parents. The ritual, the stand and sit, the same hymns over and over, and the long sermons broken by seemingly unlimited rounds of thanksgiving and offerings bored my twin brother, Taiye, and me. It wasn't until we became teenagers and discovered church was a fertile place for meeting girls that we started to enjoy going.

When Taiye and I travelled to the States to study, we found ourselves lost in a strange city. With uncles and aunts flung all over the country, we sought home in a place of worship. It was a refuge from the segregation we hadn't known existed in Los Angeles, for all its claim to diversity. We needed to find our place outside of campus without falling in with gangs, drug pushers and everything our mother warned us about before we boarded the airplane to America.

I was the one who found First Baptist Assembly. Or rather, found Reverend (Dr) August Freeman. Bored on a Sunday morning, I switched on the TV in our studio flat and there he was, smartly dressed and erudite. He spoke with vigour, yet calmly, without the fire and brimstone energy of many Pentecostal pastors. Even the way he called for offerings was a class act. 'Give if you have, but give after you have helped your neighbour get through a hard time. Don't give with a heart of sacrifice. Give with joy knowing you've done the needful on earth and for your fellow man.' I liked him instantly.

Finding out the church was situated in South Central – a bus ride from the USC campus – was like a message. I coaxed Taiye to come with me to a Sunday service and we were not disappointed. First Baptist Assembly was like a homecoming. Black folks dressed in their Sunday best, a choir that was as contemporary as they were soulful and a pastor who preached sermons that empowered you for the week to come.

We quickly enrolled as church workers – me as a volunteer personal assistant to Rev. Freeman and Taiye volunteering with the prayer ministry with the wife, Reverend Tasha Freeman – and only then started seeing the underbelly of the 'Jesus Business'. A soap opera on a grand scale. Think of any vice, it was at First Baptist Assembly. Financial misappropriation by the Reverend Freeman's brother, the functional alcoholism of the Reverend's wife, who also led the choir, not to mention the sexual predatory acts by deacons of both genders and more. Everything 'backstage' was diametrically opposed to the preaching from the pulpit. But it didn't matter. My admiration for Reverend Freeman outweighed the shenanigans of church members who Christ intoned us to love anyway because after all: *love covers a multitude of sins.*

Till today, Taiye credits First Baptist Assembly for saving us from being 'Jesus Freaks'. I credit Rev. Freeman for making me question my faith and the ease with which I'm susceptible to the charms of men of the faith. Remembering the exact day this happened reminds me of my pending shower. I stand up from the bed. Folake mumbles something. I pause, so as not to wake her. When her breathing continues evenly, I walk to the bathroom.

The Sunday service that changed everything replays as the water hits my face. The praise and worship had gone on longer than usual. The atmosphere was charged. The Holy Spirit was moving so no one noticed Reverend Freeman was not at the pulpit way past his scheduled entry point. It was my job to make sure he stuck to the programme, so I hurried to the church office. Why didn't I knock? Why didn't I make some noise to herald my entry into the Reverend's office? I burst in with the zeal of a fan eager to show my idol to the world.

'Sir, we are nine minutes over—'

My voice was cut off by the scene before me; the Reverend bending over several lines of cocaine. He looked up at me, the tip of his nose coated with white powder. His eyes were glazed.

'Come, boy,' he said, his lips stretching in a maniacal smile, 'come partake with me.'

I took a step backwards, closed the door and ran.

'I knew. Everyone knows,' Taiye said when I told him what I saw.

'And you didn't tell me?' I asked. Outraged. Betrayed all over again.

'I can't stop going there,' Taiye said, then proceeded to tell me about his ongoing affair with Reverend Tasha Freeman. I was crushed.

I never went back to First Baptist Assembly after that, although Taiye went for two more semesters and only stopped when Reverend Freeman was arrested on multiple counts of rape of minors. It was too much. Not even his infatuation with Tasha Freeman could survive the disgust everyone felt.

I didn't step into a church – Pentecostal or orthodox – for several years after my experience with First Baptist. When I got married and Folake was pregnant with the twins, we discussed the importance of replicating some of the structure, values and standards we grew up with in Nigeria. Without a rule book for parenting in America, Folake and I returned to our Anglican roots – not least because our respective mothers were convinced our children were doomed to hell if the twins were not baptised. We chose the most staid, conservative and orthodox church we could find, complete with a white Reverend and a congregation that treated us as exotic members because we were not Black Americans, but *foreigners* from *Africa*.

I felt nothing during those mind-numbing Sunday services at the Anglican Church. I knew what 'nothing' was because before getting too close to the behind the scenes at First Baptist Assembly, as just a member of the congregation, I had felt something special. Like I was connected to something bigger than me. I resent losing that feeling, so now I hover between being a lapsed Christian and an agnostic; not out of choice but from a deep sense of self protection. Experience has proven that faith practised in fellowship with others makes you vulnerable to hurt and disappointment. Not in God, but in people.

So, yes, I want this assignment over as quickly as possible. It's bringing memories of a time I want to stay forgotten.

It's reminding me of what I lost, and yet, still yearn for. It's pulling me deeper into a dark place that I fear will sever what little connection I have with the concept of a God. The more I dig into the case of the missing first lady, the more frayed at the edges what little faith I have becomes. I'd rather not know the depth of depravity which could cause a 'man of God' to be framed for his wife's murder. I don't want to know the extent of hatred the couple may have generated, that would make anyone set them up for the kind of scandal the bishop's arrest has generated.

But if Folake is right – as she almost always is – I'll be abdicating my responsibility by jumping to conclusions because I want this over quickly.

I step out of the shower and towel myself dry.

'God is not man,' I whisper to my reflection. It's what Mum says every time Taiye and I justify our disillusionment with organised religion.

Man is not God, the voice in my head whispers back. I turn away from the mirror. I am too tired to unravel what this means or where the thought even came from.

I slip under the covers and put my arm over Folake's waist. The rise and fall of her breathing relax my body but not my mind.

Man is not God. Is this a warning to me to be less judgemental? To keep an open mind if I really want to get to the bottom of what happened to Sade Dawodu?

Sleep comes just in time to halt further misgivings about getting entangled in the ugly side of the God business.

THE EYES OF MAN

Pastor George, aka Deputy Jesus at Grace Church, walks in on schedule, shoulders squared as if prepared for battle. I stand to greet him, but my smile doesn't erase the scowl on his face.

'I've lined up all the elders to speak with you for about an hour each,' he says, after shaking my hands with a perfunctory 'bless you'.

'I doubt I'll need that much time.'

Pastor George unbuttons his blazer and sits across me. 'They're all on standby, anyhow. Bishop's PA is coordinating everything.'

There's a brief silence and I gauge how best to proceed with this inscrutable man. I flip through the list he'd emailed me.

'Before we start, there's a name here, with a US phone number next to it, a LaTanya—'

'Ms Jacobson,' he says in a clipped tone. 'She's Bishop's business manager in the US.'

I look up sharply. 'Business manager?'

He raises a sardonic brow. 'Don't look so surprised, Dr Taiwo. Bishop is an important man, and Ms Jacobson manages his affairs in America. She sorts out his bookings and handles most of his international travels.'

I shouldn't be surprised, but I am. 'Like an agent?'

Pastor George shrugs. 'You could say that. She's not here, that's why I put her US mobile phone. You can call her from here. We have teleconference facilities.'

And why would you put her on the list of interviewees? I want to ask but sense that's an angle for later. To be fair, I had asked for a list of contacts of all the bishop's high-level associates. Rather than ponder on why a man of God would need an agent or even a *business* manager, I dig in.

'Tell me about your relationship with the bishop,' I say.

'He's my boss in the strictest sense of the word, but also my spiritual father.' His expression remains blank as he sits back and crosses his legs.

'I understand the hierarchy.' I leave a short pause. 'What do you really think about him?'

His face hardens. 'Does it matter? He's chosen by God to lead this church.'

'You hired me to—'

'Exactly. I hired you. Why would I do that if I am a suspect?'

'No one said—'

'Your line of questioning implies it,' he says sharply. 'What I think of the bishop is inconsequential.'

The article before 'bishop' makes me sit up. I'd thought this was my purview as an outsider. 'Is this what I should expect from the other elders?'

The scowl becomes a frown. 'What do you mean?'

'This passive aggressiveness?'

'Ooph.' He waves his hand. 'Nonsense. I'm asking you to focus on the key issues rather than irrelevant questions.'

He's arrogant, self-righteous and deliberately obtuse. I don't like him.

'Thanks for the reminder, Pastor,' I snap, unable to mask my impatience. 'But as the expert here, I'll determine the relevant line of questioning. Again, what do you think of the bishop?'

The ensuing silence is tense. I set my face in a manner I hope conveys my readiness to walk away. Right now. Pastor George looks away. He's weighing his words and I wonder why.

He lets out a deep breath. 'Look, I know some of the elders will say things have been tense between the bishop and me. But our differences have never been personal. I have the utmost regard for the bishop.'

The bishop again. Interesting. 'Can you expound on these differences?'

He cocks his head left, as if considering the import of my question. I'm not convinced.

'I've been a pastor here for thirteen years. Since the first church was planted in Lagos. I rose to become his right-hand man, and in all those years I never questioned him. I studied the Word not with my heart but through his eyes.'

'Until now?'

He smiles. 'The higher I rose, the more I found my path. It became clear that I had to have my own voice and listen to God rather than the bishop.'

'Is there a difference?'

The way he looks at me, momentarily vulnerable, makes me reconsider my initial impression. Maybe he's not arrogant. Maybe he's just searching and hiding his doubts better than most. *Man is not God.* Perhaps Pastor George is one of the few in the God business coming to terms with this truism.

'Unfortunately, yes,' Pastor George says, 'I started questioning the church's stance on certain matters. Our involvement in politics, for instance. Are we the kind of church Christ mandated, or an organisation built around the interpretation of one man?'

'This man being the bishop?' I ask and he nods.

'I made the mistake of questioning some of these inter-pretations. At board meetings, and when the spirit led me, in the pulpit. It didn't go down well at all.' He pauses as if to choose the right word. 'The bishop can be quite temperamental. I've been publicly cautioned a number of times.'

'So, there's a leadership tussle between you two?'

His dry laugh catches me by surprise. 'This is not parlia-ment, Dr Taiwo. This is a church and Bishop Dawodu is the leader. If I'm not submissive to his leadership, then I have the option of going to another church or starting my own. But to – what's the word you used? – tussle for leadership? That would be a sin and I'm not ready to tempt God.'

'And his wife?' I ask, after doodling in my notepad.

'She doesn't like me.'

'Pardon?' His frankness is jarring.

His expression takes on a 'gotcha' look and for the first time, I consider he might have a sense of humour.

'You didn't expect that, eh? In fact, she's one of the people who supported my public reprimand.'

'Why?'

He shrugs, smile gone, scowl back. 'When you find her, you can ask her for me.'

The slight sarcasm is intended to put me on the defensive and stop this line of questioning. I'll let it go. For now. 'Tell me about her.'

'She's very smart. Some think she's emotional but I find her quite real. Authentic even. I admire that about her. She speaks her mind and does not care who doesn't like it. That can be quite dangerous in a church.'

'Dangerous?'

He holds out a hand as if to halt any misinterpretation of his words. 'Not to the extent of physical harm, but more in the stress and politicking of church leadership. I think it gets to her which is why she disappears for weeks on end sometimes. The thing is, she didn't use to be that way. She was a bright light, always had a kind word for everyone, always smiling. Respectful. Volunteered for almost every department. Choir. Children's church. Ushering. Name it and Sister Sade was involved. Then she married Bishop, and as the years passed, she became, well, less approachable.'

I notice he's dropped the article before Bishop. He's comfortable. I'm asking the questions he expected. 'It's got nothing to do with her not having children?'

'I'm sure it would worry any woman her age, but I'm not her husband. I'm saying I would understand why she would need a break,' – he waves his hand around the boardroom like it is the wide expanse of Graceland – 'from all of this, once in a while.'

'And you don't?'

'I never wanted to. My calling is 24/7. She's married to Bishop but it doesn't mean she has such a calling in her life.'

'You think she's self-indulgent? Perhaps irresponsible?' I repeat Pastor Nwoko's summation to check his reaction.

He smiles sardonically. 'No, Dr Taiwo. I think she's human.'

A soft knock, and we both look in the direction of the closed doors.

'That's your next appointment. Are we done here?'

We've not exhausted the hour he claims to have allotted for every interview. I suspect he planned it so he spent the shortest possible time with me. Not so fast.

'The bishop said they had an argument before he came back to Graceland that night?'

He stands and looks down at me like my question is beneath where he placed me in his estimation. 'They are married. So?'

I search his face for any clue that he has an inkling of the bloody scene at the bishop's house. Nothing.

'I wonder who he told amongst the elders.'

'Why?'

'It seems everyone's convinced the first lady is away on her personal retreat, yet someone is using this absence to perhaps frame her husband. Someone or some people who knew they had a quarrel and she was travelling—'

'I didn't do it.'

The denial is uncalled for. Our eyes lock.

I take the plunge. 'I was at the bishop's house yesterday. You know, the crime scene.'

Pastor George cocks an interested eyebrow. 'And? That must be good, right? The police refused us entry.'

I shrug. 'I was lucky. Made some calls.'

'And?'

'It's not looking good for the bishop is all I can say now,' I lie. 'There's a lot to convince the police something very bad happened to his wife there and he's the number-one suspect.'

The pastor's shoulders slump briefly, then he squares them up as if summoning strength. Or manufacturing conviction?

'It's a set-up. I guarantee you that. He was here. I was with him.'

'And all the elders were too?'

He frowns, then nods. 'I can't vouch for that, but right now, I think it's safe to say that all the elders you met on that day we briefed you were here.'

I appreciate that he's not saying this with absolute confidence. Providing alibis for eleven elders, not counting Mrs Bucknor, would have been a stretch and he's smart enough to know this.

'Did the bishop tell you why he came back to Graceland that night? Did you know they had a quarrel? That she was travelling?'

Another slightly louder knock. It doesn't break our gazes or the tension in the air.

'Soon,' Pastor says, the scowl leaves and is replaced by a cynical lift of his lips, 'that door will open and you'll ask those elders the same question. Some might say the tension between Bishop and me would be my motivation to embarrass him like this. I assure you, it would be far from the truth.'

'But you concede you have the motivation?'

'If I had the ambition to be more than where God places me in this ministry, perhaps. But I don't.'

'Do they,' – I nod towards the door – 'know you don't have ambitions to the throne?'

This time, his smile is both sad and weary all at once. 'They see me through the eyes of man, Dr Taiwo.' He pauses. 'They don't know me at all.'

AN INTERRUPTION OF NOTE

Five male elders, a bathroom break and three hours later, I'm ready to throw in the towel. The boredom is excruciating. Each elder walks in, gives their version of what might have caused the police to arrest the bishop – three of them blame the devil's mischievousness and the other two believe it's simply a misunderstanding inspired by the first lady's rash actions. All of them insist Bishop was in church during the time the police claim his wife was being killed and that they were with him.

I've come to know interviewees with nothing to give: eager to talk, full of anecdotes, keeping the conversation around their own interpretation of what could have happened and where the investigation should be focused. It's safe to drown out their words – you can play them back later, if something jars or does not add up – and just study them. Their body language, the cadence in their voice and what is not said.

But with all the elders I've spoken to in the last three hours, none was worth the full sixty minutes allocated to each interview. Unoriginal, unimaginative, small-minded and utterly, unconditionally devoted to Bishop Jeremiah Dawodu. They all looked different, seemed diverse in their ethnic origins, but essentially, they all thought the same.

I check my watch as Pastor Coker, the current elder, speaks. Bishop is A True Shepherd who God called for This Generation. A Man of Uncommon Anointing. A Great Leader whose—

I ask what he thinks of the first lady and again, it's a repeat of the same brochure. What a Woman of God! Virtuous and A True Helpmeet! And their marriage? Perfect! Ordained by God! Shame about the no fruit of the womb but the Lord knows best. Look at Sarah in the Bible.

My stomach growls so loudly there's no way the man didn't hear. But if he did, he gives no indication. He presses on and I've no qualms about cutting him short. I tell him he has been exceptionally helpful. He seems genuinely pleased at the compliment, and goes on to give me his number in case I've more questions.

'This your task is not easy, o. Let us pray for strength.'

I wait for him to stand up so I can prepare for the next interview, then realise he meant we should pray *now*. I check my watch in a pointed manner, but Pastor Coker is not budging.

I breathe in and nod. Can't hurt.

Nine minutes and several interminable seconds later, after entreaties to the Holy Spirit to guide my investigation towards the specific exoneration of the bishop, Pastor Coker mercifully leaves.

Two more elders to go for today. I'm not sure I'll last. I still have about five minutes before my meeting with the next one, Pastor Nwoko. I drink more Grace Church-branded bottled water to fill my stomach and make notes in my notepad. Snapshot impressions a voice recorder can't capture. Questions for further research. Clarifications of church hierarchy and politics that Kenny can help with later.

I text Chika. *Any joy on S. Dawodu's call records?*

I wouldn't have noticed the door opening if not for the ragged breathing that accompanied it. A man in his mid-thirties stands half inside, fresh-faced but clearly uncomfortable. He glances behind him, seems reassured no one's there. He looks around the conference room as if checking to be sure I'm alone. Then he closes the door as carefully as he opened it and faces me.

'You're the investigator?'

'I'm Philip Taiwo.'

'You're the one I need to see.'

'And you are?' I quickly browse my list. Not an elder.

The man comes closer to where I'm seated. His eyes dart to the door as if someone would burst in any time.

'I am Victor Ewang,' he says in a rush as if I should know the name.

I stand and stretch out my hand which he takes and drops like it scalded him. I resist the urge to wipe my hand on my trousers. His palms are that sweaty.

'Pleased to meet you, sir.' I flip through my notes, frowning. I'm not due to meet him till tomorrow. 'Time is of essence. I was told you would only speak with me tomorrow.'

'Yes. Unfortunately, to beat traffic I have to leave here before four.'

'I understand,' he says, looking to the door again, then back at me. 'But this can't wait. There are powerful people who have every reason to have First Lady disappear.'

'Who are they?' My antennae are up. Three minutes until my next meeting. I can move it on.

Ewang forges on. 'She found out some things. I know because I told her. But I swear I never knew how far they'd go—'

'If you can wait just one moment, so I can move my meeting with—'

'No!' He raises then lowers his voice. 'It can't be here. We must meet here tomorrow like you planned and give the impression that you spoke to me. But what I really have to say can only be said outside this place.'

'Will you give me your number? We can set up a time—'

'Here's my card. Call me and I'll come to you.'

He slips out as quietly as he came, only pausing to look left and right before shutting the door behind him.

I read the card. *Victor Ewang. Director of Foreign Missions.*

BREAKING NEWS

Pastor Nwoko walks in without knocking. I greet him with a fake smile and slip the card into my pocket.

'Pastor, is there a place around here we can nourish our spirit and stomach at the same time?'

Although taken aback, Nwoko, who seemed primed to extol all the virtues of the bishop, takes my request in his stride and offers to lead me to the staff canteen. On the way, he gives me a tour of the administrative building – Community Outreach (one of the many departments under him), Children's Church, Old People's Support Group, on and on he goes. I check my messages as he drones. There are several: some from Kenny, one from Folake reminding me to leave Graceland early to avoid traffic and a curious one from Abubakar.

What did you do? Call. Urgent.

I frown and my steps falter. I want to call Abubakar immediately, but we are already at the canteen.

In an hour. What's going on? I text back.

'We can sit there.' Pastor Nwoko points to a corner of the large room filled with church workers, chattering as they eat. The glass-covered bain-marie is filled with dishes that

I find strangely unappetising given my ravenous state. I'm not a fan of precooked meals buffet-style.

'The chef would have prepared something special for you,' Pastor Coker says, as we walk past the queue waiting for rows of hairnet-wearing servers.

The TVs are all tuned to GraceTV. The bishop is on multiple screens, looking dapper in a light blue suit and a cravat, a matching handkerchief in his breast pocket. He's reading from an iPad on mute, while the surround sound system plays praise and worship songs by the popular Grace Church Mass Choir.

We get to the spot Pastor Nwoko has picked out. We are about to settle down when a commotion rises above the din.

'Change the channel!' a young man shouts, running and pointing at the TV screens.

I turn to Pastor Nwoko. 'What's happening?'

'The police are talking about Bishop!' the young man continues and the serving, eating and chatting stops. Instantly. 'Change the channel!'

Pastor Nwoko stands up and heads towards the animated young man.

'There's a press conference!' The young man's voice is now too loud in the hush that follows the flicker of the screens to a medium shot of a police officer in full uniform, reading from a paper.

A prepared statement. Serious stuff.

'... The bishop has been extremely cooperative, and the force remains indebted to him for his gracefulness during this investigation. But—'

The camera view widens and I can make out other police-men standing behind the officer, identified on the news bar as 'Detective Lawrence Bello of the SCIU, Lagos Island Police Force'. I see the solemn face of Inspector Dobra of CSI fame and guess what's coming. Ah. That's why Abubakar wanted me to call.

'... our investigations have shown that while the police carried out its duties with careful due diligence, such duties were based on a false tip.'

'Thank you, Jesus! God is good!' rends the canteen. But Detective Bello is still speaking, so there's a quite a bit of hushing of the early celebrants, especially by Pastor Nwoko, who strains towards one of the TV screens as if he wants to be absorbed into its flat frame.

'The information we acted on has proven to be mischievous and in poor faith. Our investigations have shown that indications of foul play in Mrs Dawodu's disappearance were deliberately contrived to mislead our investigation, resulting in the arrest of the bishop, her husband. For this, the police remain sorry, and order the immediate release of the eminent bishop from custody ...'

No amount of hushing can keep the small crowd in the canteen from shouting in riotous ecstasy. Some are crying, others rolling on the floor. Tables jostle and plates fall to the ground, and some break to pieces, but no one seems to mind. The police officer is still reading but no one cares to listen any more.

I strain to make out the rest. '... we hope Bishop Dawodu's wife returns in good health, and a more formal apology will be tendered to the bishop and the members of Grace

Church as soon as we conclude our investigation into the source of the false information.'

Someone bursts out in a praise song. Others join in, and my phone vibrates in my hand. I check it. Abubakar. I hurry towards the canteen doors to take the call and almost collide with Pastor George. Our eyes lock.

I can't decide whether the joy on his face is from the news still playing on the TV screens or because my services are no longer needed.

CASE CLOSED

You'd think Bishop Dawodu just won a presidential election in a landslide. Even Pastor George's trademark scowl is absent as he informs me that all the elders are off to bring the bishop back home. There's an emergency thanksgiving service to plan and a hundred other things to do, including an interview with CNN and other media outlets.

Through it all, I look out for Victor Ewang. I walk to what I assume is his office, following the signs on the doors. It is empty, like every office in the church office building. Everyone is off celebrating the bishop's vindication, even if his wife is *still* missing.

I call Abubakar as soon as I get on the road back to Lagos.

'I saw the news,' I say as soon as he picks up the call.

'The SCIU was asking for you.'

'Special Crimes wanted to see me? Why?'

'A*ff*arently your observations raised doubts in the minds of the CSI team.'

My respect for Inspector Dobra leaps. The guy is not only an eager student of his chosen vocation but one of the rarest of law enforcement officers: the type who owns up to his mistakes. It couldn't have been easy for him to concede that his report on the crime scene contributed to the bishop's wrongful arrest.

Abubakar continues, 'They were worried you would share your conclusions with your client without talking to them first.'

'Oh, is that why they called a press conference so quickly?'

'I told them you would never do that, but they didn't believe me.'

If my feedback to Inspector Dobra led to the release of a falsely accused man, surely no harm was done.

'Detective Bello, the lead investigator, wants to see you.'

'Why?'

'He didn't say. Something about clearing the air and giving you the *pull ficture*.'

I can hear the tension in Abubakar's voice. He is nervous. The whole thing could backfire on the college if it seemed that I had made them look like fools. I'll have to meet with this Detective Bello. My plan was to finish with class tomorrow and drive back to Graceland to continue the interviews. There's no need now. I tell Abubakar I'll be at the college an hour before my first class at 10 a.m. and he promises to pass on the information to Detective Bello.

Chika's call comes in a few minutes after the frazzled commandant hung up.

'Talk about a wild goose chase,' he says when I tell him where I am.

'I'm happy for the bishop, but no one appeared concerned about his wife.'

'I'm sure she's fine,' Chika says drily.

'Why do you say that?'

'Well, according to my contact at the telco, her phone is still on.'

'They can trace it?' I wasn't holding out much hope on the technology front. Past experience with searching databases in Nigeria has proven I'm as far from my time at SFPD as my old Prado is from mutating into a Tesla.

'Generally, yes, if they do a triangulation. But you'll need a warrant to get that information. For now, though, all my guy could confirm is that the phone is very much active. It's been switched on and off about four times in the past three days. There are no incoming or outgoing calls, but the GPS is working and registers its location as Lagos.'

'If her phone was not stolen, what will be her excuse if, or when, she finally shows up?' I muse aloud.

'Are you still on the case?'

'Not from what I saw today,' I answer ruefully.

'Then, that's not your problem.'

Fair point. But someone *did* set the bishop up for a crime he didn't commit. I am no closer to who or why than when I first drove through the gates of Graceland Estate with Kenny. Still, I can't continue the investigation if my employers are no longer interested in my services. I thank Chika for his help, and hang up rather abruptly. I hate loose ends.

Kenny's call comes in as soon as I drive past the point separating Lagos from Ogun state.

'Thank you so much, ègbón mi!'

When Kenny calls me 'my big brother', I know she's very pleased with me.

'I'm happy for your church,' I say.

'God is faithful!' she adds with a squeal for effect.

I roll my eyes. I was the one who figured out the blood pattern was staged, not God. I let her go on about the jubilation in the Grace Church missions across the world.

'Why's no one worried about the first lady?' I ask when she pauses for breath.

'We told you. She goes away like this for weeks.'

The traffic slows down before I veer on to the Maryland highway. A street hawker passes by with Gala stacked on a tray.

'Wait, sis ...' I say, as I reach for spare change and wind down my window. One Gala can hold me till I get home. The boy hands me a sachet of water, but I shake my head. There are limits to my gastronomic adventures on Lagos roads.

'I was saying,' I mumble, as I tear the nylon wrapper off the pastry snack which I suspect may be well past its sell-by date, given the stale yeast smell, 'what if she's not okay?'

'God will show His mighty hand again,' Kenny says. 'You'll see. First Lady will come home safe and sound. Then the devil will be defeated. You've done your part, ègbón mi, our Sherlock Holmes.'

The more I dwell on the missing Sade Dawodu, the more uncomfortable the compliments become. I cut off the conversation, citing heavy traffic, but it's not true. There's steady movement on the crowded road and I get home in time to supervise the kids' homework and help Folake with dinner.

At the table, the tension between mother and daughter seems to have eased.

'Dad, everyone's talking about how the police goofed,' Lara says.

'Goofed is a strong word,' I say, as I dish out diced fried plantain to go with my beans. 'They made some errors.'

'Police are the same everywhere. Always jumping to conclusions,' Tai says and there's an awkward silence. Memories of how our sons, especially Tai, became bitter about policing have been generally repressed. We don't talk about the incident that made nonsense of my position in law enforcement, reinforced my second-class status and made my wife insist we leave the States.

'But Dad found them out,' Kay points out, mouth full.

'No, no. I did my job. I looked at the way the evidence was—'

'And saw that they were wrong!' Lara declares proudly. 'Auntie Kenny can't stop sending text messages to sing your praises.'

'Yeah,' Folake says. 'She sent me a recipe for something to cook for you, and when I joked that she had better send the money for such an extravagant dish, she actually asked for my banking details!'

We all laugh, imagining the horror on Folake's face at the suggestion that she would collect funds from anyone to feed her family, even her much-loved sister-in-law.

Eating done, the boys retire to their rooms to get a game in before their mother insists they go to bed. Lara sits next to me on the sofa, still fascinated by how the blood pattern led me to postulate the bishop might have been framed.

'But is she alive?' Lara asks, as Folake switches on the TV and joins us on the sofa.

'We hope so,' I say. I'm not fond of discussing my work at home, but the popularity of this case means I can't shield my family from it.

'What if she's not?' Lara asks, her eyes wide with curiosity. 'Like, what if she was *actually* killed, and someone's trying to pin it on her husband?'

My eyes catch Folake's. How does one explain to a child that a majority of homicides are perpetrated by a family member?

'I'm sure Sade Dawodu's fine,' Folake says firmly, as she switches the channel to the local news station.

But there's no getting away from the subject because it's the evening news hour and every report is about Bishop Jeremiah Dawodu. Snippets of the press conference are intercut with a brief profile of him. Then, a cut to the front of Ikoyi Model Prison where he is walking out like he's Che Guevara. The bishop is the picture of triumph over oppression as he raises his hand and the crowd cheers. He is shaking people's hands, hugging them. Shouts of 'Praise God' and 'God is good' rend the air, almost drowning out the reporter's voice.

It is only when the bishop gets into the waiting Lexus 4x4 that the reporter mentions his missing wife. But it is brief, almost a by-the-way. A picture of Sade Dawodu fills the screen. Long weave frames her perfectly made-up face. Her smile is warm and friendly. It's one of the portrait shots I saw at her house. I wait to hear what the newscaster will say to indicate that this woman, whose disappearance is still a mystery, matters. But beyond mentioning that Mrs Folasade Dawodu is still not back at home – not *missing* – nothing else is added before the news moves on to flooding in Bangladesh.

Lara gives a deep sigh. 'I hope she's alive. She's so beautiful.'

Something in the way Lara calls Sade Dawodu 'beautiful' makes me look over her head at Folake. Her frown confirms she noticed it too. The envy – or was it longing? – in Lara's voice was unmistakable.

CONFLICT OF INTERESTS

Detective Lawrence Bello isn't making a courtesy call.

'Whose side are you on, Doctor?' he asks, right after the introductions.

'Please, call me Philip,' I say as pleasantly as I can.

Abubakar moves his palms up and down, imploring calm, but Bello does not notice. Or pretends not to.

'Answer my question, *Doctor* Taiwo.' The detective is in plain clothes, not the uniform he had on at yesterday's press conference. His sweaty, oily face likely has nothing to do with the humidity. His lips purse tight over a gap tooth that would have given him a friendlier disposition if he wasn't coiled up like a cobra waiting to strike. The last twenty hours must have been tumultuous for him.

'What do you mean?' I remain standing. I'm not going to let the agitated detective breathe down on me.

'Exactly what I said,' he snaps. 'I allowed you onto the crime scene, but you made a fool of the force.'

Abubakar raises a placatory hand towards Detective Bello. 'Now, now, Lawrence, Dr Taiwo is a—'

Detective Bello lowers his voice in deference to Abubakar, his eyes still fiery. 'Sir, I was one of those taken in by Dr Taiwo's reputation when you called me for assistance.'

I arch an eyebrow. 'You hoped I'd find something that supported your assumptions?'

The detective rounds on me. 'We took the necessary action based on evidence.'

'Then why did you release him?' I soften my voice, so he doesn't think I'm antagonising him.

'Because we *might* have acted hastily. We should have substantiated the evidence first.'

I raise my hands in capitulation. 'Then, my job's done.'

The detective takes a threatening step forward. I stand my ground. Abubakar moves between us like a school principal averting a scuffle in the schoolyard.

'What's your job?' Detective Bello sneers.

'To show the chain of evidence aligns with motives. In this case, it didn't, and you should be thanking me because – and trust me on this – you don't want it to break down in court. Any self-respecting judge would have thrown out your case.'

'We had him,' he insists. 'We knew we had to substantiate the evidence and that was why we took him into custody.'

I can't help the disbelief that must be all over my face. 'You arrested him on a *suspicion* to get him out of the way of your investigation?' I turn to Abubakar. 'How does that work?'

Abubakar shrugs, as he does when he can't justify a doubtful practice that's become standard procedure. 'Sometimes it's for their own safety, especially when they are popular like the bishop.'

I round on the detective. 'You arrest a man like that in full view of the world, on suspicion of murder for *his* benefit?'

'The benefit of the investigation,' the detective stresses, his nose flaring. 'We can't have him using his influence to tamper with evidence or witnesses.'

'But you started out assuming he *was* guilty. I don't get it.'

Detective Bello picks up a thin, ragged-looking file on Abubakar's desk.

'I was sharing this with the commandant before you came.' He opens the file. 'At 00.34 hours on 24 June, a male caller called one of our hotlines.'

He hands me a sheet of paper. The transcript is brief.

— *Hello. I have information.*

— *What information?*

— *A pastor has killed someone. I will send evidence. I will call again.*

— *Hello.*

— *...*

— *Identify yourself, please.*

— *[The connection was ended by the caller]*

Detective Bello hands me another photocopied document. 'Twenty-four minutes later, we received another call. The caller insisted he had proof and asked for a number to forward screenshots.'

I scan the call report. Bello's summary is accurate.

He goes on. 'The person gave us an untraceable number. You Americans call it a burner phone. All our emergency lines are mobile so they're text and images compliant.'

He hands me another transcript. Bishop Dawodu's name jumps out at me.

'Those screenshots are exchanges between the caller and the suspect.'

The mobile numbers are redacted, but the conversation's easy to follow. But—

'Why are the numbers redacted?'

'Because they're useless. The informant's own is a burner, like I said and the one the bishop used was not registered, so we couldn't trace it.'

I wave the sheet of paper. 'So, how could you determine for sure this exchange was—'

Detective Bello's eyes become flint. 'We couldn't until we followed the tip and confirmed evidence of foul play at the crime scene.'

'Oh, come on—'

'Will you read the transcript or not?' Bello snaps.

The man is testy. I tamp down my disdain for shoddy police work and read the photocopied screenshot.

— *I did it. I finished her.*

— *What can I do, Bishop?*

— *I need help.*

— *I can be there in 20 minutes, sir.*

— *Bring plenty of nylon bags.*

I look up, piqued. 'This person's confessing to being an accessory to a crime, unprompted, and it didn't raise suspicion?'

Detective Bello turns to Abubakar. 'How long did you say Dr Taiwo has been back in the country, sir?'

'Almost two years, Detective,' I answer, irritated. 'What's that got to do with anything?'

The detective makes a tut-tut sound, as if now that he understands my defect, he can be magnanimous. The dimples on both of his cheeks deepen as he gives me a patronising smile. 'Confessions are common around here.

Someday, someone will research it, but with almost all cases, the guilty confess without prompting.' He looks back to Abubakar, who nods in agreement.

In a weird way, it makes sense. A society where people are not aware of their rights will see a proliferation of confessions. The problem is with the false positives: those who confess to a crime to cover a larger, more grievous one or another culprit.

I wave the paper at the detective. 'You jumped to conclusions because you thought a crime was in progress.'

'We were *informed*. We knew if a murder had been committed, it was already too late for the victim. But if we could catch them disposing of the body, that would be another matter.'

Bello almost tears the paper from my hand. He gives me another photocopied screenshot of a single text message. I read, unimpressed.

– *We got rid of the body. He made me help him. You guys should have gone to his house.*

'When we called the number, there was no answer but we continued texting him and he would respond.'

He hands me three sheets of paper. Lots of text messages. I frown at the emerging pattern. The police's messages seem written in a flurry, several spelling mistakes and shorthand text. The informant's are in proper English, grammar and punctuations in order. Hardly how a panicked person would write.

The detective ploughs on. 'We ask him where the house is, he tells us. We ask where he is, but he doesn't say. Tells us we're wasting time because the bishop ordered him to go to the house and clean the place. We should hurry, so we asked for an emergency search warrant of the bishop's house.'

'So, you went there while the bishop was at Graceland?' I ask.

'We had every right, given the information we had,' the detective retorts sharply, defensive.

I hold out a placating hand. 'I'm trying to work with you here. When you arrived at the house, you saw the blood-stains, but even without a body, you felt you had enough from these,' – I wave the call transcripts – 'to make an arrest?'

'Perhaps we should have used a more experienced CSI, but Dobra was the only one on the ground, so we brought him in quickly and he confirmed that indeed, some violence had taken place in the house.'

'And how did you match the blood with the supposed victim?'

'We got this while at the crime scene.' He hands over another sheet of paper.

— *Confirm First Lady's blood Type 0 with the evidence.*

'And this didn't make you proceed with more caution?' My tone is deliberately snide. Amateur stuff. Whatever respect I might have had for the detective plummets further. 'The convenience of it all?'

'Of course, it did.' Defensiveness makes the detective's voice rise too high. Abubakar clears his throat pointedly. The detective's tone is calmer and modulated when he continues. 'But there was blood, an informant and all evidence pointed towards foul play.'

I'm not giving this charade an easy pass. I throw the paper on Abubakar desk. It falls to the ground. No one picks it up.

'It wasn't enough.' I don't bother to hide my scorn.

'It would have been, with more investigation time,' Detective Bello insists.

'That's enough, gentlemen.' Abubakar's calm voice cuts through the tension. 'We are all on the same side here.'

'I doubt it, sir,' the detective says.

I punch my index finger into the air, pointing it in the direction of the bristling man. 'You arrested a man on suspicion of murder with contrived evidence.'

'Which was why we kept him in custody for his own good. We wanted to trace the informant or even find the body—'

'*If* there was a body—' Abubakar says with a harshness that shows he has reached the limit of his patience. The detective visibly squirms. As the commandant of the police college, Abubakar's comment is practically a fail mark against the other officer's investigative skills.

'If the informant told us where the body was, he'd have been complicit in evidence tampering, sir,' the detective whines to Abubakar. Sweat marks around his armpit area widen. Abubakar's face is a stern mask.

'Commandant, sir,' I say, 'I have a class.' Not one to kick a dog while down, I try to keep my voice kind but firm when I turn to Bello. 'Being wrong isn't easy to admit in this field, but you've taken the first step. That press conference was well done and I think Dobra should be commended for admitting he made a mistake in his initial report. I shall do my best to placate my clients and perhaps be able to persuade them not to press charges.'

'Where does he think he is?' Detective Bello looks at Abubakar, then back at me with condescension. 'Dr Taiwo, this is not America. Your client may be powerful, but not enough to take the police to court and win.'

'But he can make life di*pp*icult *p*or you on the *p*orce,' Abubakar says grimly. 'Bello, this is not a career-making move on your *f*art.'

The detective swiftly dons a chastened look. 'I know, sir, and I'm sorry.'

There's an awkward pause as the commandant reaches for his cigarette pack. He only smokes in his office when distressed. That's my cue.

At the door, Detective Bello's grim voice stops me.

'Dr Taiwo, whether you like my methods or not, a crime was committed. When, how or why, I don't know, but I swear if Dawodu killed his wife, I'll find out. And if a mischief-maker was trying to frame him, thereby making a fool of me and my team, then I promise you, I'll find them. Either way, Dr Taiwo, I'm going to prove you wrong.'

'I'll look forward to it,' I say. From the surprised look on the detective's face, I must've sounded more sincere than he expected.

A FLYING VISIT

I'm not a stranger to conflicts with the police force. Eight and a half years at the Internal Affairs of the San Francisco Police Department, I butted heads with detectives on a near-daily basis. Everyone knew if Philip Taiwo got on your case, you'd be held accountable. I would scrutinise your procedure along with any connections you had to the case. I would comb through your history for any possible misconduct that would bear on the investigation. I would pore over your interrogation transcripts ad infinitum, to be sure everything from the location of the interview to the presence of legal representation had been duly followed. I was a major pain in the neck for the forensic labs. I had been known to request multiple interviews with coroners and analysts to go over their reports.

'The cops say you make them feel they committed the crime and are trying to pin it on the suspects,' Professor Cook, my teacher and mentor, used to joke when he was the consulting investigative psychologist for IA.

I didn't care. I was doing my job. Which is why the confrontation with Detective Bello rankles. Bringing in a high-profile suspect like Bishop Dawodu and uncovering enough proof to guarantee a conviction is the stuff that promotions and accolades are made of. This is true everywhere there's a police force and is one of the reasons I was extra hard on the officers at the SFPD. Lives can be so easily destroyed by a flawed investigation that places the blame for a crime on the wrong person, yet rewards the officer.

In the States, I'd have recourse to at least a dozen agencies whose job was to ensure Detective Bello's flagrant abuse of power did not go unchecked. How effectively they do their jobs is subject to speculation but the structures are there. The mere fact that the detective's eagerness muddled up what could have been a straightforward investigation to ascertain *if* a crime had been committed would have been cause for disciplinary action.

I crack my stiff neck and knuckles. On my laptop screen, my final report on the missing first lady stares back at me, inconclusive and therefore uncompleted. Yet, I have to submit it, prepare my invoice for the Grace Church leadership and wash my hands of this whole mess. The way my fingers hover on the keyboard mirrors my misgivings. I can't remember a time I closed a case with so many unanswered questions and still claimed my job was done. I take in a deep breath and start again—

The sound of a helicopter rumbles from a distance. Hurried boots pass through the corridor. Shadowy figures of cadets run past my office. The helicopter is now loud enough for me to surmise it is hovering over the college. I close my laptop. Whoever it is, I am grateful for the distraction.

Outside, cadets are murmuring excitedly, pointing at the helicopter as it lands at the centre of the college grounds; its wide rotor blade blows wild air into an otherwise still afternoon.

A Bell 407. I know this from the way the cabin is separated from the cockpit. Definitely not a military visitor. Abubakar walks in my direction, his eyes wide with curiosity.

'I take it you are not expecting anyone?' I say when he gets to me.

'No. But the Inspector General called me to say he gave clearance for a helicopter to land here. I asked him who but he wouldn't say. You?'

I laugh out loud. 'Me? Who'd visit me in a… Jeeezuz!'

The applause from the cadets and tutors almost drowns out the sound of the rotor blades. A bulky man in a dark suit opens the passenger door and Bishop Jeremiah Dawodu steps out of the helicopter, looking like a movie star in a dark-blue three-piece suit and sunshades. Pastor George follows. The man makes to follow but Bishop Dawodu motions for him to stay. He steps back. The bishop and Pastor George bend slightly as they hurry away from the range of the overhead blades.

'Why didn't you tell me he was coming?' Abubakar says accusingly. 'I could have had the media here.'

'I didn't know!' I shout over the noise of the helicopter. 'He was only released yesterday!'

The bishop waves at the cadets who are clapping and whistling while their mobile phones record his journey to where I am standing with Abubakar.

'Dr Taiwo, I hope you don't mind me dropping in unannounced,' Bishop Dawodu says with the widest and most engaging smile.

I accept his handshake. 'Dropping in is as literal as it gets, sir.' I turn to Abubakar. 'Let me introduce you to—'

'Commandant Abubakar Tukur,' Bishop Dawodu finishes, thrusting out his hand. 'Quite an honour, sir. And thank you so much for releasing Dr Taiwo to help clear my name.'

Abubakar grins like he's just been awarded the Presidential Medal of Honour.

'It was our privilege, Bishop,' Abubakar says. His voice carries further now that the helicopter's rotor noise has reduced to a din.

The cadets hoot and give loud cheers. Refrains of 'Up College!' start and I quickly usher the bishop in the direction of my office. I don't put it past the cadets to add 'Up Dr Taiwo!' to their chants. I'd rather evaporate instantly than witness that.

*

My office has never felt so cramped. Bishop Dawodu walks around, his tall frame turning this way and that, taking in the space and my wall of evidence. Pastor George stands at the door, keeping a respectful distance as the bishop surveys the jumble of Post-it notes. Abubakar smiles broadly like a proud parent. I feel like a fraud given my thoughts about the case five minutes earlier.

'You did all these for me?' Bishop Dawodu says with wonder.

I shrug, self-conscious and uncomfortable.

He turns from the wall to me. 'I don't know how I can ever thank you.'

I don't do well with public praise. 'I was just putting my invoice—'

Abubakar steps on my toes under the desk. 'The College appreciates any goodwill you can extend our way, Bishop. And of course, towards the police force. We regret—'

The bishop waves a dismissive hand. 'Think nothing of it, Commandant. Our Lord works in mysterious ways. The police were doing their job.' He turns back to the wall and reaches for the Post-it note with Sade Dawodu's name written on it. Gently, he peels off the picture of his wife from the wall. He stares at it for a long while.

I glance at Pastor George at the door. His face is a smooth pebble. It yields nothing.

'She's fine. I know it,' the bishop says in a cracking voice. He turns to us and there are tears flowing down his face.

We all try to look anywhere but at such a raw display of emotion.

'Thank you, thank you,' the bishop says over and over. I go up to him and pull him towards my chair as Abubakar makes a hasty retreat, taking Pastor George with him.

'It's okay, sir. I was just doing my job,' I say as soon as the door closes.

'Yes, yes,' he sniffles. 'I know, but without you, the devil would have won.'

'We still don't know who could have framed you. I wish I was able to get to the bottom of that.'

The bishop takes a handkerchief and blows his nose. 'I am sorry. I was just a bit overwhelmed by the Lord's mercy and favour.'

'I understand,' I say, sitting down across from him on one of the desk chairs reserved for visitors. 'You still don't know who could have done this?'

The bishop gives a rueful smile. 'Does it matter now?'

'Of course it does, sir. There's someone out there who wants to destroy you—'

'Doctor Taiwo, I am the general overseer of the fourth largest Pentecostal church in the country. There is always someone who wants to destroy people like me and halt the marching of the saints. Have you read the papers lately? Followed social media? There is always a pastor being accused of one thing or the other. Even the Catholic Church is not inoculated against these attacks.'

'Hardly unfounded,' I chip in sharply.

The bishop nods. 'Sadly, that is true. Which makes what you did for me all the more appreciated. You believed me when no one did. When all the signs pointed to my guilt and my contemporaries did not position the pulpit in a favourable light to warrant giving me the benefit of the doubt.'

'Frankly, I didn't consider all that. I was just doing what the elders were paying me to do.'

Bishop Dawodu gives me a warm smile. 'Your insistence on modesty is humbling.' He looks at the wall again, and shakes his head in wonder. 'So much detail. I'm impressed.' He turns to me. 'Please tell me your investigation led you to where my wife might be.'

I shake my head.

He sucks in air, then loudly lets it out. 'She is fine. I have to believe that. And she will be home soon.'

Gone is the charismatic preacher, the general overseer of Grace Church, one of the richest pastors in the world. Sitting in my chair is a man who almost lost it all for a crime that has been proven he did not commit. No matter how strong anyone is, how rich, how powerful, such a scrape with the law leaves you somehow diminished, helpless. I know this feeling. I've been there and because of this, I see the Jeremiah Dawodu beneath the designer suit and title. A man who knows how quickly fate can conspire to change the course of one's life, oftentimes using our closest and dearest to deliver the deadliest of blows.

'It's like you said when we met,' I say gently, 'your wife is alive and well and she'll be home soon.'

The bishop nods, grateful. Tears moisten his eyes again. 'I believe that.'

'So do I,' I say with more confidence than I feel.

HOMEFRONT BLUES

The silence in the house reminds me of the aftermath of a loss. The living room is in darkness. I turn on a light and Folake is sitting there, looking the saddest I've seen her in a long time. It reminds me of the day she demanded we leave the States. My stomach knots.

'Sweet, what happened?'

And just like that, racking sobs shake her body. I rush to her. She blows her nose into my shirt.

'What happened?' I lift her face to mine. 'The kids?' It must be, work issues don't break Folake like this.

She nods. 'Lara.'

'What did she do this time?' My heart beats faster.

'She stole.'

'What?'

Folake blows her nose again but her voice is stronger. 'She's stealing, Phil. I've been noticing money missing from my purse for a while. At first, I thought I miscounted. But after a while I saw a pattern. Two hundred Naira every other day, for weeks now—'

'And you never told me?'

'I wanted to be sure. Today, it was a thousand Naira! I couldn't take it any more, so I confronted the kids at dinner. The boys denied it, but she didn't.'

112

That's some relief. If Lara had lied, it'd have meant a downward spiral to get her to admit the truth.

'What did she take it for?'

Folake sobs louder, worry written all over her face. '*Stealing*, Phil. That's why I'm so scared, Sweet. She won't say. She's fifteen and I'm worried she's funding a habit.'

I shake my head. 'No, no. Please don't think that way.'

'It's all my fault. Insisting we come back. What if that's what pushed her to look for—'

This reasoning is out of character for my logical wife. 'Oh, come on, Sweet, it's a million times easier to get drugs in the States than here, and you know it.' I see she's about to argue, and add, 'Besides, what hard drugs can be bought on the streets for that amount of money?' I've no clue myself, but if I hoped this would calm her down, I failed.

'I don't know,' Folake says, distress making her twist out of my arms. 'All I know is she was a good, happy kid in the States and now—'

'She was happy to come back. Even more than her brothers.' My preoccupation with work had made me forget to share my last conversation with Lara. Guilt now adds to my rising sense of failure.

'Then what changed?' Folake shakes her head like she's looking for a clue that will explain how we got here. Then, as if finding none, she seems to snap out of it and anger creeps into her tone. 'But this? This I cannot take! *Will* not accept. If she has a habit—'

'Don't think like that. Please. Lara's just acting out. We'll get to the bottom of it. It can't be drugs.' My breath catches in my throat. How can I be sure? Who's to know what new chemical can be purchased across the pharmacy counters around the campus?

113

'If she won't talk to me, how will I know how to help her?' Folake's voice breaks.

'Let me talk to her. I'm sure there's an explanation.'

'This isn't one of your cases, Philip.'

Thinking back to how quickly I figured out the bishop's house was a staged crime scene and the man's gratitude earlier today, I can only accept that I'm better at my job than being a father. I can read a crime scene in seconds, determine the modus operandi of a complex crime with relative efficiency, but I can't penetrate my fifteen-year-old's mind.

'I wish it was,' I say under my breath.

Folake goes to bed before me, but I know she won't sleep. She might read or grade papers, but sleep will take a while, if it comes at all. I'm worried for her. Folake takes her job seriously, but there's no role she wants to succeed at more than motherhood.

I knock on Lara's bedroom door. There's no answer, but the light under the door tells me she's awake. Lara turns on her bed, giving me her back.

'Is it true?' I say at the door.

Silence.

'Omolara.' I call her by her full name. It's her mother's way of laying down the law. When I do the same, Lara knows she can't pull the Daddy's-little-girl card. 'Is it true you've been stealing?'

Lara turns to face me, her gaze defiant. 'I didn't lie, Dad. I told the truth like you always say I should and I'm still grounded.'

'A confession doesn't protect you from consequences.'

'What more do you want?'

'Do. Not. Raise. Your. Voice.'

Lara burst into tears. I will myself to stay put. Nah, not today, young lady. I wait for her to calm down.

'When you're done with your drama, you'll tell me what the money was for.'

'You won't understand,' Lara says between sobs.

I sit on the side of her bed. 'Try me, moppet.'

'I'm not a moppet.' Irritation breaks the flow of tears. 'I'm not a child and it's time everyone stops treating me like one.'

'Okay, okay. Lara, can you tell me why you stole your mother's money?'

She looks away. 'I can't.'

'Can't or won't?'

Silence. But no more tears.

I pull her face towards me, cupping her chin. 'Lara, people make mistakes, and that's allowed in this house. What isn't allowed is continuing in the mistake. Not telling us what you used the money for is a more grievous offence than the stealing itself. Do you understand?'

She makes to move her face out of my grip, but my hold is firm.

'Omolara, you've got twenty-four hours to come to me with the truth. If not, I'll march you to school, tell the principal what you've done and ask that your activities and those of your friends be investigated.'

The look of horror on her face is what I hoped for. I let go of her chin, stand and kiss her forehead. She doesn't move away.

'Go to sleep. It's a school night.'

I close the door behind me and rest against it briefly. It's going to be hard to follow through on my threat. I can only pray Lara doesn't call my bluff.

'Did she say anything?' Folake asks as soon as I enter our bedroom.

'Oh, she will.' I summarise our talk as I undress. Folake listens; her worry is not eased but she seems satisfied that we are *doing* something. She's not the wait and see type. I reassure her again and go take a shower.

By the time I come to bed, Folake is snoring lightly, the *Harvard Law Review* open on her chest. I take the journal, place it on her nightstand and tiptoe around the bed to my side.

I'm jerked awake by my phone vibrating on the night-stand, and I curse myself for not putting it on sleep mode. I grab the handset before the racket wakes Folake.

'Uhn?' I grunt out.

'They found her.'

I check my phone screen. Kenny.

'Found who?'

Fully awake, I realise the question is as unnecessary as the answer.

BOOK II

Pressure is inversely proportional to volume.

Boyle's Law

For nothing is hidden that will not become evident, nor anything secret that will not be known and come to light.

Luke 8:17 (LSB)

THROWBACK

We don't talk about the past. We've been meeting for weeks, planning. I give instructions. You tell me how they would be carried out. But we don't talk about the past.

Until I got my medical file – don't ask how, please – I assumed it was because you knew what had to be done was more important than remembering who and how we used to be. But, it's more than that, right?

I think it's because you know I'm so not the same person you knew back then. I'm not the same under-graduate who sang BeBe and CeCe duets with you in the campus fellowship choir. Or the girl you used to try so hard to make laugh; first after I flunked out of medical school and then when you sensed something happened between Soji and me. I never told you what happened, but you accepted this and kept trying to be a friend.

Even now, you're helping me. You have taken my word for everything. Never doubting me even before I showed you the evidence of my living hell. You see? You have not changed. And if you have, not as much as life has changed me.

That file – now safe in a place where no one can use it against me – was a revelation of sorts. The doctor had asked me to write my thoughts in a journal which I shared with him every week. I hated those exercises, but looking back, I see they were necessary. In one entry, I wrote:

I can now see that it was the weight of grief, not failure, that pushed me over the edge. I am just a girl grieving for a father whose death happened at an inopportune time. I'm not a failure because I am incapable of being a doctor. Daddy's death made it clear that I only wanted to be a doctor because of him. With him gone, I didn't want to be a doctor any more. Sadly, with him gone, I don't know what I want to be.

I read those entries now and realise how far from my nineteen-year-old self I have come. You see it too, and perhaps this is why we don't talk of the past. It's a distant place and we've come too far. I only wish I had come further before ever setting foot in Grace Church. But this is no time for regrets. Let's look forward.

My reminiscing has little to do with what we are doing – especially you, considering all you have to do for the plan to work – but I want you to know that I appreciate you, then and now. I know you have a lot of questions; yet, like in those days on campus, you are standing by me, fighting for me, even risking your career for me. You're a good friend. For all seasons and for all the right reasons. The only way I can thank you is through these letters, and sharing only what you need to know to do what you have to do. To share more, to give you answers to the questions you have, will be to put your life at risk. I cannot do that to you.

For now, work with what you have. Do as we agreed, no matter what. Let nothing derail you. Even your questions. All will be revealed soon.

A CIRCUS FOR THE DEAD

'You've reached Victor Ewang, I'm not around to—'

I let out a hiss of frustration and throw my mobile phone on the passenger seat as I step on the gas. Where's the man? From being eager to speak with me just yesterday to now being unavailable is disturbing. Especially now.

The frenzy in front of the Lagos State Institute of Pathology is overwhelming. The place is overrun by camera-facing reporters, hawkers meandering the crowd with sachets of pure water, soda, bottles of yogurt and energy drinks sloshing around in large polythene bags of melting ice.

The pavements and road leading to the mortuary are crammed with vehicles. News of Sade Dawodu's death has been on loop in local and international media since midnight. The body had been discovered floating in the Lekki Lagoon. It had drifted close to an ancient jetty where families have picnics during the day and young people party at night. Some party revellers called the police and shared the rather gory experience on social media. Graphic pictures of a body floating on the lagoon should not trend. But this does not apply when it's the First Lady of Grace Church. The media frenzy around this tragedy borders on obscene.

'I'm here,' I say into the phone, my eyes searching above the crowd for the fastest access to the gates.

'I'll come to you. Walk close to the gate,' Kenny says.

I shoulder through the crowd just as a tired-looking Kenny appears at the steps of the morgue. She waves at the security guards keeping the crowd at bay. One of them unwinds the long metal chain fastening the gates together. As soon as I squeeze through, the crowd press against them and more security guards rush to their colleague's aid, pushing back until the chain is locked again.

Kenny dissolves into my arms. I pat her back several times. She pulls away, wipes her tears and takes my hand as we walk into the morgue. Behind us, reporters shout questions. Was she murdered? What about the bishop? Did he do it?

I'm repulsed by the insensitivity, but the chain of disclosures has been skewed from the get-go. The minute the police had an inkling the body found in the Lekki Lagoon could be Sade Dawodu, they'd also begun their campaign of vindication in the media. On the heels of the public apology to the bishop, the body is proof there was cause to suspect foul play.

'We are all here. Waiting,' Kenny says, as she guides me through corridors into a reception room with all the elders seated around the distraught bishop. Another group, all women, surround Mrs Bucknor, who looks like her world just fell through a glass ceiling and she's sitting on the shards.

'Have they formally identified the body?' I whisper into Kenny's ear.

Kenny nods, her eyes filling with tears again. There's no doubt the body is that of Folasade Dawodu. I pull her closer just as I see Pastor George heading our way.

'You came,' he says when he gets to us. 'Thank you so much.'

'I'm so sorry,' I offer.

'The Lord knows best. For now, we have practical matters to discuss. That's why I asked Sister Kenny to call you.'

Kenny gives me a reassuring nod as she joins the women around Mrs Bucknor. Pastor George places a hand on my back, guiding me away while waving at the elders and the bishop across the room.

We find a bench on a quiet corridor leading to the toilets. The pungent smell of disinfectant hangs in the air. We are about to sit when the bishop and Pastor Nwoko walk towards us.

'I'm sorry for your loss, sir,' I say to Bishop Dawodu. He is the opposite of the man I met at the prison. His rumpled blue shirt has sweat patches on several parts. His breathing is ragged and his hands are shaking.

'Thank you,' he says, but his voice breaks as if he can't find the words to continue speaking. Pastor Nwoko pats him on the back and this seems to strengthen him. Bishop Dawodu points at the bench. 'Please, let's sit.'

We all sit and there's an awkward silence. No one seems to know how to proceed with the issue uppermost on our minds.

Pastor George takes the plunge. 'Dr Taiwo, the situation is very much different now that we know ...' His voice trails off. The bishop's head is bowed.

I nod.

'I still don't think this is the time and place,' the bishop says, but his protest is weak because he is shaking his head like he's in a bad dream he expects to wake up from soon.

Pastor Nwoko speaks gently. 'Bishop, the police will try to make their accusations again. Of course, we know it won't stick, but we have to prepare for that eventuality.'

'But I didn't do it,' the bishop says, agonised.

I feel for him. As much as I'm a bit appalled at the timing of what I'm sure the elders are about to ask of me, their pragmatism might be just what the bishop needs right now. He is clearly in no state to make any rational decisions. It's the megachurch version of 'lawyering up'. Attack before being attacked.

When the bishop seems to have calmed down, Pastor George looks at me. 'We want you to continue working on the case.'

'To do what?' I ask. I already know.

'To find out who did this!' Pastor Nwoko snaps, as if the answer is obvious.

'But, I'm not the police. I assure you they'll do everything in their power to—'

'Like they did when they arrested Bishop without cause?' Pastor Nwoko asks, derisive. 'They'll try to prove they were right the first time. No, no, we can't afford to leave this in their hands.'

'I'm not that kind of investigator.' I look at the men. Surely, they must recall my introduction to them less than a week ago.

'We know,' Pastor George continues. 'When we sought your services, we assumed First Lady was alive. At that time, our intention was to clear Bishop's name. Technically, you've not completed the assignment.' It's subtle blackmail but his eyes are pleading.

'I recognise that,' I concede. Darnit. 'But this might end up being a murder case ...'

'For which Bishop is going to be falsely accused.' Pastor
Nwoko sounds exasperated, as if I was being deliberately
obtuse.

It's now the bishop's turn to calm the elder. 'Maybe
we should just let them do their job. I'm sure if they do
their investigation, they'll find and bring the culprits to
justice.'

'You know it doesn't work that way, Bishop,' Pastor
George says before Nwoko can speak. 'The church can't
afford to have you arrested again. Think of the damage it
will do to morale ...'

'I don't care!' Bishop Dawodu springs up, and stands
over us. I catch a whiff of stress-induced body odour mixed
with his expensive cologne. 'My wife is dead. She's lying
there,' – He points towards the corridor – 'dead. She's not
coming back and all you care about is the church?'

His voice is loud enough to carry to the reception room,
and the silence there is proof that everyone heard him.

'The police can't arrest you again unless they have irrefutable proof, sir,' I say softly.

'We can't risk it.' Pastor George's gaze is locked with the
bishop's, like a matador staring down a raging bull. 'Bishop,
no one is asking you not to grieve. And no one here can
even claim to know what you're going through now. But we
have a responsibility that's larger than the current circumstances. As you yourself have preached in the past, this too
shall pass. What we want to ensure is that when it does, the
church is intact and not damaged.'

My dislike for the man rises to the fore. The calm way he
speaks, and the rather patronising way he is trying to force
this Machiavellian logic on the bishop is sickening.

Before I can intervene, he looks at me. 'We need to know who planted the evidence against Bishop. That was your assignment, abi?'

'Can't we discuss this later, Pastor? Perhaps after ...' I let my words trail off and look around.

Bishop looks from one elder to the other, resigned and despondent. He gives me a tired curve of the lips. 'They are right. This too shall pass. Do what you need to do, but let me grieve in peace.'

The bishop walks away, shoulders slumped, Nwoko trails after him.

I refuse to break the ensuing silence between Pastor George and me. Let the man squirm.

But he is unfazed. 'Dr Taiwo, what has happened has happened. First Lady has gone to be with the Lord. We can't afford to wait for the backlash. It makes sense to act now. And we need your help.'

'I'll have to ask the college for permission. There might be a conflict of interest if I remain on this assignment.'

'Then resign!' Pastor George orders. 'We will pay you well.'

The man is unbelievable. I raise an eyebrow that oddly seems to caution him.

'I'm sorry. I didn't mean it like that,' he says, watching for my response. 'But please, Dr Taiwo, a lot is at stake here. There's nothing we can do to bring back First Lady, but there's a lot we can do to contain the damage to the church. Help us.'

I throw out a challenge, just to see his reaction. 'What if he did it?'

'He didn't. He was in church throughout. We can all vouch for him. Besides, look at that man. Does he look like someone who would kill his wife in cold blood, dump her body in the lagoon and conduct services hours later?'

It's not the place to give the insufferable pastor a lesson in criminal psychopathology. Besides, given the information Detective Bello shared from the case file, it's likely that the bishop is the victim of a set-up.

'What if he's culpable in some way?'

Pastor George shakes his head with confidence. 'He's not. I can't afford to believe otherwise or else what's the point of asking for your help?'

'And I can afford to?' I ask.

'Fortunately for us, your job requires doubt, mine's the opposite.'

TEAMBUILDING

'Absolutely not!' Detective Lawrence Bello says, pounding a fist on his desk.

I anticipated this but not the vehemence. I'd called to request a meeting at his office. Perhaps it was to gloat but he'd acquiesced, causing me to leave the morgue hurriedly, turn on my GPS and drive to the Special Crimes Investigations Unit at the Lagos Island Police Headquarters.

His office is tiny and hardly private. Voices, clacking typewriters, beeping fax machines and whirring of dot-matrix printers filter in from other offices. The memo that we're in the digital age is taking its time to reach the police force. But we're alone, which encourages me to speak frankly.

'You don't want to make the mistake of rushing to conclusions again. I can help you ensure that your investigation is above board.'

'Your services will be paid for by my number-one suspect,' the detective snaps back.

'What does it matter if both of us are after the same thing? You are after the truth, right?'

'Don't be funny, Dr Taiwo. My career is practically on the line here. And now that I've proof that we were right all along, you want me to hand you the noose to hang me?'

His penchant for the dramatic is tiresome. 'Detective, if you make the mistake of approaching this investigation to prove the bishop's guilt, your career will indeed be over.'

'See? You are biased, and I can't grant you access to our files or the coroner's report.'

'No, Detective, it is you who's biased. I'm trying to save you from yourself. Let me in on the evidentiary trail, and I'll ensure you don't make the same mistake twice.'

'Will you help me find the killer?'

I'd rather not make any promises, but what choice do I have? 'Consider that a value-added service,' I say. 'My suspicion is, if there's a killer, we'll find them once we know why the bishop was framed and who framed him.' I put out my hand. The detective might be stubborn but we both know he needs a lifeline.

'I want to know what you know as soon as you know it,' he commands.

I nod. After several seconds, he shakes my outstretched hand.

I drive out of the SCIU offices with photocopies of the pitifully slim case file, complete with transcripts of the informant's conversation which led to the bishop's arrest. I also have a letter from the detective to the coroner, urging him to release the autopsy report to me as soon as it becomes available. But, only after Bello's team has vetted it. I can live with this.

Victor Ewang is still unreachable. I call Kenny.

'Why him?' Kenny asks as soon as I finish my request.

'Just a lead I'm following.'

'No one's seen him, but to be honest no one's looking. We are still here at the mortuary.'

'You don't have another number for him?'

'I don't have any number for him. I can ask his wife …?'

I don't want people to wonder why I'm looking for the Director of Foreign Missions so soon after leaving the mortuary, so I tell Kenny not to worry. Just as I'm about to hang up—

'Phil! Wait …' Kenny's tone makes me tense. 'You asking about Victor Ewang. I don't know him well. And I don't know if it's relevant, but there were rumours …'

'About?'

'Him and First Lady. People were implying there was something between them.'

Interesting. 'Was there?'

'I broached the subject with Sade once. I was worried her mum would hear. Anyway, she said I shouldn't mind people. That she was only taking financial advice from Ewang.'

'Did you believe her?'

'I had no reason not to, but now you're asking about Ewang, of all people. Phil, what's going on?'

I tell her Ewang was one of the interviewees I'd missed talking to on account of the bishop's sudden release. I just want to set up another appointment. Kenny seems satisfied with my answer. She promises to ask around for his whereabouts and I hang up.

I check the time. Already past three. I should be heading back to the mainland now if I hope to speak to Abubakar before he leaves the college. I can't drive to Chika's security firm in Lekki and get on the Third Mainland Bridge in time. A call will have to suffice.

'You want me to be your driver again?' Chika says after listening to my proposal.

'I don't need a driver to show me around Lagos.'

'If I recall,' Chika returns drily, 'I was much more than a driver—'

'When you finally came clean about who you really were,' I shoot back.

'You won't ever let that go, will you?'

'I'll remind you till eternity,' I reply, meaning it.

'Reminding me of my past transgressions to coerce me is called blackmail.'

'Is it working?'

'You know it is,' he grumbles, and I know I'm in good hands. Owning and managing a cybersecurity firm makes Chika and his team worthwhile partners on this case. Knowing Chika is a well-trained sniper with years of combat experience makes him the perfect protection in a situation where I can't count on the support of the police force. We've been here before.

'Any progress on the call log?'

'I told the guy to hold off when I thought the case was closed.'

'Well, bring him back in. I need that log.'

'Woah. Pushy,' Chika says, caustic. It's all show. I bet he'd already put his contact back on as soon as the news of Sade's death broke.

I insist he sends me a quote for his team's hours. After some protest, which I counter with the fact that I'm also being handsomely rewarded, Chika agrees.

The gods of Lagos traffic are in a good mood and I descend off the Third Mainland Bridge just after four, in time to see Abubakar before he knocks off for the day.

'I'm not sure you should have taken the assignment,' he says, shaking his head.

'That wasn't what you said before,' I retort, as we stand in our usual spot outside his office while he smokes.

'Then it was an o*f*en-and-shut case. Now it's a mess. All eyes are on us and not *p*or the right reasons.'

'I understand and that's why I need your help.'

Abubakar corks an eyebrow, stubs the cigarette and crosses his arms across his chest.'Proceed.'

'The police need an iron-clad case. Plus, it's important that they are seen to be doing all they can to solve the case. The detective and his team didn't like being made fools of, so Bello'll do everything in his power to find who sent them those tip-offs to make them think the bishop killed his wife. He said as much.'

'True,' Abubakar agrees, but I can see he's suspicious of my intentions.

'I want to get some cadets on the case. Get them to do some legwork and give feedback to the investigative team. A real-life case for future police detectives.'

Abubakar's face relaxes as he nods approvingly. 'Ah. I see where you're going. We get some of the heat off the college if we're seen as working with the *p*orce! Brilliant.'

I didn't expect him to say no, but his enthusiasm is a relief. Given the size and scope of this assignment, I'll need help with the research side of things. The cadets will get needed experience while freeing me up to focus on the two important questions on my mind: how and why did Folasade Dawodu die?

'Let's do it, but it had better work,' Abubakar says, lighting up again. He wags the smouldering cigarette at me. 'Or else.'

Despite the warning, I'm cautiously excited. My initial reluctance to get involved in the petty scandals of a church pales now in the face of a possible homicide. I go to my office and make quick notes for sharing tasks for some of the most promising cadets in my class. I'll brief them first thing tomorrow.

I open the manila file and the cover page makes me pause. State vs Jeremiah Babatunde Dawodu. The 'received' stamp bearing the insignia of the Office of the Director of Public Prosecution strikes me as odd. The date is the day of the bishop's arrest. They were ready to prosecute so quickly? On less than twenty pages of screenshots and an unverified crime scene report? How?

Perhaps because someone knew the first lady was dead *before* the body was pulled out of the lagoon. Someone who was sure her life had been in danger. I reach for my mobile phone.

'He lives on the estate like most of the staff,' Kenny answers in response to my question. 'Phil, I'm really concerned about your fascination with this guy.'

'Don't worry, sis. I just want to get the interviews over so I can really focus on what matters.'

'Like finding the killer?' She sounds hopeful.

'Maybe.'

She tells me how to get to my intended destination. I commiserate again, tell her to get some rest and hang up. I prepare my mind for the resistance I'll meet on the other side of the line. I dial again.

'Seriously?' Folake exclaims when I tell her my plans. 'At this time? Will you even make it home tonight?'

'I think so. It'll take a while getting there, but the roads should be clear by the time I'm done.'

'And this can't wait till tomorrow?' she asks.

I look at the card in my hand. '*She found out some things. I know because I told her.*'

'No, Sweet, it can't wait.'

DARK ELEMENTS

I drive through the gates of Graceland at just past 10 p.m. The security guards look sombre as they direct me to the residential quarters of the church estate. The flags of countries where the Grace Church is located are at half-mast in honour of the late first lady. Exodus Road which leads to the grandiose Grace Cathedral is almost empty.

It's dark inside the cathedral. The whole structure is at least sixty feet high; the gold-plated cross on the rooftop glows, almost mocking the mournful atmosphere. Tall marble pillars rise to meet the roof which juts at several points, resembling a damaged umbrella curved upwards. Rumoured to seat more than 50,000 people, it takes several minutes to drive past the massive structure and reach St Luke's Street where I slow down to read the house numbers lettered on the neatly arranged bungalows.

I park in front of Number 18 and call Victor Ewang. I cut off the now familiar voicenote and get out of the car.

I'm relieved to see the TV's flickering screen in the living room, so I knock gently. The curtains part and a woman's face appears. I wave, trying to assure her that I come in peace. Her frown doesn't ease but the curtains are pulled shut. I don't knock again. I can hear mutterings inside.

Seconds later, Victor Ewang opens the door. He is dishev-elled in his pyjamas, eyes frantic with fright.

He looks left and right, then inclines his head towards the room behind him. 'Not here.'

'You weren't picking up your calls,' I say by way of apology.

'Not here,' he repeats in an urgent whisper.

'Where?' I demand, making it clear I'm not budging.

'I'll send you a location. Wait for me there.'

He shuts the door. I wait in my car. I want him to see I'm not leaving until the promised message comes. The curtains part again. Same woman. My phone beeps. It's a location pin. I pull off the driveway, conscious of the woman watch-ing me. His wife? Does she know why her husband is afraid?

Outside of Graceland, I drive seventeen minutes on the Lagos Ibadan Expressway and take a right. The GPS confirms that I am at my destination. Ewang has chosen another megachurch – the Redeemed Christian Church of God – for our rendezvous.

I'm here. I text Ewang and wait.

He replies almost instantly.

Go to the parking area. Driving a Silver Infinity.

I follow the street signs to the parking lot. Floodlights illuminate the smattering of cars. I can see why Ewang chose here. There's no church programme today, and while the place is far from secluded, anonymity is poss-ible. I feel like I'm in some clandestine spy game on 'holy ground'.

The wait seems interminable and I'm thinking of driving back to Ewang's house. I'm about to text him this warning when the bright headlights of an Infinity SUV float into the parking lot. I flash my lights and it cruises towards my car. The driver's window lowers.

'Get in my car,' he orders.

Inside the plush interior, I go straight to the point. 'You said you have information about the first lady?'

Instead of answering, he reverses out and heads off onto another street. He drives past a football field and a kindergarten until he gets to a dark spot, crowded with construction vehicles and other tools of ongoing expansion work on the church estate. It's not his first time here.

'So?' I ask as soon as the car stops. There's no light inside, save for the reflection of the digital dials on the dashboard.

'She was killed because of what she found out about the church,' Ewang announces in a rush. His fear like heat from the sun.

'The church? You mean the bishop did it?'

'No! Bishop is not a killer.' He sounds horrified.

'But you said the church ...'

'I said what she *knew* about the church.'

'Why don't you start from the beginning?'

Ewang takes a deep breath. 'You know I head the church expansion initiatives, so I'm in charge of finances, sending money to different countries for church building, evangelism and all that.'

I nod like I'm familiar with his job description.

'The church makes an enormous amount of money. Everyone thinks it comes from tithes, offerings and donations, right?'

'It doesn't?'

'Not for Grace Church. You see, I was recruited to work in the church from a bank where I headed the Forex division. When I started, I was required to supervise the purchasing of foreign currency at the best possible price for onward transfer to church accounts in Europe and the US. It was straightforward. The church allocates funds to my department, gives me a list of the missions that need funding, and I buy and transfer the foreign currency to the respective countries.' He sucks in his breath, shakes his head and slumps his shoulders. 'It was simple.'

'Until it wasn't?' I ask softly when it's clear the man needs prompting.

He looks at me. 'When the money started coming from the missions abroad.'

'I don't understand.'

'The HQ is here but I was now required to send all monies to America. And not straight there, o. I have to go through several banks, incurring unnecessary bank charges along the way, before it finally gets to America. It was much more worrisome as the Naira depreciated.'

I suspect where this is going. The source of the man's fear seemed intimately linked to his job at Grace Church. I stay quiet. People tend to give more information if they sense the listener needs convincing.

'About five years ago – I was then in the job for about two years – I was required to move ten million US dollars from our church office in Croatia via a bank in Hong Kong then through Mauritius to the US. I was concerned. It was a highly expensive transfer. The fees for moving the money across three international banks were quite high compared to a straightforward transfer. So, I started questioning the instructions I was getting and the answers were not making sense.'

'Who were you asking?'

'At first it was my direct boss, Pastor Nwoko, who's also in charge of church finance. But he couldn't give me any answer, or why the instructions were given like that. I wrote off this as ignorance because he really is not a finance person. He started as a treasurer of the church in the early days. I was not close to Bishop, so I couldn't go straight to him. I began digging on my own.'

Ewang's hands start to shake and he abruptly presses the button that lets down the window on his side. He sticks out his head as if to gulp air.

'Are you okay?' My question sounds silly even to my ears.

'I am. I am.' He nods vigorously, but his head remains outside.

'You were digging?' I prompt after a beat.

'I shouldn't have, but my curiosity got the better of me. For one, the church in Croatia had an official membership of 234 people. When I googled the location, it was in one of the poorest neighbourhoods in Zagreb. I didn't have access to that mission's accounts, but there was no way a 234-member church in the slums of Zagreb was funding the planting of yet another mission in the US to the tune of ten million USD. Someone must have noticed my snooping because the next thing I knew, I was handed a visa and a ticket to America.'

'By who?'

'Pastor Nwoko. He said it was time for me to understand the breadth of my assignment. Two weeks later I was in

Houston, having a meeting with LaTanya Jacobson. She's Bishop's business manager.'

I nod again, as if the concept of millions of US dollars of church funds leading to an American 'business manager' was commonplace.

'She was the one who told me everything. Take the Croatian transfer, for instance. The money was a donation from an arms dealer. So, he donates the money to the church before it is transferred out of the country. The funds get to America via several links, are cleared by the authorities for "missionary work", and well, then "washed" by purchases for religious purposes including equipment, property and anything else the church can declare. Even private jets.'

'But that's a lot of money to clear without due oversight by the Feds.'

'My brother, never underestimate the power of the church in that country of yours.'

His erroneous assignment of my citizenship is inconsequential – if irksome – so I press on. Besides, the church's tax-exempt status in the States is not only well documented but abused. 'How does this involve the first lady?'

Another deep, shaky breath, but Ewang is calmer now. 'When I came back from that US trip, a new post was created for me. Head of Foreign Missions reporting directly to Ms Jacobson in America. My salary was doubled; I was given a house on the estate; I was finally able to marry my fiancée and start a family. For three years, I moved money like that. Moving donations from criminals, sending them to Ms Jacobson to wash, and then I became responsible for the returns in selected countries.'

'Some money comes back here?'

He nods. 'A lot comes back. And that was how First Lady started suspecting.'

'She didn't know before?'

'I don't think so. She came to my office one day, sat down and asked me outright what my real job in the church was. I was taken aback, and told her the public version. She smiled and told me she knew I was lying and she would prove it. From then on, it was like an assault. She would call me every day, send me presents, invite me to lunch. Always nice, but the questions never stopped. One day, she invited me to their house on the Island. Bishop was not there. I was nervous. We were alone. She was ...' He bows his head, as if shaking off a memory best forgotten. 'She was ...'

So, the rumours of an affair with Ewang are true. 'You were intimate?' I ask gently, trying not to judge.

Ewang smirks. 'You are a kind man, Dr Taiwo, but that's not what happened. A part of me wished it did. In fact, I went to that house hoping something would happen, but First Lady wanted nothing but information. And as soon as she got it, she shut me off.'

'Nothing happened?'

'Nothing.'

I search his face for untruth, but what does the man have to lose or gain by lying about a dead woman?

'What information did you give her?'

'Documents. Selected transactions. The names of the donors, their banking details, the amounts they donated and the amounts returned to them as clean money.' He reaches into his pocket and holds up a flash drive. 'This is an updated version of the files I gave her. And I'm convinced someone whose name is on that file found out First Lady knew what was going on, and had her killed.'

'That's hard to believe. I mean, she was the first lady, married to the bishop—'

'She claimed she hated him,' Ewang says harshly, like a man whose ego is still hurting. 'That she wanted to leave him. It was crazy but I thought it was to be with me. That was why I gave her the information, to give her leverage. If she told the bishop she had the list, then he must know someone on it killed his wife.'

BODYTALK

My prediction of less traffic after midnight proved true. I pulled up in front of my driveway some minutes past 3 a.m. Despite my exhaustion, I head to the study and open my laptop. It doesn't take a genius to understand what's happening. Numbers, initials, codes and city names flicker on my screen. I scroll up and down. Hundreds of transactions across dozens of financial institutions across as many cities. I will need help.

I text Chika. *Send despatch rider to my home first thing. Will explain.*

Close to 5 a.m., I tiptoe into the bedroom. Just as my head lands on the pillow, I hear Folake move.

'Got what you wanted?' she asks groggily.

I turn and kiss her forehead. 'Not sure, but I got something.' Now is not the time to think or talk of how much I hope Ewang is lying. If he's not, it seems I've been taken in again by a man of God in much the same way as with Reverend Freedman. Not a great indication of how much I've matured or learnt since my teenage years.

'Good. I'll do the school run,' Folake says as she settles back to sleep.

Not enough hours later, I wake up to an empty house. I shower, down strong black coffee and head out.

The roads seem unusually subdued as I drive towards Lagos Island. I know this is a perception brought on by melancholy. A sadness at the sudden turn of events. The prospect of the task ahead fills me with dread. My reluctance pulls everything into slow motion, blurring the edges of the reality of Lagos traffic. It's all me. Truth is, life goes on at its frenzied pace, and I'm the one less inclined towards optimism. Death calls.

There's no crowd outside the mortuary. Everyone has gone home to follow the news on their mobile phones. I envy them. Post-mortem on a body immersed in water is messier than most. Viewing Sade Dawodu's corpse is a dreadful prospect.

The mood inside is bustling and at odds with the sombreness the place deserves. Several people are outside on the steps and even more inside the reception area. Relatives of the dead mingle with purveyors for the dead.

— Ehn! That coffin is made of mahogany, o. It can't go for lower. See this one –

— Transport to the village is not a problem, but the embalming must be done here –

— Cremate? Haba! Don't you love your mother? A befitting burial is the –

A man in an off-white coat makes a beeline for me. From his purposeful walk and the way his eyes search mine for recognition, he must be the coroner. He is short, mid- to late-fifties, and without a speck of hair on his shiny head.

'Dr Taiwo?'

'That's me.'

We exchange pleasantries and he leads me down several corridors to a door with a sign: AUTOPSY. I take a deep breath. The coroner stops and looks at me with concern.

'I know you asked for pictures, but this body was pulled from the water. They are notoriously hard to photograph for effective diagnosis,' the coroner says apologetically.

'I understand,' I say curtly.

He pushes the double doors open. I follow him and stop at a respectful distance from the lone stainless-steel examining table at the centre of the room. Plastic covers the body. I grit my teeth and take a step closer.

'We worked through the night because of the importance of the case,' the coroner says, as he walks around the table. 'This is the VIP room.'

Class distinctions even in death. Only in Nigeria.

'The husband paid for an expedited autopsy,' he adds, noting my bemused expression.

'I don't understand.'

There's a hint of pity in his smile. 'We are grossly under-funded, and in a situation like this, if the family can pay for express service, we prioritise it.'

He pulls the plastic covering off. I suck in my breath when I catch a glimpse of the face. Bulging eyes, body distended with liquid, skin discoloured, lips swollen and tongue hanging.

'"She's so beautiful",' I remember Lara saying. There's no sign of any beauty now.

'Are you okay?' the coroner asks.

I manage a nod.

'No indications of strangulation,' he continues. 'We couldn't establish any external trauma due to the extended immersion.' His eyes flicker across the body to mine. 'I'll cover the face,' he adds and it's all I can do not to hug him. 'There's not much to go with there, anyway,' he says and

146

bends to pick up the plastic cover that had fallen to the ground.

Mercifully, he covers Folasade Dawodu's face.

'We started at the most obvious place.' He points at the two arms of the Y incision across the chest, connecting to the stem down the length of the stomach. 'We can confirm that the victim did have considerable amount of water in the lungs, meaning she drowned.'

'Could you ascertain any trauma before the actual drowning?'

'Not yet, although I'm still doing the internals. Rigor mortis makes it difficult to ascertain exterior trauma, except one that strikes bone.'

'There's suspicion of an attack, perhaps with a knife?' My question is tentative to avoid outright lying.

The coroner shakes his head. 'That'll be hard to confirm but we'll try. I did test that the water in the lungs is the same as samples from the lagoon: 72 per cent toxicology match.'

'That's significant.' I like the guy. His meticulous approach is reassuring and frankly, unusual for a civil servant.

'Absolutely,' the coroner nods curtly. 'I also checked the contents of her stomach.' He points at the stem of the Y. 'Rich, fatty meal. There was no starvation before the drowning. Because she was fully clothed, the sexual organs were protected so I'm checking for possible sexual contact. It's a long shot but worth a try.'

'You think you might still find something?'

The coroner takes off his glasses and wipes the lenses on his white coat. 'If there was contact without a condom, chances are we'll find traces of discharge, at least.'

Even with the most sophisticated equipment, I doubt there'll be much to go on there. 'Traces' only open lines of inquiry, hardly ever conclusive.

'Any blood work?' I ask. If the victim was drugged or had ingested an anaesthetic, it's likelier to remain in the body than organic substances.

His glasses are back on but no less smudged. 'That was the first thing I ordered from the lab as soon as I couldn't ascertain visible trauma.'

'And?'

'These things take time and it's a different lab from the toxicology one. Results haven't come back yet. I'll let you know as soon as they do.' He waves his hand around the body's mid-section. 'Here, something interesting came up.'

My heart skips a beat. 'She's not ... She wasn't ...'

'Pregnant? Oh no,' the coroner reassures me hurriedly. 'I read about the victim's challenges with childbirth which is why I found it noteworthy that she's had a tubal ligation.'

I can't hide my surprise. 'She's been sterilised?'

'And recently too because the tubes were cauterised and the scars appear recent.'

HIDDEN FIGURES

'Wow,' Chika says, as he pushes his chair away from the screen.

'Crazy, right?' I say, still peering at his laptop.

Chika shakes his head in disbelief. 'The names on this list are enough to bring down governments.'

To the uninitiated, the information on the flash drive would be just a list of names and banking transactions across multiple financial institutions all over the globe. Look closer, and it is an explosive list of personalities – politicians, well-known business people – all 'donating' large sums of money to Grace Church so it could be filtered through several locations and then returned, cleaned and untraceable.

'It's the most elegant form of money laundering I've ever seen,' Chika says, impressed. 'And it's all legal, that's what blows my mind.'

'Only because the church is outside of financial scrutiny.' I walk over to his side table and pour myself a glass of water. 'The real crime is the source of those monies.'

He whistles and pulls his chair closer to the laptop, shaking his head at the screen. 'Sade Dawodu may have been murdered after all. You don't mess with the people on this list and get off in one piece.'

'If she was uncovering a crime, we've got to consider that may be why she was killed.'

Chika snorts. 'If your informant is right, she might have tried blackmailing her husband into a divorce with this information. Altruism had nothing to do with it.'

'Are we excusing murder now?' My tone is unintentionally sharp.

'Of course not, but look at this.' Chika waves at the screen. 'Senators, governors, arms dealers, known drug cartels and worse. Even those considered legitimate business people are here. There's no one here who wouldn't kill to keep this list a secret.'

'All 117 names?' I ask, the magnitude of the task ahead becoming clearer. He nods. 'So, we have 117 suspects, but we can presume not all, but a few or an individual, did it?'

'*If* any one of them did it,' Chika says, cautions.

'Yes, yes,' I say impatiently. I'd hate to spend precious time on a dead end but what choice is there? 'So, where do we start?'

Chika is quiet but I know his head is working out all kinds of scenarios. Banter aside, we make a good team. He's a doer, crafting his next move with precision. I'm a thinker, always evaluating the best course of action before taking a step.

'I always go back to Sade herself,' I say after my thoughts lead nowhere. 'If she tried to blackmail her husband, why did she leave the house? Where did she go? Did she leave alone or with someone?'

'And the elaborate set-up to make it appear like she was violently attacked?'

'We don't know it was her.'

'Who else could it be?' Chika asks, caustic.

'Perhaps someone she confided in? Someone helping her escape?' I start pacing the office. 'Ewang claimed Sade got him to give up information. If she was colluding with someone on that list, and they worked together to set up the crime scene to make it look like she had been killed there, that would narrow the suspects to someone local. Or someone who had travelled out of the country recently, meaning we can check the names on the list with airlines.'

'It doesn't quite help,' Chika says, unconvinced. 'There are at least twenty or so names that are local, but operate globally. They could have been anywhere in the world at the time Sade disappeared. Also, how can we be sure this is the complete list of transactions? There could be more Ewang doesn't know about.'

'I agree, but I saw that guy, Chika. He's scared. He believes if Sade tried to blackmail her husband with this information, then the bishop, some LaTanya woman and most, if not all, of the people on that list, know the information came from him.'

Chika shakes his head. 'That's not how these things work. If this is a profitable venture for the bishop, and it likely is, he won't want anyone knowing their secret is out.'

'So, it can only be the bishop and this LaTanya?'

'Except we know your LaTanya is not in the country, and the bishop wouldn't have framed himself for killing his wife.'

'We are going around in circles.'

'Which is what I suspect we are supposed to be doing.'

I do a slight double take on this. 'Who would want us going in circles?'

'I'm thinking, your victim. Only she didn't plan on getting killed for real.'

He knows something. I can tell by the way he's smiling. 'What have you got?'

'I followed up on the security guard on duty the morning she disappeared. Turns out the owner of the company knows a friend who knows a friend. Anyway, I made some calls yesterday after we spoke, and the owner granted me permission to speak to the guard.'

'I would have liked to speak to him myself.' I hate my whiny tone.

'I know. You were hours of traffic away. Do you want to know what he said or are you going to make me feel bad for taking the initiative?'

I sit back on the chair and face him. 'Go on.'

'Thank you, sir,' Chika says with a slight tilt of his head, teasing. 'So, the guard apparently took over the morning shift. He said the night-duty guard – I assume that would be the bishop's number-one alibi – Samson, didn't give any incident report during the handover, so he didn't know anything happened that night. And because I knew you'll give me grief for speaking to him without you …' He waves his mobile phone at me.

I sit up. 'You recorded your conversation?'

'I learnt from the best. Do I press play or do you want to continue with Twenty Questions?'

'Please. Play.'

The interview background is noisy, but Chika must have placed the mic side of the phone closer to the security guard because the recording is much clearer when he speaks, while the questions are a bit muffled.

'I no know say na me see madam last, o.'

'E be like say na you, o.'

'Na wa, o. Na so madam just die like dat?'

The colour and layers of meaning that goes with pidgin paints a picture in my mind. I can almost see the security guard shaking his head, wondering at the mystery of life and death.

'You see am leave di house?' Chika asks. The security guard must be nodding 'yes' because Chika continues. 'Na before bishop leave or na after?'

I smile at him. He did learn a lot from watching me interview witnesses. Don't assume. Give just enough information to steer the conversation, but leave key facts hanging. Let your interviewee fill the gaps, then compare with what you know.

'Bishop no dey house, o. Im car no dey there when I come for duty.'

'So, madam left alone? Her driver no come?' Again, I nod approvingly at Chika. He's matched the interviewee's speech pattern. I lean closer. Pidgin is not my strong suit, but listening to a recording makes it easier to decipher.

'Madam don give everybody leave, o. Cook, gardener, cleaner. Everybody no come work.'

'So, the house dey empty?'

'I no look inside, o, but me I think say the house empty since everyone dey leave.' There's a trace of defensiveness and irritation in the guard's voice at having to repeat his story. But, also because despite his denial, he *did* look inside the house.

'But her car dey compound, so how she go? She take Uber?'

'No o. Na her friend come carry am.'

I turn to Chika, piqued. He motions for me to continue listening.

'Her friend?' Chika asks.

There's a stretched-out silence, and if not for the background noise, one would think the interview was over.

'Your madam don die, o.' I picture Chika inching closer, his eyes steady on the guard. Non-threatening. 'We dey find di people wey kill am.'

There's another long silence as if the guard is considering Chika's words. He must have given a cue that he's willing to speak because Chika's voice rises again. 'Dis her friend, na woman or man?'

'Na man.' The guard sounds confident.

'You know am before?'

'How I no go know am?' Answering a question with a question. Classic Nigerian, indicating certainty. 'E dey come di house well well.'

'You know im name?' Chika asks.

At this, the guard laughs. 'I wan know am die? Na everyday my wife dey play im music.'

'A singer?'

'Yes, na. Im name na Enomo Collins.'

HEAD GIRL

Folasade. Never Sade. That's how Daddy called me when he came to see us. Our flat was the smallest in the house because Mummy had only me, and the other three wives had a combined sixteen kids. I lived for those visits, when Mummy has been chosen to cook his dinner and I didn't have to share him with his other children.

Because your wealth will be the crown of this family, he promised when I asked why he gave me my name.

I especially loved it when he visited because I did well in school. One time, when I was made head girl, he came three nights in a row! I was happiest during those three days. I liked knowing I had a hand in Mummy's strut when she walked past Daddy's other wives.

Then, just like that, Mummy found Jesus and decided that the Lord's approval was more important than her husband's. She packed out, leaving Daddy with the ultimatum: if he wanted her, he must forsake all others.

The longer Daddy stayed away, the more time we spent at the church, praying for him to find Jesus. When I got my admission to study medicine, I was sure it was going to be like that time I was made head girl. He sent me a bottle of perfume and a congratulatory note addressed to 'my brilliant daughter, Folasade'.

He had never played favourites and was not about to start with us. Instead of finding Jesus, he mixed his blood

155

pressure medicine with over-the-counter Viagra and died on top of wife number 5.

The day after he was buried, I walked into an anatomy class, stared down at the naked cadaver of a man close to Daddy in age and stature, and knew I no longer wanted to be there. That semester I failed anatomy. Then biochemistry. And kept failing until the medical school told me I'll never be a doctor.

It took grief therapy and my praying mother's stubborn faith for me to finish university. I changed courses. Luckily, there was space in the Sociology department, so I went back to year one. Managed to graduate with a second class upper. Did I ever tell you that? That was also the time Mummy became a member of Grace Church. And introduced me to Jeremiah Babatunde Dawodu.

He smiled at me, and called me 'Folasade'. I was undone, soon to be doomed. But I didn't know then what I now know. And what I've now burdened you with. But enough reminiscing.

Let's go start a fire.

CALL LOG

Chika hands me the sheaf of papers he picked off the compact printer adjacent to his desk.

'So, here's the thing,' he starts, turning his laptop in my direction so I can compare the printed data with the on-screen info. 'Sade made several calls the day before she disappeared. My cyber guys are trying to match the numbers to registered SIM card databases. I must warn you it's not always accurate, but you know that, right? Some people use fake names to buy SIM cards, or they simply inherit one from a friend or relative and never bother to change the particulars with the mobile phone company.'

'I'm most interested in the calls she made on the day she disappeared,' I say, riffling through the printouts.

'Just three calls. They were easy to track. One of the numbers was dialled repeatedly but was not picked up. I've highlighted the names the numbers are linked to.'

I go to the last page. The last day Sade was seen alive. Three names. Kikelomo Bucknor against which Chika has written 'Mother'. The second name is a U. Ohaeri, and Chika has written, 'Doctor?' next to it. And then Enomo Collins, against which Chika has scrawled 'Choirmaster'.

'The singer?'

'Apparently, the church work is a side gig. He's actually quite a popular gospel singer.'

I remember the YouTube worship session I viewed several days ago. The lead singer had looked familiar. I must have come across some of his music videos on the rare days I watched other things on TV besides the news.

'If they left the house that day, you think they had set the bloody scene up?' Chika asks.

'We won't know if we don't ask him.'

Chika is back on the laptop. Typing fast. 'Says here he has a studio in Anthony Village.'

'Wait.' I pull out my mobile phone and dial.

'And we're calling who, now?' Chika asks with raised eyebrows.

The line is ringing, so I put a finger to my lips.

'Bello,' the voice announces.

'Good day, Detective.' I inject warmth into my voice, and Chika's eyebrows rise even higher. 'I hope you don't mind my calling you so late.'

'I assume it's for good reason, Dr Taiwo,' he says, his tone stiff.

I ignore the lack of enthusiasm. 'The case file. There's no mention of one Enomo Collins.'

The answer comes a tad later than immediate. 'Should there be?'

I put the speaker on, and place the phone between Chika and me. He leans away. I try to keep my voice level so as not to give away the presence of an audience. 'I'm sure you know he was the one who picked up the victim from her home on the morning she disappeared.'

There's silence on the other end of the line.

'Detective?'

'Dr Taiwo,' he says impatiently, 'how could we've interviewed someone who was supposed to have driven the victim the morning after we presumed she was dead?'

'But if you presumed her dead, shouldn't you have – ?'

'Dr Taiwo, we've established the police were set up and if this call is to point out more of my team's incompetence, I can assure you, your job is done.'

Chika moves a finger across his neck. 'Cut the call,' he mouths.

'No, no, Detective,' I make defiant faces at Chika but my tone is conciliatory. 'That was not my intention at all. We agreed we'd share information and I only just found out—'

'Put it in a report, Dr Taiwo. I can only tell you that we'll not put further resources on the case until the autopsy report is released and we can formally confirm or rule out foul play.'

He hangs up.

'He's lying,' I declare.

'Or defensive. He did concede that he and his team have been incompetent.'

'No, he didn't. He merely challenged the reason for my call. Classic deflection.'

'So, you think he knows about Enomo Collins? Like he's that good a detective?' Chika sneers. 'Your faith in the skills of our police force never ceases to impress me.'

'You don't look impressed,' I say, just as caustic. 'Look, I've met this guy. He might not be the most competent of detectives, but he's certainly motivated. His career's on the line. There's almost no way he's not discovered that Enomo Collins was with Sade that morning.'

'Yet he's claiming ignorance,' Chika points out. 'Not to mention the fact that this Enomo is walking free.'

'Perhaps he can't afford another high-profile arrest?' I suggest. 'You say this Enomo is popular.'

'He is, but someone is dead.'

'Yes, but from the detective's point of view, someone has always been dead. It was a murder case from day one. Why fixate on the bishop as a suspect when there's the possibility of another?'

'As you'd say, let's fill that gap of unknown with what we know, and see how it fits.'

I frown, always suspicious when Chika quotes me. 'What do we know?'

Chika points at the Google Maps on the laptop screen. 'Where to find Enomo Collins.'

A WILD RAGE

SonicStudio is a bungalow behind a larger house which accommodates a law firm, a hairdressing salon and a number of residential quarters. A real estate agent's sign announces that there's still 'vacant space for residential or office' in the building. But I can't figure out where these unoccupied rooms could be, going by the number of vehicles parked around the place.

The door to the studio is slightly ajar despite the 'RECORDING IN PROGRESS' sign. Chika knocks. No answer. He pushes the door open wider and walks in. We follow the sound of music down the narrow corridor. Another open door leads us to what would have been the living room that has been converted to the control room of a music studio.

Two young men are working at the console. A female singer is on a small screen that appears connected to a recording booth beyond this room.

'Let me take it from the bridge again.' The singer speaks into the oversized microphone and the whole room booms with her voice.

Chika coughs. 'Excuse me.'

The young men turn, curious but not unwelcoming. They both sport short dreadlocks, with numerous face piercings. I struggle to tell them apart.

'We're looking for Mr Collins,' Chika says.

Pierced Young Man One points to a spot behind us.

The music must be why we missed it. The low-growled snore from a body sprawled on a worn sofa behind us. I step closer. Enomo Collins emits sour alcoholic breath. His face is unshaven, mouth open, and his hair is as unkempt as his beard.

'Guys!' the singer booms from the screen. 'Playback!'

'Wait. Bros get visitor,' Pierced Young Man Two says into the console.

Chika walks over to Enomo and shakes him. Hard. When he opens his eyes, they stare right at me as though he's been expecting me. From his sneer, it's safe to assume that if I were featuring in his drunken stupor, it wasn't in a favourable role.

'Get out!' Enomo spits, causing Chika to yank him up.

'That's not a very Christian greeting.'

The two young men jump to their feet.

'Save it,' Chika orders. 'We just want to ask him a few questions.'

'It's okay,' Enomo says. The young men fall back into their chairs. 'But I'm not answering anything,' he warns us.

'Oh, I guarantee you will,' Chika says. Before I can intervene, he pulls the man by the collar of his shirt and hurls him out of the studio.

I look at the young men. 'I'm sorry.'

Pierced Young Man Two nods, worry all over his face. 'He's been acting strange lately. Is he in trouble?'

'I hope not.' I try to sound reassuring.

'Guys!' the female singer hollers through the speakers.

The young men turn to their console. I hurry out. I can't risk Chika adding assault to our growing list of misdemeanours.

My fear is unfounded. Chika and Enomo look like they've come to an understanding. Enomo lounges against the wall of the main house, while Chika faces him from a distance. When Enomo sees me, he squares his shoulders. Defensive.

'Why should I help you?' he says in answer to a question Chika must have asked.

Chika shrugs. 'Because you're the last person to see her alive.'

'According to who?'

'The security guard who saw you drive away,' I say.

Enomo raises an eyebrow. 'So, I'm a suspect now?'

'Do we look like police?' Chika asks.

'Is he not Mr Big Shot Detective?' Enomo inches his head in my direction, disdain in every action. 'The one that will save the bishop.' He laughs, dry and mocking.

'Please confirm if you were with Sade Dawodu the day she disappeared?' My voice is firm. I don't like being disliked for doing my job, especially when it's clear the singer knew about me long before I had learnt of his existence.

'What if I was?'

Question with a question. So, yes.

'But she has a driver, so why did she need you?' Chika asks.

Enomo shrugs. 'She asked.'

'That's all?' I ask, searching his face.

'Should there be?' His face is unyielding.

'It seems there was some violence in the house before she left. Did you see any of that—'

'If there were signs of violence, then there was violence. She asked for a lift, and I went to help her.'

'She was ready and waiting when you arrived?' Chika asks.

His eyes dart everywhere but towards Chika and me. 'All packed. I barely got out of the car before she came out.'

Liar. The guard had estimated that Enomo was with Sade for at least an hour before they both came out of the house and drove off.

I step closer to him, unthreatening. 'Where did you take her?'

When he answers, his face is composed, and he speaks in a neutral tone, 'Ibadan.'

Chika snorts in disbelief. 'She called you to drive her all the way to Ibadan? Why?'

Another shrug. 'She didn't want anyone to know where she was going. She trusted me.' Calm, measured tones. Another well-rehearsed line.

'Prove it,' Chika challenges.

Enomo raises an eyebrow. 'How? I drove her there, dropped her off and drove back.'

'Why didn't you come forward when the bishop was arrested?'

'I was afraid, all right? One day I was dropping his wife at a hotel in Ibadan and the next, he's being accused of her murder. Doesn't take a genius.'

'Did you contact her after his arrest?' I ask, thinking of the mobile phone that was still switched on even after Sade Dawodu's body was deep in the Lekki Lagoon.

'Yes, I did. But she never picked up. So, I assumed he followed her to Ibadan, and maybe killed her there.'

'Wow. Great detective skills,' I say. 'Except the bishop was at Graceland at the estimated time of death. He has an alibi of thousands. Who's yours?'

'We were friends, all right?' Enomo throws daggers at me. 'Why would I kill her?'

'I don't know. You tell us.' I can see he's disconcerted by my sudden closeness. While he was speaking, I've been moving closer, slowly, inch by inch, so that now our noses almost touch. My eyes lock him into an invisible cage. To move will give the impression of weakness or something to hide. He knows this, so he stands his ground. It takes all my strength not to gag from his sour breath. His gaze falters, the mask slips for a split second, and then is back. Yes, he *is* playing to a script. Written by who? To what purpose?

'So, at the house, you never stepped out of the car?' The repeated question rattles him.

'I said I was in the car, didn't I?'

'That's not what the security guard said,' Chika counters from the side.

Enomo can't hide his surprise. His gaze swings from me to Chika, then back to me. Then, just sharply, he takes a step back and bows his head. Like he's trying to bring himself to the present. I look at Chika. Give him space, my eyes say. He nods curtly. We wait for a beat, then I step closer to Enomo again and speak to his full head of unkempt hair.

'He said you were in there for quite a while,' – I fix my gaze on him – 'perhaps enough time to plant evidence to implicate the bishop?'

His body starts to shake and it's only when he lifts his head that I realise he is laughing. A bitter, raucous laugh that ends in dry sobs, then fits of a dry cough. I step back.

'I told you. She asked for a lift and I came. I don't know what your security guard—'

'Why should we believe you?' Chika cuts in, sharp and challenging. 'After all, you could be saying all that because you know you could also be a suspect?'

Enomo ignores Chika's question by turning to me. 'I went and dropped her at her destination. I figured the police knew this, and if I was a suspect, they'd call me and ask more questions.'

My eyes stay on him, unblinking. 'You could have come forward when you realised they were falsely accusing your bishop!'

Enomo breaks our eye contact and reaches into his trousers. A shaky hand brings out a rolled cigarette. He lights it, takes a long drag, blows the smoke upwards and away from me. There are traces of tears at the edge of his eyes.

'Many times,' he says, a miasma of smoke hovering over his head, 'the person who pulls the trigger is called the killer, but most times, we don't ask who placed the gun in the shooter's hand.'

Chika comes closer, his impatience getting the better of him, placing himself between Enomo and me like a referee who has had it with one of the boxers in the ring. 'Stop speaking in riddles.'

Enomo shakes his head, his eyes defiant. 'You've come to the wrong guy, my man.'

I gently pull Chika back and step forward. I touch Enomo's shoulder. He doesn't shake my hand off, but his nose flares, his breathing harsh.

My voice is gentle when I speak, inviting trust. 'If the bishop is guilty of something, then say it.'

Enomo shrugs off my hand so violently that I take a step backwards. The rage in his eyes is so intense that I feel Chika come closer behind me. I block him from stepping in front of me. The last thing Enomo needs now is to feel more threatened.

'To who?' Enomo asks, his voice bitter, his lips curled downwards. 'Who do I say it to? No one listened to his own wife, why should they listen to me?'

'Because you loved her?' I suggest softly.

It's as if the air is sucked out of Enomo Collins. He sinks to the ground like a lost child. Tears flow and mix with snot, wetting the cigarette in his shaking hand. It is painful to watch.

'Please leave,' he says, shoulders hunched and heaving, head bowed.

'If you cared about her,' Chika insists before I can stop him, 'you would help us.'

Enomo Collins looks up at me, his pain raw as a gaping wound. 'Because I care about her, I shouldn't help you at all.'

HANGING THREADS

I scribble 'Enomo Collins' and paste the square note on the wall. We'd left the choirmaster when it was clear we'd not get more from him. Despite drying his tears and saying over and over that he was okay, it was evident he was on the edge of an emotional breakdown. In such a state, a witness's reliability or a suspect's account becomes questionable.

'*Because I care about her, I shouldn't help you at all.*'

It's this tortured admission that raises the possibility that Enomo knows little or nothing of the money laundering scheme at Grace Church. Surely, armed with such damning information that could bring the bishop down, Enomo wouldn't have hesitated to divulge it, even at a risk to himself? Despite his claim to the contrary, he didn't come across as worried about being a suspect in Sade's disappearance and, later, her death. In fact, there was no fear in the man at all. Just rage.

And what did he mean that Bishop Dawodu might as well have killed his wife? Even if this statement supports Ewang's claim that the bishop knew whoever killed Sade Dawodu was on the damning list, I suspect this was not what Enomo meant. It's something deeper, more personal. My impression of the bishop as a genuinely grieving spouse is shaken in the face of Enomo's equally sincere distress. Could jealousy be the singer's main reason for hating the bishop? If my assumption that he helped Sade stage the bloody crime scene is correct, could he be the anonymous caller? But if he was, then his brokenness at Sade's death can only mean one thing. He didn't expect her to die.

The humming air-conditioning is distracting. I switch it off. I'll start sweating buckets soon, but my unsettled mind needs the silence.

I perch on my desk, facing my wall of Post-it notes. The bishop's observations had been right when he visited. A visit I must now view as a possible fishing expedition to gauge what I had uncovered in the days leading up to his release. He was right, though. To an untrained eye, there's a lot of detail here but to a trained mind, it's all data but few insights. Between interminable time in traffic, interviews, teaching and family, I've had little time to put all the information into context. There are several notes under 'red flags', and almost all the ones under 'research' have question marks next to them. From a timeline point of view, I knew a lot more when we thought Sade Dawodu was merely missing. From the day her body was found till now, every clue as to the cause of her death has contradicted almost all the information I had when I operated on the assumption that she was missing.

Missing. Missing. *Missing*.

That's it! Everything went topsy-turvy when Sade Dawodu's body was dragged out of the lagoon. Before then, I was following the protocols of looking for a missing person. When it became a possible murder, I lost my focus.

But given that Sade left home apparently of her own free will, would it not be prudent to pursue the path of assuming she was still 'missing'? Surely that would yield answers as to where she was right before she died and possibly lead to who caused her death?

In the States, I would know my next exact steps. Check credit cards. Track social security number. Even the missing person's driver's licence can provide a historical view of past destinations. Parking and speeding tickets can yield information on travel patterns, and attitude towards law enforcement. The list can be endless with numerous possible leads in a system that holds data sacred, where everything is built around Big Brother watching you. Here, the situation is as different as night from day. A national ID-card system that few trust and an economy built on cash.

I text Chika. *If I want to find out someone's financial records, how?*

BVN beeps back, almost instantly. He is at the office. No doubt poring over those 117 names and the hundreds of transactions.

The Bank Verification Number. Ah. I've no way of knowing whether the BVN system – which is supposed to track fraud and money laundering – works, but I know that every individual in the country is supposed to have only one BVN, even with multiple accounts across banks.

I text quickly. *Can you access Sade's bank statements?*

I wait, hopeful. Chika's security firm's clients include some of the largest banks in the country.

If it's a Naija bank, no yawa. Small thing, Chika texts back.

Just as I thought. *Can you get on it tomorrow?*

A thumbs-up emoji assures me. I turn to the next, and perhaps, most important red flag.

LaTanya Jacobson.

I google the name. A LinkedIn profile pops up.

Management Consultant with experience in Small, Medium and Large Size businesses.

Nothing about being the agent/business manager for one of the world's richest pastors. One would expect that if the relationship was legit, it would be at the top of a management consultant's résumé. I click on the profile picture. The heavy make-up makes it difficult to tell her age. I'd put it at mid-forties though. Her weave is styled in a bob cut, and she sports a tightly fitted blazer. Her arms akimbo like she's one of the Avengers; a trending power pose that's as ubiquitous as it is meaningless. The fake smile makes her lipstick resemble a big red gash on her face. I've no more information than before logging on. Data without knowledge; therefore, no insight.

I check the time. California would just be stirring now. I can call on favours from former colleagues at the SFPD but it's best done verbally. Sending an email to request the kind of background check I'd like on Jacobson is not a good idea. Without a subpoena, discretion is paramount. I pen some friends to call at a decent hour. If none comes right, I'll have no choice but to ask Professor Cook to use his influence at IA to make something happen. Although retired, my old mentor wields enormous power in law enforcement and when it comes to discretion, Prof, considered one of the 'fathers of investigative psychology', is a master. By the time he is done, I'd be able ghostwrite LaTanya Jacobson's memoir.

Now, to the most disturbing red flag of all. I reach for a Post-it note, then change my mind. I pick up my notepad and write the question that's too puzzling – and personal – to put up on the wall.

If Sade Dawodu was so troubled by her infertility, why was she surgically sterilised?

AFTER HOURS

Any chance you'll be home soon? I want us to have a sit-down with Lara, Folake texts.

The twenty-four-hour deadline has expired. Lara hasn't divulged what she used the stolen money for. The sudden shift in gear with the Sade Dawodu case has consumed me. Knowing how distressed Folake is about the situation, it must have taken enormous willpower to restrain herself from confronting Lara without me.

Will leave now, but don't think I'll be home in time for a proper sit-down. Perhaps tomorrow am?

Early class. Let's commit to tomorrow evening. Please Sweet. Folake's worry is evident in the choice of words. A demand presented as a plea.

I text back. *2morrow evening. Promise.*

Since working late tomorrow is now out of the question, I feel less guilty about calling the coroner well after official hours. He picks up on the second ring and there's a welcoming warmth in his voice when he greets me. I apologise for calling so late. He waves it off and tells me to 'shoot'. Besides, Man U is playing so abysmally, he'd apparently rather talk work rather than risk a heart attack watching the Premier League.

'The tubal ligation,' I ask. 'I was wondering if you followed up on it.'

'I'm afraid not. The discovery has no bearing on the circumstances of the victim's death, so I didn't investigate further. I can only say that the scarification was relatively recent. Maybe a year, not much more.'

I could argue that a complete forensic autopsy would include the possibility of suicide due to emotional distress from a possible life-threatening disease. I know the good doctor is diligent, but it'll take a lot more than a suspicion to get him to follow a line of inquiry he came on by accident. Sade Dawodu died by drowning. The only question the coroner would be asking is whether she jumped into the lake of her own free will or by force. Why she, or anyone for that matter, would do the former, is not his job but mine.

'Did you request her medical file from her personal physician?' I try again.

'Do you know how many patients I cut open every day who have had past surgeries?' His tone is sharp.

The way pathologists refer to cadavers as 'patients' perplexes me. As if after their organ dissection, the dead will get off the metal table, wipe the blood and gore off, thank them very nicely and walk out of the morgue.

'If I followed every appendectomy I discover, I'd never get anything done,' the coroner continues when I don't answer his question. 'Anyway, I did ask my assistant to contact her personal physician, and the husband did not have the name. We followed up with the mother, who is the second significant other the police referred us to, but were told Sade Dawodu didn't have a personal physician.'

'Surely, that's not possible. Not even a gynaecologist?'

'My thoughts exactly. The patient was relatively healthy and of childbearing age. For a woman of her standing, I would expect there's a family physician on record, but the family insist there's none. The husband says they go abroad for their medical check-ups. Which is not unusual, these days.'

I thank him and hang up. No personal physician for the wife of the head of one of the largest churches in the country? How is that possible? Before I consider the time and lose my nerve, I scroll through my contact list.

'Hello?' Inspector Dobra's voice comes across as tentative, not combative.

I mentally cross my fingers. 'It's me, my friend,' I greet him with fake cheer. 'Philip Taiwo.'

'I know,' he says.

I sense caution rather than resentment. I can work with that. 'I just wanted to say well done. It must have been hard for you to take another look at the evidence you uncovered, but in my experience, investigators willing to do that end up being the best in the game.' I hope flattery will get me somewhere.

'Thank you, sir. Please, o, tell this to the superiors threatening me with disciplinary action. I told them CSI is not an exact science, but they won't listen. But I know it's also because of pressure from the top. That bishop claims he's forgiven us, but we think he's asking for the heads of all the investigating officers on the case.' Dobra gives a long, drawn-out hiss.

'I'll see what I can do.' I hope my tone mollifies him. 'He's understandably upset, more so now his wife's body has been found.'

'To be honest, Dr Taiwo, I'd appreciate it. I'm not even sure I'll have a job when this is over.'

'You were just doing your job,' I say. Then sensing the moment is right, I continue. 'Which is the reason I'm calling. Remember when you said you guys confirmed the victim's blood type with her doctor?'

'Yes?' The caution is back in his voice.

I make my voice more upbeat, non-threatening, mildly curious. 'Do you perhaps have the doctor's name? It's not on file, and it's a rather delicate time to ask the husband for it.'

Dobra's relief comes through on the line. 'Ah, that one you must ask Detective Bello. He contacted the doctor, gave the samples and reported the results. I only bagged, labelled and sent them to the forensics lab. The only other thing I did was to request blood-type confirmation.'

We promise to meet up for drinks at some point and hang up. I sit back and consider the wisdom of calling Detective Bello. The man's influence over the entire investigation's value chain is disturbing but not unusual in a situation where hands are few and skills short. I reach for the case file. No mention of the source of the blood-match confirmation.

It's been a long day, and I'm too exhausted to deal with the angry detective right now. Besides, if Dobra is correct about an internal witch-hunt in the force, I'm not sure I'll get more than a terse 'put your request in writing'. I'll have to find another way to know how the police made a blood match for the late Sade Dawodu.

I breathe in deeply. Worse than viewing a cadaver is interviewing a parent of the dead. I've put off speaking to Mrs Kikelomo Bucknor for as long as I can.

PRETTY

A light tap wakes me. Folake is bending over me; her perfume hangs in the air. I smile groggily, then jerk up.

'Sorry. Overslept.'

'It's okay.' Folake straightens up, smoothens down the polka-dotted dress that I'm convinced makes her the hottest law professor on earth. 'We're ready. Just wanted you to know Lara says she's having cramps and can't make school.'

My surprise must have shown on my face. Lara has never missed a day of school.

'I know,' Folake says, nodding. 'I think she's scared we'll make good on the threat.'

I sit up. 'I intend to—'

'Not yet.' Folake gently pushes me back into the bed. 'We'll have the talk tonight. For now, I want you to sound her out. You both have the house. I think it's a perfect time for a good father–daughter talk.'

'Are you sure? I thought you'd want—'

'She's fifteen, Sweet. With her own mind. We can't give orders or threaten, and hope for the best. If she's going through something, we've got to approach it like she's an adult. From all angles. Today, do the Daddy thing. We'll take it from there when we join forces.' Folake's smile is reassuring.

Sounds good, although I'm uneasy about talking to Lara
alone. I'd hoped she'd be remorseful enough to approach
me of her own volition. But almost an hour after Folake
and the twins said their goodbyes, Lara remains holed up
in her room.

Standing at her door, I miss the days of effortless sharing. Those precious moments when Lara would burst
into our room – ignoring her mum's caution to always
knock – jump between us and regale us with whatever
her American eyes just discovered about Nigeria. In our
early days of return, everything held wonder. The noise.
The bustle. The Nollywood movies. The food. The people.
The clothes. They all fascinated my daughter, and I loved
hearing her impression of this world Folake and I should
have worked harder at making less alien while we lived
abroad.

I knock tentatively and enter when I hear a muffled
'come in'.

Lara is curled up on her bed, paying studied attention to
her mobile phone.

'Your mum says you're not feeling well,' I say with
concern.

Lara looks taken aback by my opening. She was clearly
expecting combat. She nods.

I sit next to her, touch her brow. She retreats further into
the pillow. 'No fever? Just pains?'

'I'll take Advil,' she says, turning her face away. She
reaches for her phone and starts scrolling through, avoiding my gaze.

'I'd have thought if the pain was so severe that you'd
miss school, you'd have taken it by now?' I say with a smile.

'I was waiting to—'

'It's okay, Lara. If you feel you can hold back the inevitable by pretending to be sick …' I shrug.

'I ain't pretending,' she denies primly, her eyes fixed on the mobile phone.

'You still won't say what you stole the money for?' I ask gently.

She looks at me, defiant. 'I didn't steal. I was planning to put it back.'

'From where? Your highly paid employment as a student?'

'I've got savings back home.' She sits up now, her back against the wall, where a poster of Zendaya hangs above her. I back off to avoid deflection. Folake's insistence on holding on to Lara's Bank of America debit card is a sore point, perhaps the reason it wasn't my money that was stolen.

'So? What was the borrowed money for?' My eyes warn her not to contradict me, especially since I've compromised by not using the controversial 'steal'.

Lara moves to the other side of the bed and gets up. She starts to pace and again, I can't help but marvel at how much like her mother she is. At fifteen, she is already Folake's height. Her hair, braided in tight cornrows that taper out to combed-out kinky hair reminds me of how Folake wore hers during her undergraduate days.

She stops, her eyes pleading. 'Please, Dad, you gotta promise you won't tell Mum.'

'I'll do no such thing.' My tone brooked no argument. 'But I promise to consider keeping what you say between us, if doing that has any merit. For now.'

She knows it's the best she'll get. She squares her shoulder like she's about to plunge into icy-cold waters, then bends and pulls out a cardboard box from under her bed. She places it next to me.

'That's it, Dad. What I spent the money on. It was an online order and my bae—' I must have frowned because she quickly adds, 'You know, my bestie in school. She helped me to use her debit card. I paid her back in cash.'

I read out the words on the labels on the assortment of bottles and cream jars.

'Skin lightening creams?' I'm baffled. 'You bought these? Why?'

'Because I was done with the name-calling. "Blackie", "Sunblocker". You know what they call me in school, Dad? "Shadow". To my face.'

'So, you decided to bleach your skin?'

She shrugs. 'Not a lot. Just enough not to be so dark.'

In my wildest assumptions about why Lara stole money, this never figured.

'See? It wasn't for a bad thing.' She seems to search my face, like she's looking for my endorsement of this point of view. When she doesn't find it, her face falls. 'I ... er, I just got tired of the shade. I ... I ...'

Her voice trails off. I wait, careful not to help her find the words. They must be her words, however she says them.

When she sees I'm not going to save her from completing her thoughts, Lara takes a deep breath, looks away and mumbles, as if admitting to a dark secret, 'I just want to be pretty.'

'Uhn? What do—'

'Pretty!' Her face jerks up, tears gather in her eyes, defiance radiates from her like heat. 'I said I wanna be *pretty*.'

'You're beautiful,' I say softly. And she *is* beautiful. From the second she was placed in my arms at Saint Bernard's – all 8 pounds 3 ounces of gurgling, finger-grasping joy – my daughter has been beautiful.

Lara waves a 'whatever' hand. The set look on her face makes it clear she doesn't believe me. 'You're my dad. You're supposed to say that.'

'You never worried about your skin before.'

Lara scoffs, wipes her face on her sleeve. 'Everyone worries about their skin, Dad. Some are lucky; they just need face wash or oil control.' She waves at the box on the bed. 'I'm one of the unlucky ones. So, I chose to do something about it.'

'What's different here? Why would you think you're unlucky?' I ask, perplexed. My brain scrambles for what to say. How do I fix this?

Lara comes to sit next to me. The box of bleaching creams lies between us and it takes all my willpower not to fling it across the room and pull her into my arms. I reach for her hand, but she snatches it away. I don't push.

'You know what, Dad? Back home in the States, I knew exactly who I was. I knew what was expected of me. I knew having smart parents meant I was expected to succeed. I knew these things and you know ...' – She shrugs, gives me a tired smile – 'I was sorta cool with it. You know, like when something's not perfect, but you kinda learn to work with it?'

I nod as if I understand, but I'm not sure I do. I wait.

'I don't know, Dad ... kinda weird how you and Mum put so much work into helping Tai and Kay survive being

Black in America. You guys must've thought I was learning by osmosis or something.'

'I don't get it ...' I say, but it is dawning. Slowly.

'It's not the same, Dad. I didn't know it then, but now, I ... you know, get it. Mum used to say, she wanted us to be chilled in our skin. Which is cool. But coming here, going to that school,' – Her lips curl in derision – 'where they make fun of the same skin Mum said we should be cool with, makes you kinda wonder if what you guys meant was for us to be chilled with being part of the *Black race* and not really our skin. You know?'

'We want you to be proud of being Black *everywhere and in every way*,' I say, still trying to navigate what she's saying without curating her every word.

'You don't get it, Dad. Here, it's not about being Black. It's about being, you know, like the right *kind* of Black.'

'Who told you that?' I ask, outraged.

'The nicknames, Dad,' Lara says gently, like I am slow to grasp the point. 'The shade at school sorta made it clear I ain't the pretty kind of Black.'

I search Lara's face for doubt, or anything that reassures me that this is an assumption, not a real, lived experience. Nothing. This is her truth. And how much of this terrible truth is our fault as her parents? Did we spend so much time and energy on bringing up the twins as young Black men in America that we didn't give much thought to what it meant to be a Black *girl* in America? Lara had just turned twelve when Folake started insisting we take a break from living in the States. We never worried about our daughter because by the time we should have, we were already in Nigeria, where everyone was Black.

I look at the boxes of bleaching creams and back at Lara. She wipes tears off her face. I don't want to interrupt her. She needs to be heard. And I need to understand.

'I took it as jokes at first, you know. Didn't wanna be called emo, like I'm overreacting. I wanted everyone to think I could take a joke. I didn't want them to think I'm low-key cheugy—' I must have frowned because she adds, 'uncool, you know, like, someone who—'

'I get it,' I say. I don't but I'd rather she continues talking rather than give me a crash course on Gen Z slangs. I've Google for that.

'No, you don't, Dad!' She stands abruptly. 'You don't get it. I hate it when you guys say you get something that you really can't get unless you're me.'

'Okay, okay. Help me get it.'

My conciliatory tone defeats her. Lara's shoulders slump, she sniffles.

'I'm listening,' I say gently.

She takes in a deep breath and starts again. 'When the nicknames started, I didn't see it as shade. I was trying to get into Naija life, get good grades and all that stuff. That first year was crazy. I didn't have time to, you know, like get that the jokes were on me.'

She's right. The first months of being back in Nigeria *were* hectic. We crammed so much into our orientation to make up for lost time. Lara spent weekends at my parents learning Yoruba. The boys assimilated through sports, making their mark on the school's basketball team. Folake and I worked hard to create a life that insulated them from the challenges of living in Lagos. Providing for our children took so much of our time that we barely had time to reflect on their unique challenges. Why should we? After all, we are home. Safe.

'When I started getting what the nicknames really meant, I was confused. How do I deal? Back home, I knew who I was.' She shakes her head. 'But here, I don't know.'

'You're my daughter, Omolara Adunni Taiwo.' Her self-awareness humbles me. Her insights make my heart burst with pride. Her conclusions crush me.

She smiles through her tears, as if to reassure me. 'I know that, Dad. But out there,' – She waves a hand around the room as if it's the whole universe – 'I'm just a girl.'

'Come here,' I order.

She doesn't, so I go to her and march her to the full-length mirror next to the bed. Our eyes lock in the mirror.

'Seriously, Dad!' Lara protests. 'I swear if you make me recite Maya Angelou, I'll never speak with you again.'

'You'll repeat after me: I am my father's daughter.'

Lara crosses her hand over her chest, rolls her eyes. 'This is so bourgie—'

'I am my father's daughter,' I insist.

'I am my father's daughter,' Lara says, stiff with reluctance.

'My measure is not in how others see me, but how I see myself.'

She repeats this but with less petulance.

'I am beautiful in ways little and big. Inside and outside.'

She cracks as she says the words, then turns and buries her head in my chest.

'I am magic. I am light. I am real.'

The words tumble out of my heart to my mouth. Lara repeats every word, punctuated by tears. I look around the room as I speak into her hair. The signs are all here. Posters of Zendaya, Beyoncé, Alicia Keys. Black female artists with one thing in common: their light skin. How did I miss it?

'My skin is the armour that holds my truth. And my truth is beauty.'

Her voice breaks further, the sobs are harder. My heart breaks. I don't let go. I hold her in my arms and continue saying the words that are as much for her as they are for me.

A PECULIAR GRIEF

The weight of the conversation ahead made leaving Lara at home a lot harder. By the time Kenny came to pick me up, we'd packed away the creams and Lara conceded her mum had to be told.

'I'll talk to her,' I promised. 'Then, we'll have a sit-down together.'

Lara attempted to protest, but it was weak. Her confession has given way to relief. Facing her mum seems no longer as daunting as it had. Still, she didn't want to go to school and I didn't push. The period pains may be true, but I can appreciate why she's not inclined towards seeing the school bullies today especially.

'What happened to her husband?' I ask Kenny, as her driver turns off the crowded Mobolaji Bank Anthony Way into a relatively quiet neighbourhood in Ikeja. No shops. No hawkers. No high fences, but several signs warning about guard dogs and giving the contact numbers of the neighbourhood watch.

'I told you. Widowed but they were separated before he died,' Kenny answers. 'I don't know the details. She was a third or fourth wife, and when she gave her life to Christ, she moved out.'

'Why?'

Kenny looks at me in surprise. Her face is lightly made-up; she's wearing a grey blouse with a black headscarf. Since she's taking time from work to accompany me, I hope the unflattering outfit is for the benefit of the mother of the deceased.

'She couldn't have stayed in a marriage that's a sin before God and man.'

'Kenny, there's plenty of evidence that God didn't frown on polygamy.'

Kenny waves a dismissive hand. 'Old Testament dispensation. Under the gospel of Christ, a man shall cleave to his wife, not *wives*.'

I give a dry smile. 'As I recall that quote is also from the Old Testament.'

Kenny ignores me and taps her driver's shoulder. 'We are here. Park there.'

The driver brings the car to a halt in front of a single storey house. Kenny adjusts her black scarf and heaves a sigh like someone about to undertake a most unpleasant task.

'You said she's willing to talk,' I remind her as we walk through the gates into the compound.

'Her daughter's dead. Of course, she wants to talk to the man who's trying to find the killers.'

'Technically, I'm trying to clear her son-in-law's name.'

'Is there a difference?' she asks. Under the circumstances, I can't fault her logic.

There are a number of people seated outside. Kenny greets some and I wave tentatively. This is not a time for socialising.

We are led upstairs to Mrs Bucknor's bedroom, a large room that opens to a small sitting area. She is seated on a king-size bed, two elderly women on either side of her. Kenny whispers into Mrs Bucknor's ears. The women scramble up and leave, sidestepping me at the doorway with muffled greetings, eyes sharp with curiosity. Kenny squeezes Mrs Bucknor's shoulders and follows suit but not before giving me a look that tells me to be nice. As if I could be anything but.

Mrs Bucknor stands and goes over to the door. She opens it slightly and walks back to me, pointing towards the sitting area. I follow her.

'I'm sorry I can't meet you in the more formal living room. The place is full of visitors and it wouldn't be conducive.'

'It's okay, ma,' I say, sitting down after she takes the wing-back chair across from me. 'I understand.'

I'm struck again by the resemblance between Mrs Bucknor and her late daughter. Her light skin and fashionably arranged grey hair give her a regal air. Her simple navy-blue boubou reveals a neck unlined with age. Her knuckles are clenched around a crisp, dry handkerchief, but I am not sure whether it's from arthritic pain or her way of exhibiting strength in her grief.

'I'm so sorry for your loss, ma.'

Mrs Bucknor nods, delicately dabbing her eyes with the handkerchief even though she is not tearful. Reflex?

'Mi ò ní pé, ma,' I add, hoping I can keep my promise to be brief. I bring out my notepad and pen. I can't bring myself to ask to record the session.

'It's okay. Kenny says you've some questions for me.'

I take my cue from her composure. 'Madam, did your daughter tell you where she was going on the day she travelled?'

'Ibadan.'

I try to hide my surprise at how quickly she answers. Until I spoke to Enomo, my impression was that no one knew Sade's destination on this last trip. Plus, Mrs Bucknor hadn't revealed this at my meeting with her and the elders.

'Is it somewhere she's been before?'

Mrs Bucknor frowns. 'I just know that when she called to say she was going away, I asked her where, and she told me it was somewhere in Ibadan. I told her to give me a call when she got there.'

'And did she call?'

'From there?' she looks askance and then, distressed. 'Clearly, she never got there—' She puts the handkerchief to her nose and blows loudly.

I give her some time before continuing. 'But she called you on the day she was travelling? Perhaps when she was on her way?'

Mrs Bucknor shakes her head. 'She called the night before she was to travel. In fact, she was quite distraught because she and Bishop had had a fight and I had to do a lot of counselling.'

So, she knew about the fight *before* the bishop told her.

'Did she say what it was about?'

Mrs Bucknor lowers her head, dejected. 'Not having a child was getting to her more than it was to him. She got quite emotional because she so desperately wanted to give him a child.'

'She felt it was her fault?' Does Mrs Bucknor know about the sterilisation? How do I ask?

'She was just being impatient with God.'

'They, er, never stopped trying?'

She looks up in surprise. 'How could they? There was no reason why God wouldn't have answered their prayers.'

She doesn't know. I retrace my steps. 'When these quarrels happened, did they, er, ever get physical?'

She shakes her head. 'When Sade called me, she was crying like I'd never heard before. Bishop lost his temper with her, and I think she was angry too. She didn't tell me the details but from the way she spoke, I suspect things got quite heated.'

I frown. Bishop claimed he never hit his wife, despite provocation. The security guard confirmed this. If Sade Dawodu called her mother to report the altercation with her husband, had she claimed there had been physical violence to gain sympathy?

'She never confirmed that her husband hit her?'

Mrs Bucknor shakes her head vigorously. 'Not explicitly but she wanted to come over and stay with me, and I insisted that she couldn't leave her matrimonial home because of a quarrel.'

'But if things got violent—'

She blows her nose noisily again and looks away, but her tone is defensive when she speaks. 'What was I supposed to do? Bishop is a man of God, but still a man. And her husband. I didn't want to be the kind of mother who encourages her daughter to come running to Mummy every time things aren't going well in her marriage.'

'You think she might have called the police if she felt her life was in danger?'

She looks as though the idea had just occurred to her. 'Maybe that's why the police are blaming Bishop.' Then she seems to reconsider, and shakes her head again as if clearing it of an unfathomable thought. 'But he wouldn't hurt her. I told her she was just being melodramatic.'

'But if she said he did …' I trail off when she holds up her hand, cutting me off.

Her eyes are hard when she speaks. 'Listen, Dr Taiwo. Sade could be a handful. I'm her mother. I know. Bishop has been so understanding, staying with her even without a child. Supporting her. Every once in a while, I think it's understandable if the man loses his patience. And I told Sade exactly this and it calmed her down. At least, I thought it did. She even promised to apologise to Bishop before she left for her trip.'

'She didn't tell you the bishop had left for Graceland already?'

Mrs Bucknor shakes her head. 'When she was speaking to me, I'm sure Bishop was still in the house. I told her to kneel down and apologise immediately. I'm sure she did.'

Interesting. The bishop never alluded to any apology or a call to his mother-in-law that night. I make like I'm writing something, then rifle through my notes, like I'm searching for a detail. 'Do you know a Dr Uzoma Ohaeri?'

There's an intake of breath that ends in a slight cough. I look up from my notes.

Mrs Bucknor frowns as if trying to remember, then slowly shakes her head. 'I don't think so.'

'Your daughter made several calls to him but he never picked up. I wondered if he's a medical doctor and her calls were because she was having a, er, health crisis?' I let my voice trail off, hoping my hesitancy will elicit a confirmation.

Mrs Bucknor shakes her head firmly. 'I don't know a Dr Ohaeri. Her fertility specialist was in the UK. Bishop would have the clinic's contacts, but I know she never mentioned a Dr Ohaeri. In fact, now that I think about it, Sade did call me the day she travelled. We didn't speak for long. Just where she was going and how long she might be gone.'

'So, er, Sade has never sought help for, er, mental health?'

'Why would she? My daughter was a good Christian woman. Mental health crisis is not our portion as Christians.'

I don't break my gaze until she puts the handkerchief to her nose once again. More noisy blowing. When she looks back at me, there's a challenge in her eyes. She knows I'm wondering why she claimed Sade didn't call her on the day of her disappearance until she realised I'd have access to her daughter's call log. And if she lied then, why should I believe her claim regarding Sade's mental health?

Mrs Bucknor stands. 'If you've more questions, please don't hesitate to tell your sister to bring you again. You can be sure I'll do anything to clear Bishop's name, and help to find my daughter's killers.'

In what order? The unspoken question hangs in the air. Her eyes don't leave mine. Unwavering. Yet, shuttered. I try to figure out what she's not saying. When Sade called her mother on the day she travelled, did she say something that wouldn't help the bishop's case? But the way Mrs Bucknor is looking at me, it's clear the interview is over. I stand up and search her face, hoping she can see I can be trusted.

But her eyes are dry and resolute. To continue would be insensitive. The wall around the woman is impenetrable, so I can't ask the question she must know I'm thinking.

Who's she protecting? Her dead child or her son-in-law?

THE DEVIL IN A DETAIL

The summons come just as Kenny's car draws up at the front gates of the police college. I frown at the text message. I'd hoped to put in some work at the office and Uber back home in time for the talk with Lara.

I turn to Kenny. 'Apparently the autopsy report is ready and the police have asked to present it to the bishop. Pastor George wants me there.'

'At Graceland?' Kenny asks. 'Can you get there on time?'

It's barely midday. The traffic should be less frenetic with the morning rush hour over, but in another hour, all hell will break loose.

'Take my car,' she suggests. 'My office is on the way. Drop me off, and the driver can take you to Graceland and wait until you're done.'

'But how will you get home? It might take some time before—'

'Don't worry. I'll take one of the office pool cars.'

I thank her and text Pastor George.

Will be there. May I have a word with you before or after the police briefing?'

Of course. Pastor George responds immediately.

As soon as we drop Kenny at her firm, I call Abubakar.

'That's unusual,' he says when he hears where I'm going.

'I know, right? The police going to present autopsy findings? Can you ask around?'

'I'll do that. But maybe it's an a*f*ology.'

'Apology?'

'I have the re*f*ort here. I was supposed to give it to you. It says right here: Mrs Dawodu's death is ruled as suicide by drowning.'

There's no need to tell the commandant about my chat with the coroner. 'Yes, but what's the apology for?'

'*P*or the wrong*p*ul arrest?'

Perhaps to save his career, Detective Bello is trying to get in the bishop's good graces. Delivering the autopsy report with a formal apology should count for something.

'Please screenshot the report to me.'

The five-page report is quickly read. Everything is as discussed with the coroner. When I see there's mention of the tubal ligation though, I have to restrain myself from telling the driver to hurry. Wild horses wouldn't keep me from the opportunity of seeing the bishop's face when this detail is revealed.

*

Bishop Dawodu's office looks like the showroom of an expensive antique furniture shop, decorated with so much gold it hurts the eyes. A mahogany desk takes centre stage, separating the bishop's chair – make that *throne* – from the entrance.

I'd expected to see all the elders but only Pastors George and Nwoko are there. They're sitting on a long, white leather sofa. They look like they're waiting on the results of a medical test. Tense, impatient and nervous. Nwoko soundlessly taps his fingers on the armrest. Pastor George's scowl is in place, but the way his blazer stays buttoned up, and his right leg shakes intermittently, betray his lack of calm.

Perched on the edge of the bishop's desk might be the source of their discomfort. LaTanya Jacobson looks even more formidable in the flesh than her picture suggests. Everything is too much. Make-up, eyelashes, rouge, nails, hair. The woman looks so over the top she could pass for a contestant in RuPaul's Drag Race.

The bishop himself is the picture of a commander-in-chief, all business as he walks to me, hands outstretched, unsmiling. While he isn't giving Mr Congeniality vibes, it's still hard to reconcile his purposeful gait with the broken man who identified his wife's body less than seventy-two hours ago. Is this because I now have an inkling that beneath the veneer of charm and holiness, Bishop Dawodu might not be as righteous as one would expect of a 'man of God'?

'Dr Taiwo,' he says, and gives me a brisk handshake before returning to sit behind his desk. 'Glad you could make it.'

I look around the room pointedly. 'Am I early?'

'I wanted an update on your investigations before the police arrive,' he continues. 'You know the pastors, but you've not met my manager, LaTanya Jacobson. She just flew in from Houston.'

I shake the woman's hand as she flashes a severe smile. Ms Jacobson sizes me up and I try not to snatch my hand away when her eyes travel downwards, then back up to rest around my belt. She cocks her head to the side, considering. Vulgar, I decide. Hardly the kind of person I'd place in a pastor's office. In any capacity. If I hadn't already spoken to Ewang, seeing this woman here would've convinced me something didn't add up.

'Pleased to meet you, ma'am.'

'Dr Taiwo. USC Post-doctoral. Almost a decade with Internal Affairs at the SFPD. Impressive résumé.'

'You're too kind, Ms Jacobson.'

She urges me to call her 'LaTanya' and waves her talons, nails painted in multiple colours and dotted with sequins. 'In any case, such impeccable credentials are perfect for a high-profile client like Jerry.'

Jerry? The familiarity is jarring given the reverence everyone else accords the bishop.

'LaTanya handles all my international bookings and manages my business interests in the States,' the bishop says as we all take our seats around a table. 'She has kindly come to give me her moral support.'

'Woulda been here earlier if you'd listened to me.' There's admonition in LaTanya's tone.

'There was no need earlier, but now, well, I appreciate your presence.' The bishop's response is calm, but I sense a warning. This is a conversation they've had before. Perhaps just before I entered the room?

'Dr Taiwo,' Pastor George says, his voice louder than usual, as if to cut off the ongoing drama. 'We were hoping for a progress report ...'

'It's still early stages.'

'Yes, but so far, is there a chance that when the police come, it ain't to arrest Jerry?' LaTanya asks.

'They said they're coming to present the autopsy report of our First Lady,' Pastor George says, disapproval in his tone and bearing. The 'Jerry' rankles him too. 'I think we should honour the dead by not jumping to conclusions.'

'You must understand everyone's distrust of the police, Dr Taiwo,' the bishop says with an apologetic smile at me. 'Their several mistakes have cost me the right mental space to grieve for my wife. My congregation is worried they'll make the same mistakes again or worse.'

'I assure you, Bishop, to all intents and purposes, the police are indeed coming to present your wife's autopsy report.'

'The report,' Pastor Nwoko says, 'have you seen it?'

'Not the final one,' I lie. Why is the man so jittery? 'I met with the coroner but he was still busy with the autopsy then.'

A soft knock and the bishop's secretary comes in. 'They're here.'

*

We head towards the conference room because the bishop won't meet the police in his office. 'I don't want their nonsense in my space,' he asserted, as he stood up and we all followed.

It's rather comical the way we stop behind him when he enters the room. Over his shoulder, I see why. Detective Bello is alone. Not the law enforcement entourage everyone expected.

As soon as I catch the detective's eyes, I can see an apology is the last thing on his mind. His bearing is full of confidence. There's a disdainful curl to his lips as he stands to greet us. He invites us all to sit as if he's our host.

Detective Bello makes a show of clearing his throat. 'The autopsy report is in. Your wife drowned and all indications point to suicide or accidental death.' He pushes a file on the conference table, which LaTanya deftly waylays on its path to the bishop. The detective continues, 'According to that report, there was no foul play in your wife's death.'

Pastor Nwoko's whole bearing is one of righteous indignation. 'So, Bishop's not under investigation?'

My attention is on LaTanya as she scans the report. She flips the pages, reading intently. It's fascinating to me that the bishop, eyes fixated on the detective, would let the woman read the autopsy report before he does.

'It depends on him,' Detective Bello answers, waving at the bishop. 'We must remember someone tried to frame the bishop for his wife's death. If I were him, I'd want to know who.'

The bishop's relief is palpable. He gestures in my direction. 'That's why I hired Dr Taiwo. But at that time, I believed my wife was alive. Now that she's dead, what's the point? It's time I'm allowed to mourn in peace.'

His tone is measured, as if he's on the pulpit. Not someone who's just been informed his wife died by suicide.

'I understand,' Bello says with fake sincerity. 'But can you help us close the matter once and for all? Perhaps give some insight as to why your wife would take her life?'

The bishop shakes his head, his shoulders slump. The only sound for a second is LaTanya turning the pages. A frown comes over her face. She's reached *the* page.

'I'll live with my failure until I'm called to be with the Lord,' the bishop looks at the two elders in apology. 'I couldn't share with you all that First Lady was clinically depressed. If I'd told you, maybe you'd have all joined me in prayer—'

'Jerry ...' The way LaTanya says his name makes the bishop look at her sharply. It is both a caution and a call to attention. She passes the file to him, pointing.

'So, she was the problem?' Detective Bello asks innocently.

Pastors Nwoko and George exchange alarmed looks as the bishop raises his head and stands. The image of Reverend Freeman, nose dipped in cocaine, flashes through my mind. The emperor is naked and he is the last to know. *Man is not God.*

'This can't be true!'

'What?' Bello asks with a fake smile. 'That your wife couldn't conceive because she had had her tubes tied?'

The pastors gasp. LaTanya pulls the bishop to sit back down.

'Jerry, you ain't got to say nothing—'

'They must take it out.' The bishop glowers at the detective. 'It has nothing to do with anything.'

Detective Bello puts up a hold-it hand. 'On the contrary, it does. If you claim your wife's suicide is because she couldn't conceive—'

'I said depressed!' the bishop roars.

'Calm down now,' Bello admonishes softly. He *is* mocking him. No, goading. 'Didn't you say you're a man of God? Okay, so she was depressed but it was because she could not conceive, abi?' It's not really a question, but he pauses as if waiting – hoping – to be contradicted.

LaTanya's hand rests on the bishop's elbow, a warning and a restraint. The American knows he is swimming in dangerous litigious space. Better to say nothing. I don't understand the power the woman has over him because the bishop seethes, his bearing defensive as he looks at the detective.

'Ehen, then,' Bello continues patronisingly, 'if both of you knew she was sterilised, as Christians, wouldn't you be hopeful for a miracle, and therefore live in a state of spiritual optimism that—' He snaps his fingers rapidly as if looking for the right word – 'Now, how do you say it in your sermons?'

'Enough!' Pastor George orders so loudly that everyone seems to come to attention. He's been quiet for so long, and I've been so focused on LaTanya and the bishop that I'd paid him no mind. 'My God will not be mocked, Detective. You've delivered the report, you may leave now.'

'I want it taken out,' Bishop says to the detective. 'I want that part stricken from the record.'

'Why?' Bello asks as if mildly curious. 'Are you asking for evidence to be suppressed? That would be against the law, sir. And I'm already in trouble as it is.'

LaTanya stands and pulls the bishop up. 'This is over. You ain't got to talk to him. Come.'

The detective stands too and the way he faces the bishop makes me grateful for the conference table between them.

'Before you go, could you help the police with one little thing we are still investigating? You know, that issue of who made those calls to the police.'

LaTanya shakes her head slowly, and just as she is about to give voice to her caution, the bishop waves his hand impatiently. Bad move. If I were his lawyer, I'd have gagged him ten minutes into the meeting.

'A mischief-maker, someone who wants my downfall,' he says, exasperation mixed with outrage.

'Or someone who knew your wife was about to die?' The detective looks around the room. 'You see, while the autopsy couldn't be clear about the exact time of death, the estimated length of immersion was six days, give or take. Which means it is likely that the late Mrs Dawodu was alive on the day the police got the tip-off that she had been murdered.' He turns to the bishop with a cold smile. 'Any idea why your wife would want you arrested for her death before it occurred?'

LaTanya pulls at the bishop. 'Do. Not. Answer. Jerry.'

He appears bewildered. The implication of the question seems to hit him suddenly. 'I told you she was not well. I couldn't help her. I tried,' he says, looking confused and hurt.

'Shhh. It's okay, hon. You ain't gotta say nothin.' LaTanya has managed to get him to the door, which she opens, the bishop following her like someone in a trance.

Pastor Nwoko gathers loose sheets of paper into the autopsy file, then throws Detective Bello a furious look. 'Can't you see he's grieving? Have you no compassion?'

The detective says nothing. Pastor Nwoko starts to speak again, but Pastor George stops him by gripping his elbow. There's a weariness about the senior pastor as he looks at the detective.

'Thank you, Officer, for all your work,' he says in a neutral voice. 'Please keep us updated with your investigations regarding who might have framed the bishop.' He turns to me. 'I'll be in my office, Dr Taiwo. I recall you'd like to confer?'

Pastor George and the still outraged Pastor Nwoko leave the room.

I lean back in the chair, my eyes on the detective, and let the silence between us stretch.

'Why do you hate the bishop?' I ask casually when I see his discomfort is about to give way to annoyance.

He raises a quizzical brow. 'Apart from the fact that he's costing me my job?'

'It was personal before that, and you know it.'

The detective stands to his full height, adjusts his uniform unnecessarily and makes a show of pulling the peak of his police cap forward, so part of his face is covered. Full police regalia. He had come to perform.

'Dr Taiwo, instead of psychoanalysing me, ask yourself what a so-called man of God could have done to make someone set him up for killing his wife.'

'So, we agree it's a set-up?' I ask wryly.

'We established that a while back. Your job was to find out why. Clearly, you've not succeeded, have you?'

I keep my gaze on him, unflinching at the dig at my professionalism and delivery. Besides, I don't argue with facts.

'So, before questioning how I go about my job, perhaps we'd get somewhere if you actually did yours,' Detective Bello says. Then he gives me a mocking salute and walks out.

I bring out my phone and switch off the voice recorder. I can't help but smile ruefully at the grand exit. If only he knew his challenge was a double-edged sword. To do my job successfully, I'd have to get on his case and keep going until I know why he's trying to use the police to bring Bishop Jeremiah Dawodu down.

THE THING WITH FEATHERS

Hope. I lost it in bits and pieces. Its feathers torn off me little by little until I was left with nothing to rise above the relentless winds blowing against me. To reclaim it would mean finding the strength to build myself back, feather by feather. But, if I try and succeed, where would I fly to? Who would I be? I didn't know and worse, I didn't want to know.

You will wonder why I did all these things and yet choose not to be around to savour the victory of his downfall. Now you know. I lost hope. I looked at my life beyond his undoing and saw nothing. An empty abyss where whatever the future promised will be held back by my past.

Live with purpose, they say. Purpose gives meaning. I agree. His destruction is my purpose. To unmask him. Expose him without his cloak of holiness. Naked. Bare for you and everyone to see they've placed their faith in the hands of a mere man. Not a god. Just a salesman peddling hope as the antidote for lives stripped of purpose, searching for meaning.

If my plans work, and he falls, what would I live for? I don't want to know. Whatever little hope my purpose gave me, I place in you. So, when you think of me, please take solace in everything you're doing to help me achieve my purpose.

He must fall. Don't settle for a fall that's less than loud and befittingly spectacular.

FIRED

I make my way towards Pastor George's office. The size and breadth of Grace Church can only be appreciated when one walks the long corridor of the administrative offices. From the conference room, midway between Bishop Dawodu's office and Pastor George's, I count at least twenty rooms. Then I walk past a space twice the size of the conference room. It's all glass. Several people wear headsets; some talk rapidly; others simply nod as they seem to listen to whoever is on the other side of the line. Some have closed eyes, clasped hands and appear to be praying. Even without the sign that identifies it as the 'Prayer Ministry', you'd know from the reverence in the atmosphere.

I find myself slowing my pace, moved by the scene. How many suicides are being prevented now? How many marriages are being saved? How many gravely sick people are seeking comfort after doctors have told them all is lost?

Even when I tease Kenny about her commitment to a church rather than to spiritual growth, I envy her faith. The simplicity of trusting a higher power with the complexity of day-to-day life in Nigeria is a coping mechanism I wish I could develop. Prosperity preachers like Bishop Dawodu have been criticised for living in luxury off the widows' mites of a congregation whose average income is less than ten dollars a day. Yet, looking at the prayer team, I'm reminded again how much good churches can do. Giving back, building a sense of community and, most of all, offering hope in a nation that's stripped its people of every reason to have it. When one considers that the rise of Pentecostal churches in the early 1980s coincided with the collapse of the Naira, severe austerity measures and a military junta that plundered the country's oil wealth, you'd be inclined to agree with Karl Marx that religion is an opium. Hope, a fundamental human need, is what religion offers.

I continue down the corridor. The disturbing revelations I've discovered about Grace Church make me even more conflicted. How can a place so rotten at its core, do so much good? It would be naïve to think the circumstances surrounding Sade Dawodu's death are isolated – an exception, not the rule. Truth is the absolute power arrogated to the church leaders, which almost certainly leads to abuse. The rot is the inevitable outcome of blind faith and of not holding the church leadership accountable.

I've reached Pastor George's office. He's not alone. I can make out a female form through the glass door. He has his hands on her shoulders. His eyes are closed as he appears to be praying. I take a couple of steps back and wait.

Minutes later, the woman walks out and stops when she sees me. I try to place her face to understand why she's staring at me with imploring eyes.

'Please tell him to come home,' the woman says. I recognise her now. The face behind the curtains at Victor Ewang's house. 'That night when you came to our house, he spoke to you,' she continues. 'He came back and I sensed so much relief in him.'

I'm unsure how to approach the situation. How much does she know? I stay silent.

She pulls my hand. I hide a wince as her nails dig into my upper arm. 'Tell him it's okay. He should come home. Whatever he's done, we can figure it out.'

'Your husband has not been home?' I ask.

'Since last night. Please, sir, if you know something—'

I remove her hand as gently as I can. 'Mrs Ewang?' She nods, almost apologetic. 'I've not seen or spoken to your husband since that night.'

'What did you say to him?' she asks, worried and desperate.

'I'm afraid I can't say,' I say kindly.

'That's what he tells me every time I ask him what is wrong,' she says, bewildered.

'I'm sorry,' is all I can say. I control the urge to offer comforting words which might lead to more questions. I point towards Pastor George's office. 'I have to go.'

Indeed, he has been looking at us through the glass door the whole time. Mrs Ewang seems to realise this. She mumbles an apology, bows her head and scurries off.

Is it possible Ewang is lying low until he is surer about the circumstances of Sade Dawodu's death? I'm worried he did this without a word to his wife. But then again, Victor Ewang's fear stems from what he knows. Under the circumstances, leaving his family might be his best chance of protecting them.

Knocking would be superfluous given that the pastor can see me. I walk in just as he goes around his desk to sit.

'I wonder why Mrs Ewang would waylay you like that,' he says.

'Something about her husband not coming home,' I answer tentatively, like I'm just as surprised at the woman's behaviour.

'Yes. She told me. I prayed with her for his safe return. But why you?'

'I don't understand.' I hide my face by bending to pull one of the chairs across the desk to sit.

'Have you spoken to Brother Victor?'

'He's on the interview list you gave me.' I try to be calm, but frankly, his tone irks me. Like I'm a recalcitrant employee. Me. His line of questioning worries me. As the number-two man at Grace Church, I've to assume he knows what's going on in the 'foreign missions' department.

'Yes, but *when* did you speak to him?'

'The day you practically begged me to take the case back,' I shoot back to put him on the defensive.

'Why was he the first one you went to? There were others on the interview—'

'Am I required to disclose my process?' I snap.

Pastor George looks taken aback. Then, he shrugs as if to say 'suit yourself', reaches for a paper to his right and hands it to me.

The header says it all: 'Termination of Contract'.

'You're firing me?'

'No, Dr Taiwo. There's simply no need for your services any more. First Lady's death has been ruled a suicide. Bishop is not under suspicion. The church is safe. Why should we continue raising unnecessary dust?'

I search his face. Am I getting too close to something? Does he know I know about the list? 'But we still don't know who tried to frame your bishop.'

'What does it matter now?' Pastor George says, his voice louder than I've ever heard it.

'I thought—'

'Dr Taiwo, please compile your costs today, and invoice the church with attention to me.'

'I don't like not finishing things.'

'That's not my problem, Dr Taiwo. Please close the door after you and may the Lord bless you.'

I stand up. I can't remember the last time I felt so angry. Belittled. I open my mouth to tell the man where to get off, pastor or not. I stop when I read Pastor George's demeanour. His scowl has disappeared. He has pushed his chair back to allow him room to cross his legs. His eyes are shuttered, his face without expression. He wants me angry. Pissed even. He wants me gone.

I place the letter on his desk. 'As I said, I don't like not finishing things.'

I make sure to leave the door open behind me.

DUMPING GROUNDS

My anger simmers; despite not being prone to violence, I've the urge to punch something. Anything with Pastor George's face on it. I hop into the back seat of Kenny's Range Rover and order the driver to get us out of Graceland as fast as possible. The further I'm away from the place, the better.

How dare the man? What's he hiding? Terminating my contract even before I give a preliminary report. And so rudely too. This is all Kenny's fault. She's the reason I took the case. I don't work like this. Pussyfooting around issues. Moving without questioning the shifting goalposts. Then, to be dropped like this just when things are heating up, when I've become so emotionally invested.

I check the time. 6:17. The traffic is not going to ease for another couple of hours. I'm too riled up for this. I can walk some of the distance to burn off some of the negative energy and let the driver meet up with me down the road. Common sense prevails. I call Kenny instead.

She listens to my rant with such unusual reticence that my voice starts to trail off in worry.

'Are you there?' I ask.

A deep sigh flows from the other side. 'I'm here.'

'You have nothing to say?' I accuse.

'I was waiting for you to finish.'

'What else is there to say? He fired me? I've never been fired in my life!' My ego is bruised. My conversation with Lara had started this downward spiral. This is the last straw.

'He can fire you, but that doesn't mean you're off the case,' Kenny says.

'What do you mean? He was the contracting—'

'I mean I'll pay you, Phil.'

'You can't be serious.'

'I am,' she says, so calmly I believe her.

This sobers me up. I'd called to vent, not change employers. 'Come on, Kenny. If they don't want to get to the bottom of what happened to their first lady, I don't think you—'

'She was my friend, Phil,' Kenny bursts out with so much anguish, I instantly feel bad for downloading my angst on her.

'I'm sorry, sis, but I tried,' I say gently.

'I know you did. That's why I want you to continue.'

'Against the wishes of your church?'

'If that's what it takes, then so be it,' Kenny says in measured, clipped tones. I've heard she's a tough boss, now I'm getting a sense of how she earned that reputation.

'I can't take your money,' I protest. 'Besides, there are several ethical issues to consider. For one, who are you representing?'

'What does that mean?'

'Who gives you the mandate to investigate or contract an investigator?' I say unnecessarily, knowing my sister is well versed in matters of mandates and confidentialities.

'Nonsense. This is Nigeria, bros, I gave myself the mandate to look into what happened to my dear friend.'

'It was suicide,' I say gently.

'Even if it was, I want to know why!' Kenny sobs. 'Her mother wants to know why. Those that know and love her would want to know why.'

'I know, sis, but people with mental health issues—'

'Sade was the most level-headed person I know,' my sister spits out.

'But you said she was not happy—'

'Not happy. I didn't say she was depressed, or so sad she'd take her life. You didn't know her, Phil. I did. Before she became withdrawn, she was so full of life, so positive. Something happened to her to make her think life wasn't worth living and that's what I'd like to know.'

'Whatever happened is not making your church look good, at least from what I can gather so far.'

'Remember what Dad used to say? "Truth before religion". This is the first time in my life I know what he meant. I want truth, Phil, and if that costs me the fellowship of my fellow man, so be it.'

This is a different Kenny from the one I've endured since I arrived from the States. Her constant badgering of the whole family to come to one church programme or another had gotten so out of hand, our dad had once demanded an intervention.

'I'm not taking your money, though,' I say primly. I won't admit that I'm glad that all my work won't be wasted. Or because, more than anything, I also want to know what made Sade Dawodu take her life.

*

'This is nice,' Folake says, as she settles on a raffia chair on our front patio.

I hand her a glass of wine, and sit next to her. It is nice. I arrived much later than we had agreed. When I informed Folake I had a talk with Lara, she decided it would be best if I told her what happened before subjecting our daughter to another round of inquisition. I got the wine, two glasses, and hoped this would set the stage for a nice, calm conversation. The kids are in bed, but because I know they are most likely not sleeping, I suggested we sit outside, where the chance of them eavesdropping is much less.

I'm silent for a while, pretending to enjoy the quiet of the night. Folake too seems to be enjoying the silence, moving her long locks away from her face to sip from her glass. The warm glow of the outside porch light seems to caress her cheekbones. She's taken off her make-up and her dark skin is so fresh I feel like planting little kisses on every part of her face. Concentrate, Philip, and stop deflecting.

'I'm pliant enough to listen to whatever you have to say.'

'Who says I've something to say?' I pretend to be offended, but I'm smiling. 'Can't I just want to spend an evening with my wife?'

'Not when you're in the middle of a case that's bothering you, even when the police say it's closed. And those puppy eyes you're giving me ain't because you want some. Come on, spill it.'

There's still an opportunity to change course and pick her brains for any one of the many loose strands in the case, but she'll see through it.

'Lara told me what she took the money for.'

Folake pauses with the wine glass halfway to her lips, stares at me, then puts the glass down on the stool next her.

'It's not for what you think.'

'I've thought many things, Philip,' she retorts, impatient.

'She used it for, er, cosmetics.'

'Like make-up? Nonsense. You know how many times that girl has rummaged through my things to—'

'More like creams.'

This time she doesn't speak but raises an eyebrow.

'Bleaching creams,' I say, my eyes not leaving hers.

'What?' she squeaks, not loudly, but in a genuinely incredulous way that says this is the last thing she imagined.

'She says the girls at school have been making fun of her. Calling her "Blacky" and "Shadow". And she just wanted to lighten her skin.'

'You gotta be kidding me!' Now, Folake is so loud, there's no doubt the kids have heard. So much for having the talk outside. 'Tell me you're kidding.'

My silence tells her I'm not. Folake reaches for the wine but I'm not sure if her hand is shaking from anger or shock. She touches the glass to her lips, and puts it back down.

'I tell her she is beautiful,' Folake says. 'She knows this.'

'We are her parents. Apparently, we are supposed to say that.' I paraphrase Lara's words to me earlier.

'All I ever wanted for her was to grow up a confident woman,' she says. 'She's brilliant. A fantastic student. I never thought ... I thought she was ... she's always been so ...'

I reach for her hand. To the rest of the world, my wife is a self-assured and accomplished woman, but I see her in the moments when she loses her confidence. When she falters in a world that has judged her on the basis of her gender and

213

race. In the States, we'd seen how our skin colour has been the cause of violence and fear. She has risen above all this, using her intellect and work ethics to prove she's more than her race or nationality. But it was a hard-fought battle and not without some defeats.

We've been together long enough for me to know Folake is worried that her own moments of self-doubt have been detected by her daughter and passed on like an inherited trait. And she's not alone in her self-recrimination. From the first moment I held my infant daughter, I understood that nothing mattered to me more than keeping her safe. Helping her grow up strong and battle-ready for whatever life throws her way. Despite the recent onslaught of rebelliousness, I'd thought we were succeeding. I'd thought being present parents would build the resilience we hoped would serve all our children well in life.

'She's a teenager,' I say, to console myself and Folake. 'We both know what a difficult time this is.'

Folake snatches her hand from mine and shakes her head. 'This isn't right,' she says. 'This is simply not okay.'

'You'd prefer something worse. Like drugs?' My attempt at joking falls flat, even to my ears.

'In many ways, this is worse, Philip. Don't you see? This was why we wanted to leave the States. To come back home where my children could feel comfortable in their skin.'

This is not the time to point out that 'you' was more accurate than 'we'.

'I know, but teenagers can be cruel. You know—'

'No, no.' Folake shakes her head, as if to underscore her refusal to accept my blanket assertion. 'Not like this. How did we get to this?'

'I don't know, Sweet, all I can say is that the teasing—'

'Bullying,' she insists sharply. 'It's bullying.'

'I agree,' I say hurriedly. 'The bullying was getting to her and that's why she bought the creams.'

'And why didn't she come to me?' The anguish in her voice is like a vice around my heart.

'Maybe she thought you wouldn't understand? You're always telling her how beautiful she is. Perhaps, she thought her not believing that would make you angry or even disappointed.' I know I sound desperate, but I'll say anything to make the pain on Folake's face go away.

'Actually, Phil, I'm mad.' Her voice has a hard edge to it. 'But not at her. At the bullies who messed with the wrong child. Our child. And they're not getting away with it.'

'Can we talk about this?' I try to control my anxiety at the sudden onset of déjà vu. This was exactly Folake's tone when she wanted to sue the police in Seattle. My plea against that course of action led to her insisting we leave the States. 'Just for a while, Phil,' she had said. 'We all need a break from this place. Just until the kids can navigate their identity outside of the colour of their skin. This is the time, before they get too old to learn. To change.' I agreed. Not wholeheartedly, but with this being the right time for the kids.

'Can we talk this through?' I repeat, concerned.

Folake looks at me like I'm colluding with Lara's bullies. 'What's there to talk about? That school has a no-bullying policy, and I'm going to make sure they act on it. Those girls are going to pay.'

'Sweet, it's Lara's word against theirs. We don't have proof.' As soon as the words come out, I know I have only poured petrol on raging flames.

Folake leans forward, her eyes blazing. 'My proof is in there,' she points at the house, 'ready to apply dangerous chemicals to her face because of the cruelty of her school-mates. No. I'm calling this behaviour out. Those girls need to know actions have consequences. In the States, we had to endure being treated as exotic, bizarre or, I don't know, unhuman. You know how many times in school I'd to defend my locks? How many times I said no to people who wanted to' – She does an air quote – '"just touch it"?' It was hard enough being Black in America but being darker-skinned was way tougher. And now here we are, where we should feel at home because we are all Black and it's the same thing. We're not only guilty of being Black as far as white people are concerned, we're also guilty of being *too* Black among other Black people.'

'I know, I know …' We've had this conversation many times, but it was about *our* experiences: at work, the shops, events as innocuous as dinner with colleagues and friends. Now, it's our child's happiness at stake, and it can't be discussed as dispassionately in an 'it is what it is' manner. I've no words.

'We left America for this?' Folake hisses. 'No. I won't have it!'

She stands up so forcefully that her wine glass falls, and I catch it quickly before it rolls on to the patio floor. If it wasn't night, I know she'd be heading to Lara's school this second. As it is, I know where she's heading and I stand to stop her.

'Sweet, let's talk about this before you talk to Lara. She confided in me.'

Folake rounds on me, and I take a step backwards. 'This is not about you, Phil. Our daughter needs to know that

I hear her, and support her and know what she's going through because I've been there. By God, she's gonna know that, even if I've to drum it into her head every hour of every day. Starting now.'

I know when I'm beaten. 'Can we at least agree on the next steps before you talk to her?'

'Next steps in no particular order.' She starts to count off her fingers, her eyes blazing. 'She'll name each of those girls so they can be reported for bullying. She'll return those creams to whoever sold them to her, and get her money back. Then, I'm going to sue whoever it is for selling poison to a minor ...'

'She said she ordered them online.'

Folake is on a warpath. 'Even better. That means it's an organisation, and by the time I'm done with them, they'll be paying legal bills for decades—'

'Folake, I think—'

The loud screeching of brakes cuts me off. Sudden bright lights head our way. Fast. I push Folake further into the patio. She falls, pulling me with her. Blinding lights get closer. I roll to take the fall. We both land on our sides. We freeze for a second as the lights veer off. Then, we are up, heading straight to the front door.

The squelching tyres on grass stops our scramble to the door. We both turn. The vehicle has stopped. It's a grey VW minivan. The windows are tinted. I move towards it. Folake pulls me back sharply.

'Wait,' she orders.

The door slides open. Folake and I step forward, then stop. A big lump rolls to the edge of the patio. Bright lights turn on us again. The tyres almost drive forward over the lump. We move back, but not before seeing what lies in our front yard.

The lump is a human form.

I jump over it and run after the van. It's moving away fast. I fumble for my phone. Running, checking for the camera button. It drives faster. I click on the video. Press record. I run faster, heart pounding, bare feet hurting. It's too dark to make out the number plate. I run faster.

The VW slows to make a turn. I get close enough to see there are no plates. I drop the phone to my side in defeat, just as the van disappears into the night.

No time to waste. Pulse racing, I run back to the house. My children are standing outside in their PJs. Folake is bent over the human form.

'Is he all right?' Lara asks from the doorway.

I pull Folake up and into my arms. I turn her face away and only then look down.

Victor Ewang's eyes stare back at me. Unblinking and vacant. Dead.

INTERNALLY DISPLACED PERSONS

'Inside, inside ...' I usher Folake and the kids into house and sprint to action. Keep everyone busy doing something. Best way to deal with shock. Keep moving. I ask Kay to get his camera, Folake calls the campus security, and Tai rocks Lara in his arms. I grab some kitchen gloves, Kay hands me the camera, and I head back out.

I take as many pictures of Ewang's body as I can. I try not to think of the last time I saw the man, or his distraught wife. Focus on the work to stem feeling. I'd have missed the paper in his bloodied breast pocket, if it wasn't for the Nikon 300 flash. It's tricky pulling out the note with the kitchen gloves, and trickier still to unfold it over the dead man's chest, take a picture and fold it back into the pocket.

The ambulance siren is closer. The neighbours will follow soon, emboldened by the campus security team's presence. I work faster, registering Victor Ewang's suffering with every click.

Bound. The bruises around his wrists are fresh. Angry welts. A struggle.

Tortured. Nails pulled out.

Beaten. The shirt is poorly buttoned. Stripped then re-dressed? There are bloodstains on the shirt around the ribcage.

Gagged. Discolouration around the lips, and across the cheeks.

Asphyxiated. Deep bruises around the neck. Bulging eyes and protruding tongue.

The flashing lights of the campus security cars followed by the ambulance put a stop to my impromptu post-mortem. I dash back into the house, pull off the gloves and order Kay to take the camera to his room. By the time he returns, the noise outside is considerable. Anytime now, there'll be a knock.

'Okay. I know you're all scared but stay inside and leave everything to Mum and me.'

My kids nod. We huddle for a quick family hug, then Folake and I walk out to blinking lights and curious neighbours.

*

My front lawn looks like an accident scene. Neighbours troop over, students converge and mobile phones are whipped out as the university's Department of Pathology staff wrap the body in a much-used black plastic bag and literally fling it into the ambulance. I cringe at the extent of evidence that might be lost by this callous handling of Ewang's body.

'The bus came from there?' The campus's Chief Security Officer points west. Ex-military. You can tell from his bearing: squared shoulders, spine straight. He walks around the scene with purpose, eyes squinting as if looking for details the ordinary person wouldn't notice. A policeman he's not, but the CSO's authoritative and pragmatic.

Folake and I nod. I try to make out what the two medics are doing inside the ambulance. Hopefully not destroying more evidence. It is dark, but it doesn't seem like anyone is opening the body bag again.

'And your wife and you were seated here?' He points to the two wine glasses on our patio.

I look away from the ambulance and follow his hand. I nod again, trying to hide my impatience. We've given him a rundown of the events that led to the body being dumped in my front yard twice already. I can sense Folake trying to remain calm while pretending to ignore the onlookers who are keeping a respectable distance from the scene.

'I believe we've answered all your questions,' she says. 'As you can imagine, we're all in shock; perhaps we can take this up again when you've contacted the police and they request our statements.'

'I understand, ma,' the CSO says respectfully, then turns to me. 'Dr Taiwo, the safety of the university community is my primary responsibility, so I need to ask if you know any reason anyone would do this?'

I shake my head, trying to look deadpan. 'Not a clue.'

'But you know the victim?'

'I think so.'

'Think?' The man's face is the picture of disbelief.

No way am I going to disclose sensitive information in full view of half of the residents of the University of Lagos.

'I didn't see his face properly,' I lie. 'But he looks like one of the staff at Grace Church. I've been doing some consulting work there. I can't say much more than that, sir. But I assure you that when the police come, I'll be as cooperative as my non-disclosure contract allows me.'

I don't think the CSO knows, or cares, that murder voids NDA conditions because he simply nods as if I am making absolute sense. Folake's grim stare clearly makes him uncomfortable, the ambulance is ready to go, and his presence is the only thing keeping the onlookers around. He has enough for his paperwork.

'But from what you know of the work you're doing, you don't think there's any reason for me to fear for safety on the campus?'

My voice is steadier than my heartbeat when I answer. 'I can't guarantee anything, sir, but, yes, from what I know at this present time, I don't foresee any harm coming to anybody on campus.'

My stomach feels queasy. This is my home. Ewang's body is a loud message I can't afford to miss. My safe haven is shattered. We're not safe.

'Maybe so,' he says, rightfully unconvinced. 'For everyone's sake, I think it's best I detail two or three armed guards within the perimeters of this house,' – He points at the houses on either side of ours – 'and there and there.'

Armed security will draw more attention to us, but what choice do we have? I look at the onlookers. All gawking – there's no other word for it – and speculating. I also sense distrust from our closest neighbours, people we've barely engaged with besides the most perfunctory exchanges. They don't know us enough to believe this is a random act of violence. They'll need the assurance of feeling protected by the campus security.

Either that, or we move off campus. Leave home. No, not again. I look at Folake and her expression says this is my call.

I turn to the CSO. 'I think armed security is a good idea but I'm sure everyone will be more at ease if we, er, went away for a bit. Just for things to settle down.'

Relief floods his face. He asks for our contact details and makes me promise to call him when we know where we are spending the night. I appreciate him not pressing me for an address on the spot. My mind is still figuring out the best possible place to go.

The CSO bids Folake goodnight, more warmly than when he first arrived on the scene, and summons his team. We watch the cars and ambulance, sirens blaring, drive away.

'Where will we go?' Folake asks.

'Somewhere safe.'

*

We arrive at Chika's house at close to midnight. He's waiting for us. He high-fives the twins, hugs Lara and waves away Folake's apology for inconveniencing him and Onyinye, his wife.

'Oh, come on. This is the most excitement this house has seen since we moved here,' Chika says as he starts to usher us into the house.

The twins start unloading the bags we hurriedly packed less than an hour ago. I walk over to help but Chika insists I go in with Folake and Lara. There's no point arguing.

Inside, Onyinye holds a sleepy Adaora. I've not seen my god-daughter for about two months, and I'm struck by how big she's gotten.

'Mama!' Adaora squeals as soon as she sees Folake. All sleepiness gone.

Folake takes her from Onyinye and starts planting kisses over the little girl's face. They've been fast friends since the day Adaora was born. She was a crier, but in Folake's arms, she'd simply coo and snuggle, then promptly fall asleep.

'I'm the baby whisperer,' Folake would joke as she took the baby off a tired but grateful Onyinye. It was not an easy birth. In those early weeks, with Onyinye's mother long dead and unable to perform the traditional post-partum care of Omugwo, Folake had stepped in to be a surrogate mum to Onyinye.

'Why are we standing?' Onyinye says. 'I made some food. Come and eat. You guys must be starving.'

'We've had dinner—' Lara says.

The twins walk in, carrying our overnight bags.

'Speak for yourself,' Kay cuts in. 'Where's the food, Auntie Onyinye? I'm starving.'

Tai pats his stomach. 'All my dinner's been eaten up by adrenaline. I could eat a horse right now.'

There's an uneasy laugh from everyone. The events of the past hours have taken us all to a time we'd rather forget. I plant a kiss on Adaora's forehead, make faces at her, which delights her. None of us will be going to bed soon. My god-daughter's nickname 'energiser bunny' is well earned.

I trail behind everyone as they troop towards the kitchen. Chika closes the door and faces me.

'I must say, Dr Taiwo, for an academic, you do have a knack for attracting trouble.'

'Oh, no, dude,' I say in hushed, angry tones, 'whoever pulled that stunt is the one in trouble.'

Chika pats my back, his face hard, eyes flint. 'That's the spirit, Doc.'

DECODING NUMBERS

'Dad! Dad!' Tai's voice propels us to run outside.

No matter how much I try to speed up the sequence, everything unfolds in excruciating slow-mo.

The scene outside is the nightmare every Black parent has imagined but prays to be spared. But there it is. My twin boys lying on the ground held down by two uniformed police officers, and another two training their guns at Folake and me. The corner of my eye catches her pushing Lara back into the house. My hands are up in the air, my eyes focused on the two rather large officers: one bald, the other with a full head of pasty brown hair, and on the other two, both hyper, ready to pull the triggers of the guns.

'They are our sons! We live here!' Folake shouts, fear and alarm make her voice sound strange, even to my ears.

But the officers are not listening.

'On the ground. Hands in the air.'

We kneel, and our hands are up in the air. But they keep repeating the same instructions, not lowering their guns, not removing their knees from my sons' necks.

We rented the place on Airbnb. I'm here for an interview at the university. I reel out my résumé in a fearful rush, not daring to lower my hands to reach for my SFPD ID card.

They're not listening.

'Dad! Tell them you work for the police!' Kay grunts.

'Shut up!' the policeman on top of my son shouts, digging his knee in harder, and causing Folake to let out a keeling sound, like a wounded animal.

My eyes stay on the officers, pleading with my hands in the air while trying to keep the desperation out of my voice. The fear. 'Please, let me show you my ID. I work for the police. San Francisco. Let me show you.'

'Keep your hands where I can see them!' the bald over-weight officer shouts.

My sons are struggling to breathe. My wife is crying. I can hear Lara from inside, whimpering. If only I can reach for my ID card. Show them—

The butt of the gun hits me in the face—

I wake up, my heart beating too fast, and then so slow, I fear it's stopped. I never sweat or scream out of the night-mare. Always at the same point in the dream. Just before blood trickles down my forehead, and my sons' tears and snorts are proof of my helplessness.

'The dream again?' Folake says, next to me. 'You've not had it in a while.'

'Last night must've triggered it,' I say, resigned.

She touches my arm and caresses it. 'We're not in Seattle, Sweet. We're home. In Nigeria. Safe.'

'Are we?' I ask sombrely, but don't wait for an answer. I plant a kiss on her forehead, tell her to go back to sleep, pick up my laptop bag next to the bed and pad out of the room.

*

FEMI KAYODE

Chika's house is huge. Not in an ostentatious way. It's the sheer size of it. Five bedrooms. All en suite. A kitchen the size of a football pitch. I envy his success in the past year. His security firm has been doing so well, he can build a house to his taste and ambitions. While I shied away from the glory and fame our Okriki Three case brought, Chika leveraged his connections with our wealthy client for more business. I didn't because I was still figuring out how to convince my wife that America is home. I didn't want to settle enough to need the connections to build a successful life in Nigeria.

I pull open the double-door refrigerator. I need sugar. Something sweet to wipe away the dry taste of fear and anxiety.

'Can't sleep, Doc?' Chika says from behind me.

I turn and open a can of juice. 'Look who's talking.'

It's just past six. We all went to bed well past two, when Adaora was snoring the way only exhausted children do after overexerting the adults in their life.

Chika walks over to the Nespresso machine. I down the orange juice. 'I'll have one too.'

He nods, takes two mugs from the rack where coffee capsules are neatly arranged.

'The strongest one, I assume,' he says as he inserts a capsule of Intenso into the machine.

I walk over to the dining table. My hands are shaky. I try to steady them by resting my chin on clenched knuckles.

Chika places the mug in front of me. 'You're right to be nervous.'

I don't look at him when I take the mug. 'I'm not nervous. I'm scared. How did a routine missing person case turn into this?'

228

'I mean you're right because I've been looking through that list. Something like this was bound to happen to that Ewang guy. And if they know you know, then what happened last night was inevitable.'

'I can't unknow what I know.'

'Which is why we've to narrow that list down asap.'

I tell him about Pastor George and my terminated contract.

'So this man knows you spoke to Ewang?'

'Doesn't mean he's in on it though,' I shoot back. Chika is a man of action. And I'd hate him acting on an assumption I can't prove.

'At this point, we can't eliminate anyone. Look, this guy is second-in-command, right? So he stands to gain the most if Dawodu's scheme becomes public knowledge.'

'You mean he set it all up? Even killed Sade?'

'I'm not sure about the first lady, but Ewang, I'm inching towards thinking your Pastor George knows more than he's letting on.'

'But why would he ask me about Ewang, fire me and then dump his body at my house?'

'Show of power, I guess. He wanted you to know who was pulling the strings.'

I sip the coffee, thinking. Pastor George might be arrogant, conceited even, but I don't peg him as this unsubtle. 'I don't know, Chi. What if the episodes are unrelated? What if Ewang's killer is on that list and Pastor George was just doing the right thing by taking me off a case that's been solved by the police. He did say all he cared about was the church and now that the bishop is off the hook, there was no need for my services.'

'There are no coincidences. You always say that.'

'Yes, there are interlinkages, but most times they're not deliberate.'

'You're convinced the killer is on that list?'

'You got your laptop here?'

Chika looks at me like that's the dumbest question ever.

*

The picture opens on Chika's screen. I've asked to move to his study to view my footage of Victor Ewang's body. I'd hate anyone waking up to what's now on his laptop.

The note seems more ominous as Chika expands the view further and the single typed sentence is blown up on the screen.

Dr T, We know you know. Talk and you're next.

'A4 paper.' I'm standing over Chika's head, nonetheless feeling the urge to talk in low tones. 'Folded into the front pocket of his shirt. They wanted me to find it.'

'You left it on him?' Chika asks.

'I thought it best. If the police see it and bring it up in their investigations, we can assume they know nothing about the list, eh? Besides, I can't meddle with evidence.'

'Makes sense.' He sits back on his chair and puts both palms together. 'So, despite evidence to the contrary,' he says, 'Sade Dawodu's death is not a straightforward suicide.'

I sit across from him. 'It's a safe assumption. She knew something, and someone wanted to be sure she didn't speak.'

'And it can't be the husband since he was being framed for her murder.'

230

'That's where it starts getting confusing.'

'Maybe not so confusing if we assume she tried to black-mail someone on that list and the person decides to kill two birds with one stone. Kill the wife and frame the husband for the murder. Chikena. No loose ends.'

'But he's been released. That's as loose as it gets.'

'Maybe his arrest was a message? He now knows they're on to him and he's cut a deal. Think about it. If Ewang was the source of the leak, and they still want to continue doing business with a now contrite bishop, they get rid of the Ewang and warn you off. And they can go back to business as usual.'

'If we can't narrow down the list to the most likely killer, we're all in danger.'

Chika turns to his laptop. A few clicks and names, numbers, pictures and locations fill the screen. 'Okay. This is where we are with the list.' He taps the keyboard several times. 'When you asked about the BVN code, it got me thinking. If we can use it to trace Sade Dawodu's transactions, we might be able to do the same for the Nigerians on this list. I had to call in big favours to get all the BVN codes.'

'It worked?' I ask, hopeful.

'You tell me when I show you what we found. My guys worked non-stop for the past three days. Don't worry. I separated the tasks among them, so no one had the complete picture.' More clicks. 'The list. We tracked all the accounts of outgoing funds from Nigeria and linked them to the church's BVN. There are several under different ministries, but we caught most of them. That allowed us to see trans-actions that went through the church's account and then moved to offshore accounts. Now, if you're someone on this list who knows your money laundering scheme has been found out, what would be the first thing you'd do?'

'Stop all transactions until the matter is sorted out or at least there's no more risk of being found out?'

'Exactly. So, of the 117 names on this list, with literally hundreds of transactions, almost none stopped their payments to the church over the past six months.'

'Almost?'

'Yes. It would make sense that not all transactions are consistent. Like, some are monthly, others happen three or four times in a year. That made things a lot more complicated because we'd have to study the trend of transactions for each BVN going back at least three years.'

Chika squints at the screen and types fast. I've never seen him like this. Even the stylish reading glasses he sports are incongruous with my gun-wielding sidekick of our previous assignment. I'm not sure which side I prefer, but both give off a competency that makes me feel safe.

'These ones here.' Chika uses the trackpad to trace a long list of names and account numbers. 'They consistently transfer funds every quarter of the year. A total of fifty-two names. Of these names, only two have not made any payments in the last two quarters of the year.'

The highlighted names mean nothing to me, but the figures against them have so many zeros, the mind reels.

'This guy here is a major businessman, specialising in oil, manufacturing and pharmaceuticals. The way the money comes in implies some kind of tax-evasion activity.'

Chika highlights yet another unfamiliar name on the screen.

'This one's interesting. He is currently in prison in Dubai for advanced fee fraud and identity theft. He was arrested early in the year, so we can understand why he has not moved any money through the church recently.'

A heavyset man, head to foot in Louis Vuitton, appears on the screen. I recognise him. The man's arrest at the penthouse suite of a seven-star hotel in Dubai made headlines several months ago.

'Unless he managed an escape from Dubai's most secure prison, I'd rule him out,' I point out.

'We can't rule out the possibility of his henchmen wanting the list kept secret because his assets are being seized and they don't want his monies with the church found.'

I nod my agreement. 'Yes, but it's a money laundering scheme, not asset management. They pay the church; the church washes the money and sends it back to them after taking its cut.'

Chika is typing again and tapping on his trackpad. 'We can cross off Mr Vuitton, then. We then looked at the sporadic transactions and isolated the names that haven't transferred anything in the last seven months.'

'Why seven?'

Chika looks at me like I should know better. 'Ewang said he told the first lady about the list a year ago. I reckoned she didn't act on it immediately, but her sitting on it for about three to four months seems a safe bet.'

'Nice logic.'

'I learnt from the best, Dr Taiwo,' Chika says wryly, but he's back at the keyboard. 'There are six who haven't transferred funds in seven months. Two governors, one female senator on the commission for resource allocation in Niger

Delta. The remaining two are well-known businessmen. Just to be sure, we now compared all transactions in the past full year with the whole sample size. All 117 of them. It still tallies. Everyone continued making deposits and withdrawals through the period under review, except these six.'

'So we can assume they know?' Chika nods. 'Could be any of them. They all seem high profile enough with a lot at stake.'

'Yep. Six possibilities plus these ones here.' He points at the screen. 'These make monthly payments and get paid back the washed money monthly. There were twenty-six of them. Luckily, only two have not made any transaction in the last three months. Look at the names.'

I peer at the screen. My eyes widen at the one I recognise.

'The other one you may not know,' Chika says on seeing my reaction. 'He's a justice of the Supreme Court. Presided over lots of high-profile cases where the culprits consistently got off. Now we know why. The second name, well, you know it.'

Richard Kelechi Nwoko. *Pastor Nwoko.*

I'm not completely surprised since Ewang had named the man as his direct boss. Still, Pastor George isn't here, which begs the question: why did he want me off the case if he wasn't involved in the money laundering?

'My sister wants me to carry on with it. I think she knows something is wrong.' I give Chika a quick summary of my conversation with Kenny. 'She claims it's because the first lady was her friend, but I'm thinking she suspects something.'

'Well, after what happened to Victor Ewang, let's hope all she wants is to know what happened to her friend.'

A shiver goes through me. I check the time quickly. Kenny will be awake, getting ready for work. I should call her.

Chika's hand stops me. I hate it when he reads my mind with such accuracy. I put the phone on the desk between us.

Chika sits back pointing to the laptop with a flourish and a triumphant smile. 'Before calling your sister, wait for the *pièce de résistance*. The late Mrs Sade Dawodu's financial records.'

I tense. I know when Chika is about to give information that might change the trajectory of an investigation.

'Using the BVN, we tracked her transactions over the last twelve months. There was nothing major for a while. In fact, look here, up until ten months ago, her bank balance had less than I make in a month. Then suddenly, there's this influx of cash. See there? Every month without fail, twenty million Naira was paid into her account. Guess from where?'

'The bishop.'

'Right on. From literally giving her nothing, he suddenly became overgenerous.'

'And we must never trust anything that happens suddenly.'

'Exactly. Which makes me suspect she used the information from Ewang to blackmail him, and he paid up. Told you your victim might not be so innocent, eh?'

I'm sceptical. 'And she still died by suicide?'

Chika wags a finger. '*Suspected* suicide. Besides, crime may not rest on some people's conscience as well as it does on others.'

'So?'

'I think she was planning something, and it backfired. She was soliciting help. I can't tell for what, but look

235

here.' He pulls his chair closer to the laptop and opens another file.

'Six months ago, she started emptying her account. These payments we traced to an investment account whose sole beneficiary is her mother. Now you can't blame a daughter for wanting to take care of her mother, right? Question for the mother is if she knew her daughter was investing on her behalf. It's a unit trust account and based on the value of the transfers, the investment should be worth at least forty million Naira today. Another odd transaction, actually made on the day she disappeared, was to an account we traced to an address in Ibadan. Two mil.'

I frown. 'Ibadan? And you can't figure out to who?'

'All-powerful BVN saves the day again. Wait.' He clicks and the picture of a distinguished man pops up. It is the profile page of the University College Hospital, Ibadan. Professor Uzoma Ohaeri is smartly dressed in a grey suit, complete with tie and striped shirt. He's all grey with a full head of hair combed out in all directions, Don King style. Probably in his early sixties. His position catches my eye: consultant psychiatrist.

Perhaps Bishop Dawodu was being truthful. His wife did have mental health issues. But did Mrs Bucknor know? If her daughter was being treated by a psychiatrist before she married the bishop, wouldn't she know the name of the doctor? Or was Sade seeing Dr Ohaeri in secret?

'There's one more thing,' Chika says. He's on a roll today.

'There's more?' I ask.

'Come. Sit.' He points at the screen. 'There's one more recipient of Sade's largesse. See here. Two payments. Twenty-two million Naira each. To this account.'

Chika selects the recipient account number and copies it. He continues talking while opening another program. If I didn't know better, I'd say he's showing off. 'We've this software we've been using to synthesise all transactions linked to a specific BVN. See, when I paste the account number in the search box?' He pastes, presses 'enter' and sits back for me to see the name corresponding to the BVN.

L. Bello. *Detective Lawrence Bello.*

WHO'S PLAYING WHO?

'You don't want to do that,' Abubakar says. His shock is obvious from the forgotten cigarette smouldering in his tobacco-stained hand.

'You mean I can't take what I know to the SCIU? I've to report this.' My voice is loud even to my ears. I can hear the anger tinged with fear in it. I don't like how I sound. 'A dead body was dumped in front of my house.'

'But you don't know if that's connected—'

'Everything is connected, Abubakar. My family's safety is at risk.'

Abubakar remembers the cigarette, tries to take a drag. There's nothing left, so he stubs it out. 'I hear you. But, that kind of money you're talking about must have been shared out all the way to the top. You'll meet brick walls that won't let you through to find out what's really going on.'

I don't get how this works. 'We've got to do something.'

'To achieve what?' The question sounds like a reprimand. 'If Mrs Dawodu was bribing Bello, you still don't know why.'

'But if we confront Bello, he might tell us what the money was for.'

'And I'm betting it was not to cover financial fraud that implicates the same husband the police arrested for her possible murder.'

This logic takes the wind out of me. This is something I'd have thought of if I was not so anxious for my family. Knowing the detective investigating the case I'm working on has been compromised by the victim is the least possible trigger for rational thinking.

I try another angle. 'What if the police are part of the blackmail scheme?'

Abubakar shakes his head as he reaches for his Rothmans pack. 'It doesn't add *uf*. *Ip* the police knew about the money laundering, they could have *affroached* the bishop to extort him. It's more likely the two incidents are not linked. The only *ferson* who had all the answers is the late Mrs Dawodu. If you want to know what is going on, I suggest you don't *confront* Bello just yet.'

'My family and I remain sitting ducks.' The frustration carries in my tone.

Abubakar waves his lighter at me. The unlit cigarette dangles from his lips, distorting his speech further. 'Whoever is behind all this doesn't know what you know. That will *keef* you *safe*. Use that to your advantage. Come to me with clear *froof* of the connections and I'll take it *from* there.'

*

My mind is not on the class. The same goes for the cadets. News of Victor Ewang's death and where his body was found is trending, and they are full of questions. I tell them in the firmest tones that I can't discuss the details of a live case, but that doesn't stop the murmurs as I half-heartedly take them through the forensic analysis of a case file. Fifty minutes later, I hurry out of the class before anyone approaches me.

Kenny is waiting at my office. She sports dark glasses that make her look like a grieving widow at a funeral. I'd called her as soon as I left Chika's house, but she insisted on a face-to-face meeting.

'I'm sorry,' she says as soon as I reach her.

'Come in,' I say and quickly usher her into my office.

She takes off the glasses and looks at my wall of Post-it notes. For a long while, she just stands there, taking in all the details of Sade Dawodu's death.

'I could have saved you so much trouble,' she says, her voice breaking.

'You know more than you told me?'

She shakes her head, and wipes tears off her face. 'Not really. Just that, I could have given you more information. Made you aware of the danger you might be getting into. It's all my fault. Folake will never forgive me.'

She starts to cry. I pull her into a hug, waiting for the sobs to subside.

'Folake won't blame you for anything.'

She looks at me with tear-stained eyes. 'You?'

'Depends on what you didn't tell me,' I say grimly.

Kenny pulls out of my arms and sits on a chair. I perch on the desk. The silence stretches for quite a while, then she pulls out her phone.

'The day before Sade disappeared, she sent me a text message,' she says as she hands me her phone.

There are several messages above the one she wants me to read.

Take care of Mummy for me.

'I didn't understand it. I tried to call her to ask for an explanation but she wasn't answering.'

'Why you?'

'I told you we were close. I was hurt when she started shutting me out, but one day she came to my office. Phil, Sade had never, ever visited my office. I was surprised. She asked if she could trust me. I told her yes. Then she gave me a flash drive.'

My stomach knots. God, please, no.

'She said she has information she doesn't quite understand but as an auditor, she felt I could help. I opened the file. At first, I was confused. Hundreds of transactions, running into billions across several bank accounts. I asked her how she got it; she told me it's best I didn't know. I told her to give me a couple of days to wrap my head around it. She thanked me and left.'

'Just transactions? No names?'

'No names. Just bank accounts. And the monies moved. I could have found out the names behind those accounts, but I got scared, Phil. This was my church, my place of sanctuary. If what I was interpreting got out, it would destroy many people, not to mention shatter people's faith.'

I try to hide my relief. That list of names is a death sentence as Ewang has proven. 'What did you do?'

'I returned it to her. I told her I couldn't make head or tail of the data. She didn't believe me but she said she understood. And that was when she stopped talking to me.'

'And she still sent you a message to take care of her mum?'

'I think she knew I felt guilty. She knew I'd do anything to make it up to her. I failed her, Phil. She knew something was going on in the church. I let my blind faith stop me from helping her.'

'What could you have done?'

'I don't know.' Kenny is crying again. 'All I know is that she trusted me with something, and the least I could have done was help her understand those transactions.'

'You think she went somewhere else to decode the file?'

'I'm sure she did. I think it was Ewang who did it for her.'

'Ewang gave her the file.'

She looks at me surprised, then confused. 'It's possible she went back to ask him to explain?'

'I don't think so. He claimed she cut him off as soon as she got the file. Look, sis, it is extremely important that you tell me the truth. Did you save the file?'

Kenny shakes her head.

'Are you sure no one knows she gave you that file?'

Kenny nods. 'I can't say I'm a hundred per cent sure, but she told me she wouldn't tell anyone. I never thought she'd lie, especially since she cut me off right after.'

'Why didn't you tell me when you first asked for my help?'

'I wasn't sure it had anything to do with her disappearance. She gave me that file almost a year ago. It was that text message that even made me think of asking you to help.'

'But her mum didn't want me on the case—'

'She didn't know her daughter was dead. She didn't want unnecessary attention focused on her daughter's behaviour. The elders have been painting her as irresponsible and unworthy of being first lady. That's why her mum was reluctant to bring an investigator in. I convinced her that as my brother you'd be discreet.'

'You could've told me.' I finally let the accusation and hurt out.

'I'm sorry. I'm so, so sorry.' Kenny bends her head in her hands and sobs harder, her shoulders heaving.

I pull her into my arms and rock her like I used to when we were kids.

'It's all right,' I say over and over. 'Everything's going to be all right.'

For the life of me, I don't know how.

*

It took another hour to calm Kenny. Then, another hour of quizzing. I make her face my wall of Post-it notes and insist she tells me anything that could make them make sense.

I point to one name on the wall: *Dr U. Ohaeri.*

'I don't know him.'

'He's a psychiatrist. You said Sade didn't have mental health issues.'

'I'm not an expert, but really, we shared a lot. Some things one would consider pretty intimate, and Sade never once told me she was seeing a psychiatrist or that she ever saw one. She told me about fertility doctors in India, Turkey and the UK, but never a psychiatrist. And certainly not,' – She gestures at the wall – 'any Dr Ohaeri.'

'Maybe she was ashamed?'

Kenny thinks for a beat, then shakes her head. 'Sade was not like that. If there was a subject she didn't want to talk about, she wouldn't even bring it up. As I said, when it came to her health, we were pretty open with each other.'

'How was her state of mind when she gave you the file?'

'Cool, calm. In control. It was like she had looked through it already and kind of deduced what was on it. And made peace. I didn't get a sense that she was emotionally distraught about it. Which was why it was easy for me to tell her I couldn't help her. Even when she left my office, she didn't seem particularly devastated by my decision.'

'So you think she went to someone else?' I am thinking of Detective Bello.

'I wouldn't be surprised, but I honestly don't know.' Tears well up again. 'Maybe I should have helped her. Maybe then she wouldn't have gone to people who put her life in danger. Maybe she'd still be alive.'

'All maybes,' I say comfortingly, then walk over to my laptop and pull up Sade Dawodu's call log. I start dialling.

'Who are you calling? Kenny asks, sniffling.

'The number listed for the Ohaeri guy.'

On the fourth ring, a male voice answers. 'Ohaeri.'

I put it on speaker and introduce myself in a rush.

'You're a psychiatrist?' Professor Ohaeri asks.

'No, sir. Psychologist.'

'Then you should know that I can't divulge anything about my patients.'

Kenny moves closer.

'But, sir, there's the possibility that Mrs Dawodu died under suspicious circumstances. I'm trying—'

'Are you the police?'

'No, but—'

'E má bínú, sir. My name is Kehinde Bhadmus.' Kenny sits and pulls the chair close to the phone. 'I represent the leadership of Grace Church who hired Dr Taiwo to look into the circumstances surrounding Mrs Dawodu's death. I can send you the letter of engagement as proof.'

Kenny gives me a don't-judge look. I shrug. Her ability to employ subterfuge to get her way will take getting used to. The image of my good Christian sister is tarnished, but I must confess I like this version better.

'Sir,' Kenny pleads, 'if you can send me your email—'

'Proceed,' the voice says brusquely. 'Ask your questions.'

I don't waste time. 'We see Mrs Dawodu paid you two million Naira on ...' I pause to quickly look at the laptop screen and check the date.

'Yes, she did. I didn't ask for it. I guess it was guilt money.'

'Guilt money?' Kenny asks, then quickly puts up her hand over her mouth at my stern look.

There is a long silence as if the man is weighing the wisdom of speaking further. We hold our breath.

'Look, when Sade was an undergraduate, she was referred to me for grief counselling. Her father had died quite suddenly and it affected her performance in medical school. We made good progress and I supported her re-enrolment to study sociology. She even graduated with a second class upper. That's how well she did. The last time I saw her was when she and her mother came to see me on graduation day.'

'Mrs Bucknor?' I ask.

'That's her mother, yes. They brought me thank-you gifts for my help over the two-odd years I counselled Sade. Normally, I don't accept gifts for doing my job, but these were simple mementoes. A pen and, I think, a box of handkerchiefs.'

In the ensuing silence, Kenny and I could have passed for competing athletes waiting for the judges to announce the results of a close race. It goes on for so long we both check my phone to be sure the call has not been cut off.

'Sir?' I say tentatively.

'I'm here. Still thinking if I'm doing the right thing …'

'You are, sir,' Kenny says, reassurance pouring out of her. 'E sé gan ni. You're doing the right thing.'

A long, tired sigh comes through the speaker. 'Sade made contact with me last year. I was happy to hear from her. We spoke about many things. I was proud of her, but after a while I realised she wasn't happy. The more we talked, the more I knew she needed help. But the help she actually asked me for I couldn't give.'

Another long silence. I can't risk the man shutting down so I don't wait for him to break it. 'What kind of help, sir?'

'I cannot say further. But I'll give you a number. It's for a Doctor Raimi, here in Ibadan. Tell him I sent you. His specialty is, erm … Let's just say his field of medicine does not demand the strict confidence that mine does.' He calls out a series of numbers which Kenny types on her phone. She turns the screen to me. I read it back.

'Go and see him. He won't say anything on the phone. Good luck. For what it's worth, Sade was a lovely young girl who grew into an amazing woman. I mourn her as a friend.'

I sense he's about to hang up. 'Sir, the guilt money. What did you mean?'

There's no hesitation this time, but a trace of anger in his voice. 'Sade stole her medical files from my office. I don't know why, or even how she did it, but she sent a text message to apologise. But I was too hurt. I never picked up her calls after that. I regret that. Now, please, goodbye.'

*

Kenny can't help me any more. Besides, I need my space. I start shepherding her out of my office with the proviso she keeps everything between us. I don't want to tell her about the list of names and how Pastor Nwoko and LaTanya Jacobson feature prominently in the money laundering scheme. I'm rather disappointed when she gives me a hug and apologises for bringing me into this, thanks me for trying to clear the bishop's name.

'Even after all this, you don't think Bishop Dawodu's involved?'

'How could he be? You saw him at the mortuary. The man is devastated at his wife's death.'

'All that money was moving through his church and he doesn't know?'

'It's possible. He's a pastor not an accountant.'

That's it. This blind devotion to a man rather than facts is the ultimate triumph of organised religion. I can only pray that unravelling the rot inside Grace Church serves the double-barrelled purpose of protecting my family and releasing the Church's hold on my sister.

Alone, in front of my evidence wall, I try to quell the desperation threatening to overwhelm me. My last assignment held a significant amount of danger, but I knew where the threat was coming from and why. In this case, I am at a loss.

The only person who has all the answers is the late Mrs Dawodu.

I train my eyes on her blown-up picture.

'What game were you playing?'

Abubakar is right. The one person with more answers than all of us seems to be the victim. Victor Ewang, Enomo Collins and now, Dirty Detective Bello. Sade Dawodu is the only obvious connection. Everything points towards Chika's conclusion: Sade was executing an elaborate plan before her death. But a plan towards what? I can't ask the very dead Ewang. I don't want to confront Enomo again until I've something more concrete. Abubakar has warned me off the detective. Of the two, I'm sure Bello is the one I'd have the most leverage on. Proof of payments from the victim could force him to give information regarding what the money was for. If I'd a clue about the reason for the money, I'm convinced it would lead us to whatever Sade Dawodu was doing before she died.

The set-up at the bishop's house, going to Ibadan with Enomo, stealing medical records and more. It must all have been for a purpose. Did the plan include her death? By her own hands or was she coerced into jumping into the lagoon? If she was the one who set up the crime scene to frame her husband, then I've to presume that incident activated her plans.

But you didn't figure I would come into the picture, right?

But why would she kill herself if everything was going according to her plan? Her husband was on a leash, judging by the transfer of funds from his account to hers. She'd money and men like Enomo and Detective Bello ready to do her bidding. I'm now inclined towards the possibility that Sade Dawodu may not have killed herself. If she wanted to leave the bishop, and in the process, extort the men on the list, what scuttled her plan between the setting up of the crime scene and her body being found floating in the Lekki Lagoon? What if she was drugged and then submerged in the water? The length of time the body was in the lagoon destroyed any evidence of a struggle. There is no way to ascertain whether she was forced underwater or went willingly.

I reach for my phone and dial.

'Enomo lied,' I say as soon as Chika picks up.

'You don't say.' His sarcasm can't be missed.

'He says he dropped Sade Dawodu at a hotel in Ibadan. But nowhere in all your transactions did you see any hotel payment. Now, let's assume he paid for the reservation, I don't think he left her there. I think he stayed with her, and followed her around to get something done there, and then they came back together. That guy we saw would never have left her side.'

'The point being?'

'For one that Enomo isn't telling us the truth about the last time he saw Sade and that means he's hiding something or protecting someone.'

'Or he's afraid? Especially if he knows about the list.'

'Like you said, if that guy had any information that could bring Dawodu down, I don't think he'll care about any danger to his life.'

'So, we need to prove he's lying about the last time he saw the first lady?'

My gaze is fixed on Sade's image on the wall, her eyes holding secrets she can no longer share.

'I think if we can place her exact time and place of death, we'll be closer to solving this riddle.'

'You don't think she died by suicide,' Chika says. He knows me enough not to make it a question.

'I'm saying, I don't know why she'd do that, and it's driving me nuts.'

'Where does that leave us?'

'I don't know, but it certainly leads to Ibadan. We've to retrace her steps on the day she disappeared. Plus, there's someone I'd like to speak with.' I tell him about my phone call to Professor Ohaeri.

'When do you want to leave?'

If I'd my way, I'd leave right now. But, family first.

TALK TO MY LAWYER

The drive through the gates of the University of Lagos Staff School takes me back to a similar one Folake and I took in San Francisco. Crown Heights College was not situated on a campus, but it might as well have been. It was – still is – an exclusive high school founded in the late 1950s to provide private schooling for the white middle-class families who moved into the upscale developments that had displaced scores of Black families from the Fillmore jazz district.

'I called Dr Cowan,' Folake said, as she touched up her lipstick, and I turned into the Upper Fillmore neighbourhood. 'She said they didn't get an invitation.'

'Perhaps it's only the boys' class, then,' I said, frowning. The fewer-than-normal cars parked outside Crown Heights was a good indication that the invitation to a Parent-Teacher meeting was not as widely distributed as Folake and I had assumed.

'That's strange,' she said. 'I wonder what it's all about.'

We parked the car and headed towards the school hall where Tai and Kay were waiting for us.

'What's this all about?' I whispered as we entered the hall.

'Ain't got a clue,' Kay answered. His newly acquired deep baritone took getting used to.

We almost bumped into Folake as she stopped suddenly. We looked around. All the parents and students were people of colour.

'I got a bad feeling,' Tai whispered.

From the hardening of Folake's face, it was clear she felt the same. She walked extra slowly to the empty seats near the empty podium. I wouldn't have gone so far in, but I knew better than to question her determination to make our presence loud and felt.

Principal Paul McAdams walked onto the stage. It occurred to me then that this was the first time I had seen the middle-aged man without a tie and tweed coat with elbow patches. He was also the only white man in the room. I stole a quick glance at Folake. This was not going to end well.

McAdams cleared his throat. 'Thank you, dear parents and our freshmen, for coming to this meeting. I'm sure you've all heard about the tragic occurrence in Texas two weeks ago.'

A pin would have made a loud crash if it had fallen. Jordan Edwards' picture filled the screen behind the principal. Everyone in the room was familiar with this image of the fifteen-year-old Black boy who was brutally murdered by the police in Balch Springs, Texas, ten days earlier.

'Now, while the details of this young man's death—'

'He was a boy!' a man shouted from one side of the hall.

'A child!' A woman's voice rose from the back, catching in a stifled sob.

A ruckus was developing and everyone started to speak at once. Everyone except the Taiwos. The twins and I were looking at Folake from the corners of our eyes. Her face was set hard, her right foot tapping on the ground.

'Please, please.' Principal McAdams stretched out calming hands which managed to look condescending and threatening to a roomful of aggrieved people of colour. 'I promise you, we mean well. This boy's death—'

'It was murder!' another angry voice shouted.

'Well, we have to let the courts decide that. As you know, the police account of what happened is quite damning of the boy—'

'They blew the back of his head off!' The speaker stood up. A Black man of immense girth and height with a voice to match. His outrage filled the room.

'That's what the media says,' Principal McAdams responded, like a teacher correcting the grammar of a student.

Folake's foot tapping got faster. I looked around the room. McAdams had better get to the point before things escalated. Unfortunately, like most white people of a certain age when faced with a roomful of minorities, he became as clueless as a shower head on a desert.

'We want to make sure the same thing doesn't happen to any of our students. That's why we've invited the head of community relations of the police department, Deputy Chief Aaron Black, to give our young boys of colour tips on how to behave themselves when they're in the presence of law enforcement. Deputy Chief Black, please.'

The principal gestured backstage, and ten seconds later, his clone was standing next to him. I knew Black. I avoided him at all costs, especially since he knew I was one of the people who signed a petition to challenge his promotion to Head of Community Relations at the SFPD.

Black's surname was not the most ironic thing about him. Despite being married to a Taiwanese medical doctor, the deputy chief was considered one of the most racist officers on the force. Indeed, his promotion was viewed as an image laundering act to clear the way for him to be made chief when the current one retired.

'Hey, guys, we all just want our kids safe, right?' He raised his voice like he was talking to a group that was collectively hard of hearing. 'Right?!' The silence did not bother him. 'Then, let's do this!' He turned to the screen behind him and clicked on the pointer.

Jordan Edwards' brown face faded to a PowerPoint slide. *'What to do when the police stop you: A presentation to young Black men by the San Francisco Police Department.'*

The loud scraping of the chair stopped the infuriated chatter and froze Deputy Chief Black's introductory remarks. All eyes fell on Folake as she pushed past me and the twins, our chairs making loud noises as we were forced to move back.

Folake walked out of the school hall like a super model on a runway. Head high, shoulders squared as the sound of her heels filled the room. Her rage was like radioactive emissions; the only way to avoid it was to get out of her way. The twins and I followed, less loudly. I knew then I could no longer stop the inevitable.

Seven months later, we were in Nigeria.

The same seething rage Folake had at Crown Heights seems to envelop her as she parks the Prado, and without sparing me so much as a glance, alights and makes her way towards the administrative building of the Staff School. And just like I did on that day, ten days after Jordan

Edwards was murdered by the police in Balch Springs, Texas, I follow her.

*

Folake places the box of bleaching creams on the principal's desk, obscuring her nameplate: Mrs Azuka Ojoh. Principal. We'd stopped at our house to pick up the 'evidence' as soon as Folake confirmed the appointment with the principal. Even a dead body on our front lawn two nights ago wouldn't stop Folake on the warpath she had declared when I told her what Lara used the money for.

After a decade as the head of the university's staff school, it seems nothing fazes the principal. Even the box of creams in front of her. Her reputation for discipline is well earned, and her face wears the permanent scowl of one used to dispensing harsh judgement. She reminds me of Pastor George.

Mrs Ojoh glances from the box to Folake. 'I can see why you're concerned, Professor Taiwo.'

'We're more than concerned,' Folake says, equally cool. 'This was peddled by students of this school. The bullying that pushed our daughter to purchase these chemicals is clearly a marketing strategy.'

The principal scoffs. 'I wouldn't credit those girls with that level of sophistication.'

Folake turns out her palms, eyes wide in contrived surprise. 'Are we to assume there's an adult in the picture? Someone training these girls to abuse other students to create a demand for,' – She waves a condescending hand over the noxious creams – 'these poisons?'

I've never been more in awe of Folake's legal mind than I am right now. She knows taking legal action against a minor would be a stretch, and holding the school accountable for the duty of care would be debatable. Instead of these routes, she's letting the principal know she intends to hold the parents responsible for their children's actions.

The way the principal sits back in her chair and levels with Folake's unflinching gaze, tells me the woman knows exactly where Folake is going. 'I assure you, Professor Taiwo, these girls will be punished. There's no need to—'

'Oh, there's every need. For one, I'm not even interested in them being punished. What good would it achieve? Besides, you and I know punishing them will only make my daughter's life more difficult in this school.'

'Are you suggesting they should be expelled?' The unflappable Mrs Ojoh looks unusually flustered. 'These are children of fellow university staff. I'm sure there are ways—'

'We don't want them expelled, madam,' I quickly interject to save the woman from a seizure. There's no way my wife's plan involves rusticating young girls from an academic institution.

'What we want is behaviour change,' Folake says. 'These girls have a mindset that's damaging to themselves and their future. That's what I want us to address.'

The principal is genuinely confused. 'How do we do that? This is not a boarding school. We do our best here, but these girls go home to their families and their own moral codes.'

Folake nods sympathetically. 'I understand that. I do have a proposition but I need you to tell me something first.'

Mrs Ojoh raises a suspicious eyebrow, but nods for her to continue.

'I want to know about these girls' academic performance ...'

'I can't share that without their parents' permission,' the principal stutters, horrified.

Folake waves a hand haughtily, like this concern is a minor detail. 'Just generally. Are they average students, or B, or distinction level?'

Mrs Ojoh shakes her head like one who has to accept her failure. 'I assure you, Professor Taiwo, the girls who bullied your daughter are far from distinction level, at least academically.'

'So, it's safe to suggest their performance in general subjects like, say, mathematics is significantly lower than my daughter's.'

The principal looks affronted by the comparison. 'Your daughter is practically a maths genius. I know teachers who are in awe of her mind.'

Folake smiles. 'I know. Which is why you'll appreciate my proposal.'

*

'Are you sure?' I ask as Folake drives out of the school compound.

'Never been surer of anything,' she answers, her eyes fixed on the road, lips tightly drawn, determined.

I was afraid she'd say that, but still I try. 'But to insist Lara tutors the girls bullying her is almost, I don't know, counterproductive.'

Folake gives me a side glance. 'Honestly, Sweets, for a psychologist, you can be so clueless about women.'

I'm too worried to be outraged. 'These are not women, Sweet. They're children.'

'Children on their way to being women.'

'Sounds like it'll be torture for Lara.'

Folake shrugs nonchalantly. 'At first, yes. And she deserves that as punishment for stealing in the first place. But in time, my plan might be the best thing to happen to her after having me as her mum.'

'You clearly know something I don't,' I say drily. 'Again, I ask, how will this work?'

Folake breathes in deeply and stops the car at a red light. She turns to me. 'Sweet, no matter how much you, or I, tell our daughter how beautiful she is or how special, she'll never believe us because that's what we're supposed to say.'

'We've established that, but—'

She holds her hand up. She's not done. 'If these bullies have the power to override our words, then I want them to use that power to fix the damage they've caused.'

'How?' Maybe I'm slow today. I need her to explain this strange logic to me.

'By forcing them to see Lara as more than her physical features. They'll experience my daughter's superior intellect. Maybe, they'll see they too can achieve that level of academic excellence and still be beautiful just as they are.'

It's my turn to sneer. 'It won't work. These teenagers of today. Social media has—'

'Sweets, it's not Snapchat or Instagram that made my daughter want to bleach her skin. It's not some pop star who sold a version of beauty lowering Lara's self-esteem. It's real people who might be just as damaged and need help.'

I point at the traffic light. 'Green.'

Folake presses on the gas.

'So, we're turning our daughter's pain into community activism?'

'Call it a social experiment, then. If the bullies get nothing out of it, Lara will at least get to show her superior intellect. That's a boost for her self-esteem you or I can't make happen.'

'And if the principal can't make the parents agree to this plan?' I query.

Folake throws me the look that resurrects my concern for the poor principal. 'Oh, she will,' Folake promises.

I want to point out some risks of this 'experiment', but we're now close to the Campus Security offices. Within those walls is another battle. I need my wits about me and Folake on my side.

*

The office is full of men and women in uniform; a blur of starched cotton and name tags comprising regular and campus law enforcements. I try to hide my disdain on seeing Lawrence Bello. 'Dirty Detective' Bello. It's hard to think of him as an officer of the law knowing what I now do.

'Prof! Welcome,' the CSO says to Folake. 'Thank you for coming on such short notice.'

It was short notice indeed. The message had come as we were preparing for the meeting with the principal. There was an overlap of thirty minutes in the timing which Folake fixed by calling the CSO. He moved the meeting forward by half an hour and assured us he'd inform the police who have now been officially invited to investigate the case.

'We're not investigating the death,' the CSO had insisted over the phone, as if this assertion would calm us. 'We're not equipped for that. We've called in the police to find out how the poor man died.'

So, here we are. The tension is palpable.

'Thank you for coming,' Bello says, no friendlier than he'd been the other times our paths had crossed. He smiles tightly when he greets Folake. 'Your husband and I are working on an investigation together.'

Folake says nothing. Don't make small talk with an American-trained lawyer. There's no Nigerian version of Miranda Rights, but Folake had cautioned me as she parked the car. 'Say nothing outside what happened in front of our house,' she'd warned. 'When in doubt, let me speak.'

'The Department of Pathology has released a preliminary report of the autopsy.' The CSO passes over copies of the report on the university letterhead. 'You must understand we couldn't authorise an extensive autopsy without the family's consent.'

Bello cuts in, 'As you can read, the victim was tortured and most likely choked to death. A significant amount of time seems to have passed between the time of death and when the victim was dumped in front of your house.'

'The pathologist says at least three hours,' the CSO adds.

Bello looks at him sharply; his body language seems to warn the CSO to be quiet. Then he turns back to Folake and me. 'From your statements, we could place you at your house during the presumed time of death.'

'So why are we here?' Folake asks, her face impassive as she places the report back on the table. I hold on to my copy, reading quickly to match the content with my initial impressions of Ewang's body.

'To ask your husband why he thinks anyone would place a dead body in front of his house,' Detective Bello proclaims.

I try to keep my face blank and look at him. Thinking of him as a 'dirty detective' helps.

'Everything we know we've put in our statements,' Folake says before I can speak.

'I'm sorry, madam, but your statement gives us nothing. A man is dead.'

Folake pushes her chair back and locks gazes with the detective. When he breaks the eye contact, she speaks slowly, with a deliberateness that says she won't repeat herself. It's her lecturer tone. 'We're very aware a man is dead, Detective. My husband and I only have one connection to the victim. He was a congregant at Grace Church, where my husband is on retainer, working with the church to investigate the death of the bishop's wife. It's been ruled a suicide, which means the case is closed. But you know all this, don't you?'

'Can your husband speak for himself?' Bello sounds miffed.

'In addition to being a first-hand witness to the event under investigation, I'm his legal counsel. Unless we're charged with something, I'll answer all the questions on his behalf.'

The detective looks at me, seething. 'Dr Taiwo, tell your wife—'

'I don't tell *Professor* Taiwo anything, Detective,' I reply without a second's pause.

Folake looks towards the CSO. 'Chief, does the university need our help on anything in particular?'

He sits up. 'Everything is in your statements, ma. We've handed these over to the police, and the body is being released to the state as we speak.'

'So, why are we being subjected to this?' She's not looking at Bello but there's no prize for guessing who 'this' is and her opinion of him.

The CSO looks to Bello for help. 'He says he and your husband are working together.'

'Are we, Detective? I ask, deliberately derisive on the 'detective'. 'Are we working *together*?' Folake kicks me beneath the desk.

'Have you spoken to anyone at Grace Church, Detective?' Folake asks. 'The victim's wife? The church leadership? The bishop?'

Bello becomes defensive. 'The homicide people are doing that. I'm here because of this.' He passes her a piece of paper encased in a transparent plastic file. It's a photocopy, but I can see it's the note I found on Ewang's body. I wear a curious look and wait for Folake to read it before passing it to me.

'What does this mean?' Folake asks, and I can't help but be impressed by her poker face. Right there and then, I know her plan regarding Lara will work. My wife is badass, in the best possible way.

'It was found on the body,' Detective Bello responds to her but he's looking at me. 'A note that's clearly a threat to your husband.'

I'm betting the detective wouldn't show us the note on Ewang's body if the police knew about the money laundering scheme.

'But you don't know that for sure, right?' Folake challenges.

'That's what we're trying to find out.'

'If we knew anything, you think we'd keep it from you?' I ask, testing my theory.

The detective's relief at hearing me speak makes him even more earnest. Almost desperate. 'You know something is going on in that church. You can't keep protecting them. Protecting him.'

I don't dignify him with a response. He doesn't know about the list.

Folake stands. 'Detective, we'll liaise with the university's security team to ascertain how the body came to be dumped in our front yard. In the meantime, I assure you, if Dr Taiwo discovers anything helpful, he'll contact your team immediately. For now, in the absence of anything else, I think this meeting is over.'

She goes to the CSO, shakes his hand and before the detective can protest, she is out.

I start gathering my copy of the report.

'You know there's a connection, Dr Taiwo,' Bello says, and if I didn't know better, I'd say there is a plea in his voice. Then, he ruins it. 'And if I find you're aware of something you're not telling me ...'

The list of transfers from Sade Dawodu's account to this criminal in uniform flashes through my mind. The gall of the man.

I wave the autopsy report, pointedly ignoring him. 'May I keep this?'

I don't wait for the CSO's reply before walking out.

Folake is already in the driver's seat. My proud smile fades when I see she's fuming.

'You were awesome in there, Sweet.'

She faces me. 'Fix it, Phil. I don't know how you're going to do it, but fix it. This case has come into our lives in the ugliest way, and at the worst possible time. I can't stand all the media attention, and as much as I love Chika and Onyinye, I miss my bed. I want this over and done with. Expeditiously.'

She starts the car just as I'm about to apologise and promise to do my best.

My phone beeps. I reach for it as Folake reverses. It is a text message from a familiar number, but I can't place it.

I frown at the message when it opens.

Can I trust you?

I look at the number again. Now I recognise it from hours of poring over Sade Dawodu's call logs. I whistle as Folake gets on the main road leading to the faculty of law.

'What?'

My hand trembles slightly as I turn the mobile phone to her. 'Don't freak out but I just got a message from Sade Dawodu.'

BOOK III

For a fixed mass of gas at constant pressure, volume is directly proportional to temperature.

Charles' Law

The poor and the oppressor have this in common: The Lord gives sight to the eyes of both.

Proverbs 29:13 (NIV)

STAGES OF GRIEF

You might still be in the first phase of grieving. Denial. You might be tempted to stay there, hoping and praying this is all a nightmare you will soon wake from. Don't. Denial is a dark and warm place that pulls you in with illusions of what could have been. I have been there.

I didn't know it then but my grief began on my wedding night.

Let us pray, he said when I came out of the bathroom of that luxury suite in the Maldives. It was not a request from my husband, but from Bishop.

I had envisioned a different picture of our wedding night, but I knelt. He stood over me, prayed until I lost all desire to be made love to. And then he raped me. It will take months of him taking me only when I am unwilling, to realise my husband was only aroused by my fear.

I am telling you this because if you choose to stay in that place of denial, you will end up like me. Pretending that all is well, sure that everything happening now will pass in a couple of days. Until days become weeks, then months roll into years.

Please face the truth. Nothing will change what is. It is only when your pain gives way to anger, that next stage of grieving, that you will be ready for the next, final step.

The bloody evidence we spread around the house will not keep him in custody. Neither will finding my body. But please, don't worry or fret. Remember, we're playing the long game. Doubt now surrounds him like flies on shit. We have him where we want him.

GHOSTING

Folake almost swerves off the road as I read out the text.

'Answer!' she orders as she guides the car to a stop on the roadside. 'Type something. Anything.'

I glance from my mobile phone screen to Folake. 'She's *dead*. I saw her,' I say, but there's panic in my voice.

'Hurry, Philip,' Folake says, pointing at my phone.

You can trust me. I press send.

We wait, our breathing louder than the car's air-conditioning.

You're helping a bad person beeps back.

Folake inches closer. 'Say something like "aren't you supposed to be dead?"'

My fingers are already flying across the keyboard.

I'm not helping anyone. I just want to know the truth.

I turn the small screen towards Folake. She nods.

Our eyes are trained on the ellipses of a message in progress. The response appears. *The truth can get you killed.*

Folake and I glance at each other. I take the plunge and type. *If you're dead, who is this?*

The response is quick. *Justice.*

I'm also ready.

Tell me who you are. Maybe we can work together.

We wait but nothing comes. Folake expels a breath. 'You think you scared them off?'

I frown at the screen. 'I'm not sure. We'll see.' I put the phone in my pocket, disappointed. 'I think it was a test to check how amenable I might be to their point of view.'

Folake pulls back onto the main road.

'Are you? Amenable?'

I think of the woman who empowered young girls to make independent choices. A woman who inspired such fierce loyalty in my sister that she's willing to pay me to get to the truth. A woman who must have discovered a terrible truth that cost her dearly. A woman someone is trying to avenge.

'*She is so beautiful*,' Lara had said.

'Something happened to Sade Dawodu, Sweet. Something terrible. Something that stripped her of light and left her no choice but to take her life. Even if I could walk away from not knowing why she did it, I can't walk away now that my family's in danger.'

We are now at the Faculty of Law. Folake parks the car and faces me. 'That's a lot of pressure, Phil, and I'm sorry I was hard on you earlier. You can't fix something if you don't know what's broken. But I'm sure of one thing: you've got this. You are good at what you do. If anyone can find out what really happened to Sade Dawodu, and how it connects to that poor man's death, it's you.'

'I'm not so sure. So much is happening at home. Lara needs—'

Folake leans across the gear box and kisses me. 'Let me deal with Lara. You get to the bottom of all this, so we can get our lives back.'

*

I'm too troubled to be embarrassed by the perfunctory way I teach my afternoon class.

'As research shows, the psychology of deception is grounded in a complex mix of cultural, social, even religious biases on the part of the interviewer and the interviewee.' I'm sure I sound like a robot. 'Based on the literature I shared last week, can anyone tell me some of the variables to take into consideration during an interrogation?'

Hands fly up. Most of the answers are correct – the conditions under which a lie is told, the nature of the lie itself, the consequences of telling the truth or getting caught in a lie – but I barely acknowledge them. I nod, make notes on the blackboard and finish the class minutes ahead of schedule.

'*You know there's a connection.*' Bello's words echo in my mind as I open my laptop. What is the connection between the detective and Sade Dawodu? Surely, they must have had a series of engagements before the transfer of such huge funds? Who initiated the meeting? Was it recent? Or was it purely transactional and there was a middleman who connected to them both?

The text messages from Sade Dawodu's phone coming on the heels of another meeting with the clearly corrupt detective also complicates matters. What if he's the one manipulating things? Is he working alone, or with other officers? Does he know Enomo's role in all this?

So many questions, and my head is spinning. I've to calm down. Concentrate. Focus on that thing. The connection. Connection.

I text Kenny. *You never sent the names of the first lady's friends.*

Kenny's response takes longer than usual and because I can't get over those messages from Sade Dawodu's phone, I press the dial icon on her number.

'Hi. I'm not available to take your call, but if you want me to call back, tell me what it's all about.'

Sade Dawodu's voice is as melodious as in the interviews I've watched: calm and measured. Not for the first time, I can't help thinking I'd have liked her. I debate leaving a message, but I suspect I'd be playing to the gallery. I *know* what I saw in that mortuary. Whoever is sending the messages is *not* Sade Dawodu. I'd have liked to have more to go on before calling Chika, but time is of the essence and the earlier he gets on this the better.

'I just sent you a screenshot of a very interesting exchange,' I say as soon as he answers.

'Hold on,' he says.

I check my inbox while waiting. There's an email from Professor Cook. I click on the attachment without reading what I know will be a terse message from Prof asking after the family and reminding me I owe him for this favour.

'Wow. This is what real ghosting is.' Chika's voice.

'You see it?'

'Nothing more? Just this?'

'Yes. So, the phone is back on,' I answer as I click open the folder. Scans of LaTanya Jacobson's social security card, her credit history and police records open. 'Can you trace it?'

'Not in real time. If it comes back on and you let me know immediately, we can. But for now, we can only confirm the last time it was switched on and from where. There's no guarantee it will be switched on again at the same place, though.'

272

'Uhm. Let's work with what we've got for now.'

'It's going to cost us if we don't have a formal request from the police.'

'No police for now, Chika. Not until we know who or what we're dealing with.'

'Got it. Expense account it is,' he says. His comebacks are sharper and quicker when he is nervous. Victor Ewang's death worries him.

I click on and enlarge mugshots of a much younger LaTanya Jacobson. Arrest date is 4 April 1996. The first name is the same, but the surname is hyphenated with another.

'Phil?' Chika's voice breaks my focus. 'You there?'

'Gotta go. Will tell you later.' I cut off the phone without taking my eyes off the laptop screen.

There are several documents in the folder: fingerprints, tax returns, parking and/or speeding tickets, more misdemeanour charges, bail hearings and a marriage certificate. I click the copy issued in the DC on 17 September 1995. Included is an annulment certificate due to 'irreconcilable differences' on 23 July 2017.

The name against 'Husband' on the two documents swims in my vision, becoming one.

Jeremiah Dawodu.

TURNING POINT

'But it'll be really late by the time you get there …' Folake's voice trails off and I picture her shaking her head in disapproval.

'I need to know he's got nothing to do with the threat to us.'

'If he does, doesn't that make seeing him dangerous?'

'What will he do at Graceland?' My resolve is shaken by the sudden image of thousands of churchgoers attacking me with Bibles and tambourines. 'I want to look him in the face, and I want him to know what I know. Maybe we can cut a deal. I hand off the case and he leaves us alone.'

'You and I know it's no longer that simple.'

We are both quiet. I am minutes from Graceland, having rushed out of my office as soon as Dawodu agreed to meet with me. There's no turning back now.

'Chika knows where I am,' I reassure her.

'But he's not with you.' Folake's tone says she's far from comforted.

'I don't need a bodyguard,' I snap, defensive. I'd rejected Chika's offer to accompany me when I told him where I was going. It would have meant hours of waiting for us to meet up at the college. I couldn't risk losing my nerve.

'I'm sorry,' I say into the silence. 'I just want this over and done with. Everyone's fine?' I ask to change the mood of the conversation.

Folake plays along. It's easier that way. 'We are. Onyinye's been wonderful and Adaora clearly likes having so many people fussing over her.'

'Lara?'

'She's been giving me the silent treatment since the principal called to confirm the parents agreed to my proposal.'

I can understand Lara's horror at being in such proximity with her bullies, not for a moment but for hours of study.

'I'm here,' I say. Not quite, I need to centre my thoughts before I drive through the gates of Graceland.

'You've got this, Sweet. And you don't need a bodyguard. Sorry I made you feel like that.' She hangs up.

Graceland twinkles like it is Christmas, in stark contrast to the darkness I drove through. The estate is buzzing with activity: cars zipping in and out, residents returning from work and churchgoers exiting from yet another service. It seems even mourning their first lady can't stop the business of spreading the gospel.

'He and Ms Jacobson are waiting for you, but please don't take too long. He has a prayer meeting in the next hour,' the secretary warns me as she opens the door to the office of the man I can no longer bear to refer to as 'bishop'. With or without the definite article.

Today, there's no standing up to thump my shoulder or pat the back of my hand like a politician on a campaign trail. Dawodu sits behind his desk, his face an unreadable mask. LaTanya Jacobson stands behind him, her brightly coloured nails resting on his shoulder like medals. I get it. United we stand.

'You wanted to see me, Dr Taiwo?' Bishop Dawodu asks coolly.

'I'd have thought you'd want to see me after what happened in front of my house.'

'An unfortunate situation, which we'll rely on the authorities to investigate. Or perhaps you know why my head of foreign missions was killed and his body placed at your house?'

I almost sputter at the sheer gall. 'I didn't know the guy until your elders hired me.'

'And that assignment is officially over since, as you know, the police have ruled Jerry's wife as suicide,' LaTanya says.

'And Victor Ewang's murder?'

'From my point of view, there is no link. Except if you think otherwise?' Dawodu raises a quizzical eyebrow.

I look from him to LaTanya, then back. They've figured out a narrative. They're goading me to uncover how much I know. Dawodu's dramatic visit to the police college to ostensibly thank me for my services now reveals itself for what it was: a fishing expedition. The time he spent staring at my wall of evidence was not out of admiration, but rather to analyse what I knew and what connections I had made. Fool me twice, shame on me.

I sit across from them, and don my best kindly-educate-me look. 'You're no longer interested in knowing who tried to set you up?'

'To what purpose? To punish them? Vengeance is the Lord's,' Dawodu says, his tone infuriatingly genial.

'To know the truth?' I ask just as amiably, although I narrow my eyes to let him know that if anyone spiked my drink with stupid on my way here, I didn't drink. 'Perhaps why your wife would be pushed to jump into a lagoon?'

'We know the truth,' LaTanya says haughtily.

I open my palms invitingly. 'Please. I'm dying to know.'

Dawodu leans forward. 'My wife was a deeply troubled woman, and while planning to take her life, she somehow got it into her head I was to blame for her woes, so she set it up to make it look like I killed her.'

'But what facts are you working with?'

LaTanya gives an impatient sigh and walks around the desk to look down on me.

'Dr Taiwo, we don't need this to drag out any longer. Jerry's a powerful man and he has lots of enemies. There are too many people out there who would like to use this to bring him down. Can we just close this chapter and bid each other goodbye?'

I point towards the door. 'Your elders, the congregation, do they know about your, er, union?'

Dawodu claps his hands. 'I've seen your rate card, Dr Taiwo, and I must say I think you're overpaid if that's all you've got.'

'Did your wife know that you had committed bigamy? Was that why she—'

'The marriage was annulled long before we made it official,' LaTanya says, as if bored.

'Yes, but did your wife know that?' I'm looking at Dawodu who's no longer looking as charming as I once thought he was. Stripped of the veneer of piety, the man looks like an expensively dressed pimp. A dandy who fancies himself royalty.

Dawodu shrugs. 'It wasn't information that I felt was pertinent to our union.'

'Making her complicit in a crime might be considered pertinent information,' I say wryly.

'What crime? What you call bigamy in the States is perfectly legal here,' Dawodu says, derisive.

LaTanya waves her talons daintily. 'He needed a green card, and I needed money to fund a nasty habit. I'm sure you found that out when you asked your SFPD pals to look me up.'

Dawodu stands and walks around his desk towards the door. 'It's over, Dr Taiwo. Kindly adhere to the terms of disengagement and desist from harassing me and my associates further. Might I also remind you of the NDA you signed? Please keep that in mind in case you'd like to use some of the information you discovered in the course of working for me to embarrass a man of God.'

My contempt makes responding unnecessary. Dawodu's hand is on the door handle. LaTanya toys with a huge bauble around her neck.

'And the threat to me and my family?'

'Do you know anything that would put your family at risk?' LaTanya's gaze is hard on me.

My eyes make my point: I'm not telling if they're not.

LaTanya waves her talons again, a serpentine smile spreading across her face. 'Then you've nothing to fear from whoever is threatening you.'

For the first time in a long time, I'm inclined towards violence. I walk to Dawodu at the door and eyeball him.

'My family is off limits.'

'Go with God,' he says with a smile as he opens the door.

Flashes of Folake huddled with my kids inside our home merge with memories of Sade Dawodu's body at the mortuary and Ewang's lifeless eyes. So much pain and loss, all linked to this creature.

'Go to hell,' I say and walk out.

ONE EIGHTY DEGREES

Pastor George is by my car. His trademark scowl is absent. Instead, he looks aged and anxious. I'm not in the mood to be sympathetic.

'Before you say anything, please hear me out,' he says as soon as I reach him.

'I've got nothing to say to you,' I say tersely.

'I was wrong, Dr Taiwo. I made a mistake, please hear me out.'

The man sounds desperate.

'What could you possibly say—'

'This.' He pulls my hand into a handshake. I feel the paper. 'Don't open it here. Please. I'll meet you outside Graceland.' He thumps my hand and pulls me into a hug, then whispers into my ear. 'Drive to Redeemers' Camp. It's down the road. I'll meet you there.'

I pull away, and without sparing him another glance, get into my car. I start the engine and unfold the paper. The hand-written sentence is in all caps: 'IF ANYTHING HAPPENS TO ME, CALL DR TAIWO. HE KNOWS. I AM SORRY.'

I slip the paper into my pocket and reverse out. When did Ewang write the note? After our meeting? Did someone from the church witness our rendezvous? Or was it written from a state of paranoia which would be consistent with my assessment of the man's agitation and fear. A fear which has been proven to be tragically justified.

I make a U-turn to go in the direction of where I met with the late Victor Ewang. What is it with these people and Redeemers' Camp? Do they sense there's something missing at Graceland that can be found here?

I park at the entrance gates, and wait for Pastor George.

He arrives fifteen minutes later. I wouldn't have seen him if he hadn't drawn up next to me in a Volvo S70. He makes a sign to indicate I should drive behind him. I follow through the main entrance gate and stop when he parks on the side of the main road. He gets out, looks around briefly and walks to my car. While he's not anxious like Ewang, the distress is evident in his gait.

'You can't be off the case, Dr Taiwo,' he says, as soon as he closes the passenger door.

I hold out the note. 'Who wrote this?' I ask, just to be sure.

'Victor Ewang. His wife found it in the middle of her Bible.' He searches my face with a frown. 'What do you know, Dr Taiwo?'

That's rich. Coming from him. What does *he* know? 'You terminated my contract, remember?'

'I was afraid,' Pastor George says. 'I'm not proud of it, but after that detective said he had confirmed how First Lady died, I was afraid.'

'Of what?'

'For. Not of. I was afraid *for* the church. What you might find and how it would rock the very foundations of our existence.'

'You cared more about your church than the truth?'

The man's head snaps back so sharply you'd think he had been slapped.

'I thought I was doing the right thing. Protecting the church—'

'You were protecting your bishop,' I spit out. Anger at the way this man treated me makes me uncharitable.

'Maybe. I admit it. Over the years, I've been seeing sides of him that made me doubt if I was in the right place. But I thought it was me. That I was outgrowing Grace Church, and therefore seeing only flaws. That day, when we were told his wife killed herself, and how he reacted.' He shakes his head like someone ridding himself of an unpleasant memory. 'And with that horrible woman standing next to him, I just panicked.'

Studies abound on people unwittingly pulled into the webs of deception in organised religion, but few exist on people like Pastor George. The ones who make a conscious effort to turn a blind eye to what is right in front of them. I have no pity for him.

'Judge me all you want, Dr Taiwo,' he says, and for once, I don't lament not having a poker face. I want him to know what I think of him. 'I deserve it and the only way I can make up for it, is to ask, no, beg you to stay on this case.'

'Even if it proves your leader is not who he claims to be?' I ask, my eyes intent on him. I remember our first meeting. The way he'd looked when Nwoko had claimed someone was framing Dawodu had mirrored my face. Doubtful.

'If the truth will bring justice to Victor—'

'He wasn't an innocent bystander,' I say, wondering again how much the man now knows. I could be walking into a trap.

'I'm sure he wasn't, but no one should die like that. He had three small children. Whatever he was doing, if it had to do with the church, then the church must be accountable. And then there's First Lady. What pain could push a woman of God to take her own life? What could I have averted that would have saved that young woman? What did I permit?' His voice breaks in anguish. 'Oh my Lord, what did I permit?'

Pastor George's shoulders heave. I give him time to compose himself. The silence stretches. He clasps his hands, closes his eyes and then rocks his head back and forth gently, like he is praying. I look away, and hope this won't go on for much longer. I resist tapping my fingers on the dashboard. A loud, shuddering breath makes me look his way. His eyes meet mine, his hands fall on his thighs, and he smoothens the fabric of his trousers. An unnecessary act that betrays his nervous state. Or fear? It's the most expressive I've seen the man, so I can't quite read this version of him.

He leans towards me. 'I kept asking God why He has not led me away from here. But over the past weeks, I've begun to see this is the reason. This trial of the church. And meeting you is part of that reason.' He is so close to my face I have to move back, as far as the enclosed space allows. 'That note says you know something. It's a dead man's last wish. Help us, Dr Taiwo,' Pastor George adds, then he reclines into the seat, and closes his eyes as if seeking strength.

I read Ewang's note again. It now seems as ominous as the one placed on his body: *We know you know. Talk and you're next.*

I look at Pastor George. 'It's safer for me and my family if I just walk away now.'

'None of us is safe with a killer out there,' he says with confidence.

I slump into the car seat at the truth of his words. There's no walking away.

INSIDE MAN

'Can you trust him?' Folake asks. Her worried frown makes me almost regret giving her a full account of my day at Grace Church, including my conversation with Pastor George.

I plop on the still unfamiliar but really comfy bed. 'Frankly, I don't know who to trust at this point. Even Kenny,' I add, bitterness colouring my tone.

'From what you said, she did what she thought was best.' Folake's defence of my sister rankles.

'She should've told me what she knew from the beginning,' I say, lowering my voice. We're still guests at someone else's house and it's late at night.

'Like you told me about this list?' Folake snaps.

'I was trying to protect you.' As soon as the words are out, I regret it.

Folake's frosty response is as sharp as it is immediate. 'Without my permission.'

'I'm sorry.' I try to pull her into my arms; she resists. 'I was wrong. I should have given you an idea of what I—'

'We,' she says as she pulls away.

Concede quickly and move on. 'What *we* are dealing with. But it was work, and apart from the NDA, until

Chika and I figured out the extent of the danger, I thought it was best to limit the number of people who could be at risk.'

She wags a finger at me, shaking her head. 'Nope. Not buying it. As soon as that guy's body was dumped at our house, your NDA was null and void, and you know it. Besides, I'm ready to bet my law degree that you didn't sign an NDA with Chika, right?'

'We had a tacit agreement.' I'm losing and worst of all, she knows it.

She rides on. 'You guys just wanted to play macho; figure everything out before involving the weaker sex. It's patriarchy at its most basic and self-defeating. Philip, you denied me, your partner, the right to actively participate in how our family should be protected.'

I'm hurt by the truth in her words, but still I try. 'How?'

'By keeping vital information that affects us all from me. It puts me on the back foot, which makes me assume worst-case scenarios that could have been better managed if I'd all the facts.'

'When would have been the best time to have shared all this vital information?' I scoff, guilt making me defensive.

'Perhaps right after we had to leave our home? Or when I was defending your behind with that obnoxious detective? Or when Kenny told you about what she knew? Would you like me to go on?' Her eyes are blazing, her tone clipped.

How did we get from sharing how our day went to an all-out argument?

'*You're both afraid,*' my inner, sane voice whispers. '*Fear breeds anger.*'

But I'm too angry now, my ego too bruised to heed the warning in my head. 'Do I do anything right? Can I get something right for once?'

'You wanna go there?' Folake jumps off the bed and glares down at me.

I follow suit. We're now facing each other, the bed a wide gulf between us. 'Yeah. I wanna,' I hiss out. 'Because if it's not me actually doing something wrong, it's *how* I do it right that's a problem.'

Folake takes a step back, blinks like she can't believe what she's hearing, and then nails the coffin with a disappointed head shake. 'A simple apology would have sufficed, not this whining.'

'Don't patronise me,' I sneer. 'Just the other day, you said I was the best suited to fix our situation—'

'In your job which has impacted our lives, there's a difference. It's called faith in your professional competence.'

'I get it. This is a referendum on my competency as partner and parent.'

'I'm not responsible for how you interpret my words.' She storms towards the bathroom on my side of the bed, then rounds on me. 'This conversation is going nowhere, and I can't even call it a real fight because I can't scream at you in someone's else's house.' Her voice breaks, with anger, frustration and hurt. 'I miss my space.'

She makes to turn away. I reach for her. 'I'm sorry. Truly, deeply sorry. You're right, I should have carried you along.'

We are like this for a beat, our breathing ragged, our eyes locked. Then, I lower my lips to hers.

'I. Am. Sorry,' I repeat, punctuating each word with a kiss. It takes a moment but she kisses me back.

*

Unlike Folake, I could get used to living under Chika's roof. Onyinye fusses over us. Adaora can't get enough of Lara and the twins. The cook/nanny/housekeeper is a sturdy, no-nonsense woman that makes the best pancakes on earth. The driver is available to take Folake to work and the kids to school. I find myself whistling to the pop tune on the radio as I drive to work.

My wall of evidence is the reality check I need to get cracking. Given the new developments, I've to restrategise. Kenny had earlier texted that she'd sent an email with the list of Sade Dawodu's friends and contacts. I open it.

As she'd promised, it's not a long list. Five names, their email addresses and telephone numbers. One is the chairman of the Board of Trustees of Girls in Control. I remember her from the documentary I watched before I formally took the case. There's Enomo Collins' name too, and I wonder if Kenny knows that his relationship with Sade Dawodu was deeper than friendship. I wouldn't be surprised. Everyone at Grace Church seems to know more than they're willing to let on.

I pick up on the name 'Margie Njoku' against which Kenny had typed 'Sade's best friend. They went to Uni together in Ibadan. Lives in Canada.'

I search the name online. It's easy to find her. She's on every social media platform. I click on her Facebook profile link. I can work my way through her other accounts if she's not active here.

She is. On Margie Njoku's page, pictures abound of her at work, with colleagues (she's a teacher), with her family (three young children and a husband in the military), singing in the church choir and more. I scroll to the date Sade's body was discovered. Sure enough, there's a post on her friend's death.

'Your bright smile and beautiful voice might be no more, but your memory will always be alive in our hearts. #HouseofLevy2004.'

I click on the hashtag. Tons of hits for 'House of Levy'. Seems to be a popular name for choirs around the world. But none has '2004'.

They went to Uni together. Ah. That must be it. The picture must be the university choir. I try to imagine what a younger Sade Dawodu would have looked like as I click on and enlarge the picture. She's not hard to find. Even in the choir robes, Sade is a stunner. Taller than most, smile wide as she stands between the petite Margie and a lanky, dark-skinned young man. There's something about him. He reminds me of someone, but I'm not sure who. Surely, it must be some kind of doppelgänger coincidence.

I check the timestamp on what must be a scanned picture judging by the frayed edges and the flare at the centre that's yellowed with time.

9:03 P.M. 23.10.2004.

In the times I've interacted with Bello, I've never seen him smile with the kind of joy on this young man's face. But the distinctive gap tooth is the same. The dimples on both cheeks can't be missed. The detective might have grown heavier, filled out with a mature confidence, but the resemblance to the young man whose arm is slung over Sade's shoulder is too uncanny to miss.

There are no coincidences.

I reach for the case file. My misgivings regarding how a frantic caller in the midst of a crime-in-progress could be so calm in their delivery remains, but it is the redacted phone numbers my eyes rest on.

Why did the police act so swiftly?

I google the police toll-free number. There are several seven-digit numbers including a toll-free 911. I try that first.

A static sound comes on, a click like the line is being transferred. I hold my breath. A recorded voice comes on.

'All our operators are currently busy. If you're not experiencing an emergency, please use any one of our seven-digit numbers. All calls are free.'

Three dials later, the response remains the same. There are three seven-digit numbers listed on the police website. I try them all. They are either engaged or when they ring out; none is answered. I rotate calling the numbers. Always the same. No response.

I dial Abubakar.

'I saw your car outside,' the commandant says as soon as he picks up.

'I'm in my office. I just want to check something with you.'

'Go on,' Abubakar says, slower, cautious. The tone I used to get at Internal Affairs when I called a police chief.

'I've tried to reach the police emergency line—'

'Why? What's wrong?'

'Nothing. I'm just trying to confirm something. So, I've called all the lines, none was answered.'

'Not unusual,' Abubakar says with relief. 'The lines are *p*unded by the government who sometimes *p*orget to *f*ay the mobile *p*one companies, so they cut it *opp*. When they work, they are jam-*f*acked.'

'But on the day Bello said the police got an anonymous tip, the lines worked.'

'I didn't say they don't work, I said they're—'

My pulse quickens. 'Yes, yes. But they called more than once. And each time it was answered by an officer. In fact, according to the report,' – I flip open the case file to the page I'm looking for – 'not only was it picked up every time, the police were on *standby* to receive further calls. How's that possible for emergency lines that are either not working or constantly busy?'

'You think that's what Bello was paid for? To fix the call report?'

I look at the blown-up picture of the House of Levy choir. There's no doubt in my mind that the lanky young man next to Sade Dawodu is Lawrence Bello.

I remember asking the detective. '*Why do you hate the bishop?*'

'I think it's much deeper than that,' I say into the handset.

'What's the connection?'

'Ibadan.'

OUT OF TOWN GIG

'Sometimes it feels like we are in a police state,' I lament, as we are waved past yet another unnecessary checkpoint. The first, less than five minutes past Graceland, was the anti-drug trafficking team with 'NDLEA' printed across their bulletproof vests. The idea that people would carry criminal-level quantities of hard drugs on them, knowing they'll drive past cops is something I struggle to understand. Fourteen minutes later was the Immigration, Customs and Excise team. They checked ID, confirmed our vehicle wasn't smuggled across the border and the relevant taxes were paid for its purchase. Now, we're driving past the Road Safety officials, who are in a combined task force with the police, to check for armed robbers, kidnappers and terrorists. Their process defies logic since it's hard to imagine any of these groups advertising their trade on the roads.

'Only sometimes?' Chika answers cynically, as he presses on the gas to make up for time lost at the three checkpoints.

It hadn't taken much to convince him to come with me on the trip. Folake and Onyinye had given their blessings. They'd rather we are together than everyone worrying about my American arse bumming around the ancient city,

292

trying to retrace the late Sade Dawodu's steps on the day she was supposed to have gone 'missing'.

'The timing is not adding up,' I mused aloud to Chika while explaining why a phone call to Dr Raimi won't do. 'Professor Ohaeri said Sade visited him several times in Ibadan. But not three weeks ago. Yet her mum said Sade explicitly said she went to Ibadan. Enomo claimed he dropped her in some hotel there, but he can't recall the name.'

Chika had snorted. 'We always knew that one was lying.'

'Yes, but why is everyone linked to that place? Even Bello went to the university there with her.'

'So, you think the person she might have been blackmailing on the list is there?'

'Not really. I want to recreate the trajectory of events. If she left for Ibadan in the morning, and let's assume Enomo left her there, who did she meet there and how did she get back to Lagos in time to jump into the Lekki Lagoon?'

Chika made a disgruntled sound. 'You and your obsession with recreating timelines.'

I smiled. Unrepentant. While investigating the Okriki Three case, he'd questioned my insistence on walking in the victims' shoes as they were marched to their deaths by an angry mob. Several times too, and each time with my stopwatch. I've no regrets.

'No one on that list lives or does business in Ibadan,' he'd continued, but I knew it was a done deal. He was coming along. 'Me, I say rough Enomo up a bit, and he'll sing about everything that happened that day, in soprano too.'

'To be honest, it's Bello I'd rather rough up.' As much as I detest dirty cops – and I've come across a good number in my career – figuring out Bello's motivation for his subterfuge has kept me awake since I discovered he knew Sade Dawodu. Yet Abubakar insists I can't question the detective until I have more proof. Frustrating.

We are now well past the midpoint between Lagos and Ibadan, but it seems we've been driving forever. Only farms and forests line the roadside. Occasionally, we pass subsistence farmers with yams, bananas and other fresh produce for sale, but otherwise the drive is uneventful.

Despite being a thoroughbred Lagosian, Chika seems to know his way around the city. I'm struck by how little has changed in the three decades since I was last in Ibadan. The rusted rooftops, tarred roads giving way to brown earth with such ease, you'd be forgiven to think they were planned that way.

'My dad used to joke that Ibadan must have the best mechanics in the world,' I comment as we stop at a traffic light, next to a car that must have once been a Nissan – at least from the logo on the front grill – but is now a mishmash of parts from other Japanese car brands. I can guarantee the engine has long forgotten its origins.

'Ibadan people never let anything go to waste,' Chika says, as he makes a turn under a bridge, past a busy bus stop and then on to a relatively free highway in the direction of the University of Ibadan.

The message comes as we follow the GPS instructions to the address Professor Ohaeri gave us.

This is who you're protecting. The text is followed by a rather large video file.

'Open it,' Chika says, as he brings the car to a slow stop on the roadside, not too far from the neighbourhood where Dr Raimi's practice is located. He reaches for his phone and dials. 'Calling my tech guy before they switch off again.'

I open the file, and at first, I'm confused. It starts off as a series of soundbites from Dawodu's sermons.

'Touch not my anointed, but today I say to you, He has lifted His anointed above all touch. Today, His anointed has been lifted to sit next to him, to reign here on earth as He reigns in heaven.'

'Ol' boy, the phone is on again, o. Hurry before it goes off,' Chika says. 'Yes, I know, I know. Just hurry.' He hangs up and turns to me.

'It's just a montage of sermons,' I say, frowning.

Chika leans closer and watches with me.

Another extract from a sermon. 'I am God here on earth. The one He has given all His powers to have dominion here on earth.'

It's less than three minutes of quotes like this. Different sermons pieced together like a promotional video of Dawodu and his ministry.

'Ah. That's it!' I exclaim.

'What am I missing?' Chika asks drily.

'This is the *real* Jeremiah Dawodu. A narcissistic preacher who's lifted himself to the level of God. That's what the sender is saying. He's not a man of God. He's presenting *himself* as God.'

'Hardly news. Most of these new-age pastors act like demigods. Most of them are not well here.' He taps the side of his head.

'Don't you see? They *act*. Dawodu is not acting.'

'But, Oga,' Chika starts with his moniker for me when he disagrees but is willing to keep an open mind, 'these

295

are quotes taken out of context. Shouldn't we listen to the sermons as a whole to get the full picture?'

'I think this video was spliced together to save us the trouble. This is the man Sade Dawodu married, lived with and experienced. The bishop the world doesn't know.'

'But you knew this. The money laundering, the bigamy, the lies—'

'Yes, yes, but they,' I point at my mobile phone screen, 'don't know I know.'

I press play again. The video is well put together. There's a seamless transition between sermons. It must have taken a significant amount of time to watch, isolate the selected quote, and then piece each one together with the others. Only a professional could do this. I recall Enomo's studio. The equipment and software for recording and mixing. For *editing*.

'Check with your tech guy again,' I say to Chika.

He shakes his head. 'He'll get irritated. If he finds something, he'll call. Let's go to—'

My phone beeps and glows. This time no message accompanies the files.

I open the PDF files. The marriage licence and the full court resolution to dissolve the marriage between LaTanya and Dawodu. The third is a marriage licence issued at the Ikoyi Registry to Jeremiah Dawodu and Folasade Bucknor. The date on the licence is 29 May 2013.

'She knew?' Chika asks.

'Seems like it. Although we don't know when she knew.'

'She doesn't strike me as someone who'd be complicit in bigamy,' Chika says.

'Kenny told me Sade's mum left her husband because she could not reconcile her Christianity with being in a polygamous marriage. I don't think Sade would stay married to Dawodu if she knew about LaTanya or that Mrs Bucknor would even allow it.'

'Plus, what would happen if the church knew? I am thinking again that your first lady knew enough to bring that bishop down. And hard.'

'Is that why they sent this to me?' I look at the screen again, and swipe on the PDFs as if they contained coded messages that I'm missing. 'What does it mean? That LaTanya and the bishop killed her? Perhaps this was their motivation and not the list?'

Chika's phone beeps. He looks at it, frowns and turns the screen to face me. It is a screenshot of a map with a neighbourhood circled with a red felt pen. Anthony Village. The neighbourhood where Enomo Collins' studio is located.

'Looks like Lagos is where we should be, not Ibadan,' Chika says wryly as he drives back onto the road.

'In 1.5 kilometres, turn left,' the disembodied voice of the GPS commands.

I hate to admit he might be right. It's too late, anyway. We are here already. Might as well find out what brought Sade Dawodu to this university town, a decade after she graduated and several times in the months leading to her death.

THE GOOD DOCTOR

Although Dr Lukman Raimi's medical practice is situated in the popular suburb of Agbowo, it is not meant to be seen or easily recognised. The sign identifying it as Shalom Maternity Clinic is no more than an A4-size piece of cardboard stuck on the closed gates of an unpainted building that looks uncompleted but well maintained.

'How is this a clinic?' I ask, bemused.

'It is, just not the legal kind,' Chika informs me, deadpan.

He pounds on the gates. I look around. Several beer parlours and motels line either side of the untarred road. I suspect the whole street becomes a red-light district when night falls.

'Who you be?' a voice barks from a square pigeonhole in the metal gates. All we can see is a round chin, ill-kept teeth and the lower third of a nose.

'We get appointment with Dr Raimi, o,' Chika announces.

'Dr Raimi no dey treat man, o. You no be man?' the guard asks, suspicious.

'Tell am say na Professor Ohaeri for UCH send us.'

The hole closes abruptly.

Across the street, there is a rundown building housing a beer parlour already filled with patrons. On the roof, there's a crudely made sign designating it as 'Cool Spot Hotel & Bar'. Two women of indeterminate age wave at us, unenthusiastic but hopeful. I turn back to the gate quickly. Chika chuckles at my discomfort.

'I think you're right,' I whisper to him.

'I *know* I'm right.'

The gate opens. The guard is a dark-skinned, short man with tribal marks lining his face.

'He say make you come for back,' he says and apparently expects us to know where 'back' is, since he returns to his post and lowers himself onto a mat. He picks up the open Quran and begins caressing the prayer beads he was using as a bookmark.

The front door is protected by metal, burglary proof and padlocked. We pause for a beat, Chika's eyes dart left and right, trying to figure out which side would lead to the back access into the building. He points to the right. I follow him, peering discreetly through the open windows that line the wall. I can make out the faces of women seated on long benches. About four or five are in view. There may be more. They look tired and nervous, all are staring straight ahead. Waiting.

The back entrance takes us through what would have been the kitchen. There's a nurse arranging pills into several cups. She doesn't look up from her task as she points to a door leading to what would have been a bedroom but is now an office.

When Dr Lukman Raimi rises from behind a desk in front of a wall lined with posters of the female reproductive health system, waves of tobacco hit me as he bends towards me, his hand outstretched. The man's handshake is firm but his eyes are cautious.

'Prof Ohaeri told me you'd come.'

'Thank you for seeing us,' I say politely and introduce Chika as my associate.

'Prof is a great supporter of what we do here.' Dr Raimi walks round the desk to clear textbooks and papers off the chairs and invites us to sit.

'What work is that, sir?' Chika asks innocently. My eyes rest on framed certificates on the wall. The calligraphy is in Russian.

'He didn't tell you?' Dr Raimi seems surprised, then shrugs. 'Of course, he didn't. That's Prof for you.' He looks from Chika to me; his aura becomes defensive. 'I don't know why you're here, sirs, but the services we offer here are not allowed by law. However, I feel it is my calling to help these women.'

'Help them?' Chika asks, his tone is soft, unthreatening, as if he genuinely wants to know.

'Yes, help,' Dr Raimi says to him, firm but less tense. He turns to me. 'Abortion is illegal in this country, yet do you know how many women are victims of rape, or feel compelled to commit infanticide because they cannot feed their child?'

Being situated in the middle of a red-light district cannot be bad for business, I think, wondering how desperate Sade Dawodu must have been to come to a place like this. I know of such places in the US. Many existed in states that had found ways to circumvent Roe vs Wade and suppress abortion rights. Knowing a place like Shalom Maternity Clinic is the only option available to women in Nigeria makes me sad and angry at the same time. It's not the doctor's fault, but I believe women deserve better.

'Our services are discreet,' Dr Raimi is saying, slightly more relaxed now that he senses a lack of judgement from us. 'We also offer post-surgery consultations which many other clinics like ours don't.'

'Was that why this woman came here?' I pass my phone across the desk. Sade Dawodu's picture fills the screen.

Dr Raimi gives the image a fleeting glance and looks back at me. 'I know who she is, Dr Taiwo. Which was all the more reason I understood her need for discretion.'

'But why you? There must be other clinics offering the same services,' I ask, not adding what we must all be thinking – with better facilities.

'Look,' – Dr Raimi's face hardens, and he points his index finger from Chika to me – 'I'm going to tell you everything I know on the condition you don't come back here. Everyone knows what happened to her and I don't want any kind of attention. You understand?'

Chika and I nod. Fair enough.

Dr Raimi takes a deep breath, as if considering where to start. 'Because of the kind of clinic I run, I'm not bound by the same oath a doctor like Prof Ohaeri is. My responsibility is to my clinic, the women who come here, and to keeping myself and my team out of jail. You understand?'

We nod again. Dr Raimi sits back in his chair and seems satisfied with the rules of engagement.

'So, why me? Because some years ago, her mother brought her here for an abortion. The young woman was an undergraduate and the mother was determined her daughter wouldn't have a child out of wedlock. She claimed they couldn't afford it. I didn't believe her, of course. In my position, I have seen many women in dire financial straits.

Mrs Bucknor – I only recently found out her real name – didn't fit any image of the poor. But I could see her daughter was desperate, and that she was already suffering from a lot of guilt. Even then, her mother's religious nature was clear. I've seen a lot of mothers like this. The sin of adultery can be forgiven if there is no evidence of the indiscretion. If I refuse to do the abortion, they would have gone somewhere else, perhaps a place even less safe. The mother looked like the type. So, I did it.'

'You're sure it's the same person?' I ask.

'I get a lot of patients, but it's not every day someone like that walks through here. The mother clearly wanted this to happen in the most obscure place possible. I asked few questions, but I remembered both of them because I knew they did not belong here. They could afford better.'

'This was when?' I ask.

The doctor frowns. 'She was an undergrad then. But, honestly, I can't remember the year. But definitely over a decade ago. Like I told you, I don't keep files and well, Mrs Dawodu knew that which is why she came to me again.'

'If she knew you, why did she need Prof Ohaeri's referral?'

'Because when she came to me again, ten months ago, she wanted something I couldn't do in good conscience. I knew who her husband was. She wanted an abortion and a tubal ligation.' He pauses, looks at us like he expects a question. I give him a 'continue' nod. 'I didn't have a problem with the abortion. I just assumed as a pastor's wife, she had had an affair. But I baulked at the request for permanent sterilisation for a healthy woman of childbearing age.'

'Did you ask her why she wanted it?' I ask, grateful he is forthcoming enough not to warrant beating about the bush.

302

Dr Raimi nods. 'I did. She insisted it was a valid choice. I told her that to do what she wanted, I'd need her husband's consent. After all, if she changed her mind later, who's to say my whole operation wouldn't be held liable if the spouse came after me?'

'So, she came back with a psychiatric evaluation?' I'm beginning to see how Sade Dawodu's mind worked.

'Actually, I suggested it. I told her if she could bring me concrete proof she'd gone through counselling and had undergone a proper evaluation of her state of mind, I'd do it without her husband's consent. It was still a risk for me, of course. But everything I do here is a risk.'

'So, she went to Prof Ohaeri,' Chika states.

Dr Raimi looks at him with a slight curve to his lips. 'Exactly. And he can't break confidentiality, which is why he sent you to me.'

Chika and I steal quick glances at each other. The late Sade Dawodu might be an enigma, but we now know she got whatever she wanted. By any means necessary.

'Besides, I don't keep records,' Dr Raimi reiterates. 'She knew this and so does Prof. Everything I tell you is off the record.'

'I understand,' I say. 'But tell me, when you saw her for this most recent surgery, what would you say was her state of mind?'

The doctor frowns, as if trying to recall a puzzling detail. 'You know I've seen many women over the years. Thousands, even. Many come in various states of distress. Desperate and unhappy. But not Mrs Dawodu on this second visit to the clinic.'

'How so?' Chika asks.

'That first time, she was young, and I could see her mother was pushing her. This time, she was older, and she knew exactly what she wanted. Even when I told her I needed a psychiatric evaluation, she said she would get it and doubled my fee when I finally agreed to do it. She only insisted on my discretion. In fact, she was so determined to ensure her visit here was not on record that she paid me cash. She sat where you are now, and her driver handed me the Ghana-must-go bag, filled with cash.'

Chika and I say nothing, but I'm sure we're thinking the same thing. Now we know why Dr Raimi's name didn't feature on Sade Dawodu's bank statements. At least one riddle solved.

'Driver? She didn't come alone?' Chika asks.

Dr Raimi shakes his head. 'She claimed he was her driver but he didn't look like a driver. I just assumed the guy was the baby's father.'

Chika makes quick swipes on his mobile phone and slides it towards Dr Raimi. 'Was it this guy?'

Dr Raimi frowns again. 'I'm not sure, but it looks like him. Isn't that the singer?' Dr Raimi's eyes widen. 'It is him. I didn't make the connection then, but I see it now.' He looks at us, more confident. 'That's the guy she came with.'

I don't have to look at the picture to know who Chika's showing Dr Raimi.

Enomo Collins.

THE CLEANSING

We were two years married before I told him about the abortion. Looking back, I don't know what possessed me to confess a past that had nothing to do with our present. Perhaps I thought it would bring us closer, create an intimacy that was missing in our marriage. Or maybe I felt like the wall between us was not because my husband would only touch me in public, flashing affectionate smiles for the congregation and the cameras, but never when we were alone. Was he able to discern that I had a secret which prevented him from loving me the way I needed to be loved?

I thought if I opened up to him, that he, as my husband and spiritual father, would take me in his arms and tell me old things were passed away, and all things, including our marriage, were made new.

How gullible I was! At first, he only asked us to pray and beseech his god to forgive my sin of murder. That's what he called it. Murder. Even when I told him it happened at university, when I confused sex for love. When my self-esteem was low and I was desperate for someone to show me that I was worthy of something other than failure.

He wanted to know about the baby's father. How old? How tall? Dark or light? What tribe? Where is he now? How was the sex? Everything had to be confessed for the cleansing of my past, so I could embrace a holy present.

I answered truthfully, wanting no more secrets between us. Praying that soon the questions would end.

They didn't. He moved into the guest room to intercede on my behalf. My sin was so grave, it required a time of separation.

When will I know I have been forgiven? I once asked, although what my heart wanted to know was if I was still worthy of love.

I will let you know, my husband said and proceeded with the inquisition. How many times did I have sex? When did I know I was pregnant? Who did I tell? Who took me for the abortion? How did I feel after?

To break the cycle of confession and penance, I started lying. Instead of saying I loved the baby's father, I said I now see it was lust. The relief I felt when we decided we were not ready to be parents is now an admission of my sin of selfishness. In time, the lies ended my reliving a painful past but brought judgement. I am soiled and damaged. A blight on the holy ground of our home and the church.

I prayed, fasted and begged for forgiveness of my transgressions. To be made worthy of my husband's love. It was months before my husband declared me forgiven and moved back to our bedroom. But with conditions.

I must bathe with holy water before coming to bed. He will not touch me unless I am ovulating. I cannot touch him when I am on my period.

It was all for my own good. To keep my flesh under submission. To be pure. Cleansed. After all, I am the Bride of the Church. The First Lady.

I believed him.

ARMED AND DANGEROUS

The checkpoint is unmanned, its mismatch of rusty metal drums, battered jerrycans, tree stumps, old tyres and dust-coated tarpaulin shading abandoned.

'Strange,' Chika says, scowling at the rear-view mirror as Ibadan retreats behind us.

'Maybe they moved to another spot?' I suggest, also surprised but grateful for the time saved. 'Or went to lunch?'

'Maybe,' he says with a frown. 'Normally, this one is a SARS point, so …'

The Special Anti-Robbery Squad is notorious for harassing innocent citizens. Abubakar had once admitted to me – bitter and resigned – that SARS' activities are less about curbing violent crimes than providing steady cash flow for an underfunded police force. Chika is right to be concerned. There must be something wrong if this hub of extortion is left unattended.

I'm the first to notice the vehicle behind us. There's something familiar about it, and the covered number plate worries me. We're on the highway, with several cars zipping past and only slowing down when they approach a pothole or the occasional broken-down truck.

'Slow down,' I say.

'Why?' Chika asks but he's already easing up.

'Not completely,' I say, squinting at the VW van through the side mirror.

Every car overtakes us but the VW. It hits me. The metallic grey van might have been hard to make out in the dark when Ewang's body was thrown out of it, but in broad daylight, there's no mistaking it.

'Oh,' Chika says, ever quick on the uptake. His side-eye has picked up what I'm looking at. Squinting into the rearview mirror, he increases our speed. The VW follows suit, gaining ground too quickly to be anything but threatening.

'I don't have a good feeling,' Chika says, his expression set in stone as he steps on the gas again.

'Neither do I.' Now's not the time to tell him about my first sighting of the van. 'How quickly can we get to the next checkpoint?'

'Not sure we'll get much help there. I think there's a reason the previous one was not manned. See the covered number plate? That's some serious shit.'

'They cleared the road of the police to chase us?'

'Let's hope they're just— Move your head!'

I twist to the left. Sharp. Shots ring out. My side mirror shatters. Chika starts weaving from one side of the road to the other. But this also reduces our speed, making it easier for the VW to get closer. So close that when I look to my right side, I'm staring at the barrel of a gun.

I duck. 'Down!'

Split seconds later, a round of bullets hits the side of the car. There's a sudden, loud pop, then hiss. One of our tyres has been hit.

Chika's hand reaches under his seat. 'Hold the wheel!'

Crouched below window level, I grab the steering. Chika pulls a handgun from under the driver's seat and aims over my head.

The explosion feels like it happened inside my head. He fires three more rounds. Chika's elbows send electric shocks down my back. Tyres screech.

Chika twists his body. The VW must have fallen behind or careened off the road. Chika doesn't miss.

'Can you use it?' Chika asks, as he squeezes out another shot over my bent body.

I sit upright as he takes the wheel from me. Glock 20. Not a fan. I look back. The VW is far behind. I nod. Chika hands me the gun, his eyes on the road.

'Tyres are run-flat but not for long. Don't worry if you miss. Just create distance.'

I check the gun. Chika fired what? Five rounds? Maybe ten rounds left. I close the chambers. Ready.

The VW comes back into view. All the other cars have fallen behind. No one wants to be caught in a crossfire. Even the traffic on the other side has ceased. The road is emptied, creating the perfect conditions for an execution. The chugging sound of the blown tyre is getting louder, and the Pajero's wheels wobble.

I lean out to aim, but the VW pulls back, hiding behind the Pajero. I lean out further and aim for its left front wheel. I'm thrown by the recoil. The shock to my shoulder and arm throws off my aim. The VW is right behind us, gaining ground.

'Shoot the glass!' Chika commands. 'Push them back.'

I turn, ready for impact, and pull the trigger. The Pajero's rear window shatters.

'Aim for the tyres!' Chika shouts.

I miss, but hit the headlights, causing the driver to veer to the left. I fire three more rounds. I need to hit one tyre at least to slow it down. Three, at most four more rounds to go before the Glock empties. I aim again, but the VW is using Chika's old trick, veering from one side of the road to the other. I squint, following the van's motion with the gun, ready to fire.

A sudden swerve. My head hits the roof. I lose a bullet to the air. I realise what Chika has done. He's turned the car into the bushes that line the side of the highway.

The car bumps up and down a narrow, unbeaten path. Thick bush greets us and stretches out so far that it's like we've landed on a green jungle. I look back. The VW is out of view, obscured by foliage. I face forward and hold on to the dashboard. Tall grasses prostrate under the 4x4's onslaught. Tree branches poke their way through the broken windows. I'm drenched in sweat.

I look back again. The Pajero has made a clear path through. It won't be long before the VW follows.

Chika brings the car to a stop. I look around. Nothing but bush. Then, back at him. What now?

His eyes are wild. He points his thumb towards where we came. 'You go that way.' Then to his right. 'I go this way.'

I'm trying to figure out the plan when he reaches across me to open the glovebox. He pulls out a .45 and rolls the chambers. Full. He hands it to me.

'I'll reload this one,' he says and takes the Glock from me. 'Go! Go! Go!'

I jump out, run into the bush, moving parallel to our cleared path, towards the sound of the oncoming VW. I look back just as Chika plunges a knife into the Pajero's rear tyre.

I run faster. I can hear the sound of the bus coming towards me. I crouch low, so the tall bushes cover me. I must trust Chika's instinct. Our pursuers need to think we ran off for help. The VW drives past me. I slow my pace. When the engine sound recedes enough, I stop, turn towards our car and bend low.

The VW parks next to the Pajero. Two men get out. Their gait, the way they hold the guns and the sharp turns of their heads betray military training. Looking for signs of life. Ready to kill.

'Find them!' the driver shouts from behind the wheel. 'Hurry!'

The two gunmen walk around the battered Pajero. One checks the tyres. They exchange hand signals. One points left, the other right. Both move forward, away from the car.

I wait. My heart beats loud in my ears. Please come out. Please—

The driver comes out, his gun cocked. Shades cover a large part of his face but there's something about him. The way he walks, kicking the Pajero's good tyres, then bends low to check the wheel. His face now in full view.

Samson Adamu!

Dawodu's security guard. He turns in my direction. Waits. Did I gasp aloud? I sink lower into the muddy ground. Samson points his gun and starts to walk in my direction. I check the .45 in my hand. Should I fire? What if I miss? I aim for his knees through the grass and trees.

Another pair of feet appears behind Samson's. I look up just as Chika hits the man with the butt of the Glock.

I leap to my feet, looking out for the other two assailants. I walk slowly towards the VW, gun cocked, heart pounding. Chika is faster. He drags Samson inside and gets in the driver's seat.

I start running towards him just as he reverses in the direction of the highway. I jump into the back. A bullet whips past my left ear. The sound of the moving car must have brought back the two men. I brace for impact for when Chika turns the VW towards the road.

He doesn't. He keeps reversing and shooting at the men running towards us. I can't stay steady enough to stand. I kneel and aim. I miss but slow the men's progress enough to allow me to pull the sliding door.

A groan comes from behind me just as it slams shut.

'Shoot him!' Chika shouts.

I turn. A bloodied Samson is stirring.

Chika is still reversing through the bush, shooting. Gunshots whip past, some hit the VW. I can't steady myself. Too much movement. I am dizzy.

'Shoot him!' Chika orders through clenched teeth. His voice comes from faraway, like an echo.

Everything is blurry. I can't steady myself. Something is pulling at me. I look down. Samson's bloody face stares at me, wild. He jerks at my leg, destabilising me.

'Shoot him!' Now Chika's voice is too loud. Everything is too loud. My heartbeat. The sound of gunshots reverberating in my head. The revving of the car's engine. The angry growl from the man gripping my ankle.

I raise the .45 and slam the butt straight into the space between Samson Adamu's eyes.

HOSTAGE SITUATION

Chika drives the VW onto the highway without checking for oncoming traffic. We speed away from loud horns and cars swerving off the road to avoid collisions. He keeps changing lanes, checking the rear-view mirror. The irritated honking of the other cars is reassuring. We're not being followed.

I glance from the road to Samson's prone body – if that's his real name. The man is still bleeding from his forehead, so I move towards him to—

'I hope you're not playing Mother Theresa.' Chika's grim voice stops me. His gaze holds a warning in the rear-view mirror.

I look around the VW, and find jump-start cables under the seat. They are not long enough but they'll do. I separate the cables to bind Samson's ankles and wrists. The metal ends will bite into his flesh and leave nasty bruises, but that will be the least of his problems when he wakes. I pull his legs up to tie the cables around his ankles. A mobile phone falls from his pocket. I reach for it. A Huawei. Sleek and slim. Not cheap. The screen is blank. Locked. I slip it into my pocket.

The gash on Samson's forehead appears deep. I unbutton my shirt and pull off my vest. I can feel Chika's disapproval

313

so I avoid looking in his direction. I wipe the blood off Samson's face with my vest. Blood cleaned off, I'm relieved to see the wound is not as bad as I feared and won't require stitching. I tear the vest into two strips, then wrap them around the assassin's head.

I'm almost done when Chika brings the van to a stop. He's chosen a place that straddles a weather-beaten path into the adjacent forest, shielding us from the direct view of oncoming traffic.

I hurriedly button up my shirt just as Chika gets out and walks to the front. I pull open the sliding door and join him just as he rips off the black cloth covering the number plate.

'It would draw unnecessary attention,' Chika says, as he walks around the car, leans in to check Samson is as tightly restrained as he looks, then to the rear to expose the other number plate.

I step back as Chika pulls open the back door. Bags, old clothes, Styrofoam cups and empty bottles of liquor litter it. The spare tyre lies on its side, out of its mount. He dumps it on the ground.

I take out the synthetic floor mats. An arsenal of handguns and bullets are carefully arranged in the hollow where the spare tyre should be.

'They meant business,' Chika says ruefully, picking out a hand gun and checking the chamber. Loaded. He turns his back to the highway and slots the gun into his waistband.

I'm not touching a gun again today.

My eyes catch a rectangular flat glass screen under the weapons. It's a mobile phone, a high-end Samsung Galaxy. I turn it on while Chika hurriedly puts the mats over the guns, walks round the van and throws some of the old clothes over Samson. Save for the makeshift bandage around his head, the man now looks like a passenger taking a nap.

A passing car slows, ostensibly to offer help. I wave the driver off with a thumbs-up sign. The phone is on. While it needs a code to open, the screensaver is a colourful picture of Victor Ewang, his wife and three young children. I walk over to Chika and hand it to him just as Samson stirs, dislodging the clothes covering his restraints and stopping whatever Chika was about to say about the handset. Chika jumps into the van and knocks him out with a punch so hard I hear a bone crack. The assassin goes out cold.

I pull the sliding door closed and get into the passenger seat just as Chika hops in.

'It's the same van,' I say. 'The one they threw Ewang's body from.'

Chika nods as he starts the engine, his expression implacable. 'I'd be surprised if it wasn't.'

At all the checkpoints, Chika has a 1,000 Naira note ready, his face impassive as he holds out his left hand through the window. The officers grasp his clenched fist and only release it after the exchange. Two more checkpoints later and a quick stop at an ATM to replenish cash for the rest of the trip to Lagos and we're home free.

*

Chika's team has left for the day, so the open-plan office is empty when we drag Samson out and drop him on the floor.

He starts to struggle against his restraints. His attempt to speak is cut off by Chika's sharp slap and one firm hand placed over his mouth.

'Paper,' Chika points to a nearby printer.

I grab paper off the printer. Chika makes a fist with his free hand and when it seems Samson is about to bite him, he simply removes his hand, slaps the man, takes the paper, now squeezed into a ball, and forces it into Samson's mouth. He then strips him to the waist and pulls him onto a nearby swivel chair. Chika looks around the room full of computers, servers, and all the paraphernalia of his tech trade. He walks over to one of the desktop computers and yanks the power cord off. He points to another computer, and I rush over to it, praying I don't pull out any wires that will cause undue damage.

Chika replaces the jump-start cables with the two power cords. He works fast and efficiently, leaving me feeling rather extraneous. Samson grunts. This time, when he makes like he wants to talk, Chika slaps his mouth open, removes the ball of paper and replaces it with the bloody shirt he just took off him.

He does all this in silence, with a cold precision that appals and impresses all at once.

*

'No!' I say with as much force as I can muster, my voice amplified by the acoustics of the open-plan office.

'You'd prefer we hand him to the police?' Chika's tone is ironic, ridiculing my horror at his plan.

'I'm sure Abubakar will help us—'

Chika points at Samson, bound in the chair. 'That guy and his gang were sent to execute us because of information we've on some very powerful people, Philip. I'm afraid even your commandant can't help us.'

'We can't solve a crime by committing one ourselves,' I protest as Chika checks the restraints.

'I'm not asking you to do anything.' His gaze is fixed on our bloodied hostage.

'I'll be an accomplice regardless.'

Chika walks to me, his eyes fiery. 'Phil, we almost didn't make it back to our families alive.'

'I know—'

'I don't think it has quite sunk in.' Chika taps my temple. 'This guy was going to kill you. In cold blood. They cleared police checkpoints, Phil. And if we were followed, where do you think they followed us from?'

I throw a horrified glance at Samson. His eyes shoot daggers at me as he strains against his bindings. Chika is right. They must have followed us from his house. Where our families are.

'Why didn't they attack us there, at your house, you know, here in Lagos?' I ask, thankful this wasn't the case but needing to know. 'Why follow us all the way to Ibadan?'

Chika shrugs as if the answer is a no-brainer. 'They wanted to know what lead we were following. To be sure there are no loose ends. I'm guessing they are also wondering what connection Ibadan has to everything that's happened. When they saw we only visited a back-alley abortion clinic, they figured there was no reason to wait. Besides, an out-of-town hit is a lot less suspicious than one done at my doorstep.'

Makes blood-curdling sense. I sink into the nearest chair in momentary relief. In the States, my choices would be clear. I'd hand myself into protective custody while trained officers interrogate Samson. My family would be taken to a safe place while I worked with investigators to find out who ordered my execution. But here, with all I know about how Sade Dawodu and Victor Ewang died, I've no one to turn to but Chika.

'Don't worry,' he says, reading me as accurately as only he can in such circumstances. 'The house is well protected by armed guards. I called in a favour from an old colleague. Everyone is fine.' He waves his mobile phone. 'I'll know if a bird flies into that compound.'

I lower my voice. 'You can't kill him. I won't let you.'

Chika doesn't lower his. He wants Samson to hear. 'Then you better convince him to tell me what I want to know.'

My phone rings. Folake. I walk away from Chika and answer it.

'Sorry. I should've called,' I say, trying to keep my voice level.

'It's fine. I was just worried. When are you getting home? Onyinye is worried too.'

'It's safer not to be home right now.' I try to sound offhand.

'What happened?' she asks sharply.

'Nothing major,' I say, walking further away from the racket Samson is making, groaning into his gag and strug-gling to free himself. 'I mean, we need to sort some things out before coming home.' I think quickly. A blanket answer like that will not allay Folake's fears. A version of the truth is in order. 'We think we are being followed, so Chika suggests we lie low in his office until we are sure, and not risk being followed to the house.'

'Good heavens. Are you okay? Are you with Chika?'

'Yes and I'm fine. Just waiting to be sure—'

'And he's fine?'

I look over at Chika, bent over our hostage – no other word for it. He slaps the guy a few times and grabs him around the neck.

'He's fine,' I say to Folake, praying she won't ask to speak with him.

'Tell him to call home,' she says. 'And you, you better come back here safe.'

She hangs up before I make promises I'm no longer sure I can keep. I walk back to where Chika is bent over Samson Adamu.

'Let me introduce myself,' Chika is saying to him like he's relaying the scores of a boring football match. 'My name is Chika Makuochi. In a previous life, I was a soldier available to the highest bidder. I've fought in wars and been a prisoner in a Yemeni prison for almost three years. This means I know at least a hundred ways to make you wish one of my bullets had split your skull open on that road.'

Samson struggles wildly. He is ready to crack Chika's skull.

'I'm going to take the gag out,' Chika continues calmly, 'and we'll start nice and slow.' He speaks softly, bent over Samson whose nose is bloodied and brow shines with sweat. Despite his defiant expression, I can tell he's scared. Chika does that to you.

'We will start with your name. Ready?' Chika takes out the shirt from the man's mouth. 'Your real name?'

Samson spits out blood, his eyes fiery as he looks past Chika, straight at me. 'You've messed with the wrong guy!'

Chika lands a blow on the man's chin. 'Wrong answer.'

The thug laughs, a manic, bloody grin reminiscent of Jack Nicholson's face on the poster of *The Shining*. 'You're both finished. They'll look for me.'

The pidgin and everything Samson told us at Dawodu's house was an act. Chika was right. They'd agreed on a story. The real night guard might have been one of the workers who Sade Dawodu gave the day off.

Samson struggles against the restraints again. 'Release me now! You don't know who you're messing with! They'll find me and—'

Chika is unimpressed. 'Oh, I'm banking on it. The thing is, you get to decide what they find. A dead body or one who wishes he was dead.'

'They'll finish you,' Samson says with considerably less bluster.

'You're boring me. You know what?' Chika rises up, casual and lethal. 'Let's forget the introductions. Tell me who will find and finish me.'

'You'll see,' the man promises but his grin lacks its former conviction.

Chika raises his fist again, and I've had enough. This is a hired hand. It's only a matter of time before he starts singing. Time we don't have.

'Chika!' My tone stalls the connection of fist with chin. I hand over the Huawei. 'I took this off him. If we know who he's been calling ...'

Chika takes the phone and turns to the bound man. 'You wan open am for me?'

He doesn't wait for an answer. He bends to take the bound right hand, and presses a thumb to the phone. He rises and waves the active screen at the struggling man.

I move close as Chika makes some clicks and gets to the 'calls received' menu. He hands the phone to me and walks back to the man.

'I see you made many calls to your "American Madam" today.'

LaTanya Jacobson. She ordered the hit. With Dawodu's blessing, of course. The coward is too 'godly' to get his hands dirty.

Chika goes to the cupboard in the corner and brings out a toolbox. He spreads out the contents on the floor. Slowly and deliberately. Samson is trying to hide it, but he's getting scared. I recall Ewang's autopsy report. I suspect Samson knows more than most what a screwdriver or hammer can do to the human body. The sweat is pouring down his face onto his chest, but a calm is settling in his feverish eyes. He'll break before Chika uses a single tool on him.

I call for an Uber.

NIGHTCRAWL

'At this time?' Kenny's worry makes me impatient.

'It's barely 7 p.m.' I'm not sorry for my brusque tone. Not after the day I've had.

'Yes, but it's late and I don't know if ...'

I pray for strength as the Uber descends the Third Mainland Bridge. I can't tell my sister I'm already on my way to Sade's mum's house and this call is merely a courtesy.

'You're the last person who should consider my wanting to see the victim's mother as an imposition,' I snap out, in no mood to play nice.

Kenny gets it. 'I'll tell her to expect you.'

I hang up and dial Abubakar.

Our pleasantries are brief. He knows I wouldn't call him at this time if it wasn't urgent.

'I think it's time we talk to Bello before things get out of hand and blow up in the face of the force.'

'Do you have more proof?' Abubakar asks, his tone indicating he has no interest if I don't.

'Apart from proof he knew the victim longer than he claimed? No.'

Abubakar exhales loudly. I picture a halo of cigarette smoke over his head. 'Okay. But let me be the one to talk to him first.'

'You think he'll see you today?'

'You mean tonight?'

What's everyone's sudden obsession with how late in the day it is? 'Yes, tonight.'

'I'll let you know,' Abubakar says brusquely and hangs up.

I'm grateful the Uber driver is not the chatty type. He only asks me if the GPS directions are on track. I confirm this as we turn into Mrs Bucknor's neighbourhood. There are some cars parked inside and outside of the compound, which means she is not alone.

As if on cue, my phone thrums as I enter. Kenny. *She's expecting you.*

Mrs Bucknor stands up as soon as I walk into the living room. She gives reassuring smiles to the women seated around her and waves me over.

'Let's talk there.' She points.

I follow her into a large kitchen where two teenage girls are washing plates at the sink. They stop as soon as they see us.

'It's fine. We want to talk,' Mrs Bucknor says, as they dry their hands and scamper out.

I wait a bit, to be sure we're alone. Mrs Bucknor raises an eyebrow, much more composed than my first visit here.

'Why didn't you tell me about Professor Ohaeri?'

The surprise on the older woman's face swiftly becomes irritation.

'How did you find out about him?'

'I asked if you knew him, and you said no. Why?'

Her face becomes the picture of defiance; her tone, matter-of-fact. 'Because he's a psychiatrist and I didn't want my daughter's memory tainted.'

A rehearsed line. 'There's nothing wrong with needing help with mental health,' I say.

'Maybe where you come from, Dr Taiwo, but not here,' she replies, her smile bitter. 'How is your Yoruba?'

'Good enough.'

'So, you know the saying: "wèrè dùn wò l'ójà, kòsé bí lómo"?'

I nod, stemming my irritation at the meaning. A mad person is good for entertainment when they're not one's own child. A terrible indictment on how mental health is viewed.

'There's no way I'd let my daughter's medical history become entertainment. Or fodder for gossip.'

'Even if it might explain why she took her life?'

She hisses, unrepentant. 'All the more reason! Whatever made her do what she did, it had nothing to do with a doctor she saw when she was in her teens.'

'She went to see him again. Doesn't that mean something was wrong?'

'But she's gone now.' Mrs Bucknor's voice breaks and I feel bad for doing this. For even being here. 'If something was wrong, what can I do to fix it now? The only thing I can do is preserve the best parts of her. Protect her memory.'

'She never told you anything? Anything about her marriage, or if she found out something that would have made her choose to end her life?'

Mrs Bucknor's eyes well up with tears, and she turns away from me. 'A mother should know when something is wrong, but I didn't. I should have known.' Her shoulders start to heave, her hands start to shake. 'I'm her mother, and she chose to … to …'

It would be cruel to ask more questions, no matter how desperate I am for answers. So, I do the only thing I can. I watch Mrs Kikelomo Bucknor collapse in a nearby chair and weep for the daughter she lost. When I place a comforting hand on her shoulder, she shrugs it off. I step back.

'I want to be alone.' Despite the tears streaming down her face, her voice is cold.

*

I get the same taciturn Uber driver that delivered me to Mrs Bucknor's house less than half an hour earlier. Paranoia makes me cautious. I send my live location to Chika.

He calls immediately. 'Anything from the mother?'

'Nothing we can use.'

'And the transfers to her account?'

It's hard to explain why I couldn't press Mrs Bucknor for more information. The woman was at breaking point and I didn't want to be the one to push her over the edge. Besides, people at extreme spectra of emotions tend to be unreliable. I'd rather go with nothing than something I can't work with or verify.

'I didn't get there.' I trust Chika won't press further. 'And you? Any luck with, er, our guest?'

'We're making progress,' he says so loud I know he wants Samson to hear.

'Chika, careful,' I warn.

'No, *he* should be careful. I did manage to confirm that his name is really Samson Adamu. But, wait for it. He is ex-military.'

'Isn't he too young to be retired?'

'Depends on what he retired to do.'

True. Being a hired assassin pays better the military.

The Uber turns into Anthony Village, and the irony of getting so much more done at this time doesn't escape me. The light traffic at night is in stark contrast to the chaos Chika and I drove through from Ibadan.

'I am close to Enomo's place now.'

'Greet him for me. I've got some persuading to do.'

'Chi—' I start to say, but he's hung up.

*

Enomo Collins looks even more dishevelled than the last time I saw him. He stands in the doorway, unsurprised to see me. Without a word, he turns and walks into his studio. He dismisses the same dreadlocked, face-pierced young musicians I still can't tell apart. They give me curious stares as they scramble to save files on the computer, press buttons on the console that dim digital indicators, and then they're gone.

I walk around the little space, touching some of the equipment, ignoring him. Let him stew.

Enomo's eyes follow me. 'You don't strike me as a night-crawler, Dr Taiwo.'

I look him dead in the eye. 'You didn't leave her in Ibadan.'

'H-h-how do you know that—?' he sputters.

'Because that wasn't the first time you took her there and stayed with her. Dr Raimi can confirm it.'

'Your timeline is wrong. I took her to that clinic months ago.'

It takes enormous willpower not to step back from the alcohol on his breath.

'Who are you protecting, Enomo? She's dead.'

Enomo gives a bitter laugh. 'You think I don't know that?'

'Then why are you lying?'

'Because it's what she would have wanted!'

I know a man ready to unburden himself when I see one.

'Explain.' I keep my tone curt and authoritative. Let him wonder how much I know already.

Enomo sits on a sofa and holds his head in his hands.

I bring out my phone and dial. Enomo's rich baritone fills the room singing 'Endless Love'. Enomo raises his head sharply, confused. I turn the screen to him so he can see the number I'm calling. I click on the speaker as the customised ringtone goes to voicemail.

'You've reached Sade Dawodu. Please leave a—'

I cut it off.

'It's not what you think,' Enomo says softly. He looks defeated, yet strangely relieved.

'Whatever I think, it's not looking good for you.'

Instead of answering, Enomo reaches to the side of the sofa and lifts up a battered leather laptop bag. He digs into the side pocket and retrieves an envelope. He looks at it for a beat, then expels some air before handing it to me.

'Perhaps I should have given you this when you came the last time, I don't know. I didn't trust you enough, and well, you know, it was written to me and I guess I just wanted to hold on to it just a bit longer before,' – He buries his head in open palms – 'you know, sharing it with anyone.'

Enomo's name is scrawled across the envelope in a distinct, cursive handwriting. I lift the flap and bring out a piece of paper, read so many times, it's crumpled at the edges with smudged text indicating the spots where liquid – tears? – had fallen on it.

My love,
It's funny, isn't it? Just when I gave up on love, you came into my life. But I am sorry, I have nothing to give you. You deserve more.

When you get over your sadness about everything, you will see this is for your good. You are young and talented. You need someone who still believes in good and the idea of a god. That person is not me.

For the time you shared with me here, I can only say thank you.
Sade

I shake my head, looking from paper to Enomo. 'I don't understand.'

Enomo's smile is bitter and wistful all at once. 'We didn't go to Ibadan. Not on that day. I picked her up from her house and we came here. It was the first time we ...' His voice trails off. Then, after several seconds, he starts again, but this time soft and low, like he is speaking to himself.

'I didn't see it coming. I thought she was happy with me, that we were leaving together.'

I put the letter back in the envelope. 'That's why you helped her to set up the bloody scene at her house?'

Enomo doesn't seem to notice that I'm now sitting next to him on the sofa. He stares into space, hurting. 'She told me it was the best way to stop that man from coming after us.'

Perhaps I was wrong about Bello? 'So, who called the police?'

Enomo turns to me, his eyes so tortured, so raw that I've to steel myself not to look away. 'I don't know! I was here, wondering where she disappeared to, trying to understand what that letter meant, when I saw the news like everyone else. By then, it was too late. That was when I understood the letter. Even then, there was a part of me that hoped that the police would make the suspicion stick on her husband. Because even if he didn't push her into that lagoon, he sure as hell killed her!'

'Wait,' I say. 'Start from the beginning. When did she leave here?'

'We came straight here from her house. We didn't go anywhere.'

If Sade was still alive while Bello was supposedly getting anonymous tips, perhaps she was the one composing the messages to the detective?

'When did she leave here?'

'I don't know! It must have been in the middle of the night. I was sleeping and woke up to find that note.'

'Why didn't you tell the police?'

'I was afraid I would become a suspect. I was the last person she was seen with.'

329

'And it never bothered you that no one asked to question you?'

Enomo sneers. 'Come on, the police! I just thought they were being incompetent, or the bishop managed to get them to drop all investigations since they could prove it was suicide.'

The power of the police force when they do their job is as potent as when they don't. A fact Bello and the late Sade seem to have managed to exploit to its full extent.

'And when I came to see you?'

'That was when I got really scared. Especially when you said everyone knew I was the last one to see her alive. I didn't know if I could trust you. But the way you spoke to me made me hope that I could. That was why I started sending you the messages from her phone.'

It adds up. The messages started after I confronted Enomo. I was right. They were tests.

'The file?' I ask. 'The one you helped her steal from Professor Ohaeri...?' It's a wild guess but worth a try.

Enomo looks away with a studied frown. 'I don't know where she left it. Maybe she destroyed it? She had said her husband wanted to make it look like she was mentally ill and she didn't want to make it easy for him to do that. But it's not with me. The only things she left here were that letter, her overnight bag and her phone.'

I can bet my American passport Sade Dawodu didn't destroy that file. Why go through all the trouble of stealing it only to shred it? 'Why was she so desperate to get away from her husband? Did she know something he was doing?'

Enomo holds up a hand while he clicks on Sade Dawodu's phone. 'You've to understand that until she showed me this,

I didn't believe her. I mean I wanted to, but I just couldn't believe it.'

He hands the phone to me. I press the play icon on the video file.

It takes about forty-five seconds of playtime to figure out the horror in progress. I can't stop my hands from shaking.

CAUSE OR CONSEQUENCE?

The video is crudely made. The timestamp is eighteen months ago. There are several points where there's nothing in frame. I guess it's because whatever was used to record was discreetly placed in a stationary spot, with the bed as the focus. Even when no one is in view, there are voices in the background, ostensibly praying. Naked men walk the length and breadth of the room and around the bed, coming in and out of frame, eyes closed in fervour.

Then Sade Dawodu enters, dressed in a sheer night-gown. She kneels next to the bed, and only the most careful observer will see the briefest glance she gives the camera. I suspect she selected the spot to kneel because she knew where the recording device was. The reason becomes clear a couple of seconds later when Dawodu comes into view and starts to pour olive oil over his wife's head. The other men are now completely out of the frame, but we can hear them, their praying more ardent, louder and more nonsensical.

Once Sade is drenched in oil, she raises her head to the camera again. Her eyes are cold and resigned. In that brief second, it is as if I can finally see this woman who's been so elusive to me for the past two weeks. An enigma becomes an open book and dares me to read. Her eyes are clear and challenging as they stare straight at me, just as the night-gown falls to the ground.

Now you see me, what are you going to do?

Dawodu is undressed like the other men, his nakedness as obscene as the act unfolding for the camera. He raises his voice but his words are not prayers, but commands in English, sprinklings of Yoruba and a lot of 'tongues'.

'I present this woman as a living sacrifice. Her body as a temple. As I have blessed Your church, I now place my holy hands on her womb, preparing it as a vessel for a child of the church, born of my name, for your sake.'

When the men walk into frame again, I count four. Two of them have their backs to the camera. The fourth stands next to Dawodu, his expression lascivious, and he's repeating Dawodu's words like a mantra. It's all made so much more cruel, vulgar and unbearable because I recognise him as Nwoko, and the other, when he turns around, is none other than that most boring of interviewees, Pastor Coker.

As Nwoko lowers himself onto the bed, Chika roars, 'Enough!'

I press the stop icon. I did warn him as soon as I came back from Enomo's studio. He has insisted on seeing what had me so shaken and revolted. Reluctantly, I opened the file on Sade Dawodu's phone. Now, midway into the disturbing video, I can say I've never seen Chika so pained. Or livid.

'That's what she was going through?' he says, suffused with regret. He leans back into the chair, palm to forehead. Broken. 'No wonder she wanted to die.'

We're tired. Chika has spent the three hours of my absence working on our hostage. While I hate to imagine what he did to the man, I'm relieved to see the DIY tools aren't bloodstained. Samson's face is bruised and battered, and the look of satisfaction on Chika's face tells me whatever he did was well worth it. The man is snoring loudly, still bound. All bravado gone, like a child spent from screaming after a tour of a haunted house.

'I'm not sure she wanted to die.'

Chika looks at me in surprise. 'Why else would she take her life? Look, when I was in Yemen, we went through a lot of training on how to identify suicide bombers, especially the female ones. The men were easy; it's the women who you need to be really sensitive to because most times, all you've to go with is their eyes. Did you see that woman's eyes before she laid down on the bed? They were dead. Flat. No emotions. Like a suicide bomber.'

I nod, thinking about the literature I've consumed on suicide. 'Yes, they were, but there was more, if you look deeper. Suicide bombers are quite misunderstood in popular media, but their typology is quite clear in psychology. Everyone assumes that they're on a revenge course, or they're crazy people doing the bidding of superior soldiers. But that's not quite true. Suicide bombers fit the altruistic professional theme.'

'A professional suicide is a bit of a misnomer, don't you think?' Chika's sarcasm should've thrown me off, but I'm too busy working things through in my head, so I let it pass.

'The "professional" only refers to their approach. They believe in a cause they'd sacrifice their life for. They're calm, precise; many times, clear-eyed on why they're doing what they're doing.'

'Sounds like our victim.'

'Close but not quite. A closer study of Sade Dawodu might show that she doesn't fit the model altruistic suicide or any other models either. She doesn't come across as egoistical, meaning she doesn't present with a martyr complex. Many people in this category tend to be clinically depressed, with high levels of despair and loneliness. We know she might have been depressed, but she wasn't lonely. She was making very cold and calculating choices as far back as ten months ago. Most importantly, she wasn't acting like a victim, but someone who was taking control of her circumstances.'

I pace back and forth across Chika's small office space. If I let my mind dwell on the contents of the video Enomo gave me, I'll be impotent with rage. The bound hostage is sleeping, but it's not restful as his head keeps jerking as if to prevent itself from falling off his neck. I turn to Chika. 'A lot of suicide analysis focuses on the reasons that lead to it, but not enough research goes into suicide with the consequences in mind.'

'But the suicide bomber knows the consequences. They'll be dead. That's why they do it.'

I shake my head. 'No. Too simplistic. The closest typology that Sade fits is the fatalistic revenger—'

'How can she have revenge if she is dead?'

'It's a form of regaining control over life, especially when it seems all sense of self is lost within a social contract like marriage. Still, Sade doesn't quite fit it. The most culturally relevant that I can think of ... darn, I wish I'd my laptop here.'

I go to my phone, click on the Safari icon and type in the search bar.

'Here it is,' I say sombrely, as the article I'm looking for pops up. 'Samsonic suicide.'

'Samson as in the Bible?' He points in our would-be assassin's direction. 'His namesake?' The irony hit me. How fitting it would be if my hypothesis is true.

'Yes. Remember he brought down the building he was imprisoned in, knowing it would kill him but also all the people in it?'

'Yes. But Sade Dawodu killed only herself and we now know why.'

'I think Sade killed herself to set in motion far-reaching consequences. It's actually quite common in India, China and several parts of Africa. Many women die by suicide, hoping their community will avenge them.'

'Sade Dawodu doesn't strike me as someone who'd leave further actions to the community, or anyone else for that matter.'

I'm pacing faster now. Chika's observations confirm my suspicions rather than challenge them. 'Exactly. So, she didn't leave anything to chance. She made sure she'd accomplices whom she never gave a complete picture of the situation. She manipulated everyone to do her bidding, making sure that their most important motivation would be her death. You see? She combined all the typologies – she knew she'd take her own life as a form of control over it, and instead of bringing the house down like Samson did, she found people who'd do it for her.'

'Bello and Enomo?' Chika asks.

'I think there are more.' I start pacing again to stem my agitation. 'But I don't know who they can be.'

'You're thinking someone who knows about the list?'

'Yes.' I stop and face Chika. 'Detective Bello doesn't seem to know about it, and I really think Enomo has told me all he knows, especially as he's afraid he might be blamed for Sade's death.'

'So, why was he sending those messages from her phone?'

'They were tests to see if he could trust me. My point is, if we can explain Sade's suicide by her expectation of what she wanted to happen *after* her death, then the list she got from Ewang is the missing link.' I point towards the bound Samson in the outer office. 'Any luck with our august guest?'

Chika shrugs. 'Not really. Just a hired hand. He takes his orders from Dawodu, but he suspects there are higher people.'

I'm disappointed. I'd hoped my brief foray into violence would bear more fruit.

'He did confess to torturing Ewang, which was how they knew he told you about the list.'

'Who killed him?'

'He died while being tortured. His heart gave way during electrocution. Dumping him on your front yard was the American woman's idea to warn you off.'

'That's stupid,' I snort.

'No. Brazen. And that's what got me thinking. This thing is much bigger than we thought. Ex-military men serving as assassins, clearing the road of police officers before coming after us. These guys are working for some very powerful people.'

'Someone other than Dawodu?'

'It's possible, but he,' – Chika points towards Samson – 'only knows Dawodu and LaTanya, who pay him directly with funds he then uses to pay the others.'

My eyes must look like they'll pop out. 'They do this regularly?'

'On orders. They're just muscles in a complicated machinery. Guys willing to teach people a lesson or two. But they're not the brains.'

I face the glass partition. The hostage is still deep in exhausted sleep, bloody drool falls from his open mouth. I almost envy him. It's been a long day and night, and while I've learnt a lot more today than in all the days I've been on this investigation, I am no closer to knowing how to keep my family safe. I turn to Chika.

'What do we do with him?' I jerk my thumb towards the glass partition.

Chika is settling in for the night, adjusting the headrest of the ergonomic executive chair, and moving his bum this way and that to find a comfortable posture.

'We wait.'

'For what?'

Chika leans back and closes his eyes. 'Phil, those other two have made their way to Lagos by now. They've reported what happened. So, whoever sent them know we know. They're putting an action plan together.'

'An action plan that might involve putting our families at risk. Maybe we should let him go? I'm sure I've enough to convince Abubakar to—'

'Calm down, Oga. Trust me, right now, they're discussing how to bring you on board, negotiate terms with you and get you off their backs.'

'They were willing to kill me,' I point out, panic rising again. 'Kill us.'

Chika feigns unconcern and rests back on the chair again. 'And they failed.'

My phone rings. It's an unknown number.

Chika sits up sharply. 'Pick it.'

'Dr Taiwo,' LaTanya Jacobson says. 'We'd like a meeting.'

NOT THAT KIND

I could tell you I did it because I didn't want to bring a child into the hell my life had become. That would not be the whole truth. I could use revenge as an excuse, because when I told him what I had done, his fury was the closest to happy I had been in all our years of being married.

But why? he growled.

I felt like it, I lied and smiled so wide he lunged at me, his big hands wrapping around my neck, his body crushing me. There was a moment while he was squeezing, his nose flaring and spit spraying on my face as he cursed, I could have just let him. I closed my eyes and the darkness pulled me into a warm embrace. I felt peace. It was fleeting, but enough. I knew then the only way to find that peace again would be to go into the dark. But not at his hands.

I opened my eyes and his hands slackened, uncertainty in his eyes. I calmly reminded him about the documents I had put aside as insurance. I told him I had no doubt that he could kill me right here and get away with it, but nothing would save him from the wrath of those who would come after him once the information was released.

His harsh breathing was the only thing between us for a long while. He screamed again, slapped me hard, and then, let go of me.

Before, when I thought I was the problem, that my 'sin' was the reason I couldn't conceive, I would have done anything to have a child. It was a time when I was sure if I gave him a child, he would love me. I would be worthy. I tried and tried. At the lowest point, when the weight of my guilt made me a pawn in his hands, he told me he 'discerned in his spirit' that he had inherited the consequence of my sin. After all, if 'two shall become one', it stood to reason that the punishment for murdering my child would be shared with him.

Desperate, I asked him, what I could do?

Offer yourself as a living sacrifice, he commanded.

You know those pictures where pregnant women rub their swollen bellies, smiling with expectancy? That's not me. I would lie on that bed, an offering for the sole purpose of bearing a child, and think of all the women who never questioned this path. Who had been told no sacrifice was too great to fulfil their motherly purpose. I would lie on that bed and try to picture the child that would come forth from these unions, but try as I did, I couldn't summon an image of myself mothering the result of the alliances he demanded.

Perhaps this was why it didn't take Mummy much to convince me about that first abortion in university. I don't know. Maybe I always knew this was not for me. But I was too scared of being different, or of disappointing everyone yet again. Perhaps it needed this living sacrifice nonsense to open my eyes to that fact. I am not a mother.

I could have gone along with being bred one night every month, praying, hoping, lying there. And for a while, I did. Until one day, I just didn't.

SATURDAY RUNS

The signs marking Jeremiah Dawodu's house as a crime scene are gone. 'You're still there?' I speak into my phone.

'Oga Phil,' Chika says, 'trust me, even if I wanted to go anywhere, your wife would have my head for even thinking of leaving you alone.'

He's parked on the street adjacent to Dawodu's with a bound Samson in the back of the VW van.

'I'm not letting him out of my sight,' Chika had insisted when I suggested calling Abubakar for reinforcements. The hard look on his face had forestalled further discussion. Despite knowing how much I admire the commandant, Chika's distrust for law enforcement runs deep.

'I'm walking into the compound now,' I say into the Airpods. 'It's a fortress here. There're at least six armed guards outside.'

After all I've found out about Dawodu's operation and how far he'd go to keep it going, I'm not surprised. Before passing through the gates, I was searched so thoroughly by two stern-faced security guards, you'd think I was about to enter a US embassy in the Middle East.

One guard talked into a mobile phone. 'He's clean, ma.' A pause. 'He's alone. Yes, ma.' A frown, then, 'Should we hold his phone?'

I raised my voice. 'You can tell Ms Jacobson I won't be going past this point without my mobile phone.'

The guard's face remained impassive as he listened. 'Yes, ma. Okay.' He nodded at his colleague. 'He can go in.' He hung up and turned to the closed gates, his hand on the AK47 slung across his shoulder. I'd been cleared, so not worthy of further attention.

'I'll drive closer,' Chika says, as I now make my way towards the mansion.

'Better not. Don't know how many of them he has manning the whole street. They'll notice the VW,' I advise. I'm now at the massive entrance door.

'Code Okriki.' Chika reminds me of our cypher for leaving the mobile phone on in dangerous situations.

'Got it,' I say, removing the earpiece and slipping it into my pocket at the doorway. I'd switched off the Bluetooth auto-disconnection, so the phone remains on. From the point of view of the security camera trained on me, I have just cut off a conversation. I resist the urge to sniff my armpit and smoothen my rumpled shirt. It's been a long night.

Dawodu sits cross-legged at the centre of the widest sofa in the room. His blazer is unbuttoned, his shirt open enough to accommodate the silk cravat. The picture of calm and control. LaTanya sits on a damask-upholstered wingback chair. I stand at the entry between the lobby and the living room.

'Please have a seat, Dr Taiwo.' Dawodu points to a chair. I don't move. We both know this isn't a courtesy call.

'I'll get you something to drink,' LaTanya says, standing up. 'Water? Juice? I'm having white wine.'

Indeed, she is. There's a bottle of Chenin blanc open in front of her. It's barely 8 a.m., but considering that I wouldn't mind a stiff drink right now, I can't judge.

'No, I'm fine.'

LaTanya sits back down and looks at Dawodu. 'Will you handle this, or should I?'

Dawodu uncrosses his legs, and leans in with a genial smile. 'This will go much easier if you sit and we can have a conversation.'

'This should be quick,' I say briskly. 'Let's not beat about the bush. You know I have your man, and he's been cooperative.'

LaTanya tuts. 'I didn't peg you for a violent man, Dr Taiwo.'

'I didn't either, but no one's ever tried to assassinate me before,' I say to her and turn back to Dawodu. 'We had a deal. You were supposed to stay away from me and my family.'

'That was before you started following up on the list,' he says.

I raise an eyebrow.

'Several of the banks flagged logins into their systems and they traced it to Lagos,' he responds. 'That wouldn't be you or your Rambo accomplice, would it?'

I shrug. 'I like to know what's entrusted to me but that doesn't mean I was going to use it.'

'Not a chance we're willing to take,' LaTanya says, as she daintily sips on the wine, talons wrapped around the glass stem.

'Now you know I know, I assume you want to cut a deal?'

Dawodu stands. I sense he doesn't like looking up at me. 'You're a smart man, clearly of sound mind. What we want to know is how much it would take to make you forget all this ever happened. You go your way, safe with your family, and we go ours, sure you will … remember the risks associated with making all,' – He waves his hands around – 'this go further than this room.'

We're head-to-head now. 'Why should I trust you if your own wife couldn't?'

'Homeboy had to go there,' LaTanya says, but my eyes are fixed on the bristling Dawodu. 'Chile, that girl was loony. She didn't want a deal. She wanted a divorce.'

'I'd want one too if my husband and his cronies were gang-raping me,' I say to Dawodu's face.

His eyes flare. 'It was not that! She consented so we could have a child.'

'Why must she pay the price for you shooting blanks?'

I notice his fist clench. I move closer, daring him.

'Boys!' LaTanya steps between us. 'Let's be adults here.' She looks at me. 'Jerry asked you a question. What would it take for you to forget all this ever happened?'

'Guarantees.'

'Our business associates won't like knowing someone knows about our arrangements,' she says. 'We need them to know this will be contained.'

'How can I be sure one or two of them don't already know I've the list?'

'They don't,' Dawodu spits out over LaTanya's head. 'Why do you think we went to this extent?'

I give him a cold smile. 'You tell me. I'm not used to a pastor who launders money and hires assassins.'

Dawodu steps forward. LaTanya pushes him back, but she's looking at me. 'Dr Taiwo, do you want to cut a deal or not?'

'Guarantees. You leave me and my family alone and that includes my friends too.'

'And?'

'Two million dollars to a numbered account in Mauritius,' I say, hopefully deadpan.

LaTanya and Dawodu look so relieved, they start smiling.

'Oh, not so judgy now, are we, Dr Taiwo?' she says.

I shrug. 'Everyone has a price. Besides the only way you'd trust me is if I become an accomplice. So, it's a win-win.'

'It will take me a few days to make the arrangements,' LaTanya says, so pleased she walks back to pour more wine into her glass.

'I'll keep your hitman till then.' I turn to leave. 'I must warn you, the demurrage fees are high. He's not a small man.'

'It's a weekend, Dr Taiwo,' Dawodu says like I'm being a difficult child. 'Banks are closed. Release the guy.'

'Not your Hong Kong bank,' I say. 'I'll send the account details as soon as I set it up. Transfer in forty-eight hours.'

I walk out so they know I'll not be negotiating. But, in truth, it's to stop myself from throwing up.

*

'You were awesome!' Chika exclaims as soon as I get in the VW. He punches the wheel in glee. 'Damn, I would give everything to have seen their faces!'

I turn to check Samson is still bound and gagged. The assassin is much less belligerent now. His eyes betray his curiosity though. Likely wondering if he's been sold out and his employers have washed their hands of him. Good.

I sink into the passenger seat, exhausted. It's been over twenty-eight hours of non-stop activities, with less than three hours' sleep on the couch in Chika's office.

'What's the plan now?' he asks.

I put on a contemplative face. 'We could take the money and run?'

Chika does a double take. 'I thought we're just buying time to—'

It's my turn to laugh out loud. The shock on his face is priceless. 'We are, but it's also good to consider what two million dollars could do for us.'

He hisses and starts the car. He hates being the brunt of jokes. 'I'll get you back.'

'Make sure you've got two mil,' I snap back, resting on the headrest. A quick snooze might—

My phone thrums. I pick it up as soon as I see who's calling.

'Bello will talk now,' Abubakar says without ceremony.

I don't want to contemplate why it took the commandant so long to get back to me. Suffice to say, given the choice of being Chika's hostage or being grilled by the commandant of the police college, I'd be tempted to take the former.

'Where are you?' I ask.

'In my office. Come.' Abubakar hangs up.

I turn to Chika. 'One more detour before we go back to your office.'

'Does it buy us time?' he asks, as he manoeuvres the VW on to the main road.

'I hope it will save us time,' I answer, more optimistic than sure.

*

Cadets mill around the college field. There are no classes on weekends, but drills and exercises are mandatory. Chika thumbs towards the back of the VW.

'We can leave him here?'

I wave at a cadet I recognise. He runs over.

'Keep watch,' I order in my best imitation of Abubakar. 'A fly moves close, let me know. I'll be in the commandant's office.'

The cadet nods, snaps to attention.

I turn to Chika. 'It's all good. Let's go.'

Abubakar's office is stuffy with tobacco and tension. He looks as though he's aged overnight, his normally sharp uniform unbuttoned. The ashtray overflows with cigarette butts.

My eyes swing to Bello. How long has he been standing at attention, looking like he'll collapse any second? Are those bruises on the younger man's face? Is the redness in his eyes and the swellings around his cheeks from lack of sleep or something more malevolent?

I turn to Abubakar but his face is hard, inscrutable. He puffs out smoke and waves disdainfully at Bello.

'He's all yours.'

I look at Chika and his face is as unsympathetic as Abubakar's. There's no mercy for dirty cops in this room. Not today.

'Can he sit down at least?' I ask.

'No,' Abubakar barks.

'It's all right, Dr Taiwo,' Bello says, facing forward, his voice wavering. 'Commandant says you've questions for me. I'm at your service.' Not for the first time, I imagine what an outstanding officer he could have been. The ramrod straight

back, the squared shoulders, the case file – albeit manufac-
tured with the most basic of information – that showed that
on a good day the detective knew what his job expected of
him.

'One question,' I say curtly. No need to drag this out.
'Why?'

Bello's eyes flicker to Abubakar, who nods with a scoff,
his way of giving disgraced officers permission to speak.

'We were friends, sir,' Bello says, avoiding my eyes. 'Me
and the victim went to university together.' His shoulders
slump, his eyes meet mine briefly, pleading for understanding. 'We were friends because we went to the same campus
fellowship. But when we graduated, we parted ways.'

'Were you romantically involved?' I ask, thinking of
Sade's first visit to Dr Raimi's clinic. Could Bello be the—?

'No, sir,' he answers with perplexed denial. 'She was my
friend's girlfriend in university. I know something went
wrong between them because they suddenly stopped going
out. When I asked her about it then, she said it wasn't meant
to be. That they were sinning. And that was that. We were
friends on social media before she got married, and when
she closed all her accounts, I lost touch with her. Until she
approached me about eight months ago.'

'She approached you?' I ask.

'Yes. She told me what a horrible man her husband was.
She showed me a video of what he was making her do. I
was angry. It just confirmed why I stopped going to all these
fake churches.'

'What was she paying you for then?' Chika asks from
behind me, his arms crossed over his chest as he leans
against the wall.

Bello's nose flares at the insolence in Chika's tone. I see his hand clench, his eyes flicker at Abubakar again. The commandant is not in a merciful mood because he nods again, this time pointing his cigarette at Chika to emphasise who Bello should address his answer to.

Bello half-turns to Chika, his eyes on the ceiling. 'She wanted out of the marriage, and her husband wouldn't give her a divorce. She told me she was in love with someone and they were running away together. So, she asked me to help make things uncomfortable for her husband. Just raise suspicion, make him squirm a bit and perhaps give her enough time to disappear. She needed him put away for some days, and when she was safe, I could release him as by then it would be too late for him to find her.'

'So, she paid you to set him up?' I ask.

He turns to me, his expression pleading. 'She did all the setting up, Dr Taiwo. Yes, I advised her on some of the clues to lay out to make my job easier, but she did it all by herself. I told her how hard it would be, but she convinced me that if I paid all the right people to look the other way and not question too many things, it would be fine.'

'Who did you pay in the force?' Chika asks.

This time Bello's look to Abubakar is obstinate. 'Sir, you agreed.'

Abubakar busies himself with lighting another cigarette and taking a long drag. 'Just know he settled some senior officers with the money Sade Dawodu gave him. I'll have a chat with them later, but I agreed that he doesn't have to divulge their names to you.'

I hold his gaze for a second. He's protecting officers higher up, and I know better than to question his judgement. He didn't get to where he is by selling out fellow officers.

I shake my head at Chika and he shrugs, his face set in a cynical mask. 'So, you took the money for yourself and your superiors to look the other way if yawa gas?' he asks.

Bello looks at the floor. 'I just didn't want my chain of evidence questioned. I assured them I'd release the bishop and there would be no political fallout.'

Something's always bothered me. 'The blood match. How did you …?'

Bello turns to me. 'Sade gave me a copy of her biodata from her medical file.'

'Why didn't you include it in the case file?'

Bello looks down, his shoulders droop. 'She told me to use it only if it was absolutely necessary.'

'Why?' Chika asks from the side but I don't need the answer. I now know how Sade's mind worked.

Bello looks at Chika, resentment back on his face, his shoulders square again. 'Because the records were from when she was at school, not recently. And it was signed by a psychiatrist and she didn't want anyone thinking she did all she did because she was a basket case.'

'She didn't give you the whole file?'

Bello shakes his head. 'Just the biodata page. I didn't think I would need to present it as evidence when her husband was released.'

'Then, she turned up dead,' I say.

Bello raises his head and gives me a rueful smile. 'No, Dr Taiwo, you showed up.'

I can only imagine how much of his plan I scuttled. How nervous he must have been, then afraid when Sade's body was found. No wonder he gave me the case file. He was caught off guard, perhaps needed my help as much as I needed his, while praying I never discover the extent of his involvement.

'Was that all she told you? Nothing about what was going on in the church itself? Nothing about church finances?'

Bello frowns. 'No. She only showed me evidence of the abuse she was going through.' He raises an eyebrow like something just occurred to him. 'Did she take the money she paid me from the church account?'

He doesn't know about the list. I turn to Chika again, checking if this is the right time to set my plan in motion. He nods. Go for it.

I look to Abubakar. 'Sir—'

'Never good when you call me that,' he says with a resigned smile.

'I just want to know if you can talk to Detective Bello's superiors, to be sure that his deal on the Dawodu matter still stands.'

'I'm sure I can force their hand,' Abubakar says like he is swallowing vinegar. 'Given how much they've compromised themselves.'

I look at Bello. 'We need you to make a very public arrest.'

IT TAKES A THIEF

Detective Bello looks resplendent in his full uniform as he informs the journalists of the arrest. If there's an award for best actor in police work, he would be in the running. After giving a short statement, he paraded the former Sergeant Samson Adamu for the press to see, complete with a viewing of the VW van and the guns inside.

'The discovery of Victor Ewang's phone in the suspect's vehicle is definite proof that the suspect has a hand in the murder of the deceased. We also believe he wasn't acting alone, and the police are still investigating to ensure all the accomplices in the murder of the late Victor Ewang are brought to justice,' Detective Bello says to the camera.

Chika and I look at each other, impressed by the extent to which he is following the script. We're in Chika's office, having just cleared it of all traces of the last thirty-six hours. We're now seated in the recreation room, the giant TV screen tuned to Channels TV.

Microphones are thrust at a bewildered-looking Adamu.

— Who ordered the killing?

— Is it true you were not acting alone?

— Where did you get the guns?

— How much were you paid?

The questions come from all directions, and Samson's trademark braggadocio is markedly absent. Close up, his fear is like laser beams.

I still can't understand this culture of showing off suspects to the press before they are formally charged with a crime. It seems unfair to charge a suspect in the court of public opinion. My unease is made worse by a suspect's willingness to speak about the crime without the benefit of legal representation.

'I hear you, but in this case, that crazy system is working in our favour,' Chika replied when I shared my thinking. 'The idiot is talking faster than he did when he was here.'

Indeed, Samson is talking but it's more like pleading. His expression is the opposite of the smirk he had on when Chika untied and handed him the VW keys hours earlier.

As soon as the plan was finalised in Abubakar's office, I'd made the call to Dawodu.

'I've thought about your proposal. As of now, we're releasing your thug.'

'Very wise, Dr Taiwo,' he had said. I pictured him giving LaTanya a high five as they downed copious amounts of Dom Perignon. 'You won't regret it.'

'I'm assuming our deal stands.'

'Our word is our bond, Dr Taiwo. You release Samson, we transfer the funds as soon as you send the account details.'

'You'll hear from me,' I said and hung up.

Then, we went back to the VW, drove some distance and parked by the roadside. Chika wordlessly removed the restraints from Samson. Of course, the hired assassin had assumed Chika came to his senses after pressure from the 'big guys'. He'd taken the keys with an arrogant grin and, battered as he was, got back into the bus and drove away.

Fewer than fifteen minutes of freedom were all he had before the VW was intercepted by Detective Bello and a team of police officers at a strategically positioned check-point down the road. It was apparently a random 'stop and search'. Nothing unusual in Lagos. But Samson knew he was doomed. The ammunition and the blood in the bus guaranteed an immediate arrest.

'Dem send me, o! Abeg save me, o!' Samson is now saying to the journalists, sitting shirtless on the ground, handcuffed.

Chika and I wait for a beat as the camera pans back to Detective Bello, who is now taking more questions from the journalists. He points at someone and we expel a sigh of relief when we hear the voice of the cadet in mufti we chose to deliver the rehearsed question.

'Detective, is there any link between the death of Mrs Dawodu and this arrest?' the cadet asks in that tightly wound journalistic tone.

Detective Bello is right on cue. 'At this time, the police are ready to follow all new leads. For now, we're going by the autopsy report that ruled Mrs Sade Dawodu's death as a suicide. Our thoughts and prayers go to Mrs Dawodu's family, and the police regrets any distress we might have caused Bishop Dawodu in our investigation. This suspect is currently being treated separately from Mrs Dawodu's suicide.' Bello smiles at the journalists. 'Next?'

Chika and I do a quick fist bump. Perfect execution. Indeed, it takes a thief to catch a thief. Weaponising the endemic corruption in the police force is a lesson well taught by the late Sade Dawodu.

'I'll go home now,' Chika says. 'You'll be fine?'

I nod. 'Kenny has set up the meeting with Pastor George and Mrs Bucknor.'

'I can come with you,' Chika suggests.

'No. Folake and Onyinye are too worried. Let's take them out of their misery. Go home.'

'And the list?'

'Abubakar advises that we hand it over to EFCC and let the law take its course.'

Chika laughs drily. 'You want to hand the names of people involved in financial fraud to the Financial Crimes Commission of the most corrupt country on earth? Good luck with that.'

My phone vibrates, and when I see the unknown number, I hold my hand up to stop him from speaking.

'What the hell's going on?' Dawodu's voice roars.

'What do you mean?' I ask innocently.

'My man has just been arrested by the police!' The panic in his voice is the definition of joy. 'He's being paraded to the press!'

My smile is so wide it's difficult to keep the glee out of my voice. 'That had nothing to do with me or my colleague. We released him.'

'Someone must have tipped off the police.'

'That would have been extremely stupid of me, don't you think?'

'Then who?' Dawodu asks, my logic not lost on him.

'I think you should do the lawyerly thing and tell your man to say nothing.'

From his ragged breathing, I'm sure he's aware that ship has sailed into very stormy waters.

CURVEBALL

Two days later, I sit at the desk in my home study and let out a sigh of relief. My job is done. To make this clear to all, I type a perfunctory report confirming the police's conclusion about Sade Dawodu's death, and even take it further by attaching an invoice. For good measure, I added the cost of the excess on Chika's car insurance and addressed it for the attention of Pastor George. I don't expect to hear from him soon. My debriefing at Mrs Bucknor's house had broken him. Kenny had held on to Mrs Bucknor as if both of them were sinking.

'Don't show me, please,' Mrs Bucknor had said when I told them about the video. 'Please don't kill her again.'

'Did you know?' I asked her.

Mrs Bucknor had buried her head in Kenny's chest, sobbing. 'How could I? How could I?' she kept saying. Kenny's eyes begged me to stop.

'Is it possible you're wrong? About the money laundering?' Pastor George had asked.

'You know I'm not wrong.' My tone was hard. I found the man's refusal to take his religious head out of the sand infuriating.

'And the bishop killed Victor?' Kenny asked, disbelieving.

I refused to repeat myself. I'd told them everything and only left after I made them all swear they'll never speak about the list of names and the money laundering scheme. I emphasised the danger to their lives, and their loved ones. They all swore repeatedly never to speak of them to anyone.

I stand and stretch. I'm officially done with the case of the missing, now dead, First Lady of Grace Church. I go down, and the scene at the dining table makes me pause. As soon as we got home, Folake had made good on her threat. Today's the bullies' first day of being tutored by Lara. It's not going well.

Lara alternates between working on her iPad and the notebook in front of her. The bullies, with more make-up on than you'd find in a Cover Girl shop, sit at the opposite end of the dining table. They giggle and whisper with their iPads open to YouTube fan videos of Asian pop stars.

I despair. Lara's misery is written all over her hunched back, over her laptop and notebooks. I wish I could change Folake's mind about this whole exercise, but she insisted: all three girls must learn the value of lifting each other up. I go over to squeeze Lara's shoulders. She looks up at me with a plea.

I turn to the bullies. 'Girls, this is homework time at our house.'

They put away their iPads, bring out their textbooks and move their chairs closer to Lara. The way they do this so quickly makes me pause. They are just kids, perhaps in need of a firmer hand than most as they find their paths, but kids all the same.

'I don't know if we've told you, but we are all really glad you girls are making an effort to get along,' I say, aware that my smile must be stiff on my face.

The girls look at me, flustered. Distrustful.

'Trust me, girls, if you give yourselves a chance, you'll realise this is good for you. Lara is a maths whizkid—'

'Dad!' Lara protests.

I keep my eyes on the three bullies and this time my smile is genuine. 'And I'm sure you girls are brilliant at something that Lara can learn to be better at.'

The girls look at each other and then at Lara. She squirms.

'Your eyebrows ...' One girl starts.

Lara's head snaps up. 'Whatchu gonna say about—' she retorts.

'They are perfect.' A second girl says. 'We could teach you how to tweeze them to make them fleek. Angela,' she points to the third girl, 'has an Insta page where she gives make-up tips. You could model for her.'

Lara's eyes round. The three girls exchange looks that remind me of those gay guys who give makeovers to straight men. While I'm not sure this is the kind of exchange of skills Folake and I were hoping for, it's a start. As long as it doesn't involve bleaching creams. I make a mental note to check out this Angela's Instagram page.

'You've got this,' I say to Lara and bend to kiss her fore-head. Her shoulders remain stiff but she doesn't move her head away.

As I walk back upstairs, I hear one of the girls say, 'Your dad is nice.'

Lara grunts something, but I hear the ruffle of papers. Tutoring has started.

I enter the bedroom, ready to restate my concern to Folake. She hands my phone to me.

'It's been buzzing since,' she says. 'I didn't want to disturb you cos I knew you were busy with the report.'

I frown at the message. Chika. *Doc, check truth.ng online.*

I cut and paste the website address of the popular online news service into my browser, a knot already forming in my stomach.

'What is it?' Folake asks, taking off her reading glasses.

I hand the phone over to her and horror blooms on her face. 'My God, who did this? How did they know?'

*

News of the leak is all over the media. Some are calling it 'The Panama Papers of Nigeria'. Twitter is trending to crash level. I'm at Abubakar's office, where we'd all agreed to meet.

'Samson is still in custody. I've questioned him at least ten times. He never said anything about a list and this is the first time I'm finding out about it,' says Bello.

Chika snorts. 'Why should we believe you? Maybe it was Sade Dawodu's last instruction to you?'

'I've no reason to lie!' Bello's voice is high with tension and shame. 'I've done everything you've asked me to. I know I'm in trouble already, so why would I compound it by leaking some dangerous list of names to the press?'

Abubakar puffs smoke in the air. 'He's right.'

'I believe him,' I say, 'but that doesn't remove the danger to us all if Dawodu thinks we leaked it. And it won't have to be from him. Any one of the people on that list can come after us.'

'Let me think,' Abubakar snaps.

Chika looks at his mobile phone, frowning. 'My guys at the office. They say turn on GraceTV. Something's streaming.'

There's a feverish anticipation in the way Chika, Bello and I converge over Abubakar's head and stare at his desktop screen. The commandant swears in Hausa, stubs his cigarette and asks for the website to search. Chika reaches across over his shoulders and types.

The internet service of the police college is not the best, and it takes a while for the video to load. Dawodu is well into his address by the time the feed finishes buffering.

'These malicious lies,' he is saying with fervour, 'are meant to bring the Church down. The righteous have enemies, our Lord has assured us that we wrestle against powers and principalities, but He's sure to save us from the snare of the fowler. So, I assure you the Church will march on triumphantly just as we always have. What proof is there that we, the devout and the blessed, knew anything of the criminal activities of those vile few who chose, in their bedevilment, to take advantage of the house of God? Ask yourselves why such heinous accusations would be levelled against us. Who are these sinners who take the life of one of their own masterminds?'

'Chiiiiisos, is he placing this on Ewang?' Chika asks, incredulous.

'Seems like that.' I'm not surprised at Dawodu's audacity. The man won't go down without a fight.

'Bastard!' Bello hisses behind me. My reservations about him prevent me from agreeing with him. Dawodu is worse than a bastard. A sleazy criminal with the morals of an alley cat and the mind of a dangerous psychopath.

Dawodu continues his speech of righteous indignation. 'We shall investigate and cooperate with the authorities to make sure that the evildoers amongst us, the ones chosen by the devil to betray the Church, are brought to justice.'

'He'll get away with it,' Abubakar says with a resigned air. He reaches for his cigarette pack and heads for the door. 'Mark my words. There are too many powerful people on that list.' He shakes his head and goes out.

'I'm a grieving man,' Dawodu is saying, his voice wobbling as if it takes tremendous effort to continue. 'I've lost a wife, and now, the devil is not content, he wants to shake your faith in me, in your Church. In God. But the devil is a liar!'

His studio audience repeats 'devil is a liar' a number of times while Dawodu breaks into gibberish for a minute, then continues, 'Tomorrow, I shall honour the memory of my wife here, in this sanctuary. I shall leave this travesty against the temple of God to the authorities and pray for them as they weed out the evil amongst us. But tomorrow, I shall celebrate my wife's life, and I enjoin you all to pray for me, for our Church and for my precious Folasade as we usher her beautiful soul into the bosom of the Lord.'

'He's playing on public sympathy to deflect the situation,' Bello says, sounding in awe of Dawodu's gall.

The scroll bar registers over 1.3 million people are watching. Believing this act. Abubakar is right.

'Look on the bright side though,' Chika says with a cynical curve to his lips. 'If the leak can't be traced to any one of us, we're safe.'

The silence around the room is proof that pyrrhic victory is no victory.

BRIGHT AND BEAUTIFUL

'You're doing the right thing,' Folake whispers as we're handed the programme for the 'celebration' of Folasade Dawodu's life.

I'm not sure about her summation, but I'm grateful to her for coming with me to offer moral support, as she had put it. Strangely, I feel as though I owe it to Sade to be present today. I know the truth. *Her* truth. But this ceremony would be near impossible for me without my wife beside me.

Side by side, we enter Grace Cathedral with heavy hearts, not only for the life lost but for the hypocrisy we're about to witness.

The place is filled to capacity. The service is due to start within the hour, and I scan the room as solemn-looking ushers, all dressed in white, lead us to our seats. There are overblown images of Sade Dawodu everywhere we turn. On the big screen behind the altar, a video of her life in pictures is on loop.

'I wonder if Kenny changed her mind,' Folake says as she scans the room.

My sister had been adamant that she wouldn't come to the memorial service. Even when I told her the invitation was sent to me by Mrs Bucknor, Kenny had simply snorted over the phone.

'I won't be a player in that deceitful and corrupt game any more,' she had declared. I didn't say anything, but inwardly I cheered.

I spot Mrs Bucknor, with Pastor George and several elders flanking her, all of them look drawn and tense as they wait for the service to start. Several people climb onto the stage to greet her, and she gracefully shakes hands, accepts comforting hugs and frequently dabs her nose with a handkerchief.

Nwoko walks to the altar. Dawodu follows him, looking sombre and regal in monochromatic black. Even his signature pocket handkerchief is black. A hush falls over the congregation as Dawodu surveys the hall. Many of the congregants are already standing, but he waves his hand perfunctorily, as if telling them that this is not the occasion to show him the adulation he's accustomed to. When everyone sits back down, he clasps his hands together, bows slightly in appreciation and walks to his mother-in-law. He leans in to greet her, and as if on cue, pained wailings rise from the congregation.

Mrs Bucknor doesn't look at Dawodu, but stares straight ahead, her face set like stone. The woman's steely calm in the face of what she knows this man did to her daughter is nothing short of superhuman.

Sade Dawodu's face, replicated dozens of times throughout the auditorium, seems to mock the proceedings.

'Let us stand for a short prayer,' Nwoko says.

My revulsion paralyses me.

'Sweet!' Folake bends towards my ear. 'You're here to honour her.'

I agreed to come to this sham and I might as well pay my last respects properly. I stand, focusing on Sade Dawodu's images, doing my best to drown out Nwoko's voice. What a powerful force she could have been if things had been different. If she'd found the love and peace she sought in the church. If she'd found a husband who truly loved her, instead of someone only capable of loving himself. If she'd had a mother who affirmed her value at the right time. When Folake hands me a tissue, I realise that I'm tearing up. I grab it quickly, dab my eyes and reach for her hand. I'm blessed to have this woman in my life, I think, as Nwoko finishes the prayers.

Nwoko proclaims, 'And now, to start this celebration of life, we'll call on the choir to sing our First Lady's favourite hymn, "All Things Bright and Beautiful".'

The choir's funeral procession troops past, dressed in white. They arrange themselves on the stage, and then Enomo Collins, elegant in a white suit, clean-shaven and dapper, steps in front of them. He faces the audience.

'We're here to celebrate a woman of courage and strength. A woman who most of you only knew through pictures like these.' He waves at the screen behind him. 'But who chose to live her life on her terms. Indeed, all things were bright and beautiful to her, and when they stopped being that way, she freed herself the only way she knew how.'

His voice almost breaks, but he seems to gather strength from a last look at Sade's face before turning to the choir. He raises his hand, and the whole auditorium fills with the immense power of three hundred-odd voices singing in harmony.

All things bright and beautiful
All creatures great and small
All things wise and wonderful,
'Twas God that made them all.

There's not a dry eye among the congregants. Folake's fingers entwine mine tightly. Dawodu is the only one unmoved, his eyes closed as if in silent communion with some deity, certainly not the God the choir is praising. My eyes dart to Mrs Bucknor, but her face is blank, staring unblinking into the distance. Her left hand, I notice, is in Pastor George's. The song finishes and Nwoko stands again, ready to walk to the pulpit, but stops when Enomo turns back to the audience.

Enomo's wireless microphone hisses, his harsh breath amplified. 'Thank you all once again for being here today to honour our First Lady who lived a life of courage and strength. We all knew the same woman, yet each of us knew her differently, in our own ways. Today, I want you to witness a Sade Dawodu you may not have seen or known, because she was a private person who frequently chose to bear her challenges on her own rather than upset others. But this is a time to know and honour all sides of this beautiful woman, a human being who was so much more than most of you thought. I give you Sade Dawodu, her life and the beginning of her death.'

Perhaps it was his tone, or the defiance in his stance, but a sudden tension falls over the crowd.

My heart starts to beat faster with a sense of foreboding I can't shake. I hear Folake's small gasp; I know she's also thinking the same thing, dreading what we sense is about to come. Despite my trepidation, I know Enomo is making the right choice. The courageous choice and the one Sade would have wanted. And under the circumstances, the *only* choice.

Dawodu's eyes are now open. Nwoko has turned to the big screen behind him. As soon as I hear the crackling audio of men praying, their shuffling feet padding back and forth on the floor, I bury my head in my hands. Folake grips my thigh, forcing me to look up as the video becomes clearer. Because no one can figure out what's going on yet, the silence is pregnant with anticipation. Then, the first naked man comes into view and Nwoko's face becomes recognisable. A moment later, Sade Dawodu walks in, naked underneath the negligee, and the room is filled with gasps and cries of outrage.

'Turn it off!' Dawodu's voice thunders through the hall, but no one hears him. The audio of his voice praying as he pours oil on his wife fills the room. When Sade undresses completely, the audience holds their collective breath.

'Stop it. Please!' Nwoko cries out, fear upstaging the outrage he must be trying to convey.

Just like that, it's like a spell is broken and the spirit of Babel is unleashed. Pastor George covers Mrs Bucknor with his body, shielding her from the video playing on the big screen. She doesn't move, her eyes fixed on a spot above everyone's head.

Dawodu is screaming, 'Put it off now! Now!' as though hell's fires have caught up with him but, for the first time in his ministry, no one is listening. No one wants to.

Nwoko lunges towards Enomo like a frenzied hyena, but the choirmaster is ready for him. As they struggle on the stage and choir members rush to separate them, those who aren't trying to stop the fight remain rooted, their faces turned upwards as they watch the horrific scene playing out in front of them.

Adults hurry children out of the hall, covering the eyes of the older ones as they leave.

Dawodu stops shouting. He turns to look at the fighting men on the side of the stage.

A wild, pained scream pierces the air. A Bible hits Dawodu's face. The scream and the Bible is from a woman who is now kneeling on the floor, crying like an animal hit by a poisoned arrow. A tambourine lands on the stage, missing Dawodu by an inch. The hardback Bible that comes next doesn't miss. It lands so squarely on the man's face that it draws blood on his forehead, causing him to stagger, almost falling on Mrs Bucknor and Pastor George. Winded, Dawodu lurches like a drunk towards the front of the stage. A mistake. Bibles, sèkèrè of different sizes, tambourines, bottles of olive oil and more are being thrown on the stage, all aimed at Dawodu. He covers his face, swaying as he pulls off the wireless microphone and removes the receiver from the back of his jacket. A man jumps on the stage and kicks the podium so hard it crashes on the altar floor. He makes a beeline for Dawodu. Pastor George pulls Mrs Bucknor up.

I start towards the altar and Folake grips my elbow, shaking her head. 'Let it play out,' she says softly, sad. 'You know it's what she'd have wanted.'

I nod and sit down, the church in chaos around me. Perversely, it occurs to me this could be the first time the Grace Cathedral's stage has seen any true emotion.

More men and women hop on the stage and head for Dawodu, waving their Bibles like weapons. That's when Jeremiah Dawodu starts to run. He runs through the pandemonium on stage, past the cyclorama and disappears. The exit to backstage is not wide, but that's not stopping the angry congregants from trying to get through to get to their bishop.

On the other side of the stage, Nwoko and Enomo are finally pulled apart. With a rough shake, Enomo frees himself of the men holding him, looks up at the video playing, and then turns to us with a bloodied smile, his white clothes soiled and rumpled.

'Church, meet your bride,' he says, his voice booming through the speakers, and over the animal grunts of the men raping Sade Dawodu. 'Consider what your love cost her.'

The video ends on his well-timed speech – how many times did the poor man watch it? – silence comes over the crowd. Nwoko makes another attempt to tackle Enomo, but he's held tight. Ignoring him, Enomo goes over to where Mrs Bucknor stands with Pastor George. He offers his arm to her, and she takes it. After a last glance as if to be sure the video is off, she straightens her shoulders and comes down from the stage with Enomo. As they walk through the traumatised congregation, she keeps her eyes trained forward. Her gaze locks on mine.

She nods at me, her eyes cold and sure. I'm reminded of the last time I saw that look.

'*Now you see me, what are you going to do?*'

It all makes sense now. Mrs Bucknor was the one who leaked the list of names to the press.

'How long do you think she knew what was going on?' Folake asks on the way home.

I step on the gas, eager to be home, safe with my children. 'I think she always knew, at least she knew as soon as her daughter disappeared. I'm pretty sure she was the one Sade gave the list,' I answer. 'I think she had help, though. Enomo's certainly. But I don't think Bello was working with her. I think Sade gave different instructions to different people. Some worked together, and some alone. The detective was genuinely surprised when he heard about the list. Also, if he knew about it, he could have used it as leverage to save his skin with his superiors when things didn't go as planned.'

'What a woman!' Folake says. 'That must take an enormous amount of strength. To put your grief as a parent aside and plan revenge with such care.'

'I don't think she saw it as revenge. I think she was doing what she felt she failed to do when her daughter was alive.'

'What's that?'

'Take her side.'

REVELATION

Don't confuse me for a nihilist. To survive what I have been through, I had to believe in something. I abandoned faith in a god that didn't show up for me and chose to believe in me. To put my plan in motion, write all this to you and go through with leaving this life, I had to believe I can. So, before you start blaming yourself for my choices, please give credit where it is due. Me. Not the devil or your god. I did this.

I have told you to give your grief purpose and not waste it. I hope you have. Some things will not go according to plan, but I must trust that you will improvise. You will have to.

When you look back on all you have done to give my death purpose, I hope you will find it in your heart to forgive me as I have forgiven you for all the years of pushing me, bending me and shaping me into a version of what you believed your god wanted. Because, when all is said and done, I was many things on my journey to the person writing you this. Some I kept, others I lost, but through it all, I was always my mother's daughter.

Your loving daughter,
Folasade

#BLACKGIRLMAGIC

The knock on my office door interrupts my packing up. I've to leave now if I don't want to be late.

'Come in!'

The door opens and Pastor George steps in. Surprised, I stop stuffing files into my laptop bag. The last time I saw him was almost a month ago, his head buried in his hands, shrouded in shame at Enomo Collins' dramatic reveal of the sordid underbelly of Grace Church. Since then, he has navigated a public relations nightmare while taking the reins of a broken and battered church. The toll of reputation management, keeping the congregation together and cooperating with law enforcement is written all over his face.

'Dr Taiwo,' he says in greeting.

'Pastor George,' I reply, sneaking a look at my watch.

'I hope you don't mind my showing up without an appointment.'

'No, no. Please come in. My son has an exhibition today and I was leaving early to beat traffic.'

He takes one of the two chairs across from me. I'm grateful for the thorough clearing the cadets did last week. After finalising their reports and attending a debrief at the

SCIU offices at the Police HQ, we'd all come here to file away my wall of evidence and formally close the case.

'As you can imagine,' Pastor George begins, 'things have been rather hectic.'

'I understand.' It can't be easy for him. 'How's everyone coping?'

His smile doesn't reach his eyes. 'That man left a lot of mess to clean up.'

'Does anyone know where he is?'

No amount of bluster or spin could have saved Dawodu from the evidence his congregation had seen with their own eyes. The man had disappeared after leaving Sade's funeral service. Since then, the media has been aflame with speculations regarding his whereabouts. A massive manhunt was launched after the EFCC detained his lawyers and several other people for questioning. The man was like a phantom. Background checks by Interpol and local police showed there was no record of a Jeremiah Dawodu before he secured his social security number in the US. No family in Nigeria claimed any association with him. He appeared on the grid just as mysteriously as he went off it.

Based on the information from Samson regarding Ewang's death, the state also wants Dawodu charged on suspicion of conspiracy to commit murder. The exodus of several prominent business people abroad to avoid being arrested has dominated the news cycles, but he remains at large. There is speculation that he could be somewhere in Asia or on some remote island living off the monies embezzled from the church. Even the FBI's arrest of LaTanya Jacobson on her arrival at JFK had not shed any light on Dawodu's whereabouts, although her perp walk had been the highlight of cable news for several days, inspiring a spate of memes on social media.

'Would it be insensitive of me if I said I don't care?' Pastor George asks after considering my question. 'Wherever he is, I hope he stays far away from truly devout people.'

'He won't dare start another church,' I say, but even to my ears, I sound unconvincing. The world is rife with disgraced pastors who have laundered their image and returned bigger and stronger.

Pastor George gives a nonchalant shrug. 'Some people in church think he's taken his life out of shame, but people like Bish—like Dawodu don't strike me like that.' He shakes his head.

To finalise my report, I'd done extensive research into narcissistic personality disorder in the clergy. The incidence of NPD in religious leaders across the world is higher than the population average, and a common trait binds most: a self-absorption that immunises them to shame and guilt. Pastor George is right. Jeremiah Dawodu will not take his own life.

'I spend a lot of time with Mrs Bucknor these days. Understandably, she wants to have nothing to do with the church, but I keep going to her, praying with her.'

Given the media frenzy and the legal mess, I'm impressed Pastor George is alive to the real human tragedy at the heart of all this. That he takes it upon himself to make time for Sade's mother gladdens my heart. I tell him this.

'What choice do I have? It's sad that she had to lose a daughter before we realised we'd put our faith in a charlatan. A crook and a—' He tries and fails to say the word. 'Fraud can be prosecuted, but it is grossly evil what he and the other elders did to her. And such a tragedy, a failing on all of our parts.'

Perhaps the best news was the arrest of Nwoko and the two 'elders' implicated in the video. Despite the absence of a living victim, an embattled Detective Bello – with Abubakar's support – secured charges of rape against them. Using Sade's suicide as proof that consent was never given and the video as evidence that penetration took place, the Director of Public Prosecution had sought the immediate arrest of the three.

Enomo Collins also started what promises to be a long and very public campaign against such 'men of God' who use their position to sexually molest congregants. So far, he has raised millions of Naira to formally bring charges against the four implicated men (Dawodu in absentia), claiming their assault led to Sade's suicide. Kenny and I contributed to the fund. Nwoko and the two former elders are in detention, and Detective Bello has assured me there will be no special privileges. General population all the way.

Pastor George reaches into his blazer and retrieves an envelope. 'I came to give you your check. I thought a bank transfer would be rude and ungrateful.'

'Thank you,' I say, surprised and touched. Truth be told, the idea of being paid to find out the sordid details that led to Sade's death seemed exploitative, so I never thought to follow up.

He places the envelope on my desk and pushes it towards me. 'You'll see we also covered the full cost of replacing your friend's car.'

'That was not necessary at all. It was insured, and I've paid for the excess—'

'Trust me, Dr Taiwo, it's the least we can do. Besides, we can afford it. Take it, but make sure you pay your tithe.'

It takes me a second to realise the man is making a joke. He smiles, and I'm reminded how much I've grown to like, even respect, the preacher.

'I'll definitely pay when I find the right church,' I shoot back.

'May I recommend Grace Church? It's under new management.' He says this deadpan, but his eyes twinkle with humour.

'Touché,' I say, laughing and we banter for a bit until I remind him of my engagement.

The pastor stands and looks at me with a plea. 'I know you have to go, but I have a request.'

I raise a quizzical brow. I'm not sure I want to get involved in more church drama.

Pastor George kneels and bows his head. 'Pray for me.'

Panic courses through me. It's been a while. 'I'm not sure I can.'

He looks up at me. 'With God, you can.'

I take a deep breath, about to close my eyes when Pastor George takes my hand in his. I grope for what to say, how to say it. My heart beats fast because nothing is coming to mind.

'I know the Lord's Prayer,' I say, apologetic.

Pastor George gives me a wide smile. 'Perfect,' he says, then bows his head again.

*

The school hall is full to capacity. There's a lot of chatter as students show off their work to proud parents. I make my way to the corner that seems to have garnered the most visitors.

'My exhibition is titled #Blackgirlmagic to counter the negative stereotypes of the Black skin,' Kay is saying as I inch towards Folake and Tai, beaming.

'You're just in time,' Folake whispers, relieved rather than accusing.

'Sorry,' I say, looking around. Kay's display includes six blown-up pictures mounted on the wall, each framed with plain white wood, highlighting the vibrant colours of the paper flowers that serve as a backdrop for his muse. Lara, with her luminous eyes and her lustrous dark skin.

My daughter has never looked more beautiful. Gone is the petulant teenager I'd lived with for months. In her place is a budding beauty, staring boldly at the camera. In one picture that I will carry with me till my last breath, her features are frozen in laughter, delight animating her face, pulling the viewer in.

'I added the hashtag to counter the culture of filters on social media which gives a false impression of physical beauty. I used my sister as my subject because she embodies the beauty of the Black skin,' Kay tells the crowd gathered around him. 'And now I'd like to present her to you.'

I'm tearful as Lara steps forward, encouraged by the very same girls who made fun of her. Indeed, the former bullies are the ones hooting and clapping as Lara joins her brother. They're still her reluctant students, but clearly a photoshoot is the common ground they need to declare a truce of sorts.

Tai thumps me on the back. 'How do you like our surprise?' he whispers.

I nod, moved that in the midst of all that was going on, my wife and sons found the time to rally and stage the most effective intervention in history. There'll be time enough in the future for Lara to see herself through the eyes of her parents, her peers, the people she will date and work with, the partner she will choose to spend her life with. But her brother's lens has captured her as she is now, today. Beautiful and most of all, loved. As long as there's breath in me, I'll make it my life's mission to remind her of this. Every day if need be.

Lara basks in the admiration of students and parents, waving like a pageant queen. When Kay takes a bow, Lara's eyes meet mine. I blow her a kiss as Folake rests her head on my shoulder. Lara winks at me and curtsies. The applause around us is loud but I don't really hear it.

I am lost in the magic that is my daughter's smile.

ACKNOWLEDGMENTS

Everything I heard and read about The Difficult Second novel is true. Writing this book has been a journey of self-discovery. At each turn, I was blessed with people who held my hand, guided me and offered comfort when all seemed lost. Beyond the euphoria of completing the novel, I believe I am a better person because of the support system the universe brought my way. I am grateful.

To Tracy Brain, whose compassion, kindness and gentle guidance anchored me.

To Gerard Woodward and C. J. Skuse, who took me and this book under their wings with an enthusiasm that made the journey to completion so much easier than I imagined it would be.

To my amazing Raven team, led by my UK editor, Alison Hennessey, who believes in Philip Taiwo in ways that humble and inspire.

To my wonderfully supportive Mulholland team, led by my US editor, Josh Kendall. The depth and detail of feedback never fail to challenge and elevate.

To my agent, Harry Illingworth, for fighting my battles with uncommon grace.

To Kate Woodworth, my accountability partner par excellence, grammar police, plot-checker, advocate and friend.

To Edwin Hill, Chiedozie Dike and Temitayo Olofinlua, who refined my thoughts and sentences at different stages of the many drafts of this book.

ACKNOWLEDGMENTS

To my long-suffering First Readers Circle; Idiare Atimomo, Ebben Kalondo, Ese Esosa, Pearl Osibu, Sahara Sintayo-Obende, Toni Chappelle, Sabrin Hasburn, Frank Edozien, Pheadra Farah, Susan Daniels, Bosede Ogunlana, Leye Adenle, Zukiswa Wanner, Felicitas Kakoro-Gowases, Yinka Adeleke and Nyasha Nyandoro, for welcoming Philip Taiwo into your busy lives.

To my dear friends who offered a hug, a meal, a roof, a writing desk and a soundboard; Matthias Langheld, Irmela Schnebel, the Tyce clan and the teams behind too many lodges, hotel rooms and Airbnb rentals to mention.

To dad, mum and Bose; a tripartite team of prayer warriors who keep championing my passion.

To my sons, Simi and Tomi, who keep teaching me so much about the gift of being a father.

To Nneka, my ride or die, who lived with this story long before and after I typed 'the end'.

To God, the source.